Cords of

by

J. Ewins and L. Telfer

WordHive Ltd: London

Published by WordHive Ltd, 2019

First published in Great Britain in 2019 by WordHive Ltd, 77
Victoria Street, London, SW1H 0HW.
www.wordhive.co
WordHive Limited Reg. No. 105153310.

This novel is a work of fiction. John William Sargent, known as
Jack, joined the Metropolitan Police in 1872. He worked as a
farm labourer near Battle, Sussex, before joining the police.
The Alexandra Palace Fire and the visit made by the Shah of
Persia were actual events in 1873 as was the developing
knowledge of organised crime groups.
The research into characters involved in situations are referred
to in the Acknowledgements.

WordHive Ltd: London

Other Titles in the Jack Sargent series:

The Faceless Woman,
Jack Sargent's First Murder.

Set in London 1872, Jack Sargent joins the Metropolitan
Police and enters a world of treachery, murder and love.

*

Other books published by WordHive Ltd:

The Chris Duncan Series by M.D. Wigg and Jay Heyes, available in paperback and in digital versions:

Chaos Calls to Chaos, Book one.
Set in the London of Dean's Yard, Westminster, the story wends its way across to Kensington: Chris Duncan had not expected to fall in love with Eve when he started working on the BBC project for the surfing Archdeacon.
Follow Chris, and his flatmates from Rosary Gardens, to the beaches of North Devon as romance unravels.

Unforced Rhythms, Book two.
Storm takes a chance to win the woman he loves in Melbourne with dire consequences, while Chris Duncan wrestles with his future and travels out to East Africa to meet Eve again.

*

Performance and Community workshop series: book one.
Easter Monologues for performance: **Following in the Way of the Cross,** by M.D. Wigg and Jay Heyes.

Book 2: **To the Ends of the Earth,**
Backstories for Performance: Pentecost.
By M.D. Wigg and Jay Heyes.

Childrens Books

Ermie and Azar and the Vortex: J Ewins and L Telfer.

Two children off to the park with mum become involved in an adventure of time travel on the London Underground with a mysterious Florist. Age: seven to eleven.

Ma and Me: Walk by J Ewins and L Telfer.

The adventures of Ma and Me, as they go out around their estate. Suitable for key stage one.

"The cords of the grave coiled around me:
the snares of death confronted me."

2 Samuel 22:6, NIV.

June 1873

London and Sussex

For Peter

June 9ᵗʰ 1873.

The initial quietness stunned him and Jack drowned in the tedium of it. The silence peeled off the London dock like flags fluttering in the wind.

The young constable waited for change. And so it came with a regular pattern of noise building into a monotone for five seconds in length, followed by silence. But at the point that Jack felt he could stand it no more the pattern was broken and replaced with a sound as if iron was grating against the sides of the ships. Dogs scavenged in the scene that he surveyed, surviving on the pickings of the spillages of cargo as it was unloaded. He passed a mirror and saw only his own reflection. A policeman, carrying his helmet, blonde hair awry.

In the room which Jack had entered was a fluted glass light, already displaced, hanging on its cable from the ceiling directing light in a skewed stream. The usual occupant of the room was there. The familiar rat in the corner. The creature had bitten through a sack despite Jack's presence, its progress was relentless. No matter how much noise Jack made or how he threatened it the rat continued as if Jack did not exist. It was somehow very important to him to stop the creature. To do so he must cross dank water centred in the room. It was impossible to tell the depth.

A face in the water stared back at him as it always did, only it was not the face of Emily Doyle this time. Usually it was dead Emily, as she had been when Sergeant Stan Green had carried her body from the park after her suicide. She had confessed to Jack her attempt to kill her lover's wife, choosing for herself poison rather than the hangman's noose. Emily had been too far gone to save. And he had wanted to save her.

No, it was not Emily's face. The face in his dream this time was the face of his Harriet. The dream haunted him even when awake.

—

This time he registered shock that it was the face of the woman he loved. From somewhere beyond the warehouses despite the monotonous grating of iron he could hear her calling for help. He tried to shut the sounds out just as he had attempted to do that fateful day in the cloying, London mist, as he had held Emily's child while her mother died.

The rat's face alternated this time between rodent and human. Jack made an effort to try and match the face to someone that he knew. It eluded him but the eyes were those of a rat.

Then the images were gone as he awoke. One lasting common theme prevailed each time, however. The rat mocked him because he could not prevent its activity.

It was dawn now on this June day and by rights Jack should have still been asleep. His mood varied first thing these days depending on the quality of sleep he had had. Some nights the dream did not recur. He was at a loss to find the trigger although the longer the syndrome of recurring nightmare went on the more he suspected it was linked to his avoidance of contact with Sam Curzon.

The clock on the West India Dock offices struck five o'clock and the watery sun of the early June morning pushed its way insistently through the haze of London. There was promise of a fine day in that sun but little would be seen of it once the cooking fires started. Jack lay on his bed and listened.

He had finished his patrol at ten o'clock the previous night and had lain on the top of his bed fully dressed only having slipped his boots off. The light nights kept more people on the streets and his patrol had been busy. Sleep had come at midnight despite not even having touched the beef broth that his landlady, Mrs Phillips, had left out for him. It was a rough supper in comparison to his Arbour Square days but wholesome. Now he was hungry with that gnawing gripe that clawed at his stomach and he realised that apart from a sandwich, he had not eaten since midday yesterday.

Jack could smell the fresh bread now cooking as the aroma rose from the kitchen beneath him. Rose Phillips had prepared it before she retired for the night. Always up even earlier than Jack, ready for the day at the new location of a café at Wharf Road. She had left the premises near Millwall Junction, taking a recently vacated place two weeks ago. It was near the station and engine sheds and competed with The Nelson Public House on the West Ferry Road for diners.

Not that there was any competition in Jack's view.

Rose would be off to the café by six once the smitten Harry Franks called for her. The preparation for her tureens of stew were done by seven each morning once at work with whatever meat or fish she collected on her way there. Once cooked the stew would be supplemented by most of the bread that was now baking. Rose left two of the loaves at home each day for Jack and Mrs Phillips senior.

By rights, Jack felt, Rose should have a better occupation but she had accepted the role of being her brother Ted's eyes and ears at the docks. She was to monitor those who arrived by Isle of Dogs Ferry, as they passed her new café door as they made their way to other parts. It was a rougher area and the Detective Sergeant from Shadwell, Harry Franks, was not too pleased at the risks that could present for a woman alone. Hence his appearance at the West India Dock Cottage each day to act as her escort. Magically he appeared before the closure of business as well to escort Rose home.

Now, Jack's mentor Ted Phillips, was back in New Road, Camberwell, on the south side of the river. In the first six months after Jack had joined the Met he and Ted had patrolled the areas from Leman Street. At times, when the need had arisen, they had quietly put on plain clothes, working undercover for Inspector Tom Hunt. Equally as quietly they had resumed their uniformed roles.

Ted had engineered Jack's lodging with his sister and mother in the West India Dock Cottage once the case of the Faceless Woman had been solved.

"Solved" was an interesting word to Jack as he would never agree that the case had been. Some arrests had been made but they still had not got the man at the top, Mrs Berringer's lover.

With relief, Jack had found himself out of the police dormitory, leaving the snorers of the world to their off-key ensemble. But Ted Phillips had returned to Camberwell and to promotion as Sergeant Morris recovered from the hit and run. Of the three men who had come across the river in December 1872 only Jack had remained at Leman Street. Inspector Hunt had made it clear that Jack's role there was long-term. And that had made his relationship with Harriet difficult.

The third man, Sam Curzon, was out of things for good it seemed, after the attempt on his life by Emily Doyle. He was unlikely to ever return as a Police Constable. Letters between Sam and Jack had been exchanged from time to time but Jack was finding it harder to deal with the contact. Partial guilt at this reaction and also the need to try and forget Emily Doyle's death had driven Jack to leave Sam's letters unopened. Jack was also working even his rest days. The hours he put in at the Leman street station were longer than his duty periods required. It was a cause for concern to the Police Surgeon, Doctor Brown.

Sam's place at Leman Street had been taken in February by Charlie Banks. Charlie had started on the same day last November as Jack and Sam and had been the quiet one of the three. He had been overlooked as a result. Wrongly as it happened. No one was more reliable, more dogged in the face of threat than Charlie. Inspector Hunt had given Jack and Charlie the commission to keep an eye open for leads to the corrupt "man at the top" linked to the Faceless Woman case. It was the missing link Hunt's team had not found.

Charlie had surprised Jack recently by telling him that he was walking out with Hannah, Emily Doyle's former maid of all work. Now safely working as the scullery maid in Camberwell, Hannah had been tracked down by Charlie. Once her mistress had been carried into the house, dead, Hannah had fled home to life in her mother's rural kitchen.

Jack had tried desperately to place Hannah in another position, trying all his charm with the cooks on his beat. After a few days he extracted a promise from his girl's old boss, Mrs Ardle, that Hannah could fill Harriet's old position of scullery maid, providing Jack could find her quickly.

Charlie had seen Jack's concern and by a process of elimination had contacted the agencies and traced Hannah back to the Wiltshire village where her family still lived. She had fled afraid that she would somehow be implicated in the poisoning of Sam Curzon. Much to Jack's surprise Charlie and Hannah seemed well suited. Neither had much to say but there was a glow about them when he saw them together. How either of them understood each other when Charlie spoke in his dialect from Macclesfield and Hannah launched into her Wiltshire ways was beyond Jack. Still, he could talk. His Sussex pronunciation could be broad and rather drawling. Jack would abbreviate long words and expand short ones. It was particularly obvious when tired.

Jack put his head under the pump and let the cold water soak his shirt. Then he changed and glanced at the clock. Almost time for Harry to appear.

His first encounter with Harry Franks had been as Harry assumed the character of a scruffy "Tec," in a beer stained waistcoat, and a dusty bowler hat. On the first meeting the bowler had been placed at the Detective Sergeant's elbow on a beer-soaked bar in the Mason's Arms on the Commercial Road. Harry had assumed the role of being the worse for wear as he attempted to entice the young barmaid Mary into considering him as a future husband. Mary had not bitten and who could blame her. She had greater plans to leave London and by New Year had gone to work in a hotel in Brighton. Harry Franks had been introduced to Rose Phillips by her brother and had fallen head over heels in love with her.

"Miss Rose," as Harry called her, did not seem too averse to the attention. A courtship was clearly underway. Harry Franks was not a young man, Jack put him around forty years of age and a well-seasoned police detective. He had also become Jack's main link to Inspector Hunt now Jack was at Leman Street for the foreseeable future, although Ted's weekly visits to see his mother and sister invariably brought instructions if anything was developing. Franks, although based in Shadwell police station, had moved around freely between the areas since the Faceless Woman case and provided Jack with a conduit to relay and receive information. His daily visits to the West India Dock Cottage were therefore convenient for Jack and Inspector Hunt.

The small cottage which Rose and Mrs Phillips occupied was a stone's throw from the West India Dock station. A grimy area most of the time the cottage had been granted to Mrs Phillips as a widow of a company engineer. Originally built to house the Asian seamen working for the company back in 1849-50 they had been re-fitted more recently. Local housing for members of staff had been needed. The company had decided in 1870 that engineers must be close by in order to enable the efficient running of the host of mechanical contraptions. Mr Phillips senior, as he was referred to by his widow, died two years ago. Jack's role of protector to the two ladies in Ted's absence tied in nicely with the location as he had a good vantage point of the import/export dock and across the masts to South Dock. It was also convenient for the Blackwall Railway which rumbled by on its way to Poplar and the spur down to the Isle of Dogs Ferry.

Jack rolled off his bed and crossed the short distance to the window. From there at this time of the day he could see away to the right towards Colquhoun Place and the entrance to the West India Dock Offices. The clock was quite visible and he reminded himself that his current shift pattern required him back at Leman Street Police Station for patrol at ten. A good time to get air into the room before the activity of the dock picked up and the horses fouled the air with their dung.

He pushed the sash window up and the air cooled his face. Slices of bread with the broth, once heated up, would do him fine now but there were still the after effect of the recurring dream pre-occupying his mind. He thought of Harriet waking in her shared bedroom in the servant's quarters right at the top of the house in the Grove, Camberwell, and knew that in his dream forces threatened her.

Jack had begun to associate the rat's taunting in the dream with his own sense of ineffectiveness at crime prevention. His activity, he felt, was as futile as attempts had been to stop Emily Doyle's death. He could try and catch the rat but there would always be more vermin to follow it. Then there was the face in the water. A portent of another victim perhaps? The fact that it had been Harriet's face this time made him shudder. Jack leaned out of his window and turned his face into the wind. The direction was from the west. Harriet would have said that her mother was sending love to her on the wind from Honiton. He finished the dregs of tea that he had poured for himself on his way through the kitchen last night. It was cold, of course, and he threw the last few drops out of the window onto the grass at the side of the path and stared across the dock at the masts which filled the skyline.

Downstairs was the latest un-opened letter from Sam. This time it had remained on the shelf where Mrs Phillips always placed the post for the last ten days Perhaps the gnawing rat was a prompt.

*

The décor in the kitchen would have been described as workmanlike. Walls with a lime-wash and a stone floor which received a soaking from buckets of soapy water each night before Rose retired. It was her powerhouse though and boots were firmly left at the kitchen door.

Above the range two items drew Jack's attention. One a device, a triple rack hung on a pulley. It was lined today with Jack's shirts, long john's and various female petticoats and underwear from which he tried to avert his eyes. It had all gone through the dolly tub and hand ringer on Monday. Mrs Phillips had a woman that came in every week. Jack had never met her but he saw the product of her labours in clean clothes. Tomorrow it would be ironed and his underwear and shirts would appear magically in the old wooden cupboard in his bedroom.

'Morning Jack, there's a coddled egg doing for you if you'd like it,' said Rose, turning towards him as he came in. 'I heard you moving around upstairs. A bad night?'

'Marning,' Jack answered, in his Sussex drawl. Rose registered that she had her answer as his accent became more pronounced the more tired he became.

The second area which drew his attention was a shelf above the range and Jack had stared at its three occupants each day since Valentine's day. The card with a faded violet in which Harry had written a poem. It had done the trick though and Rose and Harry had walked out together the following Sunday. The Easter card embellished with a cross covered in white lace had been Harry's next offering. Since Easter there had been fresh flowers each week. Jack was fixated on the area and his eyes always went to them. The vase had changed since yesterday indicating Harry's presence last night. More evidence of Harry Franks' intentions.

'Dog roses,' said Jack, nodding at the vase. He placed last night's tea cup on the drainer.

'Yes, from Harry,' said Rose, stating the obvious. 'How was your patrol last night?' she asked noting he was relaxed enough with her to comment. She took it as a compliment and was in the middle of covering the beef broth so readily ignored by Jack the night before. Rose moved quickly into the pantry and set it down on the cold stone slab. Jack knew the process. The fat would congeal on the top and then the dripping would be smeared on bread. He would look forward to it.

'Busy,' Jack smiled as he answered the young woman.

Rose started to cut Jack a chunk of recently baked bread to go with the beautifully decorated egg coddler she had lifted with a hook out of the pan of boiling water on the range. Two more sat in the water, one for Rose and the other for her mother. Rose wrapped a cloth over the tightly fitting lid and gave it a twist. Jack picked up the bread and took a bite before resting the slice on a plate that Rose had put ready for him. She had grown used to their young lodger's endless appetite. When he missed eating food placed for him she worried. Like the broth last night. Her mother said he was probably still growing but at nearly twenty-one years of age Rose somehow doubted this. She suspected it was years in the orphanage that had instilled a drive to stoke up whenever food was produced.

The yoke was still soft, and the top of the egg ran into the butter as Rose had lined the coddler with a yellow smear. She moved seamlessly and produced pieces of ham from the larder and Jack salivated at the sight. He laid himself a place on the opposite side of the kitchen table and drew up a rush chair from a corner of the kitchen. He turned the back of it to himself and rested his forearms along the top of the back. Sitting astride the seat, he broke the bread into smaller pieces and poked the top of the egg to cover them with yoke.

'So, last night was alright?' asked Rose, again. Jack looked up at her, surprised that she was probing. 'Only I've noticed when you are on that shift you always wake early,' Rose continued.

'Oh, have you? No, it was alright, I suppose. Mainly thugs staying out because of the lighter nights. We're unarmed, easy to identify because of the uniform, and fair game,' said Jack.

'You seem tired of late. You worked your rest day again I noticed,' Rose said. She waited but he met her gaze looking surprised she had mentioned it. As a way of trying to redeem herself for what could be taken as interference she added, 'Just that Ted always says it's not good in the long term for a man.'

'Well, it stops me thinking. If Harriet was free it might be different but she only gets the same time off each week. I'd rather be busy.'

Rose, alerted by the tone, glanced at him and detected a change in attitude from the enthusiastic young constable who had moved into the cottage in January. She picked up the latest letter addressed to Jack and placed it down at the side of his plate. She had noticed it had sat with other unopened post for more than a week. Jack glanced at it and carried on eating. He knew the hand writing and had no desire after a disturbing dream to read Sam's letter. But neither did he wish to appear rude to Rose.

'Thanks, I'll read it later. It's from Sam,' said Jack.

Rose hesitated, and then nodded.

'Tea?' she asked.

'Please, I'm chokly today, if it's no trouble to you,' said Jack.

Rose gave a brief laugh. 'You will have to give me lessons if you carry on like this. What does that mean, Jack?'

'Dry. It means dry, sorry, I suppose choking dry would be the closest you'd get,' explained Jack.

Rose smiled, 'I'll take mother her breakfast. Would you pour a cup for us both?'

'Yes, you can imagine what Harriet and I can be like together when we both get going, she from Honiton and I from Sussex.'

'Shows it's love,' said Rose with a smile. Jack nodded but looked into her eyes for just a little longer than a confident lover would have done. He wondered to himself exactly what it was. The doubt registered with Rose but she chose not to probe. Still, she would mention that all may not be well in the relationship to Harry when he collected her later. It was time to take her mother the breakfast tray.

Jack watched Rose's straight back as she edged her way through the kitchen door into the hall with the tray and momentarily thought that Harry Franks was a lucky man. Then he reigned in his analysis. Although at twenty-eight she looked pretty good Harriet's emotions would not be hard to predict if she knew he was assessing Rose's figure.

Harriet, his Harriet, if that was what she was. Clever, amiable and earthy and promising to be his wife. But not yet, always the answer was not yet. Still seized with the desire to be independent Harriet had held back again on Sunday when they were at the Alexandra Palace from naming a day. All Jack had asked for was to go with her to Honiton to ask her mother's permission to become engaged. Once that was granted he would rest easy and wait for her.

Jack pushed the plate away more vigorously than was polite. He picked up the brown teapot and poured tea for himself and Rose. He could hear Mrs Phillips calling down suggestions for a house. What house?

She came down the stairs into the hall and momentarily glanced through the window to check the clock on the office building. Five thirty.

'I had better get my things together as Harry will be here soon. Thank-you for pouring the tea, Jack. What time are you on duty today?' asked Rose.

'Ten o'clock but parade first of course. It's a good morning and I thought I'd weed that bit of a vegetable patch that Ted and I laid down before the slugs get the lettuce. I may go in early.'

Jack cast his eye over the headline in the Tower Hamlets Independent from the day before. Rose always brought a copy home and she and her mother would discuss the front-page stories over their evening meal if they were alone.

"Mr Belt wrongly arrested for drunkenness," it said. Jack felt himself tense waiting for the criticism of the police that was bound to follow.

"Clashes between police and officers of the Life Guards outside the Argyll Rooms."

So far, the journalist had been fair, thought Jack. The next news item caught his attention. He read aloud:

"The Metropolitan Police to acquire nine new stations: North Woolwich, Rodney Road (Lock's Field), Chislehurst, Finchley, Isleworth, Putney, South Norwood, Harrow and Enfield Town."

18

'Interesting this,' he said to Rose, pointing at the column. Rose glanced down and nodded.

'Yes, I think it's been on the cards for quite a while, Jack. Ted said North Woolwich was coming.'

'So, the city's spreading and with it will go the Met.' Jack made a mental note to mention it to Ted when he next saw him in case there were routes for promotion. Part of him found the growth of London exciting, but part of him longed to wake each morning with the smell of green foliage.

'I'll go and get started on those slugs and try and not to get grubby. Thanks for breakfast,' he said, smiling as he pushed his chair forward in order to stand.

'As diligent with those slugs and snails as you are at catching the wrong 'uns,' said Rose, smiling.

'Slugs are easier to find, Rose,' said Jack wryly, as he picked up a sack from the porch to drop the snails into.

'Watch the birds too, I noticed they'd been helping themselves to the peas,' said Rose.

'Sussex boys have a small Birds act of their own, "Robins and Wrens Are God Almighty's friends; Martins and swallers are God Almighty's scholars." Jack recited. 'I leave the birds a bit at the side, the rest I can cover with netting.'

Time was going on and Harry would shortly come whistling across the dock. A funny development, Jack thought, Harry whistling. He had not heard Harry Franks whistle in those early days, but that slightly off-key tone the Detective Sergeant had developed had rung around the dock each morning since February fourteenth.

Jack straightened his back and stretched his arms out to the side. The dock was busy with workers ending a shift and others beginning one. He dropped the sack on the ground in front of a bed of lettuce. Growing up as the son of a market gardener had meant this activity was normal in his childhood. Somehow the rituals established in his life by his parents were helpful. Bending to remove a snail a noise ahead of him made him look up.

He watched as two men dressed as dock workers started to climb over the railings into the West India office compound. Both wore caps pressed down close over their eyes. He heard a yell and realised it was his own. It was matched by a shout from the Watchman. Jack had started to run, all thought of snails and slugs gone as the two men pulled black covers over their faces and tied them at the back. All that was visible in the black fabric were the eye holes. Jack had not seen their faces though, but he had a feel for height and build. His memory, now better trained after six months on the job, would recall the features. His money was on the fact that the Watchman had also seen them. Together they could produce a meaningful amount of detail for the police artist.

One of the men had flung a rope over the sign fixed onto the front wall at first floor level and was up it like a monkey.

The Watchman was underneath them waving a cudgel. Jack was at the railings and noted the Watchman's age. Too heavy to move quickly and breathing hard. The second man was up the rope now close behind the first.

'Open up,' shouted Jack, gripping the railings and giving them a shake. The Watchman stared at the men above him as they smashed a first-floor window with small hammers and disappeared into the building. Jack realised that he was only in his shirt sleeves and uniform trousers and the Watchman would not realise that he was a policeman.

Behind him Jack heard the whistle announcing the arrival of the amorous Harry Franks. Jack started to shout to Harry and the Watchman joined in as the well-known Detective from Shadwell came into view. Harry broke into a run and panting, joined Jack at the gates.

'Open up, man,' shouted Jack, again.

'What's happened?' yelled Harry to Jack.

'There's been a pretty start at the offices. Two men have smashed a window and gone in. They had a rope ready to go up to the first floor and hammers to smash the glass. They've ignored trying to get in on ground level so I think they know what they're after and where it is,' Jack pushed hard as the gate finally swung open.

20

'Have you anyone else here with you?' Harry asked the Watchman as he and Jack reached the front door.

'Not at this time of the morning,' replied the Watchman.

'Keys,' shouted Jack, rattling the front door. The Watchman produced a large ring with a whole host of keys and fumbled for the right one.

'Too long,' muttered Jack, 'too long.' He glanced up at the clock. It had all taken three minutes from seeing the men climb the wall and for the door to be opened.

He and Franks were in at last. They paused as the Watchman blundered in behind them and the front door crashed back against the wall.

'Well, we've announced our entrance, now, young Jack,' said Harry, holding up a hand to the Watchman to quieten him. The three men stood for what seemed an age, waiting for the tell-tale sound to indicate where the men were. In reality it was ten seconds before there was the sound of a sash window going up on an upper floor to the left of the staircase in front of them and Jack located the noise towards the back of the building.

'Reinforcements?' Jack asked Harry.

'More likely they're making their exit. They're not on the first floor by the sound of that glass. Nicely planned this. You've no truncheon, Jack I see. Only your bare fists, and I don't carry a weapon to call on Miss Rose. But I would pay money to see you use your fists. Well, we're going up you and I.' Franks turned to the Watchman. 'You get yourself out to the front gate and make as much noise as you can to attract attention from wandering police constables in the area. You know me, don't you?'

'Yes, I do,' said the Watchman.

'Then tell anyone who comes to our aid, it's Harry Franks from Shadwell here, with the best fighter on the force. That should encourage their help. Ready, Jack?' asked Harry. He did not wait for an answer and went up the stairs two at a time.

*

21

At the top of three flights Harry, the older man, was panting. Jack noted it but passed him easily to reach an open sash window. The younger man leant out of the window overlooking a courtyard at the back of the offices. Jack could see a rope had been flung over a hoisting arm meant to unload goods. The two were finishing their descent. One had done with his mask and his blonde hair caught a flash of sunlight through the slat in the outer door. Blonde like himself, thought Jack. That made him easy to remember.

It was obvious the thieves had a shopping list as they had entered and left so rapidly from the time they had scaled the railings.

'Inside job,' muttered Jack.

The first man hit the ground running but the second one hit it hard and rolled over with a sharp exclamation of:

'Argh,' as a leg went underneath the man and the impact caused damage.

His compatriot showed no signs of waiting for him and the injured man struggled on behind the first, limping. Jack stared down at the ground at a glove where the men had landed.

To follow them quickly Jack weighed up if he could reach the rope. To do so would require him to go out onto the window sill and jump. He had half started to position himself as Harry came into the room.

'Don't do it, Jack my boy,' Harry called. 'They're away by now anyway.'

'I'll see it I can cut them off,' and Jack swung his legs down onto the office floor to make for the stairs. There was no sign of the Watchman with his keys. Jack shouted to get his attention as all the rear doors were locked but the man was not in the building.

Eventually Jack found a rear door that yielded to his kicks to the lock. The Watchman was back with two constables. Jack assessed the frame of the first one as having a stocky build and he decided the man would do.

'Come *on*,' Jack shouted.

Harry had come into the hall and beckoned to the second constable, pointing to the article on the ground outside the door.

'Pick that glove up for me will you,' Harry called.

The Watchman followed Jack and the stocky constable out into the courtyard.

'How did that come about?' he exclaimed, staring at the open rear gate.

'Was it locked?' Jack called over his shoulder. He peered up the dock for any sign of the two intruders.

'Of course, it's always locked at this time of the day,' shouted back the Watchman. 'It would only be opened as the trains bring the supplies in. It's too early for anyone to have unlocked it. The Weigh Clerk has to be in place, first.'

'Well someone's opened it for them or they had a key,' Jack said, grimly. Both men had vanished into thin air. They had moved at a pace, even if one of them was injured. Jack stood in the open gateway and listened, straining his ears to hear over the usual sounds of the working West India Dock for running feet. He held up his hand to silence the constable and the Watchman who were standing with him. In the noise of the docks it was impossible to tell if a cart or carriage was moving away. If a carriage had waited for them he would not distinguish it from others but men running at a time of day when shifts changed would be unusual.

There was nothing.

Both men were gone but another article of clothing was on the ground in the alleyway: a black mask. Jack picked it up and turned it inside out. There were a couple of blonde hairs inside which would be enough to tie the mask back to the blonde man. Presumably he had discarded it or just dropped it as he ran. Jack folded it carefully to keep the hairs in place and slipped the mask into his trouser pocket.

'Careless,' said the constable at his side.

'Yes, or just sure of himself,' said Jack, turning to walk back to Harry.

'Railway, Jack,' called Harry as he started through the back door towards the Junction. Jack was out behind him.

23

'There's no trace of which direction they went in, Harry,' Jack called. He fished into his pocket and pulled out the folded mask. Harry nodded and patted his jacket to indicate he had the other piece of evidence: the glove.

'Foreign make,' said Harry, pulling the black glove out of his inside pocket. 'The label isn't English.'

Jack took the black article of clothing and turned it over. It was made of leather and would have provided a good grip and dexterity.

'Nice,' said Jack, looking for the label. It was a heavy leather though, and not something that would have been worn in the summer.

'I don't suppose it's going to help track the man down. The label says Millau, France, as the place. It could have been bought in any city probably. That pair I had in the winter were made in Woodstock but I bought them in Oxford Street,' said Jack.

'It says they're made in England though, Jack and its likely you would have bought them here. One of those men has somehow come across a French glove, if not a pair, which fits him and which helped him grip a rope. He knew what he was about then and it won't be the first time that he's done that. We can probably assume he may be French,' said Harry.

'Ex-sailor perhaps?' mused Jack.

'Could be. Maybe with a circus even,' said Harry. 'As to where they are now, Safest place is in a crowd, Jack. They'll stand out in a carriage. Who travels in a carriage around here at this time of the day? Workers, men starting shifts or ending them. They'll have resumed an appearance that doesn't get them noticed if they've any sense. What did you get to see?' Harry asked.

'Enough to recognise the blonde one again. The other was limping as he moved off,' answered Jack. He paused as before Jack and Harry at the station entrance were a horde of workmen.

'That blonde hair will be under a cap I reckon, and the injured one won't be with him. Survival means they'll separate,' said Harry, scanning the crowd for a man walking with a limp, or showing pain in his face.

'They were fast,' said Jack.

'That's an understatement. They knew what they were after.'

'Inside job, I thought,' said Jack, squeezing past some dock workers. 'We'll have to get on, they're six deep inside the carriages. We'll never see them out here.'

'I'd not have said there would be anything worth scaling down from a third-floor window in the West India Dock Offices on a sunny day in June, would you? What could there have been?' said Harry.

'Whatever it was they knew it was there. It took them a matter of minutes, Harry. They knew where to go, how to get out and managed to lay their hands on a convenient rope, which must have been put ready for them. It's a set up so there are more than just two men involved in this,' said Jack.

'Professionals,' said Harry, surveying the men crowding into a carriage. 'Organised and in and out fast. We've got a race against time, young Jack, as once they make Blackwall there are a number of destinations that they can make their way to.' Harry had managed to get his foot inside the doorway of a carriage to stop a door closing and was starting to push his way in. Being in plain clothes Harry was meeting with some resistance.

'Quit your pushing and wait for the next train,' said the dock worker whose back had been against the carriage door and who was on the receiving end of most of Harry's determined efforts to get into the carriage.

'Police,' shouted Jack from the platform. 'Move in, please, and let the Detective Sergeant on.' Jack had a toe hold in the door now and was lending his shoulder weight to Harry's' attempts to push his way in. It was a bluff as there was nothing to identify Jack as a policeman. Harry too was over dressed for his duties, and he was sporting too smart suit to be on duty, his aim having been to impress Miss Rose into agreeing to become the future Mrs Franks. Jack's mind momentarily went to Ted's last visit when he had mentioned that Harry had paid four hundred and fifty pounds for a new house in Bow in expectation of Rose saying 'yes.'

They were on board.

Blackwall came into view and Jack pushed the door open and jumped down onto the platform before the train stopped. A whistle sounded at him and he grinned an acknowledgement at the guard's admonition. He looked up and down the carriages as the seedy morass of bodies started to unload. It was like rats hurling themselves into the Thames, he thought. Harry left the carriage and was next to him. They looked up and down the platform as men went in different directions. No blonde head other than Jack's was visible, nor anyone limping.

'They could have doubled back, we would never know in that crowd. I suggest we return to the offices and try and clarify what has gone missing. Where are you supposed to be this morning?' asked Harry.

'Patrol, at ten, so it's Leman Street for me. I've time to come back with you,' said Jack. The two men started walking

'Rose will have left by now, 'said Harry, glancing at his pocket watch, while the two men changed platform to take the return train.

'We can call in at the café,' suggested Jack, as he looked up the line for the next train to take them back. It was just visible. Harry and he waited, standing aside while the workers poured out of the carriages and onto the platform. Harry hauled himself up into the comparatively empty space and glanced around as Jack joined him. They both sat for the short journey, momentarily relaxed as the quarry was nowhere to be seen. The train began to pull away from the platform.

'How are you doing in that quarter?' asked Jack. Harry frowned slightly.

'With Rose, I mean, if you don't mind me asking,' Jack continued.

'Slow but sure, I think. My innate charm and elegant good looks are wearing the lady down. Seriously though, Jack, I think what is holding Rose back from saying "yes" to me is concern for her mother being on her own. I've decided to have a word with Ted about what we do with Mrs Phillips senior.'

Harry glanced at the clock on the offices as it became visible above the skyline and checked his own watch against it.

'Those men were fast alright,' he said.

Jack looked at the despondent man sitting opposite him and thought of his own relationship which appeared to be going nowhere. He too stared through the window at the clock and then noted that the sky was no longer as clear as it had been in the early morning. Smoke and the warmth of a June morning was already turning the brilliance to a haze. Jack watched the crowds in front of the buildings and thought of the men from the night shifts who were already spending their money in the public houses.

'They certainly were fast. It was like a military operation,' Jack agreed. He ran his eye across the faces in the crowds at the side of the railway in the vain hope that he might see the blonde man they were looking for.

'Look Harry, I could carry on lodging with Mrs Phillips senior. I could have a word, if you don't think I'd be stepping out of line and reassure Rose that her mother wouldn't be on her own,' suggested Jack.

'Thank-you Jack, but I've got my weapons stacked up ready to demolish any argument Rose may have as to why she shouldn't become my wife. You know I've bought a house with the expectation of getting married? Well it's large enough to give Mrs Phillips a bedroom and a sitting-room if I have to. I'm reconciled to having my future mother-in-law living with us if that's what it takes.' Harry pursed his lips.

'You're certain that she's keen on you?' asked Jack. From the expression on Harry's face Jack regretted the question.

'Keen? Keen? What in your vast experience of the fairer sex constitutes a lady being keen, young Jack?' asked Harry, turning his full sceptical gaze on his colleague.

'Well, after walking out with a young lady for five months I would expect a certain amount of reciprocal affection,' Jack felt uncomfortable and aware the colour was rising in his cheeks despite approaching his twenty-first birthday.

Harry's stare was locked onto Jack's eyes in a way that Jack had seen him use in an interrogation. Jack looked away and glanced out of the window. When he looked back Harry had not moved his gaze at all. Slowly the Detective Sergeant leant forward and rested his forearms on his knees.

'A kiss you mean by reciprocal affection? Is that what you mean?'

'Yes, well, more than one hopefully,' Jack said, continuing to colour and dropping his eyes to his boots under Harry's scathing look.

'I'm not familiar with your techniques with young ladies but I hope you're not bringing disgrace to the uniform that you wear in your dealings with Miss Harriet?' Harry sat back but his eyes did not move from Jack's face.

'No, of course not, Harry. I er, well, a kiss, an arm around...' Jack was interrupted by a sharp response from his senior.

'Listen, young Jack, I am not in the habit of taking advantage of a young woman.' Harry hissed.

'I would never suggest...' Jack began.

'I would hope not,' Harry bridled. 'She is not a "thing" but a person. There's time enough for that when we're married.'

'Yes, of course, but surely...'Jack was interrupted again.

'Surely what?' Harry asked.

'Rose needs to know what you feel for her, surely?' Jack tried again.

'She knows my intentions. I've written to her. Poetry.' Harry stood up and gripped the door handle. It was time to descend from the train.

Jack was so shocked at the idea of Detective Sergeant Harry Franks of Shadwell writing poetry to his lady love that he missed the fact that they had arrived at West India Dock station. Harry swung the carriage door open and Jack, unsure of the response to make, jumped down onto the pathway. Harry followed and they started to walk towards the West India Dock Offices in silence. From time to time Jack glanced at Harry, but neither spoke. Then as if the change in the thought pattern sparked something Jack gripped Harry by the arm.

'Harry, isn't it a customs office on that floor?'

They were in front of the offices now and facing the crude timber sheds leading down to Limehouse Basin. At the side labourers were queuing for the soup kitchen that had been erected by the company to avoid the risk of their workers leaving the dock during working hours.

The awkward pause that had started to develop between to the two men evaporated. Jack pulled the black head covering out of his pocket and fingered the two holes cut into it. Harry, partially embarrassed at his admission of sending poetry to Rose Phillips, focussed on the object, holding out his hand.

'Let's have a look at it,' he said.

Grateful for the change in subject back to the task in hand the two men stared at the fabric while Harry turned it over again and again. He held the underside open for Jack to see.

'It's very fair hair. Like your colour,' said Harry.

'His hair was tied back. Unusual I thought. How many burglars with blonde hair to you know, Harry?'

29

'Quite a few. But not blonde like this. As I said it's like your hair colour. The colour of a young man. It's a strong colour, and its owner is a healthy young man. He wears his hair long did you say? Hence the length of the strands. Tied back? Glove from France,' Harry said, mulling the facts over.

Jack put the evidence back in his pocket so it would not be lost.

'And someone with skills, Harry,' said Jack.

'Someone who can afford a leather glove like that, can climb, get in and out fast and who knew what they were looking for. Someone who wears his hair in an unusual way. If he has sense he'll get that cut. He'll be too easy to spot in a crowd. We need to get your description to the police artist, Jack. Where's that Watchman and young constable gone? Let's see if the Watchman got a look at them and if we can tie up his descriptions with yours.'

'He'd have the leather gloves because of the grip Harry. Maybe it's not costly where he comes from,' suggested Jack.

'If we can find out what's been taken it may tie up with why a person who would be so noticeable would be used for the theft. That might give us a lead on where he would dispose of whatever the objects were they've taken,' said Harry. He paused. 'Did you see them carry anything, Jack?' asked Harry. Jack thought, staring at Franks and half shook his head.

'No, they didn't have anything visible,' Jack said.

'It's small then, or papers perhaps. No, Jack, you didn't see anything because its small. Probably valuable, and the number dealing with valuable items is also a small world. It's a world that's close to the criminal world but the item may not be about to be sold. The thieves have skills, yes, but they won't be the ones disposing of it. They were here precisely because they could do what they did fast and then disappear. They won't be doing the trading. If indeed its traded at all.' Harry hammered on the office door and he and Jack waited as footsteps approached across a hall which, thirty minutes ago, had been the scene of a police entry.

Jack glanced at the clock. So much had happened in such a short time.

'Harry, you don't think the two men are going to trade the goods?' he asked.

'If it's a valuable item, no, not them. They're thieves paid to do what they do. If its valuable someone knew what it is and where it would be. A person with specialist knowledge about the item. The specialist doesn't do the stealing, Jack. They get someone with different skills. And our blonde friend was risky because it meant that one of the thieves is noticeable. That must mean he's good and that it was worth the risk of him being noticed. But it didn't go to plan did it?' said Harry.

'What do you mean?' asked Jack.

'They banked on the Watchman being the only person around this morning. They didn't realise that a young constable would be passing time in his local lodgings and see them. Whoever is behind this, and whoever the insider is who left that rear gate unlocked for them, didn't do their homework on the area. '

Harry paused and ran his tongue over a troublesome back tooth.

'The other factor is that one of the thieves is injured.' Harry continued. 'That must be noticeable. We need to start making some enquiries around the area for a blonde man with long hair, tied back, and a man limping or hobbling. I can do that but I'd like you to be involved as you got the look at them. I'll get a request across to Sergeant Thick this morning' said Harry.

Jack nodded, pleased at the potential break in the monotony of trudging the streets.

'There isn't much security is there. If those two men don't even care what they're stealing they must be paid well. Do you think the item is probably already in the hands of the person who employed them?' asked Jack.

'No. If the theft today involves something highly valuable it probably will change hands several times. In fact, it may already do so today so that there's distance between those men we saw and the person at the top.'

The front door swung open and the constable who had chased the men with Jack stood back to let Harry in. Jack followed noting that the dust in the hall was caught in a shaft of sunlight. He frowned at it, and then asked the constable,

'Did you notice the hair colour of the man we chased, the one who had lost his mask?'

'Yes, a bit like yours, but long and tied back. It's all I noticed,' said the constable.

'Get his name and number down Jack. Corroborates what we know. Haven't seen that Watchman, have you?' Harry asked the constable.

'He's off duty now. I got his address though,' said the constable holding out his notebook to Jack. 'He lives in Park Street at the back here.'

'Good, easy to get hold of then,' said Jack, tearing out a sheet from the back of the constable's notebook and making a separate entry on it from the details provided by the constable.

'We need to find out what was up there,' Jack said to Harry.

'We do. And we need to put the word out amongst contacts in case the trading has started.' Harry stood for a few moments staring through the open door into the dock.

'What is it, Harry?' asked Jack.

Jack waited, while Harry formulated his thoughts.

'We must go,' Harry finally said. He nodded his thanks to the constable for the help he had given them. Jack waited but Harry was leaving.

'What was that about?' Jack asked as he caught Harry up.

''Of course, it may never be sold, it may be held. It may just be held, Jack.' Harry turned and looked at Jack as reality dawned. 'Stolen items aren't always sold, Jack, they're held to trade in the criminal world. Someone may 'need' to do a trade at some point to stay free. Remember that case, "The Forty Elephants?"

'The crime syndicate case? The forty thieves?' asked Jack.

'That's the one, the female crime syndicate with the smash and grab raids. We think they're linked to a group in Elephant and Castle. Organised they are Jack, not just chance criminals. Something is stirring in my waters about this morning's theft. We're looking for more than a chance operation this morning, agreed?' said Harry.

'Agreed. It's too well organised, and the blonde man isn't a local, stands out too much and had skills,' said Jack.

'And Inspector Hunt is still looking for a corrupt senior policeman, or even higher, isn't he?' asked Harry.

'You think there might be a link?'

'It's the closest we've got since January to have a highly organised, skilled operation. But now is not the time to discuss it further,' said Harry, quickening his pace.

'Isn't it? Why not?' Confused, Jack stopped, watching his colleague marching on ahead.

'Because I have to see Miss Rose is safe at her café and you have to get to Leman Street. I can't just go "dupping" along with you. That's what you call it don't you?' called back Harry.

'Dupping? Yes, walking quickly. Harry,' shouted Jack at the retreating back as he started to follow. 'Do you seriously write poetry?'

*

Two

At the station in Leman Street Jack came off parade and looked for a rattle to take with him. He tried a sideways position with his helmet, which made it look nonsensical, not the jaunty look he had been trying for. He pushed it back to the centre of his head and caught Sergeant Thick's expression and the tight top lip below his drooping moustache in the mirror. The Sergeant was standing behind him and Jack grinned at the reflection of them both but Thick met Jack's eyes without a hint of humour.

Jack dropped the smile. The morning's activities at the West India Dock Offices had produced the adrenalin rush he had needed in order to have a sense that the job was worthwhile. However, nothing had arrived from Harry to change his orders and now he resigned himself to more of the same monotony of eight hours of walking.

'Notebook?' Thick asked, still behind him.

'Of course, sorry, Sarg.' Jack handed the open notebook across to the Sergeant, so that he could quickly find the details of the morning's activities at the West India Dock Offices.

'What time did Franks say he would get that request to release you for special duties with him across here?' asked Thick.

Jack glanced at the station clock as he handed his notebook to Sergeant Thick.

'About half past nine,' said Jack, noting it was nearly ten o'clock.

'Well we're still waiting for it so you should get going on your beat. If it comes through I'll get you relief so you can go across to the Dock offices with Franks to do the interviewing. Until then you carry on as usual, right?' Thick flicked through the pages of notes that Jack had made earlier. Jack waited.

'One thing I'll say for you Sargent, your handwriting's easy enough to read.' Thick held onto the notebook to go through it and Jack realised he needed to pick up a fresh one on his way out.

'Get yourself across to the North West Railway's Goods Depot will you but go by the Jewish Orphan Asylum in Tenter Street first as they've had an incident this morning,' said Thick.

'What kind of an incident?' asked Jack.

'Usual idiot throwing a stone through a window. Caused a scare more than anything but just in case it's a pattern of behaviour they're experiencing we should go and check. I'm sending you as you will know how to behave with your background. I make it five minutes past ten, Sargent so get going,' Thick checked his own pocket watch with the clock.

'Right,' said Jack as he leant over the duty Sergeant's desk and collected a fresh notebook.

Jack turned out of the Station and walked towards Great Prescot Street. He paused to look at a foundation stone on the building engraved as laid by the Chief Rabbi, Dr. Adler, on, as it was then, Tenter Ground in Goodman's Fields, in 1846. The building had survived and recently the Orphan's Asylum had just escaped the fire that had spread from the Garrick Theatre.

Jack lifted the door knocker and banged it three times. He heard footsteps and positioned himself a respectful distance from the door as it opened. Jack saluted and the young woman stood back at the sight of the uniform.

'Have you come about the window?' she asked.

'Yes, Constable Sargent from Leman Street, Miss er . . . ?'

'Come in,' the nameless woman stood back to let Jack walk through into the hall.

'Was anyone hurt?' asked Jack, pulling out his notebook.

'Not physically, no, but it frightened the children. They'll get used to it as they grow up.'

Jack paused registering the tone. 'It's happened before then, has it?' asked Jack making a note.

'Of course it has. We always get this when someone's out of work.'

Jack paused, frowned slightly trying to understand, then made a note.

'How many children do you have here?' he asked with a half-smile in case it would help. It didn't.

'Fifty-four, but thirty-three are double orphans and twenty-one have lost one parent,' said the woman.

'What sort of ages?' Jack asked.

'Two to eleven years. Some come from the workhouse authorities as we are a certified school now. Come through, I can show you where the broken window is. I left everything as it was in case the Sergeant sent someone.' She led the way through the hall towards the side of the building and Jack stared at a brick on the floor surrounded by shattered glass.

'And no-one was hurt?' he repeated, ready to make a note.

'Not physically.' Again the emphasis on the physical.

'Do you mean the children were afeared by the window being broken?' asked Jack.

'Of course, they were. Wouldn't you be frightened if it kept happening?'

'I didn't get your name,' said Jack.

'Abigail Cohen,' said the young woman. Jack picked up her question.

'The answer is, yes, I would have been frightened. I went into an orphanage when I was nine years old, a double orphan as you put it as both my parents died.' Jack paused and thought that no-one had thrown bricks through the windows though. 'Don't you have any idea at all who it might be?' he continued. 'Anyone making a nuisance of themselves?'

'No one I can put a name to,' said Abigail. 'It's increased though and I've seen a tract recently that one of the new residents had brought with him from Germany. A piece by a Wilhelm Marr. Since the new German state two years ago the views have got worse. There's some feeling in America in the papers that the recent depression there is caused in the financial centres by Jews in prominent positions. It incites people.'

'So you think this is targeting the orphanage because its Jewish?' said Jack, slightly frowning, slowly taking the situation in.

'Yes,' Abigail said, in her matter of fact way. Her eyes gave Jack the impression she was weary.

'Right, well we'd better call in once a day then.' He shut his notebook and pocketed the pencil. 'If you see anyone loitering let me or any constable that's on this beat, know. We'll catch them.' Jack said reassuringly and gave his half smile again.

'Will you? And what will be done with them if you catch someone?' asked Abigail. Jack could see the disbelief.

'Charge them with damage to property. That's what they're doing.' Jack looked into the young woman's eyes and had a distinct feeling that there was a hint of mockery present. He looked away and continued. 'I don't like the fact that someone is frightening children. I don't like the fact that its regular, from what you say. The law's the law and if someone is breaking the law then we deal with it. I know there's the Offences Against the Person Act, but I'll have to talk to the Sergeant about what's going on here and how it fits. Political changes, you see mean that situations have been added to the Act since 1861. It's what a lawyer would call "Harm." Look, I'll call in everyday and see how things are.'

'And when you're not here?' Abigail asked.

'I'm rarely away. As I said I'll talk to the Sergeant, make sure a visit is included on the beat.' Jack set his mouth into a firm line, his eyes stared into those of the young woman and moments passed as neither blinked or looked away. Abigail nodded, finally believing him.

'Yes, I think you will,' she said, turning to walk back to the front door. Jack followed her.

Having taken his leave and once he was outside again he was struck by the poor quality of the air at that time of the morning to the clarity there had been when he first woke. He walked back and banged on the front door.

He waited and eventually heard footsteps coming. The walk of a teacher he thought, designed for the children to know she was coming so that they stopped their antics before she entered the room. Abigail opened the door and raised her eyebrows in surprise that the young policeman was still there.

On the doorstep Jack said:

'I should have explained better. I may be wrong but I think it's like children throwing stones at trains as they pass. The law's including new situations as I said. I think it's about what the people doing it intend. Frankly, I've only made arrests where a fist has connected with a face but there's more to be considered than the action involved from what I've seen in court. This might fit and that's why I need to speak to the Sergeant. Miss Cohen, if I'm not here the constable is usually Constable Banks. I'll fill him in on what's been going on. If you have that tract you mentioned it might help me understand better.'

'Thank-you, I'll get it for you for next time,' said Abigail 'Only thing is it's in German. You'll need to get it translated.'

'Right,' said Jack. 'I may know someone who can do that.' As Jack saluted and turned for the station he left her standing at the front door pondering the contact. She watched him as he walked away in the direction of Leman Street.

*

It was half past eleven as Jack waited for Sergeant Thick to finish with the Tome he held at the duty desk. Thick was flicking through the seventy-nine sections of the Offences Against the Person Act 1861.

'I'm not sure,' Thick said. 'These changes were supposed to make things simpler. That example about children throwing stones is about endangering the passenger. The other one you flagged up to me is after Fenians left barrels of explosives to go off. That's damage to property as far as I can see. You'd need a lawyer to give an opinion, Sargent. What's this tract she mentioned?'

'I haven't seen it, but Miss Cohen said that she would get me a copy,' said Jack. 'It will need translating, by the sound of it.'

'Who's going to do that?' said Thick.

'I know a man up at the German Chapel,' said Jack.

The Serjeant nodded.

'Easiest thing will be if we caught who's doing it and then he resists arrest. We've got him that way, you can do something with a person resisting arrest. Anyway we'll keep an eye on it and you or Banks call in daily as you said. See if you can get a description from someone in the home. Chances are someone's seen him. Better get back out on the street and over to the Good's Depot.'

'Right, Sergeant,' said Jack, picking up his helmet. 'Is there still nothing from Sergeant Franks?'

'No,' said Thick.

'I'll wander into Tenter Street on my way back,' said Jack.

After thirty minutes walking through the sidings and trying the doors of the warehouses at the Goods Depot Jack started to walk back to Tenter Street.

It was time he ate something he decided. This area did not hold the delights of the many kitchens he had been welcomed into in the west of the division. Since the coddled egg at breakfast he had eaten nothing and he felt the gnawing in his stomach. Eight hours without food would not sit well with his system. Jack had neglected eating this morning and now could feel the sense of shaking starting as it always did when he went too long without a meal. He thought about his usual watering holes which had been ignored today with the focus on the Asylum.

By one o'clock an idea was forming in his mind. He had remembered that the German Chapel towards the top of Leman Street had a soup kitchen. As well as a mug of soup he may collect information on the tract by Wilhelm Marr.

All appeared quiet in front of the Jewish Orphanage and Asylum. If anyone was watching they would have seen the young constable go in this morning. True they could take their time. They may know that a constable's shift would last eight hours. And if they did they could come back at any time after it ended. Charlie would be on later though.

He looked around, a small frisson at the nape of his neck. People influenced by a tract. That was the implication of what Miss Cohen had said. Why frighten children though? The word incitement came to him. He tried to remember the case.

They may even be keeping an eye on him, thought Jack. He stopped walking and stood in front of the building, arms akimbo. He scanned the street. Just let them try something.

*

'Telegram, Sergeant,' said a constable coming to the desk. He handed it to Serjeant Thick, who took it and read.

He read it through again, this time aloud:

"Alexandra Palace on fire. Dense smoke. Between 12.30 and 1 o'clock. Telegram sent to Watling Street to the Fire Chief. Reinforcements sent for to Kings Cross. Two fire engines on their way by train to Wood Green. Police to protect artefacts and prevent harm to public."

Thick glanced at the clock. A quarter past one. Someone had moved quickly.

'Constable, get out onto the street and use your rattle,' ordered Thick. 'As men come back get them using theirs to call as many back as will hear. Then send them in to me.'

Jack had finished eating bread and soup at the German Chapel. He was disappointed that no one recognised the name of Wilhelm Marr. However so many of the men present had arrived in London more than two years ago. Draining his mug of soup he heard a number of police rattles from the direction of Leman Street Police Station. He took his mug back to the kitchen and thanked the woman there. Then he turned and started to run. Expecting to see the station raised to the ground in an explosion or under siege, he was greeted by Charlie Banks waving his rattle along with five other constables.

'Go in Jack, Thick wants us all back for a fire.'

'Do you know where?' asked Jack.

'Not yet, 'said Charlie as Jack passed him, 'must be a big-'un.'

Jack joined ten other constables and Thick peered out of the door to stop the summons.

'Come in will you, now,' Thick called to the men on the street, 'Enough men will have heard the row you've kicked up.'

40

With fifteen men before him Thick started to explain.

'We're to get across as fast as we can to the Alexandra Palace. It's on fire and our job is the protection of artefacts and to prevent harm to the public. Let's hope not many are in the way of danger today,' said Thick.

'Unlikely' said Jack, 'Today's a sixpence entry or a guinea season ticket so it will be busy. I was there on Sunday, with my young lady, and saw the notices. That's how I know.'

'Right, we go now,' said Thick, his face set. 'Men will be coming together from all divisions.'

They moved off to the Police carriage. Jack stared out of the window thinking about his time with Harriet the day before.

Sunday had been a beautiful visit. Jack went over in his mind how he and Harriet had walked in the extensive park. Her confidence had grown in her new position since that last December at the hotel in Westminster. Yet it was six months and still she would not give him an answer about dates to marry. Jack's frown added to the sombre atmosphere in the carriage as he and the other constables were driven towards Muswell Hill. He remembered how Harriet had turned and laughed at him as he pressed her again for a date to speak to her mother. They had walked by a theatre built for an audience of thousands.

'Italian, Jack,' Harriet had said, pointing to decorations of blue, gold and grey.

'Oh yes?' Jack had laughed at the firm manner as she had nodded at the stately building. 'Get a lot of Italian buildings in Honiton, do you?'

'No, silly man. I read the paper on the table in the hall the morning it all opened. It's got a nave, like a church and transepts and a dome at the centre.' She looked up at the building she was describing. 'We're to have a new church in Honiton soon. Then we won't have to climb the hill for services.' Harriet turned towards him and smiled at the thought of an easier journey in her home town.

'Are you now. Like to get married in it?' Jack seized the opportunity.

41

Harriet's face had clouded over and he saw it. He lost his smile as this was always the response lately when he brought the subject up.

'Let's just enjoy the day, shall we?' Harriet had said walking towards stone vases containing shrubs and flowering plants. And that was what they had done, although the afternoon had grown cold for Jack. Now on June 9th the building was apparently on fire.

The carriage was pulling in and Jack could see more than a hundred firemen working from the west side of the burning building as he jumped down. He started to count the number of firemen there and gave up when he reached sixty as a voice called his name.

'Jack, I wondered if you'd be here as you're a Reserve.'

Momentarily distracted as he watched a hose being pulled across a railway line it was a few seconds until Jack turned and then he was shaking Ted Phillips's hand. Bringing himself up sharply he withdrew his hand and started to salute the newly promoted Sergeant instead. Ted grinned at him and reached out for the hand.

'We'll have our work cut out to clear this,' said Ted, laughing at the confusion on the young Constable's face at how to respond to his old mentor.

'Well, young Jack, how are you?' said a voice both Ted and Jack knew and it was Sergeant Morris who had spotted Jack as he moved through the ranks of constables gawping at the destruction before them.

Morris had come in search of Ted Phillips. Despite the situation there was a reunion as it was months since Jack had seen Morris. They had both been involved in a near hit and run in Piccadilly while investigating the case of the Faceless Woman. Jack had saved Morris from being run over by the coach that had careered deliberately towards them through Piccadilly.

Morris had spent some time recovering from a broken arm and Ted Phillips had received his early promotion in order to fill the gap. Now Morris shook his saviour's hand and gripped Jack's other arm with the affection he had come to feel for the younger constable. Jack in turn pumped the Sergeant's hand up and down with enthusiasm, realising that the moustache he so admired was even bigger and now had joined the side whiskers.

'Is the Inspector here?' asked Jack, looking around for Tom Hunt. This was perfect to be back with these two men and he was aware he felt at home in their company. He continued to look around, eagerly searching out the face of the Inspector in whose team he had first gone into plain clothes. Remaining in Leman Street was one of the hardest instructions he had taken once the case of the Faceless Woman was resolved. He had waited each month for the instruction to re-join the team in Camberwell. So far it had not come.

'He is, and a few more faces from the station that you know. Here's Thick now,' Morris nodded as Thick walked over towards the small group.

'Well Sargent I see you've re-joined your old team,' said Thick. 'I'll leave him with you Phillips then?' Thick half-asked, half-said as a statement.

Ted nodded, aware of how Thick considered that Jack was a maverick, someone good to have your back but clearly with more of a preference for working in Tom Hunt's team than operating under Sergeant Thick's direction. Unpredictable and therefore a headache. Better leave him with the two Sergeants from Camberwell.

Thick surveyed the scene. 'People have poured in for that ballet and concert that was due to start at half past two,' he said. 'I saw the advert in the paper about Mr Frederick Archer playing the organ this afternoon.'

'There were performances lined up for the whole week, it was in the Telegraph,' said Ted.

'Was there anything you fancied?' Jack asked Ted.

'Not in the way of performances. Those rhododendrons over there would do me in our garden,' Ted nodded in the general direction of brightly coloured bushes.

'We saw them, yesterday, in fair beauty, Ted. You should have come. Harriet and I were here yesterday.' Jack added as a way of explanation. 'I can't believe the place is on fire now. It's only been open for a fortnight,' Jack stared at the blaze.

'So it has, just two weeks, and it's gone up like dry leaves in a bonfire. How is Miss Fildew?' asked Ted.

'Well, thank-you.' Ted noted the shadow pass over the face. Jack collected himself and grinned, 'Still avoiding matrimony,' he added.

'She's very young still,' Ted said quietly.

'Yes, I suppose so.' Jack's face screwed into a grimace. Ted wondered if the relationship was starting to run a natural course of fading. He decided to leave any further comment.

'Well, we should move and get over towards where they're laying out the artefacts on the grass, 'Morris said, as he started to usher the groups of constables from Camberwell towards where exhibitors and staff were trying to save as many of the most valuable pieces of art from destruction. Jack watched the tapestries and paintings being carried in to the park.

'Keep your eyes open for two vases, Jack, it might be the way to a knighthood, as they belong to the Queen,' called Ted with a grin.

They moved in a crowd of uniforms towards the area where pieces of art lay on the grass as numerous as buttercups on a June afternoon.

'Yes but keep your eyes on the spectators and make sure they don't get into any harm, 'called Thick as he turned back towards the small team of fifteen he had brought.

Thick walked backwards still explaining to Ted, 'There's a character that went in and out six times. The Inspector had to threaten to arrest him to stop him going in again. Brave or stupid, I'm not sure which.' Thick finally turned his back on them as he re-joined the men from Leman Street.

'There must be several thousands of people here, Ted,' said Jack looking around incredulously. 'Thank goodness the attractions inside hadn't started yet and that most people were in the park.'

'They've come in from the surrounding areas as they've seen the smoke. It was like a tower of black, blue and purple and very dense. You couldn't see the fire as it was a sunny day. The column of smoke did its work though eventually, and firemen and police have been pouring in,' said Ted.

'Funny no one thought to build a lake here,' said Morris, looking around at the crowds, taking in faces just in case he saw someone that he knew.

'Where is the nearest lake?' asked Jack.

'About a quarter of mile away,' said Morris, meaningfully. Jack looked at him as the realisation dawned upon him.

'No wells?' Jack asked. 'It's as if it was prepared to go up, like a bonfire. The wind won't help. Something in it has been quick to ignite. So, it will just burn then. There's nothing can be done to stop it.'

The men stood, listening to the sound of the live thing that consumed the building.

'That's right,' said Ted. 'Going up like a bonfire.'

'My life, five hundred thousand pounds up in smoke. They'll not get five hundred pounds for it now,' Jack said to Ted who nodded in agreement.

'Where's everything going to go?' asked Jack.

'King's Cross is what I heard,' answered Ted.

Firemen were bringing people out and they sat some distance away struggling to get their breath from the smog of smoke, some telling others their story and a woman wiping her hands down her dress to try and remove the black stains from the soot. Emerging from the miasma pouring out of every window and opening available in the building was the inky blackness of foul smoke. Jack could not believe the number of people that seemed to be milling about in front of the building.

'Do we know yet where it started?' asked Morris.

45

'Up in the centre of the dome. That's the story going around. I heard it said it was the carelessness of a zinc worker. There's a lining of Papier Mache, or there was,' said Ted.

'Good grief, they're still up there. Look,' said Jack, pointing at the dome.

'I thought most of the workers had got out,' Morris shielded his eyes against the sun.

The others followed the direction of Jack's arm. Flames were spreading and fire was falling in great flakes, scattering as it fell in waves on the ground beneath. Those nearby were in danger as the flames spread along the dome. The floor split in several places and it was clear the dome would not survive.

There in the upper and outer section of the gallery on the Great Dome, just under the flagstaff, were four workmen trying to get down. Two of them were making their way towards a ladder. Another two men, possibly metal workers, were on the outside of the Dome ready to gild it. One of the men appeared to pause, hesitate and then stopped. The coughing was audible and he seemed to turn for the ladder. The four others were clearly trying to make it to a staircase already ablaze.

Jack had already begun to move, Ted Phillips's voice a fading sound in his consciousness, calling him back.

'Jack, its suicide!'

*

A rope which had been used to lift material to an upper level still had the workman's bucket knotted at the bottom. Jack looked at the timber strut which the rope was tied to and it was still clear of flames. The heat was unbearable, and beams fell across his path. Flames moved and consumed the air as he breathed. He was already coughing. He could not see more than a few feet in front of him but was aware of finery that had been missed in the attempt to empty the building. He heard windows falling in with the ear-splitting crash as glass exploded when it found impact.

46

Jack sat on the bucket and swung himself clear one hundred and fifty feet above the flames. From there he got onto an iron column and called to the workman. The man walked a few feet and Jack could feel the smoke filling his lungs. The heat rising from the blaze below reminded him of his mother's rebuke when a child as he stood too close to the fire.

'Stand back, Jack,' she had said. What would she say now if she could see him?

'*Come on,*' Jack shouted to the workman.

His voice rose above the roar of fire which was moving like a voracious animal towards them. The man shouted back but the noise of the fire meant that the reply could not be heard. The rest of what Jack wanted to say was lost in coughing.

The man calculated the distance and walked back a few feet. Jack realised he was going to try and jump onto the iron column. He pushed himself back as far as he could without falling to make room, his right hand reaching for the bucket still knotted onto the rope. They would have seconds once the man landed. If he made it.

It was black below him now with the smoke. It was rising and the air was getting worse. They could still get out if the man would jump. Jack worked out he would give him twenty seconds and if the man had not moved by then he would have to get out himself. He started to count, 'One, two...'

He shouted again, 'Jump, man, *jump.*'

Jack saw behind the man the works of art that had not been moved out. Presumably the rescuers of antiquity had concentrated on areas that were safer. The visibility was worsening by the second. Jack shifted his weight from foot to foot to be sure of his balance. Was it his imagination or was the surface of the column getting hot beneath his boots?

Jack wiped his hand across his face as he reached number fifteen in his counting. He looked at the wetness and realised his eyes were streaming. They had been sore for some minutes. More coughing overtook him and he got ready to escape. Then the man jumped, building matter fell around Jack and the workman, the heat grew more intense.

The man landed on the column in front of him.

—

It was almost instinct, Jack later told Ted Phillips. The workman was used to moving around on narrow ledges, and he and Jack both swung clear, four feet positioned on the top rim of the bucket, and then to the ground safely. But the column where Jack had waited was engulfed in thick smoke and Jack, glancing back once, ran with the workman for their lives.

Running and coughing they were out into the sunshine, smelling the green foliage instead of choking smoke. Coughing overtook Jack and he retched, falling to the ground. He was picked up in a blanket to get him away from the building by two firemen. They carried him to an area clear of smoke, where the noise of the animal that consumed so much in the Palace could only just be heard. The air was clear of smoke and Doctor Brown, the Police Surgeon was bending over him. Jack looked back, loth to stop watching the fire, partially drawn to it as he knew he had come close to being consumed in its vicious path.

His last memory was of a fireman emerging from the building carrying a body. It was later identified as John Kelsey who had suffocated trying to look after the plate owned by Bertram and Roberts the refreshment contractors. Habit made Jack look for an identifying number on the fireman's uniform so he would remember. Then his view was filled with two welcome faces bending over him as Morris and Ted arrived and there was Ted's voice speaking into his ear.

'Jack, are you alright?' And that was all for some time.

*

'How are you feeling?' Ted asked Jack as he came round. The answer was lost in a choking cough from another person at his side.

'Pretty jawled out,' Jack managed to say. Ted shrugged, assuming it meant rough.

Doctor Brown leant across Ted and put an arm under Jack's arm pit, nodding at Ted to take the other side.

Together they sat him up and hauled him a few feet to the side until he was able to rest against a tree trunk. Jack realised that his uniform was ripped and his right arm was hurting where he had held onto the rope, using his left to steady the landing he and the workman had had.

Ted rolled up a piece of cloth and put it into the hollow of Jack's back so that he had some support. Jack realised that he was in shade, far from the burning building, within the grounds and in one of those ridiculous moments that occur at such a time, he registered how wonderful the landscaping of the grounds was and how his father would have loved it here.

Doctor Brown was pouring water from a flask and holding it to Jack's lips. 'Drink, he said quietly, but there was a firmness in the direction. 'As much as you can without coughing.'

Jack did as directed and ended in retching most of it up.

Once settled the doctor listened to Jack's heart. 'Good job you're young and fit.' Doctor Brown did not like its pace however. Morris had run for the doctor as they saw Jack carried out, which had worried the doctor more considering that Morris spent too much time behind a desk these days.

'You'll have taken in chemicals. Your airway will be swollen and irritated. You may feel confused and nauseous for a while. Drink if you can. Keep feeding him the water, Sergeant, if he'll take it. I must go over to others but I will come back soon and see how he is.'

Doctor Brown looked at Jack until the retching stopped. Jack tried to steady the breathing, aware it was noisy and not coming easily and nodded at the Doctor. Satisfied that his patient was coping, Doctor Brown patted him on the shoulder and walked to the next man laid out on the ground.

Jack felt slightly drunk and confused. The cough came back after what seemed like seconds. It was almost a reflex action that he could not stop.

'The smoke does that. You saved a life, Jack. We saw it, it was like being in a nightmare watching you go in there,' said Ted bending over him.

'The workman, he got out, didn't he?' Jack managed to get the words out before the coughing started again. This time he spat out black mucus.

'That's right get rid of it,' said Ted. 'The workman did get out. He's in much the same state as you. He's over there.'

Ted pointed to a man trying to breath rapidly. Jack glanced across and nodded.

'You'll get a commendation for this, we'll make sure of it,' Ted continued. 'Try and get more of that water down you. Doctor Brown thinks it's better stuff comes up if you can, so don't worry about retching.' Ted looked at the red eyes and cherry red skin of the man before him.

'How's the Palace doing?' asked Jack. It was the second question and he was aware his voice sounded strange.

Ted saw Jack's confusion to his own voice and for the third time that afternoon a reassuring hand was laid on his arm.

'It'll be alright, everything will go back to normal eventually, the doctor says it will. Your voice will sound funny for a bit. The Palace is gone Jack. The Royal Box is gone. Those drapes around it caught fire as the ceiling came in. Actually they probably helped the fire spread if truth be told. Did you see that crystal candelabra inside yesterday?' asked Ted.

Jack slowly nodded and decided it was not a good idea as the headache he had made him feel his head should be removed.

'It's completely destroyed. It was jewelled they say,' said Ted.

Jack nodded again and winced.

'Put up for the visit of the Shah of Persia. Well they'll have to think of somewhere else to take him now. All the dining rooms are gone. I've seen kitchen equipment burned I would not have thought would have gone up. Only area that was fire-proof was the cellars, so the stock of wine is safe,' explained Ted.

'The man that the Fireman carried out?' Jack managed to ask.

'He was already dead when they found him, suffocated. Lost his life trying to protect things of value.' Ted moved some dry twigs with his foot. 'And the night watchman. He died in the transept trying to protect life and property. Life I can understand but not things. You came close, lad, in there.' Ted's tone was slightly reproving.

'I thought I could get out,' said Jack. 'I did. Ted,' Jack looked at the people sitting around on the grass, grubby faces from the smoke, some in blankets to cope with the shivering. It was not borne of cold though and he had seen that reaction before in Barn fires. Shock, the cook at the Squire's had told him it was.

'What's a Shah?' asked Jack.

'A King of sorts. He's in Berlin at the moment but will come to London later in the month. Hunt wants to talk to you so you'd better get better. Do you hear me?' Ted took his helmet off, ran a hand through his hair, and then repositioned it. Despite his state Jack noted the concern in Ted's eyes.

'I will,' said Jack before the coughing overtook him again.

'Clean air, young man, for you for a while I think,' Dr Brown said as he walked up and set his bag down next to Jack. 'Has any more mucus come up?'

Jack nodded and said, 'Black.'

'Well its moving, which is what we want. Get it out of you so stay put for a while. At least the air over here is clear of the smoke. The man you rescued had been asleep in his lunch hour. He awoke to the smoke. You picked the right one to rescue. He's an ex-sailor so would have ability with that rope you used. Any of the other three would probably have fallen in that stunt you did. Well done. Keep spitting out the mucus as it shifts. I'll be back shortly but there's a few more men I want to have a look at.'

'I'll be fine, Doctor,' Jack started to try and get up.

'No, you won't. I'll have you sacked if you move, Jack. You stay put until I come back and then we'll decide what to do with you.' Doctor Brown gave Ted a meaningful look and Ted nodded.

51

'Doctor's orders Jack,' said Ted. 'Perhaps I can distract you. Can I give him his next job Doctor?'

'Anything if it keeps him still and in the clean air. Where are you living now?' The Doctor asked Jack.

'West India Dock Cottages, 'Jack managed to say before more coughing started. He spat and Dr Brown looked at the black mucus and shook his head.

'He lodges with my mother,' explained Ted.

'We may have to think about somewhere with better air quality than that. A stint by the sea would be the best place. Can we get him across the river for tonight? Perhaps a place in the dormitory at Camberwell, Sergeant?' suggested the doctor.

Jack almost choked in trying to say no. Ted laughed knowing how badly Jack slept in the dormitories.

'We'll sort something out Doctor,' said Ted.

'I'll be back within the hour and I want to see you in the same place and not trying to resume duties, alright?' said Doctor Brown firmly. He picked up his Doctor's bag and moved across to a small group of men with injuries.

Ted waited until he was sure that Brown was out of earshot and then turned and faced the tree that Jack was leaning against. When he was sure that no one could see his mouth in order to lip-read he said quietly, 'Hunt has to get the team together again for this Shah's visit.'

Jack leaned back against his tree. Despite the state he was in a smile started. 'Where....'he began but got no further as he was consumed with coughing.

Once the spasm had produced more mucus Ted suggested, 'Just listen and don't try and speak. As I said Hunt has to get the team together again for the visit of this Shah of Persia. Security issues are on the table.'

'Are we friendly with them?' Jack managed the question.

'We should be. The country's on the other side of Afghanistan and it's in our interests to have a good relationship with Persia. Especially with Russia on the prowl. No Russian army would risk the passes in Afghanistan with a hostile Persia on its right flank,' explained Ted.

'Get them onside?' asked Jack.

'What part of listen don't you understand, lad? But yes that's right, we get their army on our side, with a few well trained European troops and maintain peace. It benefits their king and us. It's to our mutual advantage Jack.'

'Plain clothes?' asked Jack, despite Ted's gestures to stop him.

'That's right,' said a third voice, 'Although I'm not sure this is the right time Sergeant to be giving the constable a briefing.' The voice belonged to Inspector Tom Hunt, and Jack tried to rise to attention but both Hunt and Ted firmly stopped him. Hunt joined both the men on the grass under the tree. Facing Jack he hugged his knees and waited for the coughing fit to subside. Hunt and Ted exchanged meaningful looks at the state of the young man who they both regarded as someone they liked to have their backs.

*

Once Jack was comfortable again, Hunt said, 'Dr Brown tells me you need good clean air and some rest to get over this. Apart from the post mortem which, by your actions this morning you'll be called to, you could assume special duties after some sickness days.'

Jack tried to speak but Hunt held up a hand to stop Jack interrupting.

'No, don't try and speak,' said Hunt. 'I'm aware that you're not taking leave days and choosing to work continually. I know that tendency in men without a family. Keeping busy stops the intense loneliness. Morris has said he and his wife will have you to stay in their neck of the woods for a few days as it's a cleaner area than West India Dock and I'll see you after that. Dr Brown will look in on you tomorrow.' Hunt started to get up and Jack felt an intense pricking at the back of his eyes. Blinking, he wiped a grimy hand across his face leaving a smear of grey.

'Smoke,' was all he managed. Hunt held out his hand despite the grime on Jack's. The two men shook hands until the coughing consumed Jack again.

'I'll get his things across the river,' offered Ted.

'Good. As far as the Shah goes, Sargent, your background in Sussex may be useful. There's some suggestion that he go to Brighton and Portsmouth. Both have invited him. Security is our call but we'll go into that in a few days' time.' Hunt paused as Jack had started to go red in the face and was struggling to speak. 'Lay still, man, for goodness sake,' said Hunt.

The Inspector and Ted were up and on either side of Jack as he waved an arm and started to retch. He looked into Ted's eyes and tried to point but Hunt blocked his view and defeated he collapsed back into the strong support from Ted Phillips.

'Mentally affected, perhaps,' said Hunt under his breath.

'I've seen it happen,' answered Ted as, satisfied that Jack was now resting against the trunk of the tree and calming down, he stood up and joined Hunt in staring at the young constable.

'Damn shame,' said Hunt. Both men were obscuring Jack's view now and he shook his head and stared at the sky.

For the cause of Jack's unsettled behaviour was the sight of a blonde man who wore his hair tied back. He had rolled up a small and precious tapestry or painting. Jack had been unable to see clearly. Unable to speak Jack saw him stuff it into his coat lining. Indeed Jack had been looking for him earlier in the company of Harry Franks for it was one of the two men who had made off with a small and precious object from the West India Offices earlier that morning.

Jack watched as Hunt and Ted separated and stopped blocking his view. He looked on helpless as the blonde man disappeared into the crowd.

'Harry, get Harry,' was all that Jack could say before the mist swimming in front of his eyes closed in.

Three

Settling into the spare room prepared by Mrs Morris had not been a strain, although Jack was beyond too much detail by the time they got him inside. South of Camberwell, on the City branch of the London to Chatham and Dover line, was the home of Sergeant and Mrs Morris. It was located just off the Dulwich Road at Herne Hill. The air was sweeter than around the West India Docks and the area still very green despite the increase in population. Sergeant Morris commuted daily as the branch line stopped at Camberwell and Camberwell New Road. Here the Morris family had spent the last few years, bringing up their two sons who were now both articled in the City. Of all this Jack was oblivious as dusk fell on the area.

His dreams were full of water. Water that had been needed desperately and which had dried up. As he began to emerge from the Laudanum Doctor Brown had given him to suppress the cough, Jack could see a face of someone carried out by the Fireman. Except it was not the man who had lost his life but a woman and she came into view clearly in the gas light as she approached the bed. At first her face blended with others he had known in his life that had approached his sick bed. He struggled for clarity and then started to remember.

'Mrs Morris?' he asked, not quite sure he was right.

'Yes, you've woken after a good sleep. Don't talk too much in case it starts the coughing. I'll get you water and let the lady know that you're awake.'

'Lady? Who? asked Jack. She did not answer but left the room. He half propped himself up on his elbow and stared at a dishevelled man in the mirror opposite.

Ann Black was next to him with the trained quietness of one who attended the sick.

'I thought ... 'Jack started. Ann paused in the action of caring, recollecting that there was a girl.

'I'm sorry it's not who you hoped it would be. Doctor Brown sent me across with you in the carriage.'

'My doctor,' said Jack, with an attempt at a grin.

'Not yet, Jack. And you know better than that. Don't you go getting me arrested in a Police Sergeant's home!' Ann looked at Mrs Morris who had entered with a jug of water and a glass. She either had not heard or chose to ignore the subject.

'Breathing a little better?' asked Ann. 'Who was it that you had hoped to see?'

'It doesn't matter,' said Jack, and then retched as he took too much water.

'It's getting dark, what time is it?' he asked once he could breathe again. He noticed that the window was open and that he could hear a blackbird who, like him, had escaped the smoke and smell of industry. 'How many dead? Do we know?' Jack asked.

'I only know of two by the time we left. Amazing that there weren't more. One less than there might have been, thanks to you I gather.' Ann poured water into a bowl on the table and dipped a cloth into it. Ringing it out she wiped Jack's brow.

'Now if you weren't a married woman,' he said attempting joviality.

'But I am,' said Ann with a stern, well-practised stare, used to keeping male patients in order.

'Why aren't you a doctor yet? That woman is, isn't she? I can't remember her name. Is that usual, after something like this that my head should be so empty?' asked Jack.

'That's just the Laudanum. It will wear off. And "that woman" is Mrs Garrett Anderson. She's just faced a vote to be admitted to the British Medical Association but that's not generally known yet,' Ann explained.

'Not sure I hold with such stuff, Laudanum I mean, not the lady joining the BMA. That's good isn't it? You won't have to wait too long by the sound of it now.' Jack started to prop himself up on the bed with one elbow, and the cough started again.

'Lay still, Jack, the Laudanum was only to suppress the cough while we got you across here. As to the other issue I don't think women as doctors is certain yet. I've heard there's going to be a motion on the question of women members of the BMA. Some men will vote in favour but I fear most will vote against.' Ann pumped the pillows up behind him and he sank into them again. She picked up a wrist and checked her watch.

'Am I staying the night here?' Jack asked, looking around at the comfort. 'I'm not sure I can travel tonight.'

'If you behave I think Mrs Morris might put up with you for a while longer. No making passes at married women though,' said Ann, her eyes twinkling.

Jack managed a half smile, 'It must be the Laudanum. Not my usual self at the moment. What about the fire?' he asked.

'Done, I think. Sergeant Morris will be able to tell you when he gets back tonight.'

'I needed Harry to come. Harry Franks,' said Jack.

'Perhaps tomorrow,' said Ann. Jack grimaced and she saw it.

'What's it about, Jack?' asked Ann, sensing from the reaction that it may be better to deal with the issue as he clearly was not going to settle.

'I saw a theft at the fire, well near where I was resting. I recognised the man. Harry and I were involved in something early this morning and it's the same thief. I need to tell him I saw one of the men from the West India Dock Offices theft.'

'Will a message do?' asked Ann.

'It might. If Harry comes tomorrow it may be too late. This thief is a specialist and knew what he was after this morning. I suspect it was the same at the Alexandra Palace. Harry needs to know that the man is still around. I doubt that last theft was planned, more likely to be opportunistic. Something small and precious, Harry had said this morning about what he took. The man knew what he was after alright, and I suspect he was given a last-minute shopping list for the Alexandra Palace fire' Jack shifted his position slightly.

'Alright, I'll get a message to him via Morris. Anyone else?' asked Ann, thinking again of the girl that she had recalled had been around in January.

'Yes, message for Charlie Banks as he'll pick up the patrol while I'm off. Tell him to go by the Orphan's Asylum near Great Prescot Street. He'll know where I mean. Tell him, daily, and to check all's well with Miss Abigail Cohen.' Jack said, suddenly tired. 'I promised the lady,' he added as a way of explanation.

'That's enough now. And I promise I'll get those messages through. Now rest. Mrs Morris will be up shortly with a tray for you, so eat what you can and give into the need for sleep. Harry can come tomorrow if it's needed, but tonight, my friend, no one except myself and Mrs Morris. I will be back after my round at the Hospital for Women and Children.' Ann glanced at the lights on the wall and squinted at the starkness.

'I'll get these gas lights turned down a little. Leave them on, Jack, as the effects of the Laudanum and the experience you've had today are likely to give you strange dreams,' said Ann.

If you only knew, thought Jack.

*

Despite Ann's firm rule that Jack was to rest Harry Franks made an appearance by nine o'clock that evening. There was a knock at the door and Ted Phillips came in carrying a bag with Harry behind him. Harry gripped Jack's arm and shook his hand.

'Now, young 'un, not too many heroics in future. I'd like you to outlive me,' said Harry.

'I'll do my best,' grinned Jack.

Both Ted and Harry smiled to see Jack sitting up enjoying a bowl of broth. Harry pulled up a chair on one side of the bed, and sat, resting a hand on a knee. The small valise which Ted deposited at the foot of the bed had a look of quality about it.

'A small gift for you from Inspector Hunt,' he said, sitting down on the opposite side from Harry. 'It might come in handy if you have to go somewhere. I picked up your clothes as well from mother's. There's a few extra things the Inspector thought might be needed while convalescing.'

'Very kind,' said Jack. 'Looks like leather.'

'Yes, I think it is. You'll get a good few years wear out of it,' said Ted, picking the bag up and placing it closer to Jack. Jack ran his hand down one of the sides of the valise. The feel of the leather under his touch gave him pleasure and Ted noted that the smile was back. Jack undid the clasp and peered in. Something white inside the bag caught the light in the room. He looked up at Ted.

'Not signed me up for the cricket team, has he?' he asked, half joking.

All Ted said was, 'Wouldn't surprise me.'

Ted and Harry both bore the marks of smoke on their clothing. Jack registered that Harry had also been helping at the scene of the fire. He thought they both looked drained. Neither of them had had time to change.

The door opened and Mrs Morris appeared with a tray. On it were sandwiches with thick ham bulging from the sides, and two plain white Royal Worcester mugs brimming with steaming tea.

'You must be exhausted,' said Mrs Morris as she set the tray down on the tall boy to the side of Jack's bed. 'I thought a little sustenance might be needed.' She sat on the end of the bed as the two men had taken the chairs.

'You're an angel,' said Harry, reaching for a tea spoon to heap sugar into both mugs. Ted beamed at her as he had reached the same conclusion. He took a mug from Harry and sipped the hot, strong tea, feeling the sweetness reviving him.

'Good of you to come, given the day you've both had,' said Jack. 'Did you get my message?' he asked Harry.

'Yes,' answered Harry. 'I know I'm breaking doctor's orders turning up tonight but I thought you might sleep better if we discussed what you saw now. No point going over it in your mind all night.'

—

59

'Before you get stuck into detail with Harry I wondered about letting Miss Fildew know?' asked Ted.

Jack silently stared at the quality of the valise. 'There's not much point,' he said.

Ted glanced down at him and frowned slightly. He knew Jack was working the relationship out.

'Well, I think there is,' said Ted, softly. 'But it's up to you. I'll call in tomorrow and see you. I must get home before I fall asleep standing up. It's been quite a day. I'll take one of those sandwiches, Harry, before you finish the lot.' Harry passed the plate across the bed to Ted.

'No point worrying her, I mean. It's not as if she will be able to come. Her next day off isn't 'til next Tuesday. All the time will get used up travelling here and back. Leave it, Ted. I'm not sure I can cope with her reaction seeing me like this.' Jack leaned his head back against his pillow and stared briefly at the ceiling.

'Alright, then. I'll get off home. Margaret will be getting anxious after the day's events. The press was all over the site like a disease and it will be in the evening papers. I'll see you after I've had my briefing with Inspector Hunt, Jack,' said Ted, and he gulped a little more tea and made to leave. Mrs Morris opened the door and led Ted out. Harry and Jack could hear them chatting about Ted's children as they made their way down the stairs.

Harry changed his seat for the armchair in the corner of the room facing Jack.

'I shan't sit here long otherwise I'll fall asleep,' said Harry. 'That feels good. I can't believe how stiff I am after the day. One more of those sandwiches will fortify the inner man. Are you sure you won't have one, Jack, they'll do you more good than broth?'

'Yes I will, otherwise I'll be looking a little lear,' said Jack, putting the broth down on a side table and Harry passed the plate across to him.

'And that means?' asked Harry.

'Thin,' answered Jack, his mouth full of ham.

Harry bit into his own sandwich and waited for Jack to finish before he asked, 'Well lad, what was it you saw?'

'The blonde man from the West India offices. I mind him well and he was rolling up something, a tapestry, or a painting, I'm not sure now. Ted and Inspector Hunt then blocked my view as they thought I was hallucinating. I briefly saw the man stuff the item into his coat lining. He blended into the crowd but I could see his hair as he moved off. Do you think you could bear to part with one more of those sandwiches?'

'Of course. Appetite coming back? Good sign. You tuck in.' Harry brushed the crumbs off his trousers and sat forward. Jack ate and Harry waited. Satisfied that Jack was able to talk more he took out a notebook and pencil.

'Can you give me a rough idea of any colours, size? I know this was quick but you registered sufficient to know it was probably an exhibit,' asked Harry.

'Just a mass of green and blue. There were probably so many valuable pieces of art being rescued by staff no-one would think twice about challenging him. I'd been watching people carry out watercolours, tapestries and lay them on the grass. There should be a catalogue somewhere,' said Jack.

'It's probably gone up in flames. We may never know until something precious is found on an arrest, or an owner requests their exhibit back. Well, so we know he's still around, our blonde friend. Must have received another instruction to make him take the risk after the West India Dock office burglary this morning. Whatever you witnessed being rolled up was a precious item I would guess,' said Harry, shutting his notebook. 'I'll get word out to the ports and a basic description. I doubt he'll be the carrier though, too noticeable. Wherever he's from he's a professional.'

'Any news of the other man?' asked Jack.

'Yes, a siting of a man with an injured leg on the train at Poplar. Had problems getting on the train and a guard helped him. Foreign accent apparently when he thanked the guard. Told him he'd fallen. Shows how bad the pain must have been for someone trying to lay low to open up to a guard when he's making his escape. I got a description, even down to his clothing. The guard did us proud. He thought he was Dutch or German, it was that kind of accent. I've put it out to the divisions.'

'Did the guard know the direction he was going?' asked Jack.

'He got onto the North London line which runs up through Bow.'

'Sounds familiar,' said Jack.

'I've used it to go and see the house. Goes up to Hackney Wick and you and I spent an interesting New Year up there, if you remember. Of course he could have stayed on or changed at Bow. We've yet to see if anyone noticed him after Poplar. If he did get off at Bow he could have doubled back on the Blackwall Extension Railway or gone east. Anyway, it's encouraging that we've got a positive sighting.'

'Makes you wonder how someone crosses the line like that blonde man,' said Jack.

'Why him in particular?' asked Harry.

'I mean he clearly has skills. He must know how to treat something that precious without damaging it. There was a lot of care when he handled the item at the Alexandra Palace. And the speed with which they went up those ropes and came down,' said Jack.

'Who knows. Maybe he learnt to climb like that on-board ship. No matter where he was trained, Jack, he's made a decision at some point to steal. Skills or no skills, that was conscious and that puts him away as far as I'm concerned. He may not have that different a background to you. But you became a policeman and he a thief,' said Harry.

'But doesn't it interest you what it is in someone's experience to make that decision?'

'Him less so because he does clearly have skills. If you showed me a child that stole a guinea and bought food I'd have more interest. What I'd give my energies to is the character who's behind it. Someone benefitting from devious double dealing but carries a social position of the type where the highest in the land probably want to know them. The man employing our blonde friend and the man with the limp will be audacious enough and shrewd enough to break the rules but not be found out. He'll find his specialists and look after them because he needs them. He'll pay them well and they'll work for him again and again. I doubt there was any intention of taking that artefact from the Alexandra Palace today when we witnessed the escape this morning. And then there was the fire. A gift. Do you know what that says to me, Jack?' Harry leant forward.

'No,' said Jack.

'Our man at the top is here in London and he knew what he wanted from the Alexandra Palace. That's not something the average crook would know. Think about the sort of people who have lent exhibits. Earls, Dukes. Our man knows these people and what they have exhibited. I should think he's been in their homes and seen what he fancies.' Harry stopped talking as the door opened.

Ann Black stood in the doorway and looked from Jack to his visitor.

'I'm afraid I'll have to ask you to go Sergeant Franks,' said Ann. 'Jack wasn't supposed to have visitors tonight. Can it wait until the morning?'

'Of course, Mrs Black. I looked in when I got your message in case it would help Jack sleep to know his information had been passed on.' Harry started to stand. 'I could do with getting home and removing the smell of smoke from my person. It's been a hard day all round. You must be tired yourself.'

'It's certainly been a long day,' said Ann.

'Could I escort you across the river?' asked Harry.

'Thank-you, that would be kind. Perhaps a cab at this time of night,' said Ann as she took Jack's wrist between her thumb and finger for the pulse.

'Before you go, what about the Palace now, Harry?' asked Jack.

'The whole thing's gone, Jack. I got there quite early with Superintendent Manson. The Firemen were saying that it was probably a coal falling from the Dome that set fire to something in the Cupola. Terrible thing the way it moved so fast.'

'Like a barn fire in full heat of summer,' said Jack.

Harry nodded. 'I've not seen one but I can imagine. I heard there was papier maché and a light timber frame in the Palace roof. I was trying to get the musicians out as they all wanted to go back in for their instruments. I suppose it's their livelihood. They can't work without them and it was difficult for them to understand how fast the fire would spread. What they did save is in a right state. The ballet costumes are just as bad. I kept saying human life was more important. Some of them didn't share my sentiments.' Harry stared at the bed, seeing things from the day that he could not share. 'By three o'clock the whole thing was gone. Just twisted shapes of wreckage, open to the sky. By twilight it was taking on the appearance of an old ruin.'

'Were there just the two deaths, Harry?' asked Jack.

'Yes, as far as I know anyway. One of the firemen on the spot, the Foreman actually, man called Meeks, has a fracture of the ribs and a bruised back. He's quite seriously hurt. And another man, about your age, William Bates, has bruising but not seriously hurt.'

'That's incredible there weren't more,' said Jack.

Ann placed Jack's arm back onto the sheets.

'Your pulse is a racing a little but that's probably tiredness,' said Ann. 'The house surgeon, Adam Young, got dozens of extra beds ready but they weren't needed.'

'The railway and the outer terraces weren't damaged either, so the outdoor amusements will carry on. They're talking about re-opening the park on Wednesday, would you believe,' said Harry. He started to stretch and stifled a yawn. 'Well young Jack, I must behave and leave you now or Mrs Black will have my head for dissection. Not that you'll find much of interest in there. I'll wait for you in the hall, Mrs Black.'

'Thank-you, I shan't be long now,' said Ann. 'Did you keep some of the sputum for me to see?'

Jack nodded and looked at a covered dish which Mrs Morris had left on the mantelpiece. It was dark but no longer black. Ann removed the dish from the room and the two men waited for her return.

Jack could hear the blackbird again and decided that the bird must be on the roof. Dark was closing in and Jack imagined the lively, vibrant Palace that he had walked around on Sunday with Harriet. Now it would be a bare shell of blackened bricks, threatened by every gust of wind. There would be no glass glinting in the sun. The windows would be blackened holes.

Harry was leaving. 'Rest up now Jack. Nice room this. Morris and his wife won't be in a rush to get rid of you so accept their hospitality and get better. There's to be a Coroner's hearing and you'll no doubt be called after your antics this afternoon. I'll get the police artist across to you tomorrow so you can describe our blonde friend to him. I'll mention what you saw when I see the Curator tomorrow in case they miss something while they document the valuables. At least that way we stand a chance of finding out what has gone missing.'

'I hope you have a good rest Harry. I'm grateful to you for coming. I feel I will sleep now,' said Jack.

'Good,' said Ann, standing in the doorway. 'I shan't tell him off then. Where do you go back to Sergeant Franks?'

'I'm away to see Miss Rose. I thought I'd milk the sympathy in the state I'm in and hopefully come away with a "yes" tonight,' Harry winked at Jack and the door closed behind him.

'I'll go too, Jack, unless there's anything you need to ask me about symptoms since I saw you this afternoon?'

'No, I don't think so. Just sleep now. Thanks for coming again.'

*

The Coroner's hearing was on Thursday morning. Dr Brown was against Jack attending but he was summoned to do so and therefore he was determined to go. Any bruising that he had from his antics on the rope were healing, and the danger of his breathing holding a long-term problem was fading but there was the warning of a potential problem if he did not take care of his chest in damp weather. The risk of suffocation from the smoke had receded. There was the likelihood of dizzy spells from a bang to the head when he jumped from the column but rest would deal with that.

His uniform had been mended by Mrs Morris and sponged so that the smell of smoke had gone. The one drawback was that the woman who arrived each Tuesday at the Morris's home in order to help with the ironing had packed his tunic and trousers with rose petals fresh from the garden. Sergeant Morris had given Jack an inspection when he put it on and they both stared at each other as the scent filled the bedroom.

'You smell like a woman of the night,' Morris had said, standing in front of Jack, scratching his head.

'What do we do?' asked Jack in consternation.

'Hang it out on the line for a bit. Hopefully the sunshine will take most of the smell out of it. Get it off, lad, and I'll leave it pegged out for half an hour.'

*

Still smelling a little sweeter than he would have liked Jack arrived at the enquiry just as the Coroner heard the evidence of the builder recounting the recklessness of plumbers on the roof of the Alexandra Palace.

66

Directors Kelk and Lucas were called and their account of the reasons for a want of water was heard. They left, taking the sympathy of the onlookers with them and went straight to a meeting with three other directors to decide on the programme of the season and what commercial advantage they still might have with the out-door amusements.

The death of John Kelsey was confirmed and Jack thought with sadness of the loss of life in trying to save objects. Two or three other persons were missing and there were several injured.

Jack had been forewarned by Sergeant Morris that he would be asked to explain what he had seen. And so it was.

'Explain what you could see, will you Constable?' asked the Coroner.

Jack gave his evidence and described seeing the four men trying to make their escape as smoke came up from the dome.

'Mainly smoke, sir, and fire about a hundred and fifty feet below. Flames were spreading along the roof. It fell in great flakes scattering fire onto the area. I saw the floor had split in two places,' said Jack.

'Thank you, very helpful. We hear that you rescued one of the workmen from sure death. You are to be commended, Constable,' the Coroner nodded. Jack mumbled in embarrassment. Morris had also warned him this would happen and Jack glanced to the side as there was a flurry of activity from the press.

'I'm sorry, I didn't catch what you said, Constable. Speak up for the enquiry please,' said the Coroner.

'I just said, sir that any of my colleagues would have done the same,' said Jack meeting the Coroner's gaze.

'Quite so, quite so. Thank you, Constable Sargent, that is all.' Jack stepped down and felt his head throb. So, his name would be in the papers now. He knew he was being sketched as well.

Evidence continued, somewhat endlessly. Jack focussed on the details and ignored the press.

One of the foremen of smiths was injured with badly burned legs and arms, neck and head. His leg was broken and the Coroner said that he was in a critical state. John Meeks the foreman of the Palace Firemen was mentioned and as Harry had said had fractured ribs and a badly bruised back.

Jack left at last, being advised to go home by a doctor whose name he did not catch. Like Jack he was there to give his account of the fire. But being Jack, he went instead straight to the Mansion House where the Lord Mayor proposed receiving subscriptions to help stall-holders who had lost everything in the fire. Many of them had borrowed money to start their businesses and would not be able to repay the interest on their loans. Jack gave half a crown, feeling more sympathy for the small trader than for the Directors and in a wave of dizziness turned for the London Chatham and Dover train service from the City branch back to Herne Hill.

He was aching from head to foot as he alighted at Herne Hill Station. Aware that he was in uniform and that it would not do for a constable to pass out he called a small boy over and held out a penny to him.

'Get me a cab, will you. Say it's for a police officer who is unwell and to go to the Dulwich Road. I'll be in the tea room here. Off you go now and put that penny away before someone decides to relieve you of it.'

Jack sat at a table in a corner of the room and leaned back against the wall. Trying to focus his mind on something he took in the room and decided that the station had been built to impress. It had tea rooms offering buffets, decorative brick work and a tower in which the water tank for the steam trains was hidden from view. He and Morris had caught the same train in that morning although Morris had disembarked at Camberwell New Road. The Sergeant had proudly explained that one of the men involved in the building of the station had been Joseph Cubitt, the man who had built the Blackfriars railway bridge. Moving out to Herne Hill had clearly suited Sergeant Morris and he had taken pride in how exemplary his railway station was.

The small boy was back, panting as he had run in front of the cab to make sure he delivered the transport to the young policeman who may have more pennies to spend. Jack gave him another, and with wide eyes the size of saucers the child followed the policeman and watched as his benefactor fell into the cab.

*

Four

There should not have been the light.

Whoever was shining the radiant beam into his eyes should stop but he could not make out who they were. They kept moving and changing shape and colour. Rose pink one second and then a dark blue ending with a shimmer of white so that he was blinded.

A loud noise, high pitched like a scream, told a confused Jack that it was the tolling of a death bell. Except no one had died. A portent of disaster then. Jack wanted to tell whoever was ringing it that the bell was the wrong tone and should be less of a screech and intermittent.

He sat up too quickly and his head reeled. The lack of familiarity with his surroundings produced panic. Jack swung his legs over the side of the couch and realised his boots had gone. This was not the West India Cottage, nor was it a room he recognised as Morris's home. He should be back in his room. But which room? He could remember nothing more than falling into the carriage.

In reality he was propped up against cushions on a highly patterned couch with birds staring at him. Highly coloured birds, vaguely oriental in their colours, not like an English sparrow, a finch or a yellow hammer off the South Downs. Foreign, he concluded, dangerous looking and too large to help anyone relax. Probably typical, although he had not been in one, of the furnishings of a house of ill-repute.

'I went to Pemsey last week and walked out on the Mesh. Beautiful place, surelye! No hills, no trees, nor nothing to interrupt the view.'

His father's voice was as clear in his head as if the man was sitting in the room.

There was the brightness of the light and colour again and it seemed to be compelling him to stare into it.

Who was shining the light into his eyes? Jack decided not to look but even if he closed his eyes the light bored into his brain.

The high-pitched noise had stopped at last. Obviously, the body had arrived for burial. Panic seized him that the body may be his. Jack pushed himself forward and a restraining hand held his shoulder.

'Hello Jack, you're back with us.'

Jack froze. A young man he did not recognise stood bending over him. The face was vaguely familiar and he tried to recall where he may have seen the man before.

'I'm sorry, we haven't met yet. I know who you are as Mother told us you would be staying for a while. Paul Morris is the name. I helped the cabbie get you in here. Good to meet you, but sorry to see you in this bad way.' Jack's captor held out a hand. Jack stared at it and did not offer his own. A Morris and a younger version of the Sergeant. He managed a wan smile and eventually held out his hand in response.

'It's probably the effects of the smoke still making you feel ill. Don't worry Mother says it will wear off. Sorry the light is in your eyes. I'll draw the curtains more to keep the sun out. There that's better. I'll let Mother know you've come round now. She's making tea. Sorry if the kettle boiling disturbed you.'

'The bell was a kettle?' asked Jack.

'Yes, it has a shrill whistle, sorry if it disturbed you but a cup of tea will do you good.'

'And I'm at Sergeant Morris's home?'

'Yes, in the front room. The cabbie said you passed out as soon as you got into his cab. You told him the road and he worked out you were after Sergeant Morris as you were in uniform. I think you policemen call that deduction, don't you?' Paul laughed and stood looking down at Jack.

With the sunlight now under control behind the multi-patterned curtains Jack could take in the young man. Tall, strong with Morris's height but a lighter build and dressed for an office job in the City. Why wasn't he at work? Jack looked around at the furnishings and décor and decided he did not like it. In his limited understanding of the Orient he decided it was not for him.

Paul laughed again and put a hand on Jack's shoulder. The contact in his current state was almost overly familiar.

'I don't like the room either, by the way. It's all new. Apparently, the Queen's gone a bit over the top on India and its reflected in the fashions. These prints are Mother's choice. Good job we only use this one for high days and holidays. Usually, we're all trying to avoid the room. We, being Father and brother Eddie. Sorry, Jack, I may call you Jack? I'm just home and was able to get you into the house. We put you in here as I didn't think I could get you up the stairs. Well-built chap aren't you. Play cricket at all? We need an extra bowler and you look as if those shoulders of yours would open up nicely. I'll get Mother for you. Think about the cricket.' Paul opened the door and hovered briefly between hall and front room.

'I think I've got some whites upstairs, the Inspector sent a bag over,' Jack replied, starting to prop himself up.

'Excellent! We'll get you on your feet and have a chat about the team,' said Paul. He closed the door behind him. Jack could hear him walking away towards the back of the house. He suspected that Paul was a little like himself and would be the sort that one would always hear anywhere in a house.

*

On Thursday morning two men sat in an Inspector's office debating Jack's future.

'His behaviour is unreliable.' Dr. Brown slapped the desk in front of him. It was completely out of character and the policeman opposite controlled the desire he had to push his chair backwards. The strength of feeling of a doctor regarding a patient was understandable and Inspector Tom Hunt let half a minute go by before he responded.

'Deliberately so?' asked Hunt, 'Or is it as a result of some effect of the fire?'

Behind the Inspector hung a portrait of Queen Victoria, a little dated and representing her in her early widowhood. Her expression indicated she was none too impressed at the Doctor's passion.

'Look Tom, Jack will have inhaled chemicals and we should at least try and get more of the mucus up before he goes back on duty. The very fact that he went to the Coroner's court was too soon. Even if he went straight back to Morris's home, which knowing him as I do, I truly doubt, he would be set back a week. It's all too early.'

Inspector Hunt had known Doctor Brown for years as the Police Surgeon. During that time, he had come to rely on the medical opinion more and more. Policemen being exposed to variations in weather and the rate of recovery after injury was a special interest to the doctor. Hunt had developed respect for the man's opinion especially about the effects of London fog affecting his men's longevity. More men were making their pension age from Dr Brown's treatment and care and Inspector Tom Hunt acknowledged that he himself was one of them.

'All I suggested was that we use Sargent in the Shah's visit. He has a nose for spotting a situation. You see Ted's report here.'

Hunt extracted a sheet and pushed it across the desk without exposing the rest of the report.

'Even injured at the Alexandra Palace he saw a situation of theft. Ted and I didn't see anything strange about the man rolling up an item which we now know was a valuable piece of art work. But Sargent saw it and recognised in the man someone he'd seen earlier that morning in another situation. That's why I want him on the security team for the Shah's visit,' explained Hunt. He sat back and waited.

Hunt had in mind the following week and sending Jack to Brighton on the sixteenth of June. What he really was angling for was an earlier date than he thought the doctor wanted. He was gambling on the doctor aiming for two weeks rest for Jack from now. The Inspector actually wanted Jack in position before the nineteenth.

He thought that he could negotiate the waiting period down to a week knowing that the Doctor was keen to keep Jack in clean air and for a rest period. Brighton could be presented as having both opportunities and once Jack was on the spot? Who knew what he might get involved in.

'No, no. he can't return yet to central London, Tom,' said Brown. 'He must be somewhere clean. I can't insist on this enough.'

'Shame he can't do a period down at the sea,' Tom Hunt stared at the papers in front of him and looked up as Doctor Brown took the bait.

'Perfect. A few weeks on the south coast would be ideal. He's from Sussex, isn't he? Well perhaps he still has someone that could put him up for a period of convalescence,' suggested Brown.

'I doubt it. He's an orphan. No one stepped up to the care of the child when he was nine, so I doubt there's anyone left in the family. His only friends when he was a labourer were the other servants as far as I can tell and I doubt there's a home he can go into. But I do know a hotelier, a retired policeman and his wife who manage a small respectable private hotel in Brighton. He's occasionally done me a few favours about the tariff for a man when we've sent them down for a period of convalescence. I could have a word with him and Jack could be there next week if he's well enough to do the journey. That would fit with your idea about clean fresh air and his recovery wouldn't it? What do you think?' Hunt managed to look as if the idea had been all the doctor's.

'It sounds ideal. Three weeks recuperation to fill the lungs with clean fresh sea air and he should be a long way back to full health. I must say I'm surprised Tom that you're seeing my point of view. I thought I was going to have a real task to persuade you to allow Jack the time off from duties in London, especially as the Shah arrives on the eighteenth,' said Dr Brown.

'Well I see the wisdom of Jack going to Brighton,' Hunt answered quite truthfully. 'I'll send a telegram to the hotel and ask how they are fixed. I should know by tomorrow evening. He could be there by the eighteenth that way.'

'Or even earlier if you can get him in to the place,' said Brown, enthusiastically. 'Get the cure now and we'll stop the damage building up. We can prevent most of the sensitivity to changes in the weather in the years to come as he ages if we deal with the situation now. Let me know as I'm due to call in on him on Friday,' said Brown.

'I will. In fact, I could pop over and see him myself tomorrow with your permission?' asked Hunt.

'Of course, but nothing about resuming duties in London yet. He needs to be able to rest not anticipate what he will have to do when he returns to Leman Street.' Brown stood and picked up his hat ready to leave.

'You have my word I shan't discuss anything about coming back to Leman Street, but,' said Hunt, as he held out his hand to shake the doctor's. 'Jack is not the sort of constable that will ignore something if he sees it. If we send him down to Brighton he'll need a focus and I would suggest a security assessment of the town. There's a possibility that the Shah will pay a visit as an invitation has gone forward from there. If that comes off we'll need to know what we're doing. Jack can get some fresh air and review the town for me at the same time.'

Doctor Brown shifted his weight awkwardly and dropped his hand. It was a mannerism Hunt had seen before when the man was irritated. It was soon brought under control and the bedside manner returned.

'Thank you for being so honest. You're right of course. There has to be some limit imposed though, otherwise he'll never recover and by the winter in London, once the fog moves in and he's breathing in the smoke as well, bronchitis and even worse is likely to set in. He has to beat it now, Tom, or you'll be saying goodbye to him permanently, and that would be a damn shame.' Brown extended his hand.

Hunt was always grateful for the honesty in the relationship. He was relieved to have told the Doctor the truth.

'I agree. Let me see you out. As it's nearly ten o'clock I need to make a move now but I'll get on to my contact in Brighton by telegram. Have to be a little careful as the force there aren't aware of any of this from the Met. As we'll have responsibility for moving the Shah down there, if he goes, I want to have an exact briefing about the town,' said Hunt.

'Not too much walking though at first. Can he ride?' asked Brown.

'Probably, he spent years on a farm. I think there's quite a good transport system in Brighton though,' said Hunt.

The two men walked through to the front entrance of the station at New Road, Camberwell and once the Doctor had turned into the street Hunt went in search of Ted Phillips in the room behind the Duty Sergeant's desk.

'Alright, Ted, we're on with Brighton,' said Hunt.

'Has the Doctor seen him?' asked Ted.

'No, Ann Black has been keeping an eye on things. Brown's going to call and see him on Friday. I'll go over myself tomorrow in the afternoon and brief him. Come with me, would you?'

'Yes, of course. Have you seen this?' Ted held out a letter he had been reading.

'What is it?' asked Hunt.

'It's a letter from Sam Curzon. It's bad news for the family. His father's died and he's basically asking for work as he will be the only support being the eldest son. We should answer it, Tom. He says he wrote to Jack weeks ago and hasn't heard from him. I called in to see Mother over in the dock cottages last night as she was concerned how I was after the fire. It's always better if she sees me, as it stops her worrying. There was a letter to Jack sitting on the mantelpiece. Rose said it's been there three weeks and he hasn't touched it. It's the same writing. I've got it here, as I thought I could drop it off.' Ted held out the letter and Hunt took it and turned it over. He looked at the writing on the envelope and then glanced at Sam's letter to Ted.

'I wonder what's going on there. Strange he hasn't opened it, I thought they were quite close. Let's take it with us.' Hunt read the first page of Sam's letter to Ted and then handed it back.

'It's a bad hand the lad has been dealt. I'll speak to the County Chief Constable again as Sam left on medical grounds. There's only likely to be the one pay out Ted, you know that. He's nothing stacked up in the way of contributions having only been in the force a few months. Perhaps we could do something ourselves?' Hunt looked at Ted.

'A one-off isn't going to help much. The lad needs regular work. It's a great pity, Tom. We could do with that ability to analyse that Sam has, but he'll never pass the medical now.'

'I know. Look, an idea is starting to form but I want to talk to Harry Franks first. Give me until tomorrow and I'll fill you in on the way across to the Morris's place when we go and see Jack. Get a telegram across to Sam at his home in Windsor. Just say we've received his letter, Jack's injured but will answer shortly, and Hunt has an idea. At least that way he knows he's not forgotten.'

'Jack will answer shortly? How will you do that?' Ted looked sceptical.

'It will be an order,' said Hunt, firmly.

*

In a house in the Grove the daily papers lay on the highly polished table waiting for the usual flick of the duster. It was a house where dust was not allowed to reside. The papers had been ironed by the Footman earlier and were immaculate, discouraging interested parties from turning a page.

Nonetheless, Harriet Fildew, having progressed through her own efforts from scullery maid at the age of seventeen to a change of position as parlour maid, looked around her. At eighteen years now she had technically "made it" quickly. Her new employer lived in one of the larger residences on the Grove. She looked to the right and left to ensure that she was not observed.

Her eyes scanned the front page of The Telegraph dated the 12th of June, looking for reports of the Coroner's enquiry. There was absolutely no mention on the front page.

Harriet had scanned every column despite having been told that there was a headline and that she would not find the article on the front page. The last thing she wanted to do was to start opening the paper up as she knew that was chancing her arm to turn it in case she spoiled the appearance before the master, Mr Pendle, opened it himself. However, that was exactly what she was going to have to do. Harriet kicked herself for not having asked the Footman, Henry, where exactly in the paper he had seen Jack's name.

The house was quiet. Breakfast would bring Mr Pendle down and the two young men staying in the house, but Mrs Pendle would have a tray in her room. The young ladies of the house, Lily and Hilda, would be back from their rides shortly. Before that Harriet would take the chance to turn the pages of the paper. It would be dismissal if they caught her.

'I told you,' the Footman had said. 'It's there in black and white. "Constable Jack Sargent, Hero," it said. He gave evidence at the Coroner's enquiry he did and was commended for rescuing one of the workman trapped off the roof of the Alexandra Palace. Said he would be given a medal for sure. What you getting upset for, girl? I'm telling you, your young man is a hero, aint I?'

Harriet wiped the tears and blew her nose and stuffed the handkerchief back up her sleeve.

'But he'd *tell* me. Where's the paper?' Harriet had started to raise her voice with distress.

'It's in its usual place at this time of the day. Don't you go creasing it now,' Henry called after her as she picked up a feather duster and started to climb the stairs from the servant's hall.

'And as for telling you, how could he tell you?' Henry called up the stairs after her. 'You girls are all the same. You tell a bloke not to come and then expect him to anyway. Oh, and the paper said he was injured himself, so how could he tell you?'

Harriet turned on the stair and starting to come back down, now angry. As always when emotion took over, Harriet's Honiton accent came to the fore. She rounded on Henry.

'Henry, you're *despicable*. You know I'll get sacked if I get callers at the door. You know he can't come here and I don't get enough time off to see him that much. You've read the article, haven't you and you're just drip feeding me bits and getting a real pleasure from seeing me upset. Just because I prefer Jack to a lazy layabout like you. Jack will go somewhere in his job and we'll have a home together one day. Not staying in service like I would if I took up with someone like you. Yoh's a bit maize if you think I would. How's he injured, *tell me.*' Harriet shouted at the man.

'Can't remember,' Henry smirked. 'You'll have to read it yourself, won't you?'

'What will she have to read?' Mrs Atkins, the Housekeeper, asked in a tone which was as starched as her immaculate white cuffs and collar, the only contrast to break up the pure black that she always wore.

Henry stood to attention and stared at the wall. Harriet gripped the iron bannister and breathed trying to calm herself. She dropped her eyes and hoped the high flush that she could feel on her cheeks would not be noticed.

'Just books to better herself, Mrs Atkins,' said Henry.

'That's not what it sounded like to me.' The Housekeeper continued to stare at the Footman for a further thirty seconds. Henry did not move or change the direction of his gaze. Slowly, like a snake in the sun, Mrs Atkins turned her head towards Harriet and stared at her new prey.

'As you are carrying a duster, I assume that you intend to start your duties. Get along then as you are already late.'

'Yes, Mrs Atkins,' Harriet turned on the stair and, keeping her back straight walked up each step and controlled the desire to run up to the top.

In the hall Harriet had fished out her handkerchief and blown her nose. The temptation of the paper in its pristine state was too much for her. Slowly Harriet had turned the front page and allowed it to lay on the hard surface. She looked on page two.

Nothing.

Page three and there it was.

"Recently Recruited to the Metropolitan Police, Constable Jack Sargent of Leman Street Police Station, is the Hero of the Hour."

Harriet read as her eyes swam with the emotion produced by the words,

"he was injured himself,"

Although the reporter had not explained what injury Jack had. Most of the report did not register, as the tears dripped onto the paper and with horror she knew she was in trouble as the wet stains spread. She saw the words "hero," "commended," and "to be awarded a medal for bravery," and that was all as a hand was placed on her arm. Alarmed she looked into the horrified stare of Mrs Atkins.

'What do you think you're doing? Get below, *now*, and I'll see you in my sitting room.'

With a sob Harriet blurted out, 'Yes Mrs Atkins,' and as she turned she looked into the eyes of the master, Mr Pendle. He was coming down the stairs, looking bemused at the antics of his Housekeeper and maid with his morning paper. Harriet disappeared through the door to below stairs stuffing her hanky into her mouth to stifle the distress. The sound of her choking sobs, however, were quite audible and Mrs Atkins adopted the expression of every good servant.

'I do apologise, Sir. She'll be dismissed this morning.'

'What on earth is going on, Mrs Atkins? Is that my paper the girl was pouring over?' asked Mr Pendle, knowing the answer.

'I am very sorry, Sir, it will not happen again. I will see the girl is dismissed today. She's very young and was encouraged in it by another servant who had seen her young man's name in the paper. I'll ensure Mr Clark deals with him.'

'If you're reporting another servant to Clark and if it's my paper it will be the Footman who places it there for me. What's Henry been up to? Goaded the girl into it did he? What's her young man done? Up before the magistrate, is he?'

'Given where the tears are on the paper, Sir, I suspect it's the young policeman mentioned in the article from the Alexandra Palace Fire,' explained Mrs Atkins, gesturing towards page three.

'Policeman? She was upset. Not dead, is he?' exclaimed Mr Pendle, putting on his glasses to look.

Mrs Atkins stood to one side, as her employer bent over the article, now discoloured in several places. He scanned the columns and came to the part where Jack was proclaimed a hero.

'Well, good man. Says here he saved a life and is to get a medal. I think we should congratulate the girl on such a fine young man. What's her name?' asked Mr Pendle.

'Harriet, Sir.'

'Well don't be too hard on her, Mrs Atkins, understandable in the circumstances. Says he's injured himself in saving the other man. Does he call on her here?' probed Mr Pendle.

'Oh no, Sir. The staff understand from day one that we don't allow callers. It would be dismissal,' Mrs Atkins clasped her hands in front of her and stared at a picture on the wall.

'Well, perhaps we can make an exception in this case. She's probably worried about him. Give her the benefit of the doubt and an afternoon off today and let her go and see he's alright. I'd like to hear the story so I'll see her at breakfast tomorrow, same time as today, on my way into the Morning Room, and she can briefly tell me about it. Alright, Mrs Atkins, that will be all and, er, get Mr Clarke to have a word with Henry, will you? Footmen are his responsibility.' Mr Pendle picked up his paper and met the eyes of the Housekeeper. Both had an unwavering stare, the middle-aged widowed Housekeeper and the wealthy Industrialist.

Mrs Atkins controlled her response and then inclined her head and dropped her eyes to the floor with a brief, 'Sir.' Mrs Atkins made her way below stairs.

He watched her go and then Mr Pendle tucked his Telegraph under his arm and went to start his breakfast.

Harriet stood, with her hands behind her back while she was given a dressing down about allowing herself to be led on by the Footman. In the end she found herself being sent upstairs to complete her tasks and then ensure that she changed, with an extra afternoon off, in order to see Jack. In the doorway of the Housekeeper's sitting room Harriet paused and turned back.

'Thank you, Mrs Atkins.'

'It's not me you should be thanking. If I had my way you would be dismissed.' The comment was harshly said.

Harriet paused wondering if she dared take the chance of saying more. Mrs Atkins smoothed the skirt of her dress with her two hands which were immaculately framed by her white cuffs. She glanced up and continued, 'Finish your tasks and then be off by one o'clock. I expect you to help lay fires for tomorrow when you get back as Clara will have to make up your work this afternoon. You can help her in turn.'

'I will gladly. I wanted to say that I can't help thinking that you must have said something to help though,' said Harriet.

'I merely explained the truth. You came highly recommended by the servant's agency and the cook at your last employment said that you showed promise. You're a hard worker and you show commitment and loyalty but watch out for Henry.' Mrs Atkins raised a finger and looked with an unblinking stare into Harriet's wide eyes. Mrs Atkins took a deep breath so that her nostrils flared. 'I'll speak to Mr Clarke, he will deal with Henry. Where do you have to go to?' asked Mrs Atkins.

'I'm not sure where he is. Jack transferred to Leman Street but if he's hurt he may not be at work. His lodgings are at the West India Dock area. I'm not sure I can get there and back so I thought I would go and see the Sergeant at New Road Police Station, Sergeant Phillips, and see if he knows where Jack is. If it's too far to get to in the time I can just give the Sergeant a note,' explained Harriet.

'*Go to a Police Station.* You will not. No servant from this house is going to a Police station. We'll send the Boot Boy with a note,' Mrs Atkins opened a drawer and produced a pen, notepaper and an envelope. She sat at her table and looked expectantly at Harriet. 'Well?' she said, pen poised.

'To Sergeant Phillips, Camberwell New Road,' said Harriet.

Mrs Atkins began to write:

"Dear Sergeant Phillips,

My employer, Mr Pendle, has kindly allowed me to have a half day today in order to see Jack as he was extremely impressed with the account of Jack's bravery in the Telegraph. I am free from one o'clock. Please can you let me know before then where Jack is.

Sincerely yours,

Harriet Fildew."

Mrs Atkins read the note to Harriet, held out the pen to her, and Harriet moved quickly from the door to sign it.

'Well, get along then. We'll send the Boot Boy with it to the Police Station and wait for the response. I've mentioned Mr Pendle as he's a friend of the Chief Constable. And make sure you have a story from the Sergeant if you don't see your young man. Mr Pendle is expecting a full account of your Jack's exploits from you before breakfast in the morning,' said Mrs Atkins.

'From me? Mr Pendle wants to know about Jack? From me? Oh, I couldn't, Mrs Atkins,' stammered Harriet.

'You can, and you will. And mind your accent when you see the master. He's making sure I don't sack you,' a half smile at the corners of the housekeeper's mouth gave away the fact that she was half-human.

Harriet turned to go. Mrs Atkins final words had resumed the tone of ice.

'You will be there in front of the Morning Room, looking spick and span, with a full account of the heroics of your young Constable. Now get on with your tasks so that you can go at one o'clock. I have work to do as well and I can't spend any more time on this business.'

*

The Boot Boy arrived at the Police station in New Road, Camberwell, by ten o'clock. He wore a grin which did not impress the Duty Sergeant. As a result, the boy removed his grin and wore instead a surprised look more suitable to present before a Policeman. He had learned to be adaptable in his twelve years. This was a key effect from acquiring the simple mathematics and English in the last three years since the Elementary Education Act 1870. In fact, his mother had objected strongly to the concept of educating her cheeky little blighter and had insisted to the local vicar that it would make him worse. But to school he had gone.

Mr Pendle had been quite taken with him and the boy was on a promise of a job in manufacturing. He could read and make measurements and Mr Pendle had joked that with such a work force there would be no fear for Britain's status in the world. Mr Pendle had decided to introduce the boy to Mr Gladstone when he next visited the house in the Grove as proof of the military benefits of such an education. After the success of the Prussian army in the Austro-Prussian war and the unification of Germany in 1871 it was generally believed that Germany was ahead of England in its elementary education. Gladstone was firm in his view that education was needed and the boy would be living proof that he was right.

Ted Phillips and Inspector Tom Hunt were finishing their discussion of Sam Curzon's health when they were treated to the surprised look of the Boot Boy, as the Sergeant brought him in with the letter.

'Got a young 'un here, sir, with a letter to Sergeant Phillips from a house on the Grove. Given the Chief Constable's frequent visits up there I thought I'd better bring him straight to the Sergeant.'

Clutching the note drafted by Mrs Atkins and signed by Harriet, the boy was invited to take a seat.

Ted handed him a Constable's helmet to wear.

'Cor, thanks Sergeant,' said the Boot Boy.

'Have a biscuit while I read this and we'll see if there's an answer to go back with you,' said Ted, offering an open paper parcel to the boy.

''Scuse me asking, Sergeant, but are they fresh?' asked the boy.

'Straight from my wife's kitchen this morning,' said Ted, glancing at Hunt. The Boot boy took one, as did the Inspector.

The helmet and biscuit worked. The Boot Boy no longer wore the surprised look and was back to the cheeky grin that his mother despaired of. He had wished to enter manufacturing, but since acquiring a police helmet for ten minutes, and a biscuit, he was moving in his aspirations to become a Sergeant in the Metropolitan Police. In the meantime, Ted Phillips had been reading the letter.

85

'It's from Harriet Fildew, Jack's young lady. The boy's brought it from a house at the Grove. I knew she'd moved but I had no idea where to,' Ted paused while he finished the note. Resuming his explanation for Hunt he explained, 'Somehow, she must have found out that Jack's hurt and her employer has given her this afternoon off to see him. I offered to let her know but Jack said her next day off was next week so that there was no point.' Ted turned to the Boot Boy and said, 'I can meet Miss Fildew at half past one at New Road railway station for the train to Herne Hill. Can you repeat that?' asked Ted.

'Yes sir, but it will be no good me remembering it. You have to write a note. Housekeeper's don't believe the likes of me. And you should always answer using the same type of communication as you received,' said the Boot Boy.

'Did they teach you that last bit in school?' asked Hunt.

'Yes, sir. You have to write a note.'

Ted stifled a laugh and Hunt said, with a twinkle in his eye, 'How would you like a job cleaning boots here?'

'Joining the police?' the Boot Boy's eyes had gone wide.

'In a manner of speaking. As a civilian, then when you're older we can have a chat,' said Hunt.

'How much?' the Boot Boy ran his tongue across his bottom lip in case any crumbs had escaped. But he kept his eyes on Hunt's face.

'Well there's a lot of boots in a police station. They have to shine and they have to be done every day,' Ted Phillips said, winking at Tom Hunt.

'I would think we could run to, say, six days a week,' Hunt controlled his face. 'The seventh day you rest and the officers can polish their own.'

'Bed and board? I get my bed and board in my current position in the Grove. I'd have to get my bed and board, there's no room at home any more,' said the Boot Boy, standing his ground.

'Isn't there? I see. How much do you get now?' asked Hunt.

'I don't get it, sir, Mother gets it. Ten bob a month.'

—

'I will write to your Mother, a note as you call it, explaining that you're offered a civilian position in the police with a view to becoming a recruit when you're old enough. She'll receive ten shillings a month, or ten bob as you say. But we will keep another ten shillings a month for you in a tin in the safe. When you need new clothes and so on you tell Sergeant Ted here and he can help you buy them from that. On your day off you and Ted can decide how much of that ten bob you can have to spend. How's that for you?' asked Hunt. The boy waited. Hunt looked at Ted. Ted raised his eyebrows and shook his head. He had no more idea than the Inspector what the boy was waiting for. Then it dawned.

'With bed and board,' reiterated Hunt.

The boy spat into his hand and held it out to the Inspector. Ted scratched his chin and stared at Hunt. Hunt spat into his own hand and the deal was signed in a handshake.

'Can you get the note to your Mother? Where does the family live?' asked Hunt.

'In Camberwell. I can take it later when the Butler lets me go.'

'What were you to become after being a Boot Boy?' Tom Hunt held the door open as he indicated to the Duty Sergeant that he wanted three sheets of paper. Once he had them he sat down and started to write.

'A Footman. But there's no future in that,' said the boy.

'Why's that?' asked Ted.

'It belongs to the past. My teacher said. Industry, she said, get yourselves into industry. Well, Police is better isn't it?' asked the boy.

Hunt and Ted looked at each other and then at the twelve-year-old in front of them.

'Some would say it is,' said Hunt. 'For me it is. You'll have to see. When are you thirteen?' He started on the note to the Boot Boy's mother and paused. 'And what's your name?'

'Percival Green, Percy to them that knows me, I'm thirteen on Saturday,' Percy replied.

'Then Percy, civilian in the Police, New Road, Camberwell it is.' Hunt looked around for envelopes and then handed three letters to Percy. 'Give this one to your mother and then give your employer the second note giving notice. The third one is for Miss Fildew.'

'She's Harriet,' said Percy.

'If you join the police any young lady is "Miss." Especially the maids. Therein lies the route into a warm kitchen, a hot cup of tea and something from the cook's oven. Don't forget that,' said Hunt.

Percy nodded, putting the three notes into different parts of his clothing. 'So's, I don't get mixed up,' he said to Ted.

'We'll see you in a week's time, bed and board and ten shillings a month to Mother and ten shillings saved for you. Now off you go and discharge that duty. The Inspector's a busy man,' said Ted.

Percy delivered Harriet's note to Mrs Atkins on his return to the Grove.

'Take the note to Harriet,' she ordered Percy who duly complied.

He remembered Hunt's instructions and called her "Miss Harriet," which made her laugh.

Harriet opened the envelope and gave the former Boot Boy a kiss on the top of his head. He decided he would go straight to the Butler to start his notice with Tom Hunt's note. Then he would ask permission to run home with the letter for his mother once he'd finished sharpening the kitchen knives. She would be proud, he knew.

*

Five

Ted Phillips looked around at the passengers waiting at the entrance of Camberwell New Road Station. The entrance was at street level into a yellow brick building three storeys high, a trade mark look for the inner London stations of the London Chatham Dover Railway Company. The railway had been built on a viaduct and now had four lines. Ted had been up on the platform already and had had a word with the signalman in the two-storey signal box at the Blackfriars end of the island platform. The man had a child in the same class as Ted's youngest and had recently moved to the area.

It was six months since he had seen Harriet and that had been after the attack on her outside her employer's home as she had walked from the tram. Mrs Ardle, the cook of the house that Harriet had worked in had accompanied her with Charlie Banks and Ted to the Police Station. There she had given a description and a drawing had been made by the Police Artist of her attacker. An arrest had followed of a detective. It was all part of the interwoven web of organised crime that Hunt was trying to crack.

No one present in front of the station fitted the picture Ted had in his mind of the distraught young scullery maid, with red eyes and a red nose from crying.

Slowly, a young, well-dressed, lady walked towards him, her rich brown hair pulled away from the sides of her face and then piled high under a coquettish, brimmed, straw hat of the style that he had seen in Margaret's lady's magazine. It was being worn tipped forward. He glanced away scouring the faces of other women until he heard his name called.

'Sergeant Phillips?' Ted found himself saluting.

Two bright eyes stared into his and the owner of those eyes would not have been out of place as a guest herself in one of the houses in the Grove in her current attire. However, she had got that dress, thought Ted, it became her.

Harriet's figure showed the gradual return to a narrow silhouette and a V shaped neckline. Ted thought that she was losing the girlish posture and understood why Jack was anxious to get the engagement underway.

'Miss Fildew, how well you look,' said Ted.

'Harriet, please. I was Harriet to you six months ago when you were so kind. And again, meeting me and helping me see Jack is kind of you, Sergeant Phillips. I was so happy to hear you had been promoted. No one deserved it more than you. How is your family and Mrs Phillips?' Harriet asked. Ted remembered the rich, friendly accent now, from Honiton.

'Well, thank you. I should mention that Jack and I did speak about letting you know but he was concerned that it would worry you. He knew, you see, that your next day off wasn't to happen quickly and that there would be nothing you could do about it. Kind of your employer to give you the afternoon off. Shall we move for the train?' suggested Ted.

'I see. Now I understand. I thought.... Never mind. I was almost dismissed for reading the Master's paper this morning but Jack's heroics saved my bacon. Mr Pendle, that's the Master, is very interested to hear how Jack is so I will have to have a full account of what he got up to,' Harriet smiled and the shadow that had crossed her face initially vanished. Ted wondered what conclusions she had been drawing from Jack's silence. 'The home, where's that to?'

Ted gave her a very confused look.

'I mean where is Jack staying?' said Harriet correcting her way of saying things. It made complete sense to her but not to Ted.

'Herne Hill,' said Ted, and added, more out of a desire to fill the silence, 'How is your family?'

He did not know them but remembered Jack saying that Harriet had a large family of Fildews in Honiton and her mother was establishing a successful dairy.

'Well thank-you. I'm to go back for five days in July, which will be wonderful. It will be the first time for a year. I'll be there for hot pennies day and the fair.'

'You must miss them all,' said Ted.

'Yes, I miss Mother, but my sister is in London and soon a brother will come as an apprentice hairdresser so that will be better.' Harriet laid a small hand on Ted's arm and, surprised, he looked at the excited face and realised it was a natural action of a girl caught up in a story without any consciousness of her action. The hand was gone as quickly as it had been placed but Harriet carried on with her explanation of "hot pennies and the fair."

'I missed the fair last year. All the boys and maids try to catch the Hot pennies which are thrown into the crowds from the upper windows of the taverns in the town. It goes back years when the rich did it to aid the poor. And then the Town crier and the Mayor start the festivities of the fair. The Town Crier carries a floral baton and a golden glove around the crowds and then shouts: "The glove is up, God save the Queen." And the fair starts.'

'What's the glove for?' asked Ted.

'Ah, well, while the glove is up any criminals are not prosecuted,' explained Harriet.

'I'm not sure I agree with that,' said Ted, chuckling.

'No of course not, but it's just fun now,' Harriet giggled at the predictable response from a policeman.

'It's quite a town, I hear since the railway opened from London. Near Axminster isn't it?' asked Ted, trying to place the town in his mind.

'Yes, there's Axminster with its carpets and Colyton station, but Honiton returns two members of Parliament and we produce lace of a fine quality. The town is on the main route for Exeter you know, has its market and wool and the pottery of course. Then there's the lace. Queen Victoria had Honiton lace for her wedding, even though the fashion was for Brussel's lace. It helped the town no end. Then Princess Vicky wore it at her wedding. Oh, Devon is beautiful and we've hills that swell up before you. I wish you could see 'em. You should take the children, Sergeant Phillips, there's a rich landscape and a soft climate. Sea sides like Sidmouth are the place for you!' Harriet said with her eyes shining.

91

'I must look at a map, I think,' said Ted pulling out his ticket for the collector.

'Yes, do, Sidmouth is about ten miles from Exmouth, such a lovely watering place. It just nestles in the bottom of the valley with two hills, country on one side and open sea on the other. There are boarding houses and hotels and the town has gas and water now. You'll find it warmer than London I can tell you. Oh, my ticket,' Harriet fumbled in the little bag she carried and held out the ticket for the collector.

Together they walked to the platform for the Herne Hill direction and waited as the roar of the steam alerted them to the imminent arrival of their train.

*

Jack was laying on his bed half propped up with pillows playing Rummy with Paul Morris when Ted and Harriet arrived. He laid his hand down with three fours and four sevens, said, 'Rummy,' as loudly as he could. Paul's mouth had dropped open but not at Jack's winning hand. Jack turned on his side to see what had made Paul react.

Mrs Morris had opened the door and ushered Harriet quietly forward to give Jack a surprise. Paul reacted as if his Mother was bringing a Christmas gift.

'I say,' said Paul, and stood up.

'Harriet,' exclaimed Jack and then coughed slightly as he caught his breath. A frown crossed Harriet's brow, taking in how pasty Jack's normally ruddy complexion was.

'Here's an unexpected visitor,' exclaimed Mrs Morris. 'Oh Paul, I had forgotten you were in here and bound to give it away. Can you come down to the sitting room, Jack? I'll take your young lady down and set up some tea.'

Proud in front of Paul that the fine looking young lady who had followed Mrs Morris into the room was his Harriet, Jack drank Harriet in and smiled at her.

'Yes, Mrs Morris, thank-you,' said Jack. He looked into the shining eyes and asked Harriet, 'How did you come to be here?'

'Long story, but it suited Mr Pendle at the Grove for me to come and see you to get the full story. I've to give him an account of your adventures in the morning, Jack. Oh, and Jack, you're in the Telegraph as a hero!'

Jack smiled at her excitement. 'New dress?' he asked Harriet quietly.

'Yes, first time on and worn for you. Georgina finished it last night. Good job she did, otherwise I'd be in me black and pinny. It's not too finicky? It was quite plain at first but she added the aprons at the front for the fashion out of left-over silk.' Harriet extended her hand and swinging his legs off the bed a little too quickly, he steadied himself before taking it. Harriet noticed the stagger though. He saw the brow furrow but relax again as he touched her fingers. Jack looked at her and was glad of her older sister's dress-making skills.

'It's perfect,' he said, and Harriet relaxed into a smile. Jack remembered that Constable Arscott Ward had said he and Georgina were to be married when he had met him in December. Jack had meant to ask Harriet when the wedding was to be and had forgotten each time they had been together. 'How is Georgina?' He asked.

'Very busy, which is good as she and Arscott will need the money,' said Harriet.

'Come on down to the front parlour and we'll have tea. Paul lead the way for Miss Fildew,' said Mrs Morris.

Propriety in mind Mrs Morris opened the door and ushered her son out, followed by Harriet. She pulled the door behind her while Jack steadied himself with a hand on the table at the side of his bed.

When he reached the sitting room, the chaise longue had been left free for him. Ted was standing by a tall lamp, his helmet placed on the top of the piano. Jack shook hands with Ted and said quietly to him, 'I did say I didn't want her to know.'

'Not guilty, it's all in the papers, Jack. Harriet had no choice either. Her employer Pendle has given time off for her to come and hear your story and report back to him. We got a letter arrive at the station, apparently drafted by the housekeeper, which Harriet signed. He's a friend of the Prime-Minister, so you've been noticed by those who move in high circles. It would have been a poor response if we'd not brought her here,' Ted said, quietly.

Jack nodded, and looked around the room, now full of life because Harriet was there. She was sitting on an arm chair with one of the highly decorated bird cushions peeping out behind her. Somehow, he didn't mind the décor any more.

Paul had joined Ted by the piano. Jack realised that they would know each other as Ted and Morris had worked together for years. Paul and Ted exchanged a few words and then Jack realised that Harriet had all of Paul's attention. Glancing at her Jack saw that Harriet was looking at the décor but was not unaware of Paul's gaze. However she turned only to Jack, and he found himself bursting with pride.

A strange thought came into his mind that if something happened to him in service there would be, just possibly, someone else that would love Harriet. Jack glanced at Paul, taking in his appearance and wondering whether a woman would find him good looking. Then he started to ponder about if Harriet found Paul attractive? Strangely, Jack found it comforting that if he had died there would have been someone like Paul to notice her and she would not be alone.

Mrs Morris was pouring tea and she nodded at Paul to hand the plates to everyone for the slices of bread and butter.

Harriet took a plate and the tea that Mrs Morris offered. Ted helped Jack to a plate, remembering his young colleague was always hungry, but in this instance, Jack shook his head. A sure sign that he's not yet right, thought Ted.

'How long will you be staying, Jack?' asked Harriet, hoping that it would be for some time as it was easier to see him south of the river.

'Well that rather depends on Dr. Brown's visit on Friday and how long Mrs Morris can put up with me,' answered Jack, with a smile at Mrs Morris. She glanced briefly at him as she stood, poised, about to pour his tea and smiled in response.

Ted quietly stood to one side, and fingered the raised patterning on the tea plate, knowing exactly that Jack's time was limited and that he would be going to Sussex before the sixteenth of June if Tom Hunt had his way. But he had no desire to spoil the brief time that the young couple would spend in each other's presence by saying anything.

Jack was not the only one in the room who had noticed the impact Harriet had had on Paul Morris. Ted had registered Paul's interest and decided he would try and broach the subject with the young man if there was an opportunity before he left, just to put him straight on the depth of understanding between Harriet and Jack.

The respectable tea continued and Jack found himself feeling impatient for time alone with Harriet. The gathering reminded him of the last time he had entered an afternoon tea, a time before murder and poison had destroyed the oasis of Arbour Square. Then, as now, tea had been poured for him. In Mrs Morris's place he saw Emily Doyle. Perhaps it was the weakness, or the remaining chemicals from the smoke, that made him see Emily's smile as she poured him tea. A shadow of sadness at the charade passed across his mind as he thought of the dead American Berringer, who had destroyed her life and the desperate measures Emily had taken to kill his wife and remove Sam Curzon once he knew the truth.

'Diabolical woman,' had said Harry Franks of Emily Doyle. Was she? Or had the balance of her mind been affected by a desperate need to clinging to some hope of future happiness? Mrs Morris came back into focus. Jack took his tea from her and saw the concern in her eyes.

'Try and sip some now, if you can, all the excitement is wearying you, I'm afraid.' She slipped a slice of bread and butter on to a plate and set it down next to him. Bending towards Jack, Mrs Morris said, 'Just try and take a few mouthfuls for strength.'

95

Jack nodded and took a bite. He remembered the letter from Sam sitting on the mantelpiece at West India Dock Cottages. How could he have ignored it? Ted exchanged a look with him but Harriet's questions came thick and fast, eyes alternating between concern and a shining pride and Jack tried to pull himself back to the present to recount his rescue of the workman.

'Didn't you feel afraid once?' asked Harriet.

'There wasn't time,' Jack replied.

'It will be nice for me to know that you're closer to Camberwell than across the river. Perhaps the Inspector will let him stay now?' Harriet asked Ted with something of a pleading note in her voice.

'Perhaps,' said Jack, also glancing at Ted, who made a focussed study of his plate. 'Dr. Brown has said that I need to be somewhere for a while with cleaner air than in the docks,' Jack added.

'Nice pattern,' Ted said to Mrs Morris. 'I think Margaret would like this tea set.'

Ted transferred his gaze to Jack and said, 'The Inspector thought he'd call in tomorrow to see you Jack,' and then to Mrs Morris, 'If you don't mind having us back here?'

'Of course not, I haven't seen Inspector Hunt since Christmas, so it will be nice to catch up on the family. Paul, take Miss Fildew's plate, will you?' said Mrs Morris.

Paul's hand lingered a little too long next to one of Harriet's fingers as she passed her plate to him.

'We'll get him right, Miss Harriet,' said Paul. And for the first time Harriet and Paul looked into each other's eyes. The mutual impact was not lost on Jack.

Jack moved to stand, and his head swam, and he kicked himself for having gone to the Mansion House instead of coming straight back to the Morris's home after the Coroner's enquiry. But Harriet was up and moving past Paul to help him, her eyes full of love and concern, as she gripped his elbow. Ted was next to her. 'I'll help him, don't you try and take his weight,' he said.

'I need to go otherwise I'll be in the soup if I'm late. Would you mind if we go Sergeant Phillips?' asked Harriet.

'Of course, I should be making a move myself anyway shortly,' said Ted.

'Do you think you could walk me to the gate?' asked Harriet looking at Jack. Jack had every intention of doing so even if he was on his knees.

'Thank-you so much Mrs Morris. I love your house. I hope I will have a room like this one day. I'll wait by the gate for you Sergeant Phillips,' said Harriet.

'I'll be out in five minutes,' Ted said once he had got Jack through the front door.

They stood by the garden gate which was hardly private. Jack risked taking Harriet's hand and said, 'You look beautiful, Harriet.'

'I do feel it when I'm with you,' she said. Her eyes were full of life and Jack wondered if he should press her again about them going to see her Mother but decided not to as he was hardly in a state to make a journey to Honiton. This meeting had been one of the best for some while. Harriet was relaxed, and clearly revelling in the status Jack was acquiring. The strain he had imposed in the last few months had evaporated as he had not mentioned the subject of an engagement today. Jack raised her hand to his lips and looked into eyes full of vivacity and anticipation. No, he would savour the time and not destroy her mood and so he stayed silently holding Harriet's hand until Ted Phillips coughed behind him.

'Better make a move, I think,' said Jack.

'Shall I come on Tuesday? asked Harriet.

'I'll send you word tomorrow after I've seen the Doctor and Inspector Hunt, then we'll have a better idea where I'll be.' Jack turned to Ted. 'Thanks for this time, Ted, and for seeing Harriet back to Camberwell,' he said.

'My pleasure,' said Ted, with a smile. 'You rest up now, Jack and I'll see you tomorrow with Tom Hunt.'

*

On Friday morning at half past eight Dr Brown sat in the chair opposite Jack and rested his hands on his knees. He had listened to Jack's chest with his stethoscope and looked at the sputum in the jar. Using his eyes he took in the state of his patient making a realistic decision about the idea he had shared with Tom Hunt. Youth and vigour in the young man's life would mean he would not be careful in the future. There would be a weakness probably especially in winter weather. Dr. Brown could advise and keep an eye on him to a certain extent as the Police surgeon but he suspected that Jack would learn a hard lesson before he would take care.

'Of course, it will depend on what you've inhaled,' said Brown, dropping some of the sputum in a jar.

'Ann will see to the tests and I should have some results before I go away. Just for another week try and limit your exertion. Are you still getting headaches?' asked Brown.

'Not so much,' said Jack. 'I catch my breath after climbing the stairs.'

'That will be what you've inhaled. We've known about gases being released for many years now thanks to scientists like Priestley and Black. But I can't help thinking there's more in it than just gas. Any reduced alertness?' asked Brown.

'I am having problems concentrating,' said Jack, 'especially when I'm tired.'

'A change of air is what you need, Jack. I've been doing work with Firemen in the city and there is some correlation with certain conditions developing the longer they work and are exposed to smoke. That leads me to think there are chemicals in the smoke and that they are settling in the lungs. I've been doing some experiments on getting Firemen away for three weeks to the sea. They come back breathing much deeper, with their concentration restored and the headaches stop. Do you know what they tell me Jack?' said Dr Brown, enthusiastically.

Jack shook his head.

'People die in fires before the fire gets to them. That says to me they die in the smoke. Why I ask myself'

Jack looked at the Doctor and shook his head. 'Because you can't breathe, you know that Doctor. When you're in a room and the chimney is blocked and the smoke comes back into the room it makes you cough.'

'But *why*, Jack? That's what we're trying to get at. What's in it? We will understand properly one day.' Brown stood up and picked up his bag. 'We should get you to the coast and away from an expanding city. Some would also say trust in the Almighty.'

'I thought I was having a change of air here and I do trust in the Almighty,' said Jack.

'Well I think we can do better than here. I want to ensure that you are completely away from smoke and fogs so no more foul air for you from the docks, at least for a while. I have your permission for Ann to do some tests? I assumed rather than asked you. You know that she studied in Paris?' asked Brown.

'She did a medical degree there didn't she?'

'Yes, and she studied under Louis Pasteur for part of her time. No? Not heard of him. That doesn't surprise me. There have been few advances in Britain as medical work is rarely scientific. He had a brain stroke in '68 but carried on his research.' The Doctor placed the jar in his bag.

'Was Ann there at that time?' asked Jack.

'Yes, and Pasteur celebrated his seventieth birthday at the Sorbonne in Paris and Ann was there along with a British surgeon, Joseph Lister. I'm telling you this for a reason. Lister followed Pasteur's germ theory of disease based on identifying micro-bacterial organisms and used antiseptic on his ward. Ann will do some tests on your sputum and try and identify what micro-organisms could be present.' said Dr Brown.

'And sputum is what I coughed up for you?' asked Jack. The Doctor nodded. 'So, you think the smoke has these micro whatsits in it? She's not going to get into any trouble doing it is she?' asked Jack.

'She's merely carrying out some tests for me. People have been doing experiments on smoke for centuries. As far back as Leonardo da Vinci in fact. Have you heard of him? Yes? Good, so you know it was centuries ago. Fresh air helps my Firemen and I've had more recent success with moving patients down to the sea for a month or two and away from London,' said Dr Brown. 'I think I'm gaining evidence that the lungs can recover.'

'How can I do a few months Doctor? I'll be back on duty next week.'

'The Inspector is coming later I believe. We've had a chat and come up with a suggestion. He'll brief you later. But one thing, Jack, no matter what you do in the next few weeks you must give yourself time to recover. I want a promise from you, the same one I get from my Firemen.'

Jack waited. 'If I can I'll make the promise but I also have to obey orders,' he said.

'So, I must advise Inspector Hunt and influence the orders,' said the Doctor. 'Which is what I believe I've done. Promise me, Jack, that you will not go back into the Docks without coming to see me first and that you will rest every afternoon for the next three weeks.'

'I'll try, Doctor,' said Jack.

'No, not good enough,' said Brown, quietly. 'Will you promise me that you'll come and see me before you resume duties back north of the river? Or, if you can't get to me, you will go to Ann?' insisted the Doctor.

The Doctor was so intense in his desire to help that Jack decided that he should say yes, no matter what happened.

'Yes, I promise.'

'And that you will do your best to try and rest every afternoon?' the Doctor reiterated.

'If I can, depending what shift I'm on,' said Jack.

'There will not be a shift. As I said I can influence the orders. Promise me, Jack. I don't want an early death on my conscience.'

The phrase "early death" was enough to put fear into Jack's being. He sat back and stared at Brown. Either the Doctor was going mad or there was a real reason for all this. Out of respect for the man and because he did not want to leave Harriet, Jack decided to agree to what he asked.

'I promise. If you can influence when I'm working and where I will have a rest in the afternoons. How's that?' asked Jack.

'That's good, very good. Now I must go to the rest of my patients. I'll see you in a few weeks.'

Jack looked at the man who was packing away his equipment. He thought he had seen him look better. The man looked thinner than when they had first met six months ago.

'And you, Dr. Brown, are you well?' asked Jack.

'I could do with an assistant to relieve me for a few weeks myself. The heat in the city is something I find wearying more and more each year. But apart from that, yes, thank-you Jack, I am well.'

'And Ann can't assist you?' asked Jack, realising that he already knew the answer.

'And Ann can't do that for the usual reason, as yet anyway. I need a stooge for Ann to work under and then I can take a holiday. I think I have found one for a few weeks. Not a bad option but not in Ann's league. If he agrees, she'll carry on my work as his assistant and I will get out to the country. Now, as for you, enjoy your rest here, but I shall suggest to Inspector Hunt that you go to the sea-side quickly. I will see you in a few weeks if things work out for the both of us.' Brown closed his bag and opened the door.

'Thank-you Doctor Brown. I hope you manage to get away and rest too,' said Jack.

Jack swung his legs over the side of the bed and sat on the edge of it as Tom Hunt and Ted Phillips walked in.

*

101

Hunt doubled back to the landing as Brown left Jack's room to check how the patient was.

'We have a compromise,' said Brown.

Hunt nodded and waited. Brown put his bag down and faced the Inspector. Hunt registered the very earnest look.

'I've explained to Jack that I have some success with the treatment of firemen,' Brown began. 'I'd like to get him away as soon as possible to the sea, for three weeks, no shift pattern to his stay there, some exercise building to more by the end of three weeks. He's to rest every afternoon. He agrees to this providing it fits with orders. If you and I can agree to his work pattern in Brighton he can go tomorrow as far as I'm concerned.'

Hunt almost laughed as this was easier than he had hoped.

'Then let me tell him that you and I are in full agreement and he can go on Monday to Brighton. It will be as you wish Doctor,' said Hunt.

'And, one more thing Tom. He must see either Ann or I before he resumes duties in London. Leman Street may not yet be possible even in another three weeks.'

'Agreed,' Hunt said, smiling. The two men shook hands and Brown started to make his way down the stairs as Tom Hunt opened the door into Jack's bedroom.

*

Ted had taken a chair in the corner of the room and Jack asked him if Harriet had got back to the Grove alright.

'She was fine,' said Ted. 'Interesting that Mr Pendle, her employer, was interested in you. He's a good friend of the Chief Constable and that won't do you any harm.'

Hunt had seen the way that Jack had staggered as the constable had leaped to attention when he walked in.

'Now, now, no need for that,' Hunt had said, while he gripped Jack's arm to steady him. Ted's smile came back as this was Jack's normal behaviour. The intention showed he was mending, even if physically he still should not have tried.

Tom Hunt pulled up the balloon backed chair to the side of the bed. Ted noted how more relaxed Jack was than yesterday. Harriet's visit had been the morale boost he had needed.

From his bag Hunt pulled a sheaf of papers. Among them was a telegram from a hotelier called Burgess in Brighton and he held it out to Jack. It confirmed that a room was ready and that he would give Jack any assistance he required. Jack looked up after reading the brief message, his eyes astonished.

'Brighton? On Monday?'

'That's right. Do you know it?' asked Hunt.

'No, not really. I went once as a child. 'Twas a bit of a way and my parents were always working, given their livelihood was a market garden business. Father was native to Bexhill and generally preferred the quietness there to the noise of Brighton,' explained Jack.

'When would that have been?' asked Ted.

'I was coming up to nine,' Jack frowned, trying to recall, 'the summer before they both died.'

Hunt paused, allowing the memory its time out of respect. After some moments he said, 'So not much to recall about it apart from probably seeing the sea?'

Jack nodded, but in his memory, he could see his parents laughing while he stood on the water's edge skimming pebbles. He could see the flat, flinted pebble do four skims over the surface of the sea and he had turned proudly to where his parents stood. They had missed it as Father had put an arm around Mother's waist. He had called to them and they had looked towards him while he shouted, 'I got a four!'

'Do it again,' he could still hear Father say. And he had. He had turned back knowing the acknowledgement would be there, and Father had smiled at him and nodded.

Hunt watched his Constable's face, seeing the mind wander into past memories, some country that the Inspector could not enter. Again he waited, exchanging a look with Ted.

——

'No,' said Jack, 'Not much to remember about the town.'

Hunt searched his memory for something in his own past which would give him the empathy for Jack. All too easy in their line of work to ignore emotion and treat everything as functional. Trauma, like the experience of the fire, he could relate to. It was not a fire though in his case, but a young woman he had seen regularly on his beat. He had been fond of her and had been one of a pair of constables called when she was found garrotted. It was months after he had joined the Metropolitan Police. 1851 it had been and Fairbrass had taken him on one side and given him a pep talk shortly after the training for policing the Great Exhibition. Hunt remembered being one of the four hundred policemen on patrol each day inside the Crystal Palace for which Fairbrass had trained a thousand men. That time was mixed up in his memory with the dreadful murder of the woman however, and just as Jack could not share Hunt's memory fully, Hunt knew he could only have a glimmer of what Jack had experienced in the fire. One trauma was likely to recall another for Jack and Hunt knew the link with Brighton had revived memories of a nine-year-old boy whose world had ended dramatically. They should speak of loss this morning for their mutual health, he decided.

'Could I go on Wednesday, Inspector?' Jack was asking something and Hunt's attention switched back to him.

'Wednesday? Why ever would you want to wait?' asked Hunt.

'It's just that I'm supposed to see Harriet, I mean Miss Fildew, on Tuesday,' said Jack.

'No, I'm afraid that's out of the question. Doctor Brown is quite insistent that you must go to the fresh air of the sea for three weeks as soon as possible and he and I have agreed you'll go on Monday. From the team's perspective we need you there with enough time before the Shah arrives. Plus you will have to be rested and able to start doing a reconnoitre of the town, the shore line, and the Parade. Wednesday's too late.'

'Three weeks is a long time,' said Jack.

'Send Miss Fildew a note that you've no choice in the matter and you're under orders to convalesce in sea air. It's completely true anyway, and only for three weeks,' said Hunt.

'But...' Jack stopped as the hard expression came into the Inspector's eyes. Ted had looked up sharply as well. Jack nodded compliance.

'Good,' said Hunt. 'If the feelings for you are real, she'll understand. You saw her anyway this week.' He went back to trying to recall what it was that Fairbrass had said to him? Hunt searched for the words. Ah yes, that was it.

'Look, Jack a man who trained me gave me some good advice following a difficult case. It wasn't a fire but a woman I was fond of was murdered. I share it with you with the same intention he had.' Hunt paused as there was a knock on the door and Mrs Morris appeared behind a tray of tea and biscuits.

'No doubt you're thirsty by now. I'll leave you to help yourselves,' she said as she set the tray down.

'Many thanks, Violet. What time is Morris home today?' asked Ted.

Jack hesitated, bemused that Mrs Morris was a Violet.

'He won't be long now, unless something has developed,' Violet Morris answered.

'That's a lovely name,' said Jack and she smiled at him. He could not quite bring himself to ask if he may call her Violet. It was, after all, the age difference he realised. She had sons of the same age as himself. Once she had let herself out of the room Tom Hunt took a sip of the tea that Ted had poured for him and chose a biscuit. After that he picked up his theme again.

'Have your tea, lad and listen,' said Ted offering Jack the plate. Jack picked up a biscuit although he had no appetite but Ted had a look about him that was not going to accept a refusal.

Hunt had seen the way that Jack had staggered as the Constable had leaped to attention when he walked in.

'At this sort of time where you're recovering from something the mind can do some strange things. Its common, and many have said the same, that memories seem to get triggered in a situation quite unpredictably.' Hunt paused to take another biscuit from the plate.

'I've found it myself when I've gone into an arrest. Suddenly there's a very clear picture of another time,' Hunt continued. 'It can be difficult and I've thought to myself to be ready for it as there can be that moment's hesitation otherwise which can make all the difference in bringing something to a conclusion. I mention it as the fire may bring things to mind which are difficult for you. Another time perhaps and memories of something hard come back into your mind. Mention of Brighton today will have revived memories of your family time there. It's a time linked to a very difficult period for you and that may recur while you're there. Some of the situations you've experienced already probably play on your mind from time to time as well. All of us have it, Jack, and it's important to recognise it and realise you aren't the only one,' said Hunt.

Jack glanced from Hunt to Ted, who nodded. Surprised but immensely reassured he smiled at the Inspector.

'I've been having dreams, strange dreams, people in it all mixed up. Some nights I don't actually want to go to sleep. Thanks for the advice, Inspector, it helps to know it's not just me. I've thought at times I was going mad. It's like I look alright but inside it's like a house near Rye called Mock-Beggar-Hall. It looks alright on the outside but within its poor and bare.'

'Well, scars aren't always visible. That's what I wanted to say. If it gets difficult know that the men working alongside you will have gone through similar experiences. We also have a very good Police Surgeon who has some understanding himself of the wounding of the mind. Now, let's get on. There are two objectives in sending you to Brighton. Doctor Brown will already have told you that sea air is part of your recovery?' asked Hunt.

Jack nodded.

'I've let the Doctor lead on this,' continued Hunt. 'It frankly suits us that we have a man down there as we have the responsibility for the Shah of Persia's safety. Ted mentioned him to you the other day I believe.'

Jack nodded.

'The team will be in the background, Jack, and I need an assessment of the town's security in case the Shah accepts the invitation from Brighton to go on a visit there. He arrives in London in a few days-time so, I want you on the ground and an assessment of potential problems if he decides to go there. This, of course, is under-cover work and you will not be in uniform. No liaising with the local force either as they won't know we're there, is that clear?' Hunt waited.

'Yes, sir,' said Jack.

'The hotelier, Burgess, is a retired policeman. He did twenty years with the Met, and, like most of us, was brought in to police others from the same class. Like you he's from a labouring background. I remember him fit and strong. You'll find him over-weight now but he can still put his shoulder to a door. He has a good understanding of areas and characters and their intentions. Spend some time with him and give him credibility for what he can pass on to you. He's dealt with hard people, both men and women. Like you he's put on the uniform and at times, gone into plain clothes. I worked with him often,' said Hunt.

'Why did he retire? If he's the same age as yourself I mean?'' asked Jack.

Ted cleared his throat. He waited to see how the Inspector would handle the question.

Hunt had paused, mulling over the right words.

'It's important to understand the times, with what I tell you. You see, going back a few years there were high hopes about the idea of prevention of crime by putting uniformed men on patrol, and driving offenders away. The public would know who the policeman was because they would see his number,' said Hunt.

'Yes, sir, I know,' replied Jack.

'Of course you know this. Once a policeman becomes hard to identify he's considered to be a spy. The whole subject of going undercover is a difficult one. Then there's a question of background. When you look at me, and Ted here, and yourself, there's little difference. We're from the same class. If we start to question what is thought of as our elders and betters, flushing out criminal types in the middle classes and tracking down those linked to crime groups regardless of who they are in society, we're probably for it. You've gathered the man we've been after while you've worked with us since the Faceless Woman case is not from our class. He's too protected.'

'I hadn't thought of that, sir,' said Jack.

'No? Well, Burgess got too close, was criticised over a long period and it broke him. I remember you read Wilkie Collins's "the Moonstone?"'

'Some time ago, yes,' said Jack, smiling.

'The dogged detective in that story was Sergeant Cuff. So-called "Respectable Society" likes the idea that the law is applied to everyone equally in a novel. They don't like the reality when it's applied to one of them,' Hunt stopped and picked up a spoon. He allowed it to rest in the sugar for a few moments and then put a heaped spoonful into his tea.

'Does Burgess know who we're after then?' asked Jack.

'He believes he does, and I'll come to that shortly,' said Hunt.

'Is he right though, Inspector?' Jack continued, eyes more alert than they had been for several days.

'It's not a question of whether he's right, Jack, it's a question of proof. We haven't any,' said Ted firmly.

'But is he *right*?' asked Jack, looking from the Sergeant to the Inspector. Hunt breathed in and stared out of the window.

'We believe he is,' answered Ted, almost in a whisper.

'So it's coming down to his class, and he's being protected, and we can't collar him. Harry thinks there's a possibility that the theft I witnessed at the Alexandra Palace is connected. And the West India Dock theft. Do you know what was taken there yet, sir?' asked Jack.

'Yes. Franks was right that it was something small and precious. Most of what we deal with is petty theft, isn't it? We also know that poorer people don't bother to report a theft to us. But this theft is different. This was a commission, a robbery set up by a collector,' said Hunt.

Jack waited.

'It was a watch, a gilt brass verge watch signed by G. Ferlite of Geneva. He worked between 1590 to 1635,' said Hunt.

'What's a verge watch?' asked Jack.

'It's the earliest known type of mechanical device. There are some technical explanations about it. Believe me its clever and it's about the mechanism and moving the clock's hands forward at a steady rate. From what I gather they were before the invention of the pendulum and balance spring, which came in after Ferlite stopped working. You have a pocket watch Jack, don't you?' asked Hunt.

'Yes,' said Jack, glancing at the bedside table. Hunt followed his gaze to the watch.

'Well the item that was stolen would have preceded what you use now. It's a collector's item and was on its way to a museum in London. It was high workmanship for its time. That's its value. Someone talked about it, probably at a dinner or some large event. The type of event that certain classes get to hear about across a dinner table. Like the item you saw stolen at the Alexandra Palace, it was on a shopping list of the type of person who we find difficult to touch. A man at the highest echelons of society who buys policemen such as the detective who attacked Harriet, Jack. A man who commissions murder when a mistress becomes troublesome and who we still have not caught.'

And you know who it is,' said Jack. 'Burgess knows and you know, so why isn't he under arrest.'

'No proof,' said Hunt. 'He dances through crime like a ghost.'

'There *shouldn't* be any difference,' Jack had leaned forward. Resting his elbows on his knees he grasped his hands together. The earnestness of his reaction was not lost on Hunt or the Sergeant.

'No, there shouldn't,' said Hunt, quietly. 'And to you and me Jack, and Ted here, there isn't. But reality is different. Anyway, until the day that we can act without members of the team being killed, or made ill through being humiliated, we will play the waiting game. What we've told you this morning is more than we intended to do. You know now that you can trust Burgess and he'll help you so be open with him. Don't tell anyone in the local police why you're there.'

'The man you're reporting to, sir, does he know all this?' asked Jack.

'Yes, but not the identity,' replied Hunt, 'because I can't trust him not to make a mistake.'

'Can't he do anything?'

'Not yet, and you have to accept that.' Hunt and Jack stared at each other like two stags about to lock horns.

'But...' Jack started and then looked away, the sense of frustration making him desperately try to think of a solution. He could not and looked across to Ted.

'One day,' said Ted.

Hunt moved the situation on.

'If you have to get hold of me, contact Harry as he'll be in the town as well,' explained Hunt.

'Harry's going to be in Brighton?' Jack responded with a grin.

'On leave, for his future mother-in-law's health. That's the story. No stained waistcoat for this job, Harry looks very dapper and this time they're in a swanking hotel. Mrs Phillips senior has been persuaded to lend us some of her time. She benefits from good sea air and Rose Phillips will be accompanying her,' said Hunt.

Jack looked at Ted registering the phrase, "future mother-in-law." Ted started to smile anticipating Jack's next question.

'You mean that Harry Franks has finally proposed and had an answer?' asked Jack. 'And Rose has agreed to be Harry's wife?'

'She has,' said Ted.

'So, no more looking nunty, he's smartened up. The poetry worked!' stated Jack.

'Poetry?' laughed Ted, and Tom Hunt guffawed.

'Never mind, I shouldn't have said anything. Don't let on you both know,' said Jack, controlling his expression as the corners of his mouth started to twitch.

'Oh this is too good to let slip. I shall dine out on this one. Harry Franks, Detective Sergeant Shadwell, and Poet,' Hunt slapped Ted on the shoulder and the two men almost became hysterical.

'Oh dear,' said Ted, taking out a large handkerchief and wiping his eyes. 'Wait until I do the speech at the wedding. I shall stand in for father, in more ways than one, and the father of the bride speech will be mine. I shall have fun with this story.'

'So, Ted, you'll be the Old-Father. As to poetry, I think it was shared as a confidence,' said Jack, looking from one to the other.

'Too late, Jack. This is too good to miss. The poetic detective,' said Hunt and he was off again, laughing uncontrollably. It was infectious and all three men were doubled up with the ludicrous picture before them of the tough detective winning his lady with poetry. It was a relief to laugh. The humour began to subside and Ted pulled an envelope from a pocket inside his tunic.

'Talking of Rose, she passed a letter to me that was waiting at the cottage for you. I think it's Sam Curzon's writing. Perhaps you could open it while we're here as we've also heard from him,' Ted held an envelope out to Jack, quite casually between his thumb and forefinger.

Caught out, his smile vanished and Jack felt the burning in his cheeks. He wished beyond anything that the tendency to colour which he still had was over at his age. He took the letter from Ted and without looking at either of his two colleagues tore open the envelope. The letter was just one side of a page and it was signed by Sam. Jack read it and looked at Hunt.

'Sam says his father's ill. He needs work otherwise they're likely to end up in dire straits'

'That letter is a little dated, I'm afraid Jack. His father died a week after he sent it to you. I'd like you to telegram him and tell him that you and Harry will see Sam in Brighton on Monday, that I'm arranging rooms for him, and his mother if she would like to stay in Brighton with him, and to come to the Ship hotel. I have work for him. Paid work to advise me. While Sam can't go back into uniform Harry will liaise with him because of the analytical skills Sam has. He'll work for me as a security advisor, Jack.'

Jack nodded, picking up a pencil on the side table next to his bed and writing down the Inspector's instructions.

'Charlie Banks also sent an envelope for you. I had a quick look but it's in German apparently. There's a note as well,' said Ted, handing over a pamphlet. 'I didn't know German was one of your skills, Jack.'

'It's not. Charlie was covering my beat,' said Jack as he looked at his name on the envelope. 'It's something one of the teachers at an Orphanage I call in at said she would let me have. I'd found a man at a German church near Leman Street who was going to translate it. But that's no good now.'

'What's it for?' asked Ted.

'It's a tract by a man called Wilhelm Marr. She, that is Miss Cohen, thought it had something to do with inciting the damage to the building and frightening the children. She said that sort of behaviour was getting worse. I wanted to try and understand what was making people do this to children anyway but also because she truly believed it was because they were Jewish orphans. Sounded like she believed that there was a sea change because of things in this,' Jack waved the pamphlet.

'Possibly something we should be aware of then,' said Hunt.

'That's what I thought,' said Jack. 'Now it's difficult though without a translation.'

Jack thought for some seconds and then said, 'Although if the Parson is still in Simpson I might be able to get him to have a look. I haven't seen him sen I was a child. He was good with languages Father said. I thought a visit was timely if I was in Brighton.'

Hunt nodded. 'Is Simpson near Brighton?'

'Not too far. Closer to Lewes. Its spelt Selmeston if you're looking on a map,' Jack explained. 'The Parson and my father got together from time to time to chat about the Sussex way of saying things. Called it a dialect he did from what I can remember although there was some argument about that. My father said he was a very clever man and at that time he was documenting the ways people spoke in East and West Sussex. He left the parish where we were before my parents died. I heard he was living at Simpson. I could look him up and see if he's still around. Perhaps he could take a look at it.'

'Yes do, but don't get side tracked. Remember why you're in Sussex. How will you get there?' asked Hunt.

'Train, as there's a branch line from Brighton to Lewes,' said Jack.

'Alright. If you pick up a translation from your old vicar let me have it. Link up with the other four in Brighton and make sure not to over-reach yourself at present. Understood?' said Hunt, firmly.

'Yes, Inspector,' said Jack, grinning. 'I'll do the telegram to Sam now.' Jack paused and then asked, 'Who is number four?'

'Rose,' said Ted, quietly.

'Does Harry know?' asked Jack, his eyes twinkling at how much of a handful Rose was likely to be for Harry.

'No. You know and that's enough. Rose has been my eyes and ears in the Docks for years, Jack, you know that. She can get into places that you and Harry can't. If she needs help or uncovers something she'll tell you. Keep an eye on her for me as you have over the last six months,' said Ted.

*

Seven

On Monday, the sixteenth of June, Jack looked at the resort that had at one time lured Princes and their court to take up residence. Brighton had clouds like a blanket as he arrived and a squall was visible on the horizon.

He mulled over the rest of Friday's briefing and thought of the impending visit of the Shah. In his luggage Jack found Hunt had even placed photographs of the man.

Arriving in Brighton he was taken aback by the number of hotels but the one that Jack was bound for was the Ship. He boarded an omnibus at the station as there was a regular service meeting every train. In his pocket was a banker's draft from Tom Hunt for the Manager of the hotel, Burgess, and Jack noted the number of banks in the town as he travelled. The London and County Bank was the one he needed.

Looking back at the station he noted the clock on the front structure and altered his pocket watch, registering that it was on a building with pillars and a portico which looked like drawings he had seen of Rome.

At last the route brought him to the hotel that would be his home for the next three weeks. He jumped off the omnibus without thinking and immediately regretted it. The coughing that consumed him left him leaning against a wall and to his surprise he was moved on by a policeman and warned about being drunk.

'I was abouten going in,' was all Jack managed to say, pointing towards the Ship Hotel before he brought up mucus. The appearance on the doorstep of the Manager Burgess, was timely and the man took the constable to one side as a porter collected the fine leather bag Jack had dropped. After a brief discussion the constable was satisfied that Jack was unwell and not drunk and left him to the care of the Manager.

'Charles Burgess, Metropolitan Police, retired. As you noticed it helps for that to be known by the local force,' Burgess said, taking Jack by the elbow and supporting him across the step.

'Jack Sargent, Tom Hunt said you were expecting me.'

'We are indeed. We're a short distance from the Royal Pavilion and the Pier, here. A good walk for you no doubt in your condition at present but something to aim for while in Brighton. You're a fit young man usually by the looks of you. I'm sorry for the effects on your health that your bravery has had. But we'll get you right in your time here, my Alice and I.'

A stout woman appeared from a door off the hall and smiled a welcome. She had a very direct gaze and the eyes were full of life.

'This is my wife, Alice. Named for the Queen's daughter she was.' Burgess looked proudly on as the woman wiped her hands on her apron and nodded to Jack.

'How do you do, Mrs Burgess,' said Jack.

'Alice, please. If I may, as you're police and Charles served twenty years with Tom Hunt I'll call you Jack? Tom said you were local to here.'

Jack registered the level of the relationship between the Burgesses and Inspector Hunt. He relaxed in the thought that the man's advice would be worth taking about the security issues of the town but he was also determined to try and get Burgess to talk about the man behind both the murders of the American couple, the Berringers, and ultimately responsible for damage to Sam and Emily Doyle's suicide. He smiled at Alice Burgess.

'Yes, please do call me Jack. It feels like we're family, police family. Well, I'm local to Bexhill really. Kewhurst and Hastings were the parts that I got to, to fish with my father. I think I came to Brighton once as a child on a day out with my parents, but they died when I was nine and life changed from then on.' explained Jack.

'I see. I am sorry, it will feel hard for you coming back today. Duty takes us down some difficult roads,' said Alice. 'But I think you couldn't be in a better place to convalesce from your injuries in the fire. We'll feed you up and help you in any way we can. I hope you'll enjoy the Marine Metropolis as Brighton is being called and will bring back some happy memories of that day with them. It will be different to what you saw with your parents, but I suspect that you were more interested in the sea and penny ice-creams at the age of nine than fine buildings.'

'You're very kind. I'm sure I will,' said Jack. 'It certainly looks different to how I remember it. But the sun is usually brighter than London although today you would not know that. I can smell the salt again and that's agreeable. It was good to hear the sea-gulls crying as I stepped off the train.'

'I'll get you a cup of tea and some arrow root biscuits. Charles will show you your room and I'll bring it in to you. How is your recovery progressing?'

'It's just the coughing after the effects of the smoke,' explained Jack.

'Tom's telegram said the police surgeon's advice was that you were in need of sea air and would be with us for three weeks.' said Alice. 'We often have a policeman down from London who needs a little time to get right again. Sometimes they have a few things to do for Tom as well.'

'Now Alice, don't go giving away too many secrets,' laughed her husband. Turning to Jack he added, 'I'll show you along to your room and you can get settled in. There's some magnificent houses to be seen on a walk from here. See how you are later and I can show you some a short distance away.' Burgess led Jack down a corridor stretching away from the reception to a ground floor room. He brought a large set of keys forward from a chain at his side and selected one to unlock the door. He swung it wide and Jack looked into a room that he would imagine could be bright on a sunny day with light pouring in through tall, casement windows framed with draped curtains.

'We thought doing without a flight of stairs would be best for you at present,' continued Charles Burgess. 'This room is usually reserved for our bath-chair residents but I didn't think you would mind that as there is a bathroom to yourself as a result. It's nice and spacious and you can see that you have a sitting room area as well. You're closer to get assistance and should you need it press the button here on the wall.'

'A bathroom to myself? I may never go back to London,' Jack's face showed how delighted he was and Burgess was equally pleased at the genuine response.

'Come and join me when you've settled in. Alice will be along with your tea shortly. I'll be in the room at the back of the reception for the next few hours as I've accounts to do. We can exchange stories about the police when you're ready. There's no hurry, as you're probably tired after the journey.'

'I think I'll try and sleep for a short while,' said Jack sitting down and starting to unlace his boots. 'Doctor's orders every afternoon,' he added as a way of explanation in case Burgess thought him weak.

'Quite so, just the ticket. Alice will bring in your tea tray shortly. There's a key to the room in the side table drawer. The front door to the hotel is open until ten o'clock each night and then there's a night bell by the front door. Have a good rest,' said Burgess, as he pulled the door behind him.

Jack pushed the door of the bathroom open and looked around. It was the first one he had seen with a visible harmony to the fittings. The bath, washstand and toilet were encased in mahogany panelling. The bathroom was also clearly connected to a house drain so there would be no need for his water to be emptied by a maid. Laughing at the innovation's impact on him Jack turned on a tap and free flowing water from the taps highlighted how easy it would be for him to bathe.

Jack thought of the communal pump in the street used by his parents, and even of Hannah, the maid of all work at the Arbour Square house, staggering up the stairs with jugs of hot water twice a day. As much as he loved living with Rose and Mrs Phillips in West India Dock he hated the privy housed in a lean-to shed at the end of the yard. In hot weather it stank as the privy was just a wooden seat with a round hole. Beneath was a drain into a brick lined cesspool. This bathroom was completely up to date with the latest innovations.

Jack saw the towels and a gentleman's dressing gown neatly folded on a chest to the side of the bath. It felt grand and although weary from the journey he wanted to enjoy the room before taking his rest. A knock on the door announced Alice Burgess with his tea, and he swung it open wide.

'Here we are, this will put you right after a long journey. Sugar?'

'Thank-you, two please.'

She poured a cup of tea for Jack and handed it to him. 'I'll leave you to rest now and Charles says you and he are going to catch up on stories from the police later. We may get some rain, by the looks of the cloud,' said Alice, peering up at the greying sky.

'I'll set the window open for coolthe,' said Jack. 'I mean for coolness of the air,' he added realising the tiredness was overcoming him.

'Of course, I'll leave you to it,' said Alice

One thought had started to plague him though. Had Sam arrived in Brighton?

'Mrs Burgess, I mean, Alice, has Sam and Mrs Curzon arrived?' asked Jack.

'Mr Curzon? Yes, he and his mother arrived a few hours ago. Would you like me to let him know you're here?'

'Thank-you, I'll rest first and come and find him later,' said Jack, taking a few mouthfuls of sweet tea. After Alice had left the room he dipped a biscuit in the tea and managed to get it into his mouth before it fell apart.

Dismissing the thought as well he could that he must put things right with Sam, he pushed his boots off with his toes, flopped back on to the pillows and turned his back to the window. Within a minute he had submitted to sleep.

When he opened his eyes it was four o'clock in the afternoon and Jack was sweating and breathless. The air was close and announced imminent thunder. He sat up sharply, both unsure of where he was and what had woken him and gripped the side of the bed as he looked around the room. Jack swung his legs onto the floor and the action brought on a coughing spasm. Although these had got less in the last forty-eight hours he was racked by this one and fell back into his pillows.

A sea gull's cry reminded him that he was in Brighton and staying in the Ship Hotel. He pushed the sash window up higher and breathed in the cooler air as the rain started to fall.

Another bad dream and again Harriet had been the subject and he a guest at her wedding. This time she was not at risk but things were out of order as Jack was not the man marrying her. The groom's face was unclear but, somehow, he had known it was Paul Morris. The flowers were white and he had seen the detail on Harriet's bouquet. In his dream Jack had walked up a line of staff members from the house in the Grove. Although he had never met the people that Harriet worked with he could clearly make out a Butler and Housekeeper. In the background he had heard the sea crashing. Ridiculous as it sounded, he could remember all this detail. He had started shouting in his dream, but Sergeant Morris had blocked him from reaching Harriet. Jack could almost hear Morris's words, 'What do you expect?'

Then he had come to with a start. Jack leaned over to the bed side table and felt the teapot which was still warm. He poured the liquid into the cup and spooned in the sugar. There were two biscuits left and he devoured them hungrily, washing them down with gulps of the tea.

119

A gentle knock on the bedroom door brought him to his feet. He stared around the room taking it in again. The experience was strange and the place unfamiliar. All was now quiet and he went into his bathroom and ran water in order to splash some on his face in an effort to wake up before he opened the door.

Again a knock.

Jack called out, 'Just a minute.' He glanced up at himself in the mirror, wiping the water off with the back of his hand. No doubt there was a good explanation for that last dream. He and Harriet should have been meeting tomorrow, Tuesday, for a few hours only, at Greenwich. However that would have been better than nothing. Instead Jack had sent her a handwritten note on Sunday to explain that he was being sent away to convalesce by the sea, under orders, and would be in Brighton from Monday for three weeks. He had added a suggestion that if it was possible she might come down by train and join him for a day out when she had a day free.

There had been no response from her before he had left on Monday and he had deliberately omitted to say where he was staying in Brighton in case he was breaking his cover. Now she could not contact him. Harriet was resourceful though and he knew she would try and get a message to him via Ted.

Again a knock.

He made his way across the room and opened the door to find Sam Curzon on the mat. At least he thought it was Sam as the figure was slightly stooped and bent almost in a supplicatory manner. The hair loss was staggering. The eyes were Sam's but the life had gone and, in the smile, there was a shade of uncertainty as he looked at Jack.

'Sorry, I got here earlier and couldn't wait any longer to see you. I rushed down the stairs and just need to get my breath back. It seems rude to disturb you but the excitement got the better of me. Yes, it is me, I know I look different from the last time you saw me, but I'm the same man inside, just need to rest a little more, unfortunately,' Sam held out his hand and Jack responded.

'You're not alone in that,' said Jack and then remembered his manners and opened the door wide and smiled, 'Come in,' he said.

Jack picked up the chair by the side of the bed and placed it in front of the window by a table for Sam. 'Alice said that you had arrived. This is marvellous to see you but let me say how very sorry I am to hear about your father.'

'Thank you, Jack. It was hard towards the end. But we all hope for the best. My young brothers need to stay at school and bit by bit we can get them placed in work. This job now will make a big difference to me and our situation. Mother will work with an undertaker, helping to prepare bodies for burial. At least there will always be work for her there.' Sam clasped Jack's hand but the grief was in the eyes.

Caught between the desire not to admit weakness and horrified that his avoidance was being hailed as heroism Jack felt sick. He looked at Sam, still finding it hard to believe what state the man was in.

'I should have been more support to you all. I should have come.' Jack bit his bottom lip and ran a hand across the edge of the table.

'It was so quick. Father seemed strong and healthy and I thought he would go on for years yet. It's been a shock to Mother, of course. I'm hoping she'll pick up while we're here,' muttered Sam.

Jack looked at his friend and thought what a shell of his former self he was. He had hoped that Sam would fully recover and now realised that he had been fooling himself. Sam was speaking.

'And you, how are you? I hear you've been badly affected by the fire at the Alexandra Palace. I understood why I didn't hear from you when I read the article in the Telegraph. I said to the family, that's our Jack, thinking only of others.'

Jack grimaced and in order to say something he picked up the subject of his own health.

'It all happened so quickly in the fire. I didn't think what I was doing. At the moment there's a cough which is all consuming when it starts and Dr. Brown is running some tests on me. He thought sea air for a while would be the best thing. It fitted in with Hunt's plans as regards the Shah's visit.'

Jack dropped his eyes ashamed that he felt unable to tell Sam the real reason he had not responded. Sam was oblivious and caught up in renewing the old working relationship. He carried on explaining as he sat down.

'It's a good opportunity for me. Mother's with me as a cover partly but also because Inspector Hunt has kindly arranged for her to come away to the sea. That way she will get a change and some good sea air. The younger ones are with our grandmother in the country. There's a whole family of young cousins and they'll lift their spirits. It's so great to see you again and to be *working* with you Jack.'

'Your strength was always thinking, Sam. Hunt's glad to have you back. I was always too quick to be off, but you were the brains,' said Jack, sitting on the side of his bed.

'If I'd used my brain I would not have gone to see Emily Doyle that afternoon. You were the one that worked out that it was Emily who poisoned me,' said Sam quietly. The mention of the name made them both go silent for a short while. Jack nodded.

'I still have bad dreams, Sam, which I'm sure are triggered by what she did. That house was the loveliest place I ever knew, and it was the most destructive.' Jack paused as he saw the effect his words were having on Sam. 'Listen to me, you'd think I had been the one made ill by that time. I have no right to be so affected when you were the one....' But Sam waved away his concern.

'It's alright, Jack. There are different ways of being affected. You and me, we both loved Arbour Square, the house, Emily Doyle and little Sarah. The home we were absorbed into through being on placement there for the job held a wealth of kindness. But madness was in its walls without being obvious. Sam paused and for they were both there briefly walking the corridors, sitting at the dining table.

'And who's to say that the poor woman was the most wicked in the case? She was used by that American, Berringer, and was too young and unprotected to find her way. By the time Matthew Doyle came on the scene she was already involved as Berringer's mistress.' Sam's face looked grey.

'Sam its done now, don't distress yourself,' said Jack.

'No, I'm alright. You know, I've thought about this so often in the last six months. Neither of us have the right to be so affected when you think what her actions did to her poor husband. Doyle's gone completely white they say. We're alive and we weren't the ones who were betrayed. The poor man, he must think he's going mad when he considers the adultery, and murder... What is it, Jack?' Sam stopped at Jack's expression.

Jack dropped his eyes and shook his head. 'He didn't know about the adultery. I'm sorry about Inspector Doyle but Sam, how can you say that when Emily tried to kill you? She'd tried to kill Mrs Berringer and was only prevented from succeeding by the fact that someone else battered the woman to death before the poison took effect. She tricked Doyle into marrying her. That's two planned deaths and would have ruined his life and left him if Berringer had divorced his wife. Murder in her heart even though she didn't succeed. Thank God she didn't in your case. She still attempted it though, Sam.'

'She wasn't right in the head, was she? Can't have been. At times it probably seemed that her plans had worked. But she must have been in incredible distress. And killing me didn't work, did it, thanks to you,' said Sam.

'Good grief, Sam,' said Jack, exasperated. 'She had the thought to destroy another human being and tried to carry it out. The fact she didn't succeed in either case was sheer chance. But she dealt with you abusefully. And look at you, Sam. Your career's gone and you've no strength still. No, I won't let her off so lightly, I haven't got the forgiveness in my heart to match yours.'

Jack stood up and walked to the window. He stared out at the people moving on the street opposite, taking in an exchange between two men.

Sam sat forward, his elbows on the table in front of him. His hands clasped almost in an attitude of prayer as he stared at Jack's back. Deciding to change the subject he said, 'Harry Franks has arrived this afternoon with Rose and her mother. There was a boy came with a message. We're to join up for tea in a fashionable hotel on the front. Called the Royal. Do you know it?'

'Struth! I know of it but it's not the sort of place I would have been welcome in. I'd better change and so had you. Have you anything else with you?' asked Jack.

'There's some things Inspector Hunt sent which look like they fit the ticket,' Sam said.

'Yes, me too, but I thought they were for cricket. If it's the Royal on the front we had better look the part. Burgess may have a local paper and we can check who's staying there. I'll meet you in reception and we can walk up.' Jack laughed, suddenly seeing the funny side of taking tea in the Royal Hotel. Sam frowned slightly, trying to understand Jack's sudden change.

'The farm labourer and the clerk in the Royal. Father would have laughed,' said Jack as a way of explanation for his humour.

'Times change, and you're not a farm labourer anymore, although you can sound like one, which you do need to be careful of,' said Sam as he started to open the bedroom door. 'I'm a security advisor, thank-you very much, but I take your point. Taking tea amongst lords and ladies is going to need some concentration for both of us. Looking as if we're part of them will be very helpful. I'll meet you shortly in reception.' Sam nodded as he left the room.

Jack, still grinning, pulled the bag from the wardrobe where he had put it quickly. Only having glanced in it briefly when he had received it he did not know exactly what was in there. As he lifted the articles out he found there were two sets of clothes. He had been right that there were cricket whites in the bag but he put those carefully to one side. He knew what he was doing with those, from the days of playing on the Squire's team in Battle before he had left for London.

It was the clothing underneath that caught his breath. His mother had told him that 'manners maketh man,' but he was coming to the conclusion that the right fashion and bearing would have a lot to do with it as well. The strides in manufacturing now meant that there was no need to have a tailor or items sewn at home. He would have a respectable wardrobe for Brighton and the summer.

Hunt had seen to everything as indeed he had previously when Jack had gone into plain clothes. Jack felt his confidence growing and that he could emulate men who were his social superiors. If he watched his accent and worked at not using the local way of speaking he felt he could pull off tea at the Royal.

He ran his fingers over the fabrics and smiled spontaneously. With the widowed Queen having withdrawn from much of social life the Prince of Wales, having no political duties, had become an arbiter of fashion. Styles were following his example. Jack pulled out two shirts, six pairs of cuffs and six collars. With no true exercise and manual work he reckoned that he could make the two shirts last four days. The cuffs and collars would help that. No doubt Alice Burgess would be able to get things washed for him. One thing he needed to do before he tried anything on was to bathe.

*

It was stormy by the time that Jack was ready. He closed the window as the air smelt of impending rain.

He knew he had taken more time than usual but once he had climbed into the bath and felt the luxurious warmth of the water any possibility of rushing had been out of the question. Now half the hour had gone by. Pleased with his appearance and bursting with confidence he locked his bedroom door and turned for the reception.

A sole individual stood at the reception desk talking to Charles Burgess. Another guest, well-heeled by the look of him. Jack wondered how long Sam would be.

He stopped and bent down to put a lace into a double knot.

An inelegant thing to do but a matter of social survival for Jack whose laces always came undone. The man was explaining something to Charles Burgess in almost a whisper. As Jack approached he recognised the voice as Sam's. He too had spruced himself up in the clothes provided by Hunt.

'Look, I've met a young sailor in the hotel lounge.' Jack heard Sam explain. 'He showed me a picture of his sweetheart in case I came across her in Brighton. She seems to have disappeared. The man has been serving on HMS Amethyst and has been away some time. He was to marry the girl on his return. Only they were delayed with the fighting and it's been a year since he left. You can imagine the state he's in.' Burgess nodded.

Jack did not respond at first. He was taking in Sam's suit and its cut and realising that Hunt must have accessed Sam's old measurements to get all this ready in time. So Hunt had decided to bring Sam back before news of Mr Curzon's death was known. He should have realised. Of course Sam would have kept in touch with others apart from himself. Sam turned and looked Jack over too.

'Ho, Jack, quite a sight we are, the two of us. We'll both fit the Royal in these get ups from what Charles says.'

'We will I hope. No one should look down their noses at us but I'd leave off drinking your tea from the saucer, Sam,' said Jack, with a grin.

Burgess chuckled and extended an arm to usher them both into his office. He pushed the door to.

'Sam was just recounting a story from a young man who came in ten minutes ago. I've not spoken to him yet but will do. It's a missing person issue by the sound of it.'

'So?' asked Jack.

'So, we could help him,' Sam said

Jack spun round and faced Sam, 'He can go to the local police,' said Jack.

'He did, they're not interested,' Sam stared back at Jack.

'Well, why would they be? How long did you say he's been away?'

'Just over a year. They told him she's probably met someone else,' said Sam.

'Exactly.' Jack answered.

'But …' Sam started.

'Now you listen to me, Sam, the last thing we're supposed to do is get involved with local issues. It might seem hard for the sailor but the girl may have decided to marry someone else. She may have a good reason not to be found. Leave it alone,' said Jack, sharply.

'Why are you getting worked up?' asked Sam, sitting back in his chair.

'Because we can't get involved in a local matter and, like you, I find it difficult to ignore something. The orders from Hunt were clear. At least to me they were,' Jack glanced at the clock on the mantelpiece. 'We should be going.'

Burgess looked from one to the other and said, 'It may seem odd to the man but sometimes a woman doesn't want to be found. She may have decided she wouldn't wait any longer for him.'

'Exactly,' Jack cut in. 'She can decide what she wants to do without us poking our noses into the situation.'

'But why are you angry with me?' asked Sam.

'Because, you could get yourself into something that you can't cope with now, and because, I'll end up bailing you out. And I'm angry at the state that we're both in, frankly, not with you.' Jack saw the hurt register. He exhaled softly and then shook his head. 'No, it's not just that. I hate what Emily did to you. And I hate what it's destroyed in me. Frankly I'm not sure either of us are up to picking something else to look into at present. And I'm afeared of what might happen to you if we start down a road that's demanding. We should stick to the reasons why we're here and not take anything else on.' Jack stopped as Sam glanced in the mirror above the mantelpiece, looking at himself. Jack sighed, 'Alright, talking to him won't hurt I suppose. I don't want to spar with you Sam. Where is this sailor?'

'In the lounge, waiting. I told him I'd get my friend. He doesn't know we're police,' said Sam, smiling at Jack.

'*We're* not. *I* am. You're acting as an advisor according to Hunt. Any action would end up being by me, remember that will you? That's not what I, or you, are here for. He should let it go after this amount of time. What about her family?' asked Jack.

'They won't talk to him, he says,' answered Sam.

'There you are, then. That shows she's met someone else,' said Jack.

'Come and have a chat with him Jack and see for yourself. It's got a smell to it,' said Sam.

'Oh don't start that stuff with *smell*. Anyone would think you're Inspector Hunt. It's a Brighton Police issue. Don't you agree Mr Burgess.'

'No,' said Burgess, softly. 'I don't.'

*

Eight

Harriet Fildew had slipped out from the house on Monday. It was a day, she thought, with a sky that was as black as a hat. She did not have permission to leave the Grove and had been waiting at the Police Station in New Road for an hour to see Ted Phillips. Clara had said that she would cover for her but Harriet knew she was already over time. Luncheon would have gone up and Clara would have appeared in her stead and given the excuse to the Butler that Harriet had sickness.

The Pendle family usually had a quiet luncheon, and today was no exception. It was just Mr and Mrs Pendle and their two unmarried daughters. Clara would cope and was quite a proficient liar. But Harriet knew that she must be going soon.

Harriet had discovered Clara's skills a few months ago when she saw her slip out and meet her young man on the other side of the walled garden. It was out of view of the main rooms of the house but not from the upper storey occupied by the servants and Harriet had frozen as she watched the exchange of a kiss. Later Clara had told her with a giggle when Harriet challenged her that it was not the first time she had taken that risk. Harriet had been shocked, more at the risk to the girl's job and reputation and had thought that she could never do such a thing. It was more an attitude of mind as Harriet had told herself that she could never lie and was sure that she would give herself away. Clara on the other hand was the picture of innocence. And now here she was taking exactly the same kind of risk over a man.

Standing in the waiting area Harriet looked at the Duty Sergeant as he moved back and forth. Such a nice man he could be if he only let himself. He had made a great pretence of ignoring her for the last twenty minutes.

Harriet found herself wondering if Jack would make Sergeant soon. She caught her reflection in the window. At eighteen, not too old or fat, all her teeth still in place and a good job. Her savings were mounting in the post office and she had a good man who wanted to marry her. It was just that he wanted it all a little too quickly.

And Jack, who declared himself practically every time she saw him. Nearly twenty-one and fine and strong. Clara said he was too.

'Don't you go keeping him waiting too long. A man like that can always get a girl, so you think about what you're doing, young Harriet.' Clara's words had gnawed at her.

Several times she had almost agreed to the urgency in Jack's tone when he pressed her to agree to go to Honiton with him to ask her mother's permission to become engaged. She doubted her mother would agree. She even doubted her own feelings at times, especially when away from him. It was too young, too soon, and she had other things to do. But she did like the fact of him, if only he would be more patient.

And now Jack had gone away. The note from him had arrived on Sunday evening. Harriet had put it to one side thinking that it was about arrangements for meeting at Greenwich on Tuesday. By the time she had finished helping Miss Hilda to get out of her finery it was too late to get an answer to him on Sunday night. He would have been off early for Brighton she assumed on Monday morning and she had missed her opportunity. And he had not said where he was staying. Ted Phillips was her only hope.

The thought of not seeing Jack unless she could go down for the day was quite upsetting. But there was no way of getting an answer to him that she would come on Tuesday without Ted.

He would be able to tell her where Jack was. But Ted was late. The wait was going on far too long. If the Housekeeper got to hear that Harriet was sick she would go up to her room to see her. Harriet knew that she had about ten minutes before she would have to start back to the Grove.

To try and occupy herself she stared at the occupants of the waiting area. The girl opposite her was much the same age as herself. Her talents were not the kind Harriet wanted to have though. Harriet turned her head away to shut out the consequences of not having a respectable job. Think of something else.

Her sister Georgina's wedding to Arscott, was sounding a grand affair. Mother had the date arranged in St Michael's at the top of the hill and it would be a big occasion as Arscott's family were Devon people. Harriet had not mentioned the day to Jack. It was unfair of her, she knew, but her mother had not suggested him coming and she did not want him broaching the idea of an engagement if he was there.

A temperate wind blew from the doorway and Harriet looked round. The sky was just visible and the threatening storm had passed. A policeman entered and she saw that it was Sergeant Ted Phillips. Harriet stood up quickly and walked to him determined to say her piece that she had rehearsed before he disappeared into a back room.

Ted was coming on duty, tired from the heat on the train, into a police station full of commotion. He caught the eye of several people waiting and then glanced across at another woman who was walking doggedly towards him.

'Miss Fildew,' Ted exclaimed, drinking in the earnest expression and realising that it would be about Jack. Of course it would, nothing else would bring the young maid from the Grove to a police station in the middle of the day.

'Sergeant Phillips, I know you're busy but I must be quick or I'll be dismissed. I've had a note from Jack that he's gone to Brighton. I've it 'ere, if you'll take a look,' Harriet slipped a folded paper out of her pocket and Ted took it from her. Realising they were attracting the attention from the Duty Sergeant's desk, Ted indicated with an arm they should go outside. Once there he read the note, stopping at the endearments at the bottom and handed it back to Harriet.

'I don't know where he is if I'm to go tomorrow or how I can send him word. I came to you as you've always helped us.' Harriet sounded upset.

Ted took a breath and looked at her.

'This time I cannot because Jack must focus on why he's there. He had already mentioned to the Inspector that he wanted to go later in the week so that he could meet you at Greenwich but that was not to be. Inspector Hunt said no. In fact he suggested that Jack write a note to you, but not this sort of note. He's in danger of not obeying an order not to see you by sending you this, but I'll overlook that. It is only three weeks Miss Harriet and then he will return,' said Ted, trying to disguise the irritation that he felt with Jack.

Harriet erupted into tears, partly through the risk that she had taken to come to see Ted. Turning she started to run, Ted, shocked at the display of emotion suddenly, called after her not wanting her to leave while she was upset. Jack would not thank him for making her cry.

'You're maize, Harriet, maized as a bezom, risking everything for a man,' she said to herself. She stopped running when she turned into the Grove. It would not do for the occupants of the. houses to see a maid from Mr Pendle's house running. Expecting to find herself on the carpet before Mrs Atkins she slipped in through the side door to the scullery. Splashing cold water onto her face and tidying her hair she looked at herself in the mirror and controlled her breathing. Pink eyes and nose stared back at her. Glancing through a partially closed door Harriet saw the servant's meal was at the stage of pudding being served. She made her way swiftly and silently up the back stairs to the top of the house and into the room that she shared with Clara. A few minutes later the handle turned and Mrs Atkins entered.

*

When Sam and Jack entered the hotel lounge a young man looked up from the photograph that he held. Sam acknowledged him but steered Jack towards a lady in mourning sitting by a window. Other guests were involved in a mix of activities from sleeping, writing letters, or reading.

The lady looked up with a gentle smile and Sam responded by walking as quickly as he was able across to her. He bent to brush her cheek with his own. Jack had realised that it was Mrs Curzon. She had clearly taken tea and a woman appeared to clear away the tea things while Sam had a quiet word with her. Jack noted the changed relationship of adult child become carer at a time when the poor woman suffered bereavement. Sam looked up at Jack with the intention of introducing him.

'Mother, here's Jack Sargent to meet you,' said Sam and Jack moved awkwardly forward to take the extended hand. He thought that the Queen, still in black after more than ten years of widowhood, was not doing anything for the rest of the widows in the nation as they all copied her. Jack's thoughts went back to the ninth of June and the fire at the Alexandra Palace. On that day the Queen reputedly had been staying at Balmoral and had been making sketches of local beauty spots with one of her daughters. Still clothed in mourning. He recalled the photograph of her in the paper looking wretched. He asked himself if he would want anyone to grieve like that for him after ten years? He took the extended hand and said, 'I am so sorry for your loss, Mrs Curzon.'

'Thank-you. I am happy to meet you at last Mr Sargent. Sam is very fond of you and glad to be working with you again. It's quite lifted us, coming here.' Dropping her voice she continued, 'You both look the part, I must say.'

'That's encouraging, thank-you. Sam and I were reg'lar Dutch cousins. I was quite at a loss without him. Perhaps you would walk with me in the morning Mrs Curzon? I've a stroll to take each day to start building my strength again. Some company would be good.'

'I would like that, thank-you.'

'Mother, Jack and I will have a word with the young man over there before we go out,' Sam explained.

'I hope you can help him, Sam. He's done nothing but look at the photograph since you left the room,' Mrs Curzon turned her head and looked at the sailor.

'Hello again,' said Sam as he and Jack walked over. The sailor stood as the two finely dressed young men joined him.

'I mentioned to you I had a friend here. This is Mr Jack Sargent,' said Sam.

Jack glanced down at the fine face in the photograph on the side table. Looking back at the man Jack saw the worry in the eyes bordering on despair and wondered how he would behave if Harriet had gone missing.

'Mind if I look?' asked Jack, holding out his hand. 'Just in case I come across something while I'm walking.' He smiled broadly, one of his most winning smiles and as a way of explanation added, 'I'm here for my health and I've got to build up again by long walks.'

'Of course, here,' the sailor passed the picture to Jack.

'Have you been away long?' Jack asked passing the sketch back.

'Nearly a year. We were the lead ship in the Ashanti war.'

'Navy by the look of you,' said Jack, in a friendly way.

'Yes, lead ship of the corvettes. We put the wedding off twice because I didn't come home. Then she, my Grace that is, stopped writing after the first couple of months. I'm due to go to the South American side of the Atlantic. We'll be the senior officer's ship you see. I've got to find Grace and marry her before I go. There's something wrong.' The anxiety was clear in the voice.

'Sam and I are a couple of broken parts. Here for our health. Not sure what use to you we are, but we'll keep our eyes open, won't we Sam,' Jack said.

Sam smiled and nodded, 'We certainly will.'

'Nathan Long,' said the sailor, shaking their hands. 'Thanks, its good of you. No one will help. I thought her parents would tell me because we'd been betrothed but they just shut the door. Her mother was the worst, shouting that Grace was dead as far as they were concerned. They'd changed so much.'

'Is it possible that she may have met someone else who they don't approve of?' asked Jack.

'Not Grace. She's true. I was welcomed at one time and they were keen on the marriage. Her mother was angry and for her to say that about Grace. They were always so close. I went to the Police but they won't help either. The Sergeant I spoke at Brighton said much the same sort of thing as yourself. I'd been away so long she's probably found someone else and that her parents don't approve of him. He said they're probably angry because I didn't marry her and she's taken up with a wrong'un. He said it's all gone wrong and Grace doesn't want to know me but it wasn't like that. Something's happened to her, I feel it.'

They were starting to attract interest from other guests. Remembering that Burgess had said he would have a word with the young sailor Jack looked at Sam and then suggested that Nathan come and have a chat with the hotel manager. He readily agreed and followed them towards reception. Sam made the introductions and Burgess showed the three men into the room at the back of the reception. Other guests were coming through on their way out and the reception had become overly busy suddenly. Burgess called Alice and she took over dealing with other guests. He joined the three men and closed the door behind him, indicating for Nathan to sit in a seat on the opposite side of a table,

'Thank you for your time,' said Nathan, perching on the edge of the chair, earnestly looking at Burgess.

'We are late for a tea engagement at another hotel in the town. Forgive us if we go. If you leave your address in Brighton with Mr Burgess we can contact you if we find anything helpful,' explained Sam.

'Of course, thank-you, you're the first people who have believed me.' Nathan Long shook hands with Sam and Jack and they left the room.

Sam leant his arm on the reception desk and gave Jack a knowing look.

'What do you think?'

'Well, He's a clear eye, nothing shifty about him. He's on a fighting ship and sounds authentic to me. The fact he's alive after those months of war says something about him. And the girl's face is fine,' said Jack. 'I meant what I said, we can keep our eyes open as we move around, nothing more. Burgess has contacts in the local Brighton force and I suspect he'll make enquiries.'

'Something funny though isn't there? I mean the parents behaving in that way,' said Sam.

'Perhaps they didn't like him. Perhaps the Sergeant in the local force is right and they've been disappointed.'

'But for the mother to say the girl was dead as far as they're concerned suggests one thing to me,' said Sam.

'Yes, I know.' Jack thought. 'He said her letters stopped after a couple of months. Just long enough for her to confirm that she was expecting.'

'Quietly, he might hear you. I know where you're going with this Jack. Yes, all that occurred to me. I've heard families react like that before. It's usually the reason a girl is thrown out isn't it? Could be the reason why she disappeared too. Burgess seems to be spending some time with the man so it should stop him jumping off the pier.'

Jack looked sharply at Sam. 'Why do you say that?'

Sam shrugged and looked away. 'Desperation does funny things to the mind,' he said.

*

Jack and Sam turned to the right out of the Ship and started their walk along the promenade to the address Sam had been given by Harry Franks. Jack glanced at the sky.

'Let's hope the weather holds up for our walk.'

'You know Jack this is the first time I have been out of London and Windsor. I know nothing of your home county. The train journey brought us through some beautiful scenery. I've seen pictures of course of Brighton but the air! It's like wine.'

136

'You think? There's a tang of saltiness to it. To me there's a bracing bleakness to the wind. I'd prefer somewhere more sheltered. Bexhill, now, has bracing air but it's on rising ground and not far from the sea. You'd find the country there beautiful. And if you want some excitement there's St. Leonards and its Eastern style hotels and libraries. Lovely esplanade as I remember it.'

They continued the walk. Sam glanced at Jack. 'Would you ever return?' he asked.

'To Sussex? No, it's not to be. There's naught here but labouring for me. Poverty and no home of my own. London is where my future lies,' answered Jack.

'You could try the force here,' suggested Sam.

'What change the Metropolitan Police for the Brighton force?' Jack laughed at the idea. 'Why would I do that?'

'Clean air, rolling hills, some nice little woman in a neat cottage.' They laughed together.

'Sounds like the one who fancies the idea is you, Sam,' said Jack. Four children ran around them.

'Harriet's from the country, isn't she?' Sam asked.

Jack nodded, 'Devon.'

The four children were on their way back past them to their people up ahead. Jack and Sam separated briefly to let them run through the middle of them. The smallest child could not keep up and started to cry. In a moment Jack had lifted her and started a fast walk, forgetting the potential on his breathing. He set her down more because the coughing consumed him than having reached the other children. It was a dreadful sound and the little girl started to cry.

Sam stood quietly by him until he had his breathing under control. As a way of apology Jack gasped out, 'I forget.'

'Good you can Jack. At least you don't give up that way.'

'And you, Sam? Have you given up?' asked Jack.

'At times, yes. Not now though. The family need me now Father's gone and I have to keep going for them. Also, Jack, I can share this with you, earn a living, laugh again. Otherwise I might turn into a real irritable burden on everyone.'

'What has Hunt asked you to do? Jack asked.

'Have an overall view of the information as we acquire it. Compile a strategy before he gets everyone's feedback. He called it intelligence.'

Jack looked at Sam shocked. 'Sam, you're in charge! I wonder how Harry will feel about that?'

'No, no, no, it's not like that. It's sifting through information and forming a view, like I would have done with the business accounts in the office before I joined the police. It's just reading the information, like you know how to read the horizon and the sea, Jack. Harry's fine with me. Says we all have strengths.'

'Not all of us anymore,' said Jack, ruefully.

'You'll recover, Jack. Just use these three weeks and do what the doctor says.' Sam turned so that his back was to the sea. He surveyed the buildings in front of him and then looked to the left and the right. Jack followed his gaze and they stood together in silence for a while taking Brighton in.

'What are you thinking?' asked Jack following Sam's direction of gaze.

'Frankly? Its occurred to me that it doesn't matter where I live anymore. I could travel to London when Hunt wants to see me. Other men do it. There was an office worker in the tea room at the London Terminus. Mother and I got talking to him. He lives at Croydon, travels into London Bridge every work day, travels back in the evening. He has his Sundays at home, and lives in the middle of beautiful country. He told us he has a mile to walk to the station and there are two banks in the town. You remember the flooding last Christmas in Windsor?'

'Yes, of course,' Jack answered.

'We're tired of it Jack. We've lived there because of Father's work. The other thing is that it's a tied cottage and we have to go eventually. They're being very good about it and I'm not trying to hurry Mother but within three months we'll have notice,' explained Sam.

'And you're thinking of here?' Jack asked.

'Why not? I'm not like the man from Croydon, I don't have to go up to London Bridge every day. You know, by the time we emerged from the streets and houses of that mighty warren of London we were seeing beautiful views of hills and woods. There are schools everywhere for my brothers. Mother could have a lodger instead of washing dead bodies, or have paying visitors in the summer. I can use my mind, Jack, and my eyes and I can work for Hunt for as long as he wants me to but it doesn't matter where I live.'

'Sounds a bit fanciful to me, living in Brighton. You might find it a bit pricey.' Jack pointed along the front. 'I can see the Royal, Sam.'

Pleasure-seekers hurrying down to the beach as the rain had held off were everywhere mingling with the bath chairs of invalids trundling along the Esplanade. More children, full of sea breezes and health, avoided the grabbing hands of nurses and their mothers and generally got in the way of the two men.

*

The Royal Hotel was finer than the Ship and had a pleasant environment. It was near Old Steine, which consisted of two grassy squares with a road cutting through the middle. Jack remembered that somewhere around it there was a view of the Royal Pavilion.

'Sam, if we go up here I think we can see the Pavilion. It won't take too long.'

'Really? It's not too far then,' said Sam.

'Well, if my memory serves me right it was wide of the road. It's a long time since I was here but there's something about the two gardens that's familiar. I think there was a statue of someone up here. There we are, looks like he could do with a bit of a polish.'

They walked to the statue of George IV erected by the town in 1828. Domes and minarets came into view.

Sam's mouth dropped open at the sight of the Royal Pavilion.

'Poor taste, eh,' said Jack, grinning at Sam's face.

'No, it's amazing. I've never seen anything like it. Is this what India is full of?' Sam asked, to no one in particular.

'Shouldn't think so. Looks a bit of a mock-up to me. No wonder her Majesty doesn't bother with it,' said Jack. He pointed to the streets ahead.

'Up there Sam, look how wide the streets are. There's a lot of lighting, see. We should come at night as I reckon that Dome will light up quite an area.'

'I've not seen anywhere with so many shops except London. Look at how well paved it all is, and all the street lighting. Yes, let's come tonight. I must show Mother, it will quite lift her spirits,' said Sam.

As they turned back and made their entrance into the Royal Jack was aware they were being scrutinised both by staff and guests. Jack nodded at a man in livery on the door, loth to speak in case his accent gave him away. Sam was carrying it off better than he, which, he concluded would have been his clerk's training. Jack scanned the faces of people sitting in groups in the long hall which ran from the entrance. There was no sign of Harry or Rose. Sam asked for Harry Franks or Miss Rose Phillips.

Jack and Sam were led through a double door on their left into a spacious lounge half full of small groups of well-dressed people sitting, some with tea things in front of them, others writing or reading and yet others deep in discussion. Jack remembered that he also was well-dressed and was relieved to see that Hunt had matched the quality of their suits exactly to the standards around them. Trying to have the confidence that he did not feel, Jack nodded to several men, who returned the gesture without question. He also caught the eye of a waitress standing in the shadows.

There were several areas off the main room. Jack and Sam were led past tall windows and comfortable arm chairs to a passage leading into a Conservatory. Tables were laid with white table cloths and china and fine palm fronds and ferns acted as subtle room dividers.

Sitting at a table laid in a spacious area was Rose. Coming through the open glass doors from a terrace Jack saw Harry Franks with Mrs Phillips on his arm. She was limping slightly and Jack registered that her hip must be playing up. He was aware of a small palm tree suddenly brushing the side of his head and wafted the greenery away with his hand.

'Ah, cousins Jack and Sam, you're here,' Harry called across to them.

'We wondered if you'd had problems,' said Rose standing to embrace Jack on both cheeks. She held out her hand to Sam and he touched the finger tips with his hand. Jack was a little taken aback that Sam seemed to know how to behave. He nodded and smiled and a waiter pulled out a chair for him.

Harry Franks, dressed to the nines, almost exploded with life. He pulled out a chair for his future mother-in-law before the waiter could get to her and then sat himself. He rested his hand on the top of Rose's and Jack saw her full smile at her fiancé. He was pleased for them and not a little envious. The ring was in place on the third finger of her left hand. Although Jack did not know much of these things, he thought it looked a decent ring from the stones that he could see.

'Well, Jack, you are unusually quiet. There's sufficient distance between us and the next table if you are worried about keeping up appearances. I wouldn't. There are some extremely wealthy people here who are industrialists and the staff can barely understand them. They also are not as well-mannered as you, but they're paying so, while the staff look down their noses they still have to serve them,' all this was said by Harry sotto voce. Then louder he announced, 'Oh here we are. Tea,'

Harry paused while ladies in black with immaculate white pinafores hovered behind each of the party holding trays of silver tea pots. Sandwiches and cakes were deposited in the centre of the table and Jack found a man at his side trying to put a white serviette on his knee. He sat back trying not to laugh with the embarrassment. Sam sat on Mrs Phillip's left and they were chatting quietly. Jack realised that she had enquired about his father's passing and then patted Sam's hand.

'Have you eaten anything since you arrived?' asked Rose on his right.

'Not really,' Jack answered, looking up. 'Just sandwiches Mrs Morris put up for the train and some tea and biscuits at the Ship Hotel.'

'Well we'd better feed the young,' said Harry, as a waiter manipulated fork and spoon to lift several different types of sandwich on to Rose's plate. He moved across to Mrs Phillips who sat back to allow him access.

'I'm fine really,' said Sam putting a hand over his plate to stop the waiter giving him a selection, 'but a cup of tea would go down well.'

'Congratulations to you both,' Jack said to Rose. 'Ted told me before I left London that Harry had prevailed and was about to become the best fed man in London.'

'You mean the happiest. You should follow my example, Jack and get Harriet up the aisle,' Harry looked at Jack meaningfully.

'I would if I could,' said Jack, with a rueful smile.

'Ah well, I'm not so sure I can rival Mrs Beeton but I shall enjoy cooking for one man instead of a roomful.' Rose touched Harry's hand with her finger tips and Jack watched him melt.

'I'm seeing a different side to the man I know,' said Jack, winking at Sam.

'A better man,' Harry cut in, as he stirred his tea. Jack tried to work out what was different about the way that Harry was doing it. Of course, the spoon did not touch the bottom of the cup. Harry simply moved the tea around.

'May I see the ring, Rose,' Jack asked. She looked at him and controlled her surprise.

'Of course, kind of you to be interested, most men aren't.'

'Well, I'm learning,' said Jack and Rose laid her hand on the table's edge between them.

'Harry, you've done it properly, I see,' said Sam, who had finished talking to Mrs Phillips. Harry glanced across the table at Sam with a smug expression.

'Not too bad actually Sam, thanks to the Gold rush and South African diamond discoveries! I think, more tea and I shall move onto the cake,' said Harry, making a sign to staff at the other side of the room for attention.

'And the stones, why are they different colours?' asked Jack.

'Because it spells a word, "Dear." The stones are diamond, emerald, amethyst and ruby.' Rose explained.

'And you are happy, aren't you, Rose?' ventured Jack.

'I am. So happy,' she responded, smiling at him.

'You do look it. What is it that you're happy about?'

'Do you ask because you want to learn again or because you have doubts about Harry and I?' Rose asked.

'For to get it right with Harriet,' Jack said.

'Because of Harry, because of the fact of he and I. The future together, being loved so much.' Rose's smile had developed while she explained and Jack had no doubts. Harry was speaking.

'Now the early signs of hunger are assuaged, I can tell you a few things that you need to know over the next few days. But first I think we'll have the tea refreshed.'

'I will go up and rest I think. How about you, Rose?' asked Mrs Phillips.

'I'll stay a little longer, Mother. A policeman's wife is often called upon to give some help.' Harry patted her hand as a cough was heard behind him. Jack looked at the waitress who had come across with a tray of fresh teapots and then froze.

'Mary,' he exclaimed.

*

143

Here and there a few tables were clearing. The sky had lifted from its glowering presence and the Seagulls that had been driven in over the town had returned to the water's edge as the fish was brought ashore. Other bird song could be heard from the gardens at the front of the hotel.

Mary from the Mason's Arms on the Commercial Road in London had told Jack last December that she had taken work in Brighton. There had been nothing between them. She had been an interest of Harry's before he met Rose but had never responded to the attempts by a Detective Sergeant playing the part of a man in his cups to interest her in a future as his wife.

'You look very well,' Jack said, eventually breaking the silence.

Mrs Phillips was standing to go. 'Put the tea down here, dear,' she said to Mary, who had frozen. She was staring with disbelief at the two customers of the Tavern. Harry Franks, minus the stained waistcoat, and looking as she had never seen him, his hand on that of a lovely smart young woman wearing an engagement ring. Then there was the young man she had called "Farm boy," who had been newly arrived in London in December. Someone with looks but no money. But yet he apparently had from his appearance today.

'Is this where you work?' A stupid question given she was carrying tea to their table but all Jack could think of. Out of courtesy he stood up.

'Please Sir, don't draw attention to the fact that you know me. The Sommelier has noticed us talking and is coming over.' Mary dropped her eyes.

Jack had no idea what a Sommelier was but saw a man with the air of a Manager walking towards them, concern on his face. Jack walked across to where Mrs Phillips was standing. She had quietly been watching the interplay between Mary and Jack and was blocked in between the palm and Mary. Jack used the situation to help her into more space.

'Would you like an arm to the stairs,' he asked.

'That would be kind,' said Mrs Phillips. As they walked away they heard Mary sent away and all seemed normal.

144

'How did you know that young waitress?' asked Mrs Phillips as they walked through the now crowded lounge to the hall.

'She was a barmaid in a tavern that I went into, undercover. I was new to London and pretended I had come in to seek work. Harry was playing the drunk as it was a good way to hear things discussed at a bar between men. I met him there. She was gone to Brighton after my second visit and a better life for a girl hopefully. It never occurred to me that it would be this class of hotel that she was working in. She knows Harry's a 'tec, but she just thought I was a farm boy looking for work. That's what I would have looked like in my old clothes. Our cover's blown, looking as we do. Once she gets over the shock that we're here she'll work it out that I'm in the police as well and we're here together, Harry and me, for a reason.' Mrs Phillips took her hand from the cleft of his arm as Jack finished explaining.

'Will it matter?' she asked, turning to look at him.

'What? That she knows?' said Jack.

'Yes. In a few days once the Shah arrives everyone will expect more security. If a waitress in a hotel knows there're two Metropolitan Policemen here why would that matter?'

'That's true,' added Jack. 'Still I'll have to let Inspector Hunt know and see what he wants to do.'

'I will take myself and this sorry hip of mine up these stairs and hope to see you later, Jack,' said Mrs Phillips with a grimace as she put a foot on the first stair.

'Yes indeed. A lovely tea we've had,' he called back.

As he made his way back to the table, Jack decided to make a detour towards the man Mary had described as the Sommelier. Jack smiled as he approached and tried to adopt a casual air.

'Marvellous service,' he said and turned away.

'Thank you, Sir,' the Sommelier replied to Jack's back.

Harry was quieter than before as Jack arrived at their table in the Conservatory. He resumed his seat and caught Rose's clear gaze.

'So, that is Mary,' she said.

'That's right,' answered Jack.

'I wonder how Harriet would feel about this,' said Rose.

'What?' asked Jack a little louder than he should. Several eyes swivelled towards them. Jack looked at Harry, who was no help. Harry had a concentrated look focused on Rose's face.

'Were you close?' Rose probed.

Jack looked exasperated. 'I was undercover, she thought I was a farm labourer, I met her twice pulling pints in the tavern. That was it.'

'You didn't mention Mary,' said Sam. Jack looked at him. He drew a breath.

'There was no Mary. She was a bar maid in a pub I went into to meet other policemen on a job. In fact you were one of them, weren't you, Harry.' Jack's tone had a statement of fact about it.

Harry jerked his head towards Jack, recovered and made a pretence of thinking. 'Yes that night we did the raid, New Year, wasn't it? Didn't you say she was moving to Brighton for work? Of course the thing now is the fact that she knows who we are.'

'Yes, I said that to Mrs Phillips. She made a good point that once everyone knows the Shah is coming they will expect police around. Still better mention it to Inspector Hunt though.'

'And on that subject, we had better get down to the details.' Harry moved the topic along deftly. 'If I may, as tables are clearing and we can't be overheard.'

Harry moved the sugar around with the spoon. He looked up at Sam and Jack, squeezed Rose's hand briefly before letting it go and sat back in his chair.

'The Shah is due to arrive on the eighteenth of June in London. So, we've time here as if he does come to Brighton it will be as part of the visit to Portsmouth. We're waiting for the schedule for his visits,' explained Harry.

'Right,' said Sam. We need to do a full reconnoitre of Brighton, the hotels, their position, who's staying for the season, who's coming down before and during the visit.'

'Get lists of people Sam and you can do the background checks as we collate information. Jack you've got to get some exercise according to what Hunt says so check out potential bad spots on the streets, but make sure you get a rest each afternoon. That's an order. Is that clear for you my handsome?' Harry raised his eyebrows.

'Yes Harry.' Jack answered.

'Harry, I could go to Lady's groups with Mother. You obviously can't attend those and I can find out who's there and so on,' Rose looked the picture of innocence.

'But no risks,' said Harry.

'I can't imagine there would be any in an art group but if there is I have three of you to come to my protection,' she smiled at him and Jack looked at Rose, remembering his conclusion that she was going to be a real handful for Harry.

Oblivious her fiancé patted her hand and carried on his briefing.

'The Royal Pavilion is opening to the public on June nineteenth. There'll be exhibitors from all over so we need to all be there for that.'

'That's three days from now,' said Sam.

'I know. Best we can do is to go, and keep an eye open. There's also a couple of cricket matches bringing people in,' Harry looked at Jack.

'That's why I've got the cricket whites, isn't it?' said Jack.

'That's right but after your breathing problems we don't want you running around so you'll be Long-off and at the boundary. The matches are on the twentieth and twenty-first. No walking those days as the games are in the afternoon. Rest up in the morning.'

'Won't it seem strange someone they don't know stepping in. Who am I playing for?' asked Jack.

'You'll be for the Sussex Rifles who are playing Brighton. A Captain will develop a fever and ask if his cousin can take his place. I'll get you his name by tomorrow and a bit of background. The second match is between Horsham and Cranleigh. We've got the Horsham Captain to agree to be impressed with your performance with the Sussex Rifles and he'll ask you publicly to help them out. Of course that was before we knew you were going to be injured in the fire. We'll think that one through.' Harry sat back and Jack looked at him.

'I'm not likely to do anything impressive as Long-off,' said Jack, frowning.

'Well we hope for the best. I'll think of something before then to make it sound authentic,' said Harry.

'There's something I must do for an orphanage back in London. It's on my beat. I need to go over to an old parson near Lewes. I've a worrying German Tract, which we think might be inciting violence and I think he might be able to understand it. I cleared it with Inspector Hunt last week,' Jack added.

Harry nodded. 'Fine, he did mention that you'd some personal visits to make. All I ask is to wait until after the twenty-first of June. We'll have a better idea of security problems by then and what to expect with the Shah. For your own health as well limit yourself to Brighton for the next week.'

*

Nine

What Jack had not expected was exactly what happened.

On Tuesday morning he went to the reception and asked if there were any messages. Alice Burgess checked the log of early post, considered if any of the staff had taken a telegram and finally, looked up from the register at Jack and shook her head.

'No, I'm sorry, there's nothing arrived for you. Was it important? I can send a boy to the local postmaster if it was.'

'No, it's alright, it was just a friend who might have been able to come down from London today.'

'There's still time. I'll bring it to your table if anything comes while you're breakfasting,' said Alice.

Jack had hoped that Harriet would at least let him know if she could come or not. He kicked himself of course for not telling her where he was staying but had thought it a step too far in bending the rules. She had always gone to Ted before for help to get a message to him and he had assumed she would this time. Ted could then have sent a message on.

With breakfast before him he determined not to let the situation with Harriet distract him from the task of the morning and made himself eat well. His appetite just was not there. Jack had estimated that surveying the security of the town and its outskirts would take two mornings and he had made something of a start the previous night around the area of the Royal Pavilion. Before they retired for the night Jack, Sam and Mrs Curzon, had been quite fascinated by the small lanes and the variety of shops. As they separated for the night Mrs Curzon had agreed to walk with Jack at half past nine this morning.

Jack had thought that if the Shah came to Brighton he would board a launch to take him onto Portsmouth and the best way to start his survey this morning was from the sea. He also had a fancy to feel a sea wind on his face. The only inhibiting factor was if Harriet arrived this morning. Jack could kick himself for not thinking things through.

Harriet might still get word to him if she could. He had planned the morning on the assumption that she was unlikely to arrive before midday. If Alice did not receive any other post while he was in breakfast he would push Harriet's visit to the back of his mind and spend his rest time that afternoon writing his report.

Sam and Jack had shared a table as Mrs Curzon decided to breakfast in her room.

'I've got details of all the notables visiting Brighton,' said Sam. 'I'll be well-occupied for the morning on looking into who's who and the backgrounds. A reception is planned if the Shah comes with the mayor and all the councillors. Burgess got hold of a list somehow. It's as long as your arm. Made me wonder if there's a bit of a back-hander going on to get an invitation.'

'How does he get hold of the information?' asked Jack.

'Question of knowing people locally, I would guess. The mayor was irritated by the suggestion that they may be a threat but his clerk gave in eventually.'

'What about the more fashionable society?' asked Jack.

'Ah, that's in the papers,' said Sam. He adopted a different expression and recited as if his mouth was full of marbles:

'The Earl and Countess of Lisburn have taken apartments at the Bedford, while the Baron and Baroness de Sternberg have set up in the Grand Hotel. The latter have become quite familiar with an Admiral Mason.'

'You'll have some fun checking them out without blowing your cover,' said Jack. 'One more piece of bacon and then I'm done.'

Alice approached their table with a smile, holding aloft an envelope. She gave it to Jack with her eyes twinkling. 'Lovely scent,' she said.

Jack felt himself colour as he took it.

'From Harriet?' asked Sam, raising his eyebrows.

Jack looked up and grinned.

'Hope so,' he said as he opened it and glanced down at the signature.

'No, it's from Rose,' he said, trying to keep the disappointment at bay. 'I should have known it wasn't Harriet's scent. I've just got used to smelling it every-day with lodging with Rose and her mother.' He scanned the content and passed it to Sam.

Sam quietly read out the key details:

'I've befriended the companion to Lady Bruce, the wife of the Home Secretary in Gladstone's administration...... She says they had a walk together along the Chain Pier .... Apparently, there's a reading-room at the end. Mother would love that, I must tell her.' Sam glanced up at Jack and continued:

'Rose says she's found they both have an interest in portraits and they've promised to sketch together later. Rose collected her sketches when they returned to the Royal in order to show them to her new-found friend. The woman was so taken with them that she convinced Lady Bruce it would be delightful to do portraits together this afternoon in the lounges as the different members of their party have arrived. Clever Rose.' Sam passed the note back to Jack.

'Yes, isn't she,' Jack said. 'That way we get names and profiles.'

*

'Good news?' asked Alice, as Jack passed the reception.

'In a manner of speaking, yes. Just not what I'd hoped,' Jack said.

'I'm sorry. Perhaps your friend can't get away,' said Alice, sympathetically.

'Probably not,' Jack agreed.

Mrs Curzon waited for Jack in the hotel lounge, outwardly displaying her grief in her mourning clothes. Jack detested it. He had hated the feel of crepe as a child. Gathering her things together she faltered at the door and half turned to go back.

'What is it?' Jack asked.

'Perhaps I shouldn't go out. It won't seem right to be in society so soon.'

'I'm not society and fresh air can only do you good. We can walk as much as you like and always turn back. Even the Queen has had fresh air at Balmoral and the papers say she has been out sketching.' Jack offered an arm and after a moment's hesitation Mrs Curzon accepted.

'Where did you want to walk, Jack?' she asked.

'I think straight along the front this morning. Sam thinks there's something at the end of the Chain Pier that you'd take a fancy to so we'll walk down if you like. I could do with seeing the Coastguard at their station which is just past the fish market. There's a man in the service that Father knew and I want to enquire if he's still working. After that we go in the direction of the West Pier and finish at Brunswick Square. I think that will give me enough of a feel for any approach to the sea front that could be made without us both becoming dog-tired.'

They walked through the busy reception area and the departing guests that morning were milling around the luggage. Burgess had relieved and stood at the desk enquiring after the health of his guests. He quickly excused himself when he saw Jack and Mrs Curzon and caught them before they left.

'Good morning to you both. I hope you passed a good night?' asked Burgess.

'Thank-you, yes,' replied Mrs Curzon. 'After the excitement of seeing all the magnificence of the shopping area last night with Sam and Jack, I fell asleep quite early. A major improvement on how I have been sleeping.'

Jack nodded. To his surprise he had slept straight through the night.

'Sea air no doubt,' said Burgess. 'Would you excuse me a moment, Mrs Curzon? There is a matter that I need to speak to Jack about.'

'Of course, I'll wait for you, Jack,' said Mrs Curzon, sitting.

Burgess drew Jack aside. 'There's a man I want you to meet who is useful to us. He'll be here over luncheon and I'll eat in my office with him. Can you join us?'

'I should think so. Can you tell me who it is?' asked Jack.

Burgess wiped his nose with a capacious handkerchief. 'Time enough over a meal together. Good of you to walk with Mrs Curzon. Forgive me now, I must attend to the guests.' Burgess patted Jack on the arm and walked back towards the octogenarian at the desk who had launched into a volley of complaints at the sight of the Manager.

Jack and Mrs Curzon stepped out amongst the rest of Brighton, into the fine sunshine. People were hurrying back and forth determined to enjoy themselves and go everywhere possible. Despite the true reason for being there Jack could not help feeling caught up in the general excitement around him. Had it not been for his own physical weakness, still manifesting itself in coughing and the lady in mourning on his arm, he was sure that he too would have rushed around as fast as he could, moving between the piers, the market area and the windmill. Out of respect for both his health and Mrs Curzon they ambled at a gentle pace.

'How long the Esplanade seems,' said Mrs Curzon. 'Look how fashionable those men are.'

'Are they? I wouldn't know,' said Jack.

'Oh, yes, the latest styles.'

'They look pretty determined to cover miles this morning,' said Jack. They stopped to stand and stare at the wide span of sea seeming to go on endlessly and breathed deeply the reviving breezes.

'Sam mentioned that you'd a taking for reading in the last few weeks and we found out that there's a reading room at the north end of the Chain Pier. It's within easy reach of the hotel and I thought it might become a regular walk for you,' said Jack.

'It's a very fine-looking way to walk. That's kind of you. I did pick up a book of essays in the hotel lounge by a writer and philosopher called Hazlitt. Have you ever heard of him, Jack?' asked Mrs Curzon.

'No, I can't say I have, said Jack.'

153

'I hadn't either. I don't think he's much published now. It was an old copy. Led a bit of a life by the sound of it, knew people like Wordsworth, Coleridge and Keats. He was very much in favour of Napoleon and I suspect may not be popular as a result. There was one phrase though that stuck in my mind if I recall it exactly.' She thought, as if rehearsing something in her mind and then quoted:

"There is something in being near the sea like the confines of eternity. It is a new element, a pure abstraction."

Mrs Curzon paused as if checking she was correct in her recall.

'I think that's how it read. I worked at memorising it as I thought it was lovely language,' Jack noted how animated her face had become. He smiled and picked up the theme.

'I've not read too many books as yet. Where I worked near Battle, the Squire was good enough to lend me a few and that's how I grew interested in police work. He had a copy of a novel about a French detective, quite an old copy, and Dickens, of course. He taught me a few things about buying books for investment, and I like that idea. Perhaps you could show me the book when we get back?' asked Jack.

'I will. Can we stand a little longer? I'd like to stare at the stretch of sea,' asked Mrs Curzon, withdrawing her hand from Jack's arm.

They stood together listening to the repetitive crash of the tide against the beach.

'There's something reliable about that sound,' said Mrs Curzon, eventually. 'It says life.'

Jack nodded. Eventually, aware of time moving on he again offered an arm and asked, 'Shall we walk to the end?'

Mrs Curzon smiled and slipped her arm through his.

'Sam would enjoy this,' said Mrs Curzon. 'He's very taken with the town and seems determined to move us here.'

Jack looked at her with surprise.

'Has he mentioned that already? I'm surprised he's broached that idea now,' said Jack. 'Shall we go into the reading room now?'

'Yes, I'd like to see it,' replied Mrs Curzon.

The room was a lounge surrounded by the sea. A few people sat absorbed in novels.

'I think I could happily come here. 'It's almost like being afloat and it's not too busy. People would understand I think that I wanted to read,' said Mrs Curzon said.

'Fresh air and exercise and a read of a good book. I know nothing better. It may not be long sen Mr Curzon passed away but no one would begrudge you the company of a book. Nothing can change what's happened but some things help us through the tragic loss. It's a handsome place to come to and the walk is healthy. If you're to live here it would be good for you to know some parts and feel comfortable in them.' Jack partially turned towards the door and Mrs Curzon followed.

They walked through boisterous holiday-makers, until they were on the Parade near the Aquarium.

*

Climbing down the steps to the fish market Jack gave Mrs Curzon his hand to help her down and walked backwards in front of her. The smell of freshly unloaded fish from the beach-based activity surrounded them and was overwhelming.

Jack exchanged a few words with a gaffer about the price of a large Sole which lay, twitching in the bottom of a boat. Having struck a deal and handed over a few coins the man agreed to get it delivered to Burgess as a gift for the luncheon.

'You know a good fish when you see one, Jack,' said Mrs Curzon.

'I had a share of that kind of fishing with Father off Cooden, just up the coast from here. For a market gardener he loved the sea. We never went home empty handed.'

Seeing the sailing boats could be hired Jack drew Mrs Curzon's attention to them.

'How would you like a short voyage along the coast. I suggest it as I can see the lay of the land better from a boat.'

'Should I really do this?' Mrs Curzon asked.

'I don't see any difference to the Queen's activities when she goes to Osborne. She has to sail to get there. There'll be a fine view of the hills, a tang to the lips and a good breeze. I need only twenty to thirty minutes. We can hire a sailing vessel here but I don't want to make you do anything you consider to be disrespectable to your husband.'

Mrs Curzon nodded and Jack walked over to a fisherman and agreed that the man would take them out for half-a-crown for just twenty minutes.

He paid the sailor a shilling on the understanding that the man would get the rest on their return. Drink was usually involved but Jack had selected the man carefully as on his boat there was a seated area in shade and the man did not stink of liquor. Jack nodded in the direction of Mrs Curzon so that the fisherman realised the delicacy of her situation. He nodded and Jack walked back in order to bring her down to the boat.

'Is it safe?' she asked.

'Yes, I'd say so. We need to go now as the tide is flowing sufficiently for the boat to move,' said Jack.

As they walked together the fisherman peered at the woman in mourning, thinking it a strange thing for her to do. He called to Jack, 'Will you want a line, mate?'

'No, not today. I'll take in the view,' Jack smiled at Mrs Curzon realising that despite his good clothes the fisherman had worked out from Jack's accent that he was a local. Jack was in first and Mrs Curzon stepped in firmly. Jack nodded at her in encouragement at her determination and heard a gasp as the boat shifted with a wave. A moment later she was in and once seated, the fisherman pushed off.

Jack surveyed the scene, seeing the way the town was placed to descend from the area of the railway station, gradually towards the south-east. He had studied a map late into the night and was now putting flesh on the picture in his mind.

There was sloping ground, like a furrow towards the Steine and then it rose again towards the east. From where he thought the railway was positioned he could see the area was swamped by development. Jack took the map from his pocket which Burgess had left for him.

It would be difficult to pursue someone in a few of the areas.

Up to the eastern boundary he could see Kemp Town and across towards the village of Rottingdean. That far by boat he discounted as a potential problem as it was too far out of the town. Black Rock showed a raised beach and he could see an old cliff-line coming down to the shore. He made a mental note to get to Kemp Town for a vantage point to see down the coast.

There did not appear to be a navigable river from what he could see. The piers could be landing places if a helm knew what they were about. It would take a local to know that. He recalled a crossing to France some years ago from the Chain Pier but he had no recollection of it on his family's visit. Perhaps it was there, perhaps he was confused. Clearly nothing was in place now.

The Aquarium was new, barely a year old according to the local information. It had meant a new sea wall to the Chain Pier and promenade. These would all have to be closed on the day of the Shah's visit thought Jack.

A memory pulled up a tale of a Battery on the western edge of the town. There was nothing visible in that way now. The road ran out to Shoreham, he thought, checking the map.

The buildings in the squares looked imposing as they faced the sea. The sun reflected off the white buildings and the square was open to the sea. It was too wide an area to protect and they would need to block the mile-long esplanade off if the Shah went anywhere near it. Better he did not, concluded Jack. He thought of the narrow lanes that they had enjoyed last night illuminated by the great Dome. Too many clusters to find someone in if they decided to disappear there. He would feed all this to Sam later.

Jack noticed the lady in the boat was trailing her fingers in the water.

'It's *cold*,' Mrs Curzon said, surprised. Distracted by the temperature she withdrew her fingers. The odd bit of spray came over the bow. Jack turned his face to catch the droplets realising this was what he had missed in London.

Time came flooding back with each pitch and toss of the boat. Again, a wave of nostalgia hit him as did a longing for a relationship lost, of parent and child. But not just that but what the relationship could have been now. Those very activities enjoyed with his father such as this, trawling the sea for bounty to take home for dinner. It had been in essence what they did together, that and tending the market garden. He realised that being on the sea was part of him. A sudden desire to cast a line gripped him.

'I've changed my mind, I'd like to fish,' said Jack, taking off his coat.

'Just under the board there,' called back the fisherman, pointing to the tackle. 'I'll turn her out a way more.'

'Give me your coat, Jack, I'll hold it for you,' said Mrs Curzon.

'That's better,' said Jack feeling the freedom of movement as he threw the line.

Five minutes without a bite the fisherman called over, 'Well, mate, you said twenty minutes and I should be turning in to the shore now.'

Jack glanced at the man, nodded in agreement, called back to the work he had to do. He concluded that he would find this fisherman and his boat again.

*

'I so enjoyed that. More exhilarating than on the river,' said Mrs Curzon, passing Jack his coat.

Jack had paid the fisherman and enquired how often he could be found on the shore at Brighton. In the back of his mind was the possibility that the man might be willing to take him to Cooden.

'Well, was that of use?' asked Mrs Curzon, as they walked up the beach together.

Jack looked at her rosy cheeks. She looked so much better, and, he strongly suspected, he did too.

'Yes, it was. As we're near the Coastguard station would you still be up to a visit there?' Jack asked.

'I feel I could walk forever,' smiled Mrs Curzon.

'You like the town?' asked Jack, while they walked.

'Yes, I do. Sam is very keen to start making changes and I think he may be right. We have had terrible floods as you'll remember Jack, and the only reason we were in Windsor was because of Mr Curzon's work. Now he has gone it may be good for us all to leave the area. We have to move soon anyway as we will lose the cottage.'

'That's hard for you to leave your home,' said Jack.

'Well, I thought it would be when I was told we would have to leave within three months, but now I'm coming round to believing it may be a good thing. I'm not sure I want to stay in a place where I have the expectation of seeing Mr Curzon come round every corner.' Mrs Curzon paused and Jack heard the break in the voice.

He stood respectfully by her as she stared out to sea. After a few minutes she continued. 'Sam says that he can expect regular work from Inspector Hunt and that it's more common for professional people to live out of London now and travel into work.'

'Yes he told me about that this morning while we breakfasted,' said Jack.

'While he would have to go into London from time to time he would be able to live anywhere along a railway line south of the river and have a reasonable journey into Camberwell. Why not here? I could run a boarding house for visitors most of the year and my younger boys can still be schooled and perhaps apprenticed in the railway workshops. Brighton is cheaper for us, and we would have the Downs and the sea.'

Jack registered that Sam had obviously been offered steady work by Hunt. He nodded.

'I think you have helped me greatly this morning, Jack.'

'And you I. Perhaps you'd accompany me again tomorrow?' Jack asked, smiling. 'I need to inspect the railway links to Portsmouth,' he added, offering her his arm again.

Mrs Curzon nodded and slipped her hand into the crook of his arm as they reached the Coastguard Station.

*

159

It had gone past twelve when Jack and Mrs Curzon returned to the Ship Hotel. A feeling he had not experienced for a while had overwhelmed him. He was hungry for the first time since the Alexandra Palace Fire. Mrs Curzon was clearly in better spirits after the walk but he sensed that she did not think she should be and she withdrew to her room to rest before luncheon. Jack expected Burgess to appear soon to collect him for lunch and decided to remain in the hotel lounge.

He opened his notebook and wrote down the date and the time and the location. Breaking the morning down into periods of time he set to and wrote details of all he had seen from the walk and the boat. Eleven years had passed and the man would not be too old to have continued working. As with most small boys it had been the tales of smugglers that Jack had remembered. He sat on a window seat in the lounge jotting down notes ready to expand it into a report later for Sam.

Jack had confirmed his view of the Esplanade as he and Mrs Curzon made Brunswick Square their last stop before turning to walk back to their hotel. He was sure that it was too open to police and trying to prevent an attack against the Shah and perhaps others in the party would be a nightmare. The only effective way to control the area would be to close it which would hardly go down well with the residents.

Burgess was in the doorway beckoning Jack to follow him. Jack's stomach gave a lurch and thankfully, he thought, he would be able to satisfy the hunger pains soon.

'How was your morning?' asked Burgess as they walked down the corridor together.

'It was good. I went out in a boat to get the lay of the land. Very useful,' said Jack following Burgess into his office.

A man sat on one side of the table set for three. Jack assumed this was the person that Burgess had wanted him to meet. In the centre was the large sole Jack had sent up to the hotel.

'You see your fish arrived.' Burgess waved a hand towards the platter in the centre. 'Good of you. Did you catch it by any chance?'

———

160

'No, although I did try my hand this morning briefly to fish but without any luck.' Jack smiled at Burgess, and then looked at the man opposite.

'I thought we'd start with it,' Burgess continued. 'But first let me introduce you to Sergeant James Field of the Brighton Police. Sergeant Field has worked in Brighton for the last ten years.' Burgess extended an arm towards the man at the other side of the table. Jack felt surprised but tried to keep his sense of balance about the fact he was invited to lunch with a member of the Brighton force. The man was not in uniform. Had he have been Jack would have paused in the doorway. But Hunt had said that he could trust Burgess.

The man opposite him had a penetrating gaze. Depending on when he had joined the police he may have already worked twenty years. Hunt and Burgess had logged away some time themselves.

Field in turn ran an eye over Jack's face and build. It was brief and Jack realised that Burgess would already have explained Jack's background. Nonetheless, Jack had a feeling that James Field would assess someone accurately without a briefing. Trying to match the coolness Jack extended his hand.

'Good to meet you, Sergeant Field,' he said.

'And to meet you, although I had already read about you,' said Field. Jack had his accent. East Sussex. Probably a labouring man like himself at one time, early forties, a little heavy now. Jack doubted much happened in Brighton to cause the Sergeant to break into a run.

In spite of his attempt to control his feelings Jack felt wrong-footed. 'How is that?'

'The reports in the paper. The fire,' James Field reminded him.

'Curse that report, it's already got me noticed in ways that I don't want,' said Jack, thinking of Harriet's master, Mr Pendle.

'Well, the press either love us or vilify us. You're fortunate it's the former this time, eh Burgess?' Field said, and Jack glanced at the Hotel Manager, remembering Hunt's explanation of how depressed he had become. The comment had registered but Burgess showed no sign of picking up the topic and instead clapped a hand on Jack's shoulder.

'I should think you're hungry after trying your hand at fishing this morning. Let's eat.' Burgess set too to apportion the sole between the three of them. Jack and Field made casual conversation on how busy Brighton had become, the effect of the wet Spring on the crops and gardens.

The Sergeant asked: 'Are you going to attend the Summer Exhibition in the Royal Pavilion on Thursday?'

'I'd like to, said Jack. 'Do you know where the exhibitors were from?'

'I do, but as the roses had only just started to bloom after the wet spring, I would have thought it would be as good this year,' said Field.

Jack was forming an opinion of the man opposite him. Here was a policeman with a complete focus, an exact application of the law and someone who was also forming an opinion of Jack. He guessed what that would be. He had given some flippant answers earlier whereas Field was always exact. Jack was attempting to dodge providing too much information. Field had lined up his knife and fork exactly level with each other. Field would know that Jack was hedging, was uncomfortable at the contact but not the reason why. Hunt had clearly said to have nothing to do with the Brighton force. Jack had spent the lunch feeling that he was being played with. It had made him dig his heels in more.

Jack assumed business would start after the meat.

And it did.

'How was your assessment of Brighton? Any suggestions for us?' asked Field.

'I'm sure I have nothing fresh to add to a man with your eye,' Jack said.

Burgess laughed and looked from one to another.

'You see I told you that you would have problems getting anything out of him. James is here because I asked him to come. I pass the odd situation onto him as I become aware of it. The sailor, for example, trying to find his young lady. It might tie up with something that's been going on. That's why James is here. He's enjoying meeting you Jack.'

Field nodded and lent forward placing his elbows on the table.

'The young lady that's disappeared is not the first in the last year,' he said. 'There's been a number of them. All Sussex women. Once we dig for details with the families we've established each one has had a child out of wedlock, been thrown out of home, friendless and alone. In all cases the fathers have not remained in the area. Possibly unaware, like the sailor, that the girl was with child, although it wouldn't take too much imagination for them to conclude that would be the outcome of their amorous intentions. But there's more to it than that.' Field paused while he took a sip of the madeira Burgess had poured intended to accompany the pudding. Burgess waved the bottle at Jack but he shook his head. He had no taste for it.

'The disappearances coincide with an increase in child deaths in the area. It may be a coincidence. However, I don't believe in coincidence and view such a statement as an excuse to do nothing. Each child death is certified by the same Doctor. That also is too much of a coincidence. Here,' he said, taking several new paper cuttings out of an inside pocket. 'Have a look at these.'

Jack picked up the cuttings and glanced at the heading. Doctor Elm had certified death in two cases recently, death by burning and one overlaid. The deaths were in the Hastings and St Leonards areas.

'You're the Brighton force,' said Jack.

Field smiled, 'So I am. And you're the Met.'

Jack returned the smile and said, 'That's right. So, neither of us would be picking this one up. But in your case the woman called Grace is a local. And you think there's a link?'

'Yes. I'm picking them up because no one in Hastings and St Leonards is noticing a pattern. And as you say certainly one of the women is from Brighton.' Field paused as the pudding arrived. He sipped the madeira and nodded appreciation at Burgess. Jack could see there were no barriers between the Hotelier and the Police Sergeant.

'This young sailor, Nathan, who you spoke to the other day isn't the first one to find his sweetheart is missing. However, he is unusual in as much as he has returned to claim his lady love. There's a pattern to these girls being thrown out of home and after a little digging I think I can tie up the number of baby deaths with patterns of putting the child for adoption. I may have a lead on who is arranging that activity.' Field nodded to Burgess as he offered him the rich pastry dish covering fruit brought in from the kitchen for pudding. Elaborate fancy edging and painstaking designs of flowers had been worked into the pastry with hand stamps before it had been baked. Never able to refuse a pudding Jack nodded in turn when Burgess raised enquiring eyebrows at him.

'The other pattern, of course, is that the certifying doctor is the same in each case and I would place a bet that he was called into wherever the young women had their babies. Likely to be the poor house but it may be anyone of a number of local charities with or without midwives and I haven't enquired deliberately.'

'Why not?' asked Jack.

'The simple reason is that if someone is working with the doctor I don't want them being notified. I have a feel to where these women are being steered but I don't have a strong lead.'

'A pattern?' asked Jack.

'A rumour which we've been unable to get underneath and bring to something more solid. Patterns are useful but I don't like them. I want to shake this one up. Frankly I mean it when I say that I would be interested in knowing what your opinion of the security issues for the town are, as I respect a man who will put his own life on the line and save another. You went into that fire having made some judgements. You made them fast. I think you'll have looked at my town in the same way.

———

164

There was a natural pause while Field took a spoonful of the pudding and savoured the explosion of tastes in his mouth.

'I'd also like to work with you and Burgess on these baby deaths as a situation has been brought to your door, so to speak. I'd start by finding out if the child's birth was registered. That might tell us the area. There's another couple of points.' Field paused.

'What is it?' Jack dared to ask.

'None of these mothers are around when their babies die. There's no grieving mother. Mother's aren't silent when a baby dies. I've also not found a record of a funeral for any of these children either. We have a certified death and nothing else.'

'Why would a doctor kill babies?' asked Jack. 'How would the mothers disappear? They're going to show up in Poor House records, somewhere, aren't they?'

'I didn't say he was killing the babies. The same doctor is certifying the deaths. I don't know if there's actually a child in the area in any of those cases. The mothers are missing. Keep an open mind on whether they're using the Poor House. I don't think they are. I don't have bodies in those cases either. Those are the facts. I can surmise more but it wouldn't be a fact,' Field sat back in his chair.

'We should get Sam in,' said Jack to Burgess.

'Good,' said Burgess. Jack stared across the table at Field, his mind racing. Field looked back at him and the two men understood each other.

'I've to go across to Kewhurst to see a Coastguard who was Father's friend. The only thing is that I can't go until after a couple of Cricket matches in the next few days and I've to finish the assessment of the town for Inspector Hunt. When I do go I'll be in the area for St Leonards and Hastings. There's a grave I want to visit at Bexhill and I've a Parson to see who may be helpful. I can ask some questions,' explained Jack.

Field nodded.

'On the history of these other cases of missing women and the number of deaths of children, do you think the women are dead?' asked Jack, looking from Burgess to Field.

Burgess sucked in air through his teeth.

Field shook his head. 'We don't know.'

'Do you think the women might have had the children christened? Because in either the case of registering a birth or a christening there would be a record,' said Jack.

Field nodded.

'I'll let you have a copy of my report on Brighton once I've written it for Sam. Your eyes only, mind,' said Jack.

Field smiled and again made a slight nod.

Jack stood up and looked at Burgess. He suddenly felt very tired and his throat was tight.

'If you'll forgive me gentlemen, I'll decline pudding as I'm under orders to rest each afternoon. That's what I'll do now and I'll draft the report later. Good to meet you,' Jack shook hands with Field. 'Can I contact you through Mr Burgess here?'

'Always,' said Field and this time he stood up.

Jack nodded to Burgess and took his leave. In his room he gave in to the aching head and vague sense of sickness and sank onto his bed.

*

Ten

Early on Wednesday the eighteenth of June, two men, waiting in London, received information concerning the Shah's visit to England.

One man was a Metropolitan Police Inspector, of medium height, smart but heavy eyed with lack of sleep, who had been awaiting a telegram about the actual date and time to have his men in position. The Shah had delayed his arrival and the effect was a team that had been kept on stand-by. Now the telegram had come and the Inspector's manner had an edge to it that morning. The notice was short. The Inspector was Tom Hunt, a man depended upon by two eminent people: a Government Minister and a grieving widow who happened to be a Queen.

Now moving his men into position had to be fast.

The Inspector sent three telegrams: one to a hotel in Brighton to a Detective Sergeant Franks, who was hoping to breakfast early with an attractive woman and her mother. The others were to his Sergeants, Morris and Phillips. The latter two had their men ready to police the area around Charing Cross Station at a moment's notice, and Detective Sergeant Franks would return to London ready for the Shah's final segment to Buckingham Palace. As for Hunt himself he had a specific role to play in protecting the Prince of Wales. He only hoped his equestrian skills were still up to it.

The second man awaiting the arrival of the Shah was an alderman and he had a highly decorated menu placed before him. The occasion was to be an entertainment to His Majesty, The Shah of Persia, at the Guildhall. The date on the menu was Friday, twentieth of June , 1873. There was some discrepancy in the date as the Shah, as far as the alderman knew, still had not arrived in England and he had yet to be informed the man was on his way.

The alderman ran his eye over the detail. It was mainly in French as was the custom.

'Purée De Volaille.   Potage À La Victoria

Saumon À La Royale,'
he read it aloud and liked the sound of his own accent.

'And so on, lamb cutlets with peas, salads, pâtés, jellies and on and on it goes,' he muttered.

His eye wandered to the middle of the sheet.

'Peacocks displayed! Good grief. Yes, yes, I assume it will be what's expected, although the Queen won't be there. How many are invited?'

'Three thousand, sir,' said a secretary. The response was an explosion.

Minutes passed with the alderman staring out of a window. He turned a list of names over which had been sent from the Under-Secretary of State for Foreign Affairs. The list concerned gentlemen selected by the Government to attend on the Shah during his visit. Eventually he turned and waved the list at his secretary.

'Load of ex-military men appointed to attend on the Shah during his visit. Then we've got a Lord-in-Waiting, an Equerry-in-Waiting and a Groom-in-Waiting attending on him on behalf of the Queen. There's a cryptic comment that we are to be mindful of the etiquette of positions at the table with this lot. Damned cheek. Treating us like a shop-full of grocers, as if we don't know these things. Do I give this to you?' asked the alderman, looking down his nose at the list.

'I expect so,' said his secretary, coming forward to relieve him of the detail.

'I suppose it's fine and we have to go ahead. The cost, my goodness. This had better be worth it.'

'And the medals, sir, could you check the detail and let me know if you are happy with the design?' asked his secretary putting two drawings in front of the alderman. He looked at the design of the proposed bronze medal of Nasr-ed-Din, Shah of Persia, wearing a Persian fez which was extremely highly decorated head-gear. The reverse was to be of a woman dressed in Roman garb embodying Londinia. She stood before St Paul's Cathedral and the Tower of London and held an inscribed scroll.

168

'What's this?' the alderman pointed to a crest. His secretary came forward and peered at the design, frowned and referred to some notes he held.

'That's the crest of Persia and the other one is .....'

'Yes, yes, I know the arms of the City of London.'

'It says June 20th. What happens if he's later than he already is?' asked the alderman.

'I think it has to go to production.'

'But the date now? And the detail? Is it correct?' Again questions for which the secretary did not have the answer. He looked at his employer and moved a hand in some gesture which indicated he was about to answer. The clock ticked waiting for a solution.

'I have no idea, I've never met the man who did the design. I assume they know what they're doing. Do we have access to someone who knows about Persia, somewhere in the country?' asked the secretary.

The alderman glanced at the list of the three men appointed to attend the Shah on behalf of the Queen.

'You could presumably try one of these. If not try Oxford or Cambridge if there's nobody in London. There's usually some expert there. Get hold of some of these military types off this list if you can't find anyone else. They're getting a free dinner out of it. I have absolutely no idea what the man looks like but we don't want to drop a brick so make sure, will you, that the detail on the design is correct. Also make doubly sure the spelling is right. I've got two different spellings here, look.' The alderman jabbed at the paper with a stubby finger.

'Nasir. On the medal it says Nasr. Look, look, this is spelt differently as well to the detail on your sheet. This says Nasir Od-Din. For heaven's sake make sure it's right. So easy to offend someone before we've even started talking. Would he wear that sort of Headdress, etc. I don't know.' The alderman passed the design back and waived a hand of dismissal.

The secretary gathered up the design and the proposed menu and had partly reached the door when the alderman said:

'I suppose he will actually come? I no longer see the point. Last thing I heard was Gladstone was in two minds to cancel the visit as the man has delayed arriving. Too good a time elsewhere.' He sighed and glanced towards the Bank. His secretary waited. The alderman carried on. 'The Queen's got the right idea, she's going to be holed up in Windsor. I believe she's letting the man and his entourage have Buckingham Palace. She's greeting him at Windsor in some Quadrangle or other.'

The secretary fingered a corner of a paper:

'Are you going to be in the party to meet him?' he enquired.

'Not if I can help it, she's got the Princesses and two of the Princes with her. I've got too much going on here. The latest is he's landing at Dover and will be met by members of the Royal Family, then he'll be put on a special train and there's an escort to the Palace. We're not involved until the reception at the Guildhall and that's in a state of flux as far as the date is concerned.'

'Well, I suppose the point of it is we need to counteract Russian influence, so it's all very necessary,' said the secretary, turning the door knob.

'Of course, that's why he's coming. The Shah wants to balance Russian influence with British political influence. The whole point of the trip from his position is to make ties with European powers. Balance of power, that's what it's about for Persia. He's after self-protection and to do that he's coming to persuade us that Persia's a modern state. And then there's India, of course.' The alderman looked at his secretary.

The young man waited. Nothing else was forthcoming. 'I'd better get on,' he said.

The alderman nodded a dismissal and gave his attention to the papers on his desk.

*

In Sussex Jack rode up to the station on the omnibus with Mrs Curzon.

'You're quiet this morning, Jack,' said Mrs Curzon.

'Oh just something yesterday that mithers me,' said Jack, trying to smile. Wednesday morning had found him, once again, deeply troubled. It was the discussion with Field and Burgess the previous day that had unsettled him. But this lady had more problems than him.

'Not sleeping too well. Can't seem to get a night where I don't wake with worries,' he continued. Jack had spent a restless night. As a result of little sleep the cough had been troublesome that morning.

He had decided, no matter how tired he felt each afternoon he would no longer take a sleep during daylight hours. It seemed to be affecting the quality of the last few nights. Rest as instructed after midday he should do, because it was an order, but he would try and stay awake.

Jack had knocked on Sam's door at seven that morning but there had been no reply so he had slipped the pages of his assessment of Brighton under Sam's door. He had copiously annotated a second copy for Sergeant Field and left this in an envelope with Burgess on his way into breakfast.

Wondering where Sam was he had asked Burgess:

'Have you seen Sam this morning?'

'He finished breakfast by seven o'clock and left the hotel shortly afterwards,' said Burgess. 'Some early meeting he said.'

Jack had nodded, taking it that Sam and Harry would be working together.

His subconscious desire to make a difference through his work as a policeman was starting to become a realisation to him. The conversation with Field had highlighted to Jack how trying to save young life was clearly being met with abject failure, either through ignorance or a poor approach by his colleagues in another force. Would he do any better? He thought he could. Questions had been going around in his head through wakeful periods most of the night.

What of the living conditions the missing women had endured? He thought. Why was it a seemingly endless cycle that love led to a casting out by family once it's natural conclusion became apparent. He had spent too long amongst orphans or those who were unwanted to seriously doubt the conclusions society and religion were drawing. And the men? Could he criticize his own sex? He rather felt that he could.

He thought of his own feelings for Harriet and the occasions that he had longed to take her. Holding back had become harder the longer they delayed the engagement. If he just had a date that they would marry.... But that morning he vowed to himself that he would not put them in the same position as Grace and Nathan. No possible outcome of a child of his would be disowned nor born in shame.

Thinking about his own time in the orphanage had led on naturally to Miss Cohen and the orphans in London under her care. Her phrase, "twice orphaned," rang in his ears. Like him, despite difference in religion. Frankly, he wondered if the differences mattered a jot. Those children had the same rights to be protected, to grow, to develop, he thought. He had suffered the stigma, been told it was because of sin that he was orphaned and other ridiculous statements. They had had the effect to drive Jack on, not crush him, but he had seen others cowed.

His mind went to how lucky he had been to have his parents until he was nine. He could read, understand money coming in and read the basic account of it in a record, thanks to Mother. He had been schooled, grown strong with the work on the market garden and the fishing with Father. Friends of theirs had taken an interest in him while his parents had been alive but all he had of them were vague memories of a name or two and their faces. They would be older now and may not know him. May not choose to know him, such was the stigma he knew being orphaned, carried. No relative had come forward on their deaths and as far as he knew he was completely alone in the world. But without those first nine years where would he be now?

Jack's mind brooded on how hit and miss it seemed for most and how society needed to change. Some, he knew, helped others as they found them. It might at one point in his life have been true that he could do nothing. That was not true now. He had every intention of reaching as high a position and with that would come changing the status quo.

'Do you not wonder, Jack, how strange it is that one day can alter one's whole life? Asked Mrs Curzon.

'Frequently,' said Jack. His mind went to how he had taken his strength for granted and now it failed him. He had attempted push ups that morning to see what he could do and had collapsed in a heap, coughing. His tactics needed to change and instead of relying on his physical strength his motives of entering situations in order to change them needed to rely on using his intellect more. That's what Hunt would do. Sam too now, as there was no other option for him.

Sergeant Field had said that in going into the blaze at the Alexandra Palace Jack had been capable of a quick assessment of the situation. He had started to realise that was true. It was the same with the assessment he had carried out. It would be the same today. He was developing confidence in other abilities he realised he had, not just shifting a barn door.

Mrs Curzon glanced at her travelling companion from time to time as they sat on the omnibus together. Sam had been delighted last night over dinner at the Ship that she had done so much with Jack. She and her eldest son had talked about their mutual decision that Brighton would be a good place for the family and Sam had been determined to start making enquiries about a house.

'Jack, I think the next stop is for us,' Mrs Curzon prompted.

Jack came out of his reverie aware he had been poor company. Smiling, he gave Mrs Curzon a full smile a hand to help her up.

'Forgive me, I was adle-headed earlier and not attending to what you were saying. You mentioned Sam's young brothers were coming next week. Sam told me when we first met of all their antics. Perhaps a fishing trip like we did yesterday with them would be the thing?'

'That would be a real pleasure, Jack'

'One place we haven't seen yet is the theatre in New Road,' said Jack. He noted Mrs Curzon's expression change and realised she was uncertain about such an activity as she thought of her mourning. He persevered.

'Perhaps when the younger Curzon boys are here we can have a look inside to see the changes the theatre Architect made. Perhaps as you're bringing them here with a view to settling in the town it would help for them to know by Christmas they may have a pantomime?'

'Yes, I'm sure you are right it just seems so early after losing their father to think like this.'

Jack settled them into a comfortable carriage rather than subject Mrs Curzon to third class. Another woman of a similar age to Mrs Curzon was already in the carriage with two young ladies. Conversation struck up between Mrs Curzon and the women and Jack settled into a seat by a window in order to assess the area as the train took them towards Portsmouth.

Brighton blended into Hove and Jack could see the Downs with the fine view of the countryside. The line followed the shore with the village of Kingston-on-Sea on the right and its wharf and harbour. A Saxon church, also on the right, looked as if some restoration had been done.

'That's Old Shoreham,' said one of the young woman to Jack. He had been aware she had watched him for some minutes. As she spoke to him he shifted his position towards her and smiled, trying to place her accent.

'I can see you're very taken with the country,' she added and holding out her hand in a very determined manner introduced herself. 'Eleanor Davies, formerly of Cardiff and now of Worthing.'

'Jack, formerly of Battle and now I live in London.' Jack stood up and moved across the carriage and they shook hands. Resuming his position by the window he said, 'It's some years since I was in Brighton.'

'We go as far as Worthing. Have you been over this way before?' Eleanor asked. Jack thought she had a musical voice and she reminded him of a little bird.

'No, I haven't, it's interesting. Would you know if there's a harbour?' Jack asked.

'Yes. There's a harbour about a mile from New Shoreham and you'll see another fine church soon that still has some of its Norman architecture.'

' Thank-you,' said Jack, and turned back to the scenery as the train passed a one storey wooden structure known as Swiss Cottage with extensive gardens. It was clear that the coast was difficult to access from the Downs on this stretch to Portsmouth. He was also aware that Eleanor Davies was still watching him, her head cocked on one side and then on the other, like a sparrow weighing up the approach to a piece of bread.

'I'm sorry for your terrible loss. Your mother said that you'd been injured recently as well?' Jack looked sharply back at Eleanor and then glanced at Mrs Curzon who was involved in her own conversation.

'I, er,' Jack frowned and then let his face relax. No point in unravelling the confusion. Mrs Curzon had obviously been explaining why she was here and had mentioned Sam's injury. There had been an assumption that Jack was her son as they were travelling together. He let it lie, and smiled and nodded his thanks. The likelihood was they would never meet again.

' What brought you to Worthing?' Jack asked.

'Work. I'm a music teacher. I work at this great place over there,' Eleanor pointed to the expanse of buildings in the distance and then the scene changed. 'But also I give music lessons to the children of the nobility in Brighton. Tone deaf and completely disinterested, they'd much rather play on the beach but perhaps something one day will register with the little dears. It pays very well and Mother and Betty and I get to do some shopping.'

They were through Lancing station and a few miles further on a larger town loomed in view. He assumed it must be Worthing as Eleanor, Betty and Mrs Davies, started to gather their belongings together.

———

A card was pressed upon Mrs Curzon and Jack was glad for her that she had struck up an acquaintance on the journey which may help her to settle if Sam moved the family to Brighton.

Eleanor Davies paused in front of Jack. Her sister pushed through the space between them.

'You know I do feel I've seen you before somewhere. Never mind, it will come to me. I hope you all settle in Brighton well. No doubt we'll meet again as we're going to have you all to tea when you've moved to Sussex.'

'How nice, very kind of you,' said Jack, smiling at how things might develop for Sam and his family with new friends. He stood and helped Mrs Davies with her parcels from the luggage rack.

'Thank-you for your kindness to the family,' said Jack to the older woman.

'Well, I'd better move or I'll be coming onto Portsmouth with you. Get better!' said Eleanor, leaning forward with the firmness of the teacher in her tone.

They were gone from the train with as much chatter amongst themselves as there had been in the carriage, shopping bags banging against the carriage door as they climbed down. Jack pulled his watch from his pocket and said to Mrs Curzon, 'If you meet that family for tea they will have a surprise as the young woman I was chatting to thought I was your son.'

Mrs Curzon sat back and put her hand to her mouth. Then she laughed and said: 'Oh dear.'

'There's five minutes before the train leaves. Would you like to step off for a few moments?' asked Jack.

'No, I don't think so, I'll enjoy the quiet after all that conversation,' said Mrs Curzon. 'She'll be disappointed when she doesn't see you again.'

'I have a feeling Sam may suit her better,' Jack said with a grin as he opened the carriage door and climbed down onto the platform.

In the brief time he had before he must return to the carriage he looked up and down the platform for a porter. One came towards him pushing a large number of cases, and Jack waved him down.

'The town? Is it down there?' he asked, pointing.

'Yes, it follows the line of the sea,' the man replied without stopping. 'But you won't make it if you're on this train.'

'Thank-you. I wondered how close to Brighton we would be here at the coast?'

'Quite afar-off but you can see the gas-lights of the town of Brighton. It's pretty, looks like a continuous string of lights.' The porter leaned back to slow the trolley and finally brought it to a stop.

'And the main places from here to Portsmouth?' asked Jack.

'Arundel, Duke of Norfolk's castle, now its restored, Chichester with the racing and the Cathedral, then you're at Portsmouth.' The man was impatient to move on with his bags and Jack tipped him for his help and asked before he moved away and the man's impatience evaporated.

'At Portsmouth station can I get a feel of the place before taking a later train to Brighton?' asked Jack.

'Best take an omnibus from the station. What's your interest?' asked the man.

'The Harbour and the town,' replied Jack.

'You won't get near the Harbour. It ranks first in England for security. Don't waste your time if its short. The town has little to offer in interest, there's nothing beautiful there. If you're interested in fortification and seeing sailors and soldiers you'll get a feel from the omnibus. You can't get near the ramparts. The rest is suburbs with some bathing places, history to do with Nelson, of course. You could get a thousand vessels at anchor in the stretch of water at Spithead between Portsmouth and the Isle of Wight. It's quite a view when you see it. Frankly, if you were staying I'd point you to take the steamer to the Isle of Wight.'

'Thanks, I shall give it a miss then,' asked Jack.

The Porter had started to move the trolley again, with much effort he put his back into it. He called over his shoulder:

'There's better places for a day out. If you stop at Arundel you'll enjoy the view of the castle and you can find a fair plate at the Norfolk hotel. There's usually a cart from the station meeting each train. You've under ten miles to Arundel now.'

Swinging himself back into the carriage Jack had made a decision. 'We should have a view of Arundel Castle as we go past. That's under ten miles from here. I've taken some advice from a porter about Portsmouth. We know the Shah will go under naval escort. We just don't know when yet. It seems from what the porter said that there's little point in going on any further as it's so fortified the place is probably the least likely for something to happen. The man recommended stopping to eat at the Norfolk Hotel and then going back to Brighton from Arundel.'

Mrs Curzon nodded and turned to look out of the window again. Jack realised she had been lost somewhere in the past and he had interrupted her brown study.

Mrs Curzon was a sensible woman in everything and she was enjoying Jack's company and the part that she was playing in helping his work. She would above all things have liked to put the clock back five years when her husband was well, and when Sam came home every-day from a safe employment and her other sons were at her apron strings. Since December she had realised that she could not protect them anymore.

Travelling and walking with this young man and having his confidence because she was Sam's Mother was a great compliment. More than this she had found the last two days exciting. Feeling ashamed that she had slept soundly and woken refreshed that morning she had thought about how her husband would have reacted to what she was doing. She drew breath. Dare she assume he would be glad? The thought of the castle and lunch at a hotel and the prospect of living in Brighton was better than any other situation available for her. She raised her eyebrows at herself and felt a flush to her face. Looking back at Jack she said:

'I'm happy to fit in with you, Jack.' It was the most that she could say, as she felt it a privilege to be there.

Jack looked at her to make sure he was not pressing her to do something that she would find upsetting. On the contrary, he thought, there's a light in the eye. It's doing her good.

Jack smiled and said, 'Good, we'll take the cart to the Norfolk at Arundel and eat there. We can catch the afternoon train back to Brighton.'

*

In London, in the House of Lords, the Earl of Camperdown had risen to his feet.

'I thought it might be for the convenience of their Lordships if I were to state that His Majesty the Shah of Persia will leave London for Portsmouth at 8.30 on Monday morning, and would reach Portsmouth about 10.30. A.M. The "Simoom," has been set apart for such of their Lordships as might desire to attend the naval review, which would leave the Dockyard at 9.30; and I believe arrangements are being made in connection with the House for a special train.' He paused, scanning the document in front of him.

'The tickets, which will be issued by the Admiralty tomorrow, will not be transferrable.' Again he scanned the sheet.

There was a general 'here, here,' at this.

The Earl continued.

'The Admiralty were anxious to consult their Lordships' wishes as to ladies,' this was met with guffaws and general uproar. The Earl stared down his nose at several of the ribald comments. He waited for the noise to abate.

'As to ladies,' he attempted to continue. But his fellow peers had no intention of allowing him to get away with the subject. He scratched the back of his neck.

'As to ladies....' He attempted again.

'As to ladies, a certain number of tickets will be provided; but much will, of course, depend on how many of their Lordships put their names down as intending to go, and I should be glad if any Peer who does not wish to take a lady with him would intimate the fact.' Camperdown looked at the next sentence from the Admiralty and thought it could only have been written by a sailor. He drew breath, focused on the opposite wall to avoid the eyes opposite and read out:

'In any case, no more than one lady would be allowed to accompany a noble Lord.'

General guffaws echoed around the chamber.

*

Eleven

The weather was calm in Kent by half past two as a man emerged on deck at the end of his journey from Ostend to Dover. He was described in the papers:
".... as swarthy, with eyes seeing deeply into all things,"
A fleet of iron clads acted as escort lacked the grace of the old men-of-war but certainly portrayed more power.

Inspector Tom Hunt later said that the Journalists had built in as much romance as possible in their descriptions of:
"... a manly figure dressed in military uniform and swathed in a cloak."

Apparently, women sighed deeply at the sight of him. Hunt couldn't see the attraction. A comment Ted heard from one lady he was near was that the sighing was more due to the flame of rainbow coloured light produced by the jewellery on the man's scimitar. However there was silence initially until the thundering of the guns was heard and then people were aware who they were greeting.

The man was the Shah of Persia, recently in Prussia, Germany and finally, Belgium. There were a good many diamonds on the uniform and when the Shah threw his cloak off the light caught the diamond epaulettes. There were more on his hat and diamonds and rubies on his buttons. The contrast therefore with the royal princes there to greet him was extremely marked.

He was met by the Corporation of the Cinque Ports representing the region which, on many occasions, had been the most vulnerable area of England to invasion. However, that afternoon this particular invasion in process was headed by a small man, diamonds flashing, being greeted by relatives of Queen Victoria.

As the Shah landed salutes were fired from the land and the fleet. The Mayor made doubly sure they had finished before he started his address. The Shah responded to this layer of unfamiliar democracy and said that he felt among friends and the party left for the special train to London.

Later that afternoon in London, Sergeants Morris and Phillips were in plain clothes in the Strand. Their men had been waiting for the arrival of the Royal Party at Charing Cross Station. It had been a long day since Tom Hunt's telegram had notified them that the Shah was actually going to arrive and the expectation now was that the special train would pull in at Charing Cross at six o'clock. Flags and flowers were everywhere and the platform at which the royal party would arrive was covered in a crimson cloth. The Prince of Wales, Duke of Cambridge, Prince Teck and Prince Christian were the welcome party at the station.

In the throng of people men in plain clothes could only go by appearance and behaviour and watch the movement of anyone near them in the crowd that was remotely suspicious. But in Ted's experience, people never fitted stereotypes.

It had rained heavily but despite this the crowd had surrounded the station and spilled into the adjacent streets. It was such a press of bodies that Ted tried to stoop down at one point to get a view of hands and the satchels held on hips but he was in danger of being pushed to the ground. He straightened up and worked his way back to Morris who had positioned himself on a step in front of the ornate Charing Cross Hotel. It had given Morris some elevation over the heads. His men could see him at least. While the rest of the team were in amongst the crowd the instruction was to check what Morris indicated, to keep him in sight at all times and make their way back to him.

Ted joined him pressing his way on to the step below: 'Can you see the others?' he asked.

'A few, but the crowd is pressing down to the left and I think some of the men have been taken with them.' Morris's keen eyes spotted a space open up.

'We'll have a job to muster them if its needed,' said Ted.

'I think we can only do our best. This is bigger than anyone expected. Particularly as the Shah was delayed. In some ways this jovial lot are not so much of a problem. They're hemmed in themselves and if anything, we're in danger of a crush.' Morris eyed a man who had positioned himself directly in front of him. Tall, dark-haired with lines of age prematurely in his face. He turned and gave Ted and Morris an amiable, lop-sided grin. Morris dismissed him. There was no potential problem there, but stepped up one more level so that he was again visible. Ted managed to follow and used his elbows more than once.

'I'm more worried about the people at the upper windows and a few across the way who have got up to the roof tops,' said Morris. He saw one of his men in plain clothes pushing through the crowd to come back towards him. When the constable was close enough to see clearly Morris nodded to the roof opposite and the man followed the gaze and changed his direction.

'Did you say Tom Hunt will be in the Prince of Wales's party?' asked Ted.

'I understand he is, dressed up as goodness knows what. Somewhere, Harry and his men should be in the crowd as well,' Morris explained as he continued to scan the scene.

Ted laughed spontaneously at the idea of Inspector Hunt dressed as a coachman, or some other role. 'If Tom's not careful he'll find himself back at the Palace washing laundry,' he said.

'Not him.' Morris said as he swung round at the shouts from a noisy group who liked the sound of their own voices. He watched them for a minute and concluded there was nothing there to worry about.

'If you're looking for Harry and Stan my money's on them being in a doorway of a tavern, singing, waving a tankard and Harry will be wearing a bowler hat and his stained waistcoat,' said Ted peering through the crowd. Morris smiled at the idea.

'Fancy a wager as to who sees him first,' suggested Morris.

'Margaret's biscuits against Violet's?' said Ted.

'Done,' said Morris. He scanned the buildings and gave Ted a poke in the ribs. 'Up there, Brewer's Lane. See him?'

Ted followed the line of sight and it was the bigger man, Stan, Harry's sidekick from Shadwell, that he saw first. As usual Stan had Harry's back, face glowering in his best off-putting expression. In front of him was a smaller man, waving a tankard and singing. Harry Franks of Shadwell was giving a good performance.

'Did Harry come up from Brighton this morning?' asked Ted.

'Must have done.' Morris replied.

'How long's he here for?

'No idea. Depends if he's part of the duty for Buckingham Palace tomorrow. I should think he needs to get back to Brighton to coordinate the team though,' said Morris.

'They'll be alright without him. Can you get your watch out to check the time? I'm so pressed in I can't move my arms,' said Ted.

Morris turned slightly to the right to free up his left hand. He pulled out his pocket watch and said, 'Ten minutes and the Shah's train should be in.'

*

Earlier that morning Harry Franks had been at breakfast in the large, elegant room of the Royal Hotel in Brighton, when the telegram from Hunt had arrived. Rose and Mrs Phillips had not come down and Harry was in the process of buttering toast.

There was something sacred about breakfast to Harry. He seldom had the opportunity to sit at this time of the day and eat. So, when a boy brought him the telegram, he dropped his knife with a clatter on the plate and received a disapproving look from several matrons. Their faces relaxed as Rose arrived at the table, such had been her skill with the portraits on the previous day.

184

Harry got up and pulled out a chair for Rose. He bent to kiss her hand and quickly spoke into her ear to explain. She nodded and he moved quickly out of the breakfast room to the open door of the Royal. Rose casually picked up his napkin that he had dropped on the floor and laid it on the seat of the chair, indicating to a waiter, who approached the table.

'Mr Franks has had some news. I will be back shortly but if Mrs Phillips comes while we're not here would you let her know that I am coming back.'

'Of course, Ma'am.'

Rose walked coolly towards the reception area, nodding to a few of the ladies she had met as she went. At the door from the lounge she glanced right and left and then saw Harry just starting to come back in. He acknowledged her and waited.

'Can you step outside with me a moment?' he asked.

'Of course,' said Rose with a smile.

Standing with their backs to the building Harry handed Rose the telegram.

'Today!' she exclaimed.

'Yes, no warning, just arrived at Ostend and as he was already late we're wrong-footed. I should be seeing Sam in about thirty minutes but I must go straight away. My instructions were to be at Charing Cross and observe the crowd. I'll see Hunt later but I'll go straight to London Bridge and gather the team and then, my dear, I shall don my old beer stained waistcoat and be the man that the young lady, Mary knew.'

'Hopefully this time the difference will be no roving eye,' said Rose.

'You guessed?' Harry asked, shocked.

'Of course, but you hadn't met me then. I knew Jack was covering for you. He'd never pick a bar maid, too ambitious long-term and you wouldn't either if you'd met me first,' Rose tilted her head and raised an eyebrow.

Harry stood back and then squeezed her hand. 'I admire the confidence. But you're right. Old age coming on and panic about loneliness. When I saw you though it was love at first sight.'

'It's your life I care about now,' said Rose. 'Be careful in London and no heroics. Will you be armed?'

'If you mean will I be carrying a gun, no. However, I'll have Stan with me so, in some ways the answer is, yes. Stan doesn't like crowds, they have a bad effect on him. Makes him touchy. I'll take orders from Hunt as the telegram says but I hope that I'll be back by Friday evening. Would you do two things for me while I'm gone?' asked Harry.

'Of course.'

'Sam will be here shortly. He should see those sketches that you did and get any of them we would be unsure of as to identity across to the police artist. Jack's off travelling today along the line to Portsmouth and is unlikely to be back before mid-afternoon. Sam should go through Jack's findings for both days. We still don't know if the Shah will come to Brighton nor when the visit to Portsmouth will be. I should have a better feel later, at the worst, tomorrow. I'll get word to you. Would you pass it on to both Sam and Jack?'

'Yes I'll go over and see them both,' said Rose.

'The second is to get a telegram across to Detective Sergeant Stan Green at Shadwell to meet me at London Bridge Station with the usual constables: Percy, Arthur, Alf and Henry. All in plain clothes. Stan's to bring my suit, the usual suit. Destination is Charing Cross. I would have liked to share breakfast with you,' Harry added, distracted by the closeness of Rose. He put his arm around her waist while motioning to a doorman for a carriage.

'We will share many soon,' said Rose, aware of her own ache.

*

Harry Franks started his fifty mile journey from Brighton towards the London Terminus at London Bridge regretting not having eaten. There was no time now and he would hope something would be brought onto the train. Harry looked around at the other passengers. There were six people in the second class carriage and he was glad there were no more. Built to seat eight it would have been cramped.

Three of the passengers were men travelling into London to work. At one time they would not have lived further out than Dulwich and they wore the air of the regular commuter to some Merchant's establishment. In the corner sat a bony woman with a daughter of about twelve, both carrying covered baskets and whispering to each other.

Harry settled in to stare out of the window as the train passed Ditchling Beacon, it's green hill-side pitted with sheep. His telegram from Hunt had differed slightly to the ones sent to Morris and Phillips. Hunt had a meeting that morning with the man he directly took instructions from in trying to bottom the corruption. In order to meet Harry by midday to give him orders for the nineteenth and twentieth of June Hunt had suggested they meet by the Lodge on the edge of Green Park, to the side of Horse Guards Parade.

Harry's chin slowly settled onto his chest. He had long thought that Hunt was working for someone high up, possibly in a Government Department. Harry ran a picture through his mind of buildings located close enough to enable Hunt to make a midday meeting with himself. Whitehall, he thought. Admiralty, no he discounted that. Home Office, possible, or Treasury. A frisson went through him as the map played out in his mind. Privy Council and then, Downing Street. An adrenalin rush woke him up properly and he stared at the brilliant reflection of the sunlight on chalk hills until there was darkness as the train entered the Clayton tunnel and emerged to stop at Hassocks Gate.

He was lost in thought from then on and came to as the train ascended through a series of cuttings to the London Terminus of the Brighton Railway.

It was a convenient place and Harry bought a quarter of a Coburg loaf, pulling pieces of it apart and eating it as he walked. He looked up and down for his team. No sign yet but they should not be long. London Bridge was full of commuters. He took a tea from a stall and poured sugar into it. The station had certainly expanded from the years when commuters came in on the Greenwich line on a fare of 6d. Now there was furious competition between different lines and suburbia was spreading.

'One suit, as instructed Gov,' said a deep voice and Stan Green was behind him with a bag. Harry turned round and stared straight into Alf's face.

'You've caught the sun,' said Alf, who was dressed like a Costermonger.

'The benefits of good sea air. Ready for the fray?' asked Harry.

'Aren't we always,' said Stan, 'I take it we're here because the Shah is coming in? Duty Sergeant had word this morning. Miss Phillips's telegram arrived shortly after. Nice to see you've got her working already. They think the streets will be packed. It was a bit short notice but I managed to get this bunch of reprobates reassigned on an order. Could we make a move soon? I really don't like crowds.'

'Yes Stan, I know they have an interesting effect on you,' said Harry as he slapped his colleague on the shoulder and surveyed the other men.

'Good to be with you again, lads,' said Harry. 'We'll take the London Bridge and Charing Cross line over to Charing Cross Station. That's where the Shah's train will arrive. I don't have the time yet so we may have a lot of hanging around. That will be the fastest route from here.'

'Then what?' asked Stan with a scowl.

Then we do what we do best, blend and keep our eyes open,' said Harry. 'But I have a need of breakfast once we get into the area and had you all have looked more respectable I would have suggested Simpsons in the Strand.'

This was greeted with a general guffaw from his team.

188

Harry continued: 'However as I doubt that they will let us in now, despite the fact that I am a member...' there was a mixed response from his men. Harry held up his hands for the noise to abate.

'Yes, I am a member, a guinea a year and I get to play chess and drink coffee with some pretty interesting people, I can tell you. However that is not to be today.'

'We're too early for most of the places near the theatres,' said Percy.

'We could hole up in Bow Street Police Station?' Henry suggested.

'Not really,' said Stan. 'We're under cover so we don't show up at another Police Station.'

'I fear, gentlemen, given the way we are to be dressed for this lark today the only places we can go are parks or taverns. Green Park has a nice little café, as does The National Gallery. Both place us well for the Strand and later, Charing Cross Station. So, let's make a move, shall we before my stomach thinks my throat is cut.'

The men walked in twos, and Harry placed himself with Stan. He slowed his pace deliberately and a gap opened up between them and the two constables Percy and Alf who were in front. There was a favour that he wanted to ask.

'I've a meeting with Hunt at midday. Orders for tomorrow, that sort of thing. I shall slope off from the team and meet him at a lodge on the edge of Green Park opposite Horse Guards.' Harry paused.

'Right, I wondered why you wanted to place us over that way so early,' said Stan.

'Once we get across and we've got established for a while where we can get food and drink, come with me for some reconnaissance work, will you?'

'Yes, of course. Over towards the station?' asked Stan.

Harry paused. 'Not really,' he said.

Stan gave him a look.

'Later for around there. I want to know the direction Hunt comes from to meet me. He'll be expecting to see me but not you. I'll walk to the lodge from the direction of the Admiralty as if I've come from Trafalgar Square. I'd like you to watch from near the Home Office. There's a passageway where you can get a good view of the Treasury, Board of Trade, and the Privy Council. I only need to know if Hunt comes out of one of those. Or if he comes from somewhere else,' explained Harry.

'Such as?' asked Stan.

'Downing Street, or the Foreign Office. There's also a police station on King Street.' Harry hoped that Stan would not ask too much more.

'What's the problem, Harry?' asked Stan.

Harry stopped and let the other four men walk on. They were all in conversation and unaware of the gap opening up between themselves and the two Sergeants.

Harry drew a breath. 'This undercover stuff we've got involved with since the Faceless Woman case, I'd feel more comfortable knowing who it is that's calling the shots. The location today says to me that it's a politician. I'd like to shorten the odds about who it is. That's all.'

Stan raised his eyebrows. 'Have you got any ideas?'

'I have, but it seems ridiculous. That's why I want you there.' Harry walked on and Stan followed him.

'And if you don't like who it is, politically I mean, given our oath and all?' Stan took out a handkerchief and blew his nose.

'We'll need to have a chat,' said Harry.

'Damn right,' Stan looked at him and said 'Don't hold with politics.'

'Depends what sort of position it puts us in. Look on the bright side. All we're doing today is taking in the lay of the land and being better informed. Then we can make a decision.' Harry quickened up the pace and Stan fell in beside him.

*

He had waited a long time for the meeting that morning and it had come because Inspector Hunt had dug his heels in. He had asked for it three times via the Commissioner since the Faceless Woman murder once it became clear that a serving policeman had been Harriet's attacker. He had received a snub each time in the last six months as a reply. Hunt had gone to the Home Office without invitation and nearly blown his own cover. It had become apparent that Bruce, the Home Secretary, was completely in the dark. Hunt had passed it off as mistaking the room, wandered about the corridors, masquerading as a buffoon who was lost. He had quietly been determined not to accept defeat regardless of snubs from above. Indeed at times he believed that his own career was under threat. However, he remained determined.

Then the summons had come and as a result Hunt had never been more astonished. It promised nothing but a meeting with the "Minister" at the Treasury on the eighteenth of June. Hunt was still none the wiser as to the identity of the man he was to meet. He had run through the Government Ministers in his mind and had come up with a disappointing selection.

He reached the Treasury at eleven o'clock, as arranged. The enormous exterior stretched down Whitehall, which was still busy with the traffic of horses and walkers. He had an hour before he had to meet Harry. Hunt remembered the difficulty of not being observed here due to the wide space. Mounted soldiers were exercising, presumably for later as part of the escort for the Shah and the Prince of Wales. He flinched as he thought of what his own part in that was to be by command of the Widow of Windsor.

Hunt could see the odd man hanging around in a passageway beside the buildings towards Downing Street. There was nothing unusual in their behaviour and the local constable had them in his sights.

Hunt climbed the steps to the Treasury and was admitted. His name on a list he noted. He was shown into a waiting area off a meeting room and invited to take a seat.

'The Minister will see you shortly, Sir,' said a secretary and he was left alone.

The door to the meeting room door was slightly ajar and he could see the back of several heads. Voices, too low to determine the content of the conversation, became quieter still it seemed the more he strained to listen.

The door opened and a man he did not know came through it. He looked expectantly at Hunt and the Inspector felt he should stand. 'Forgive me, you have the advantage over me, we haven't met and I have no idea of your name,' Hunt started as a way of attempting an introduction.

The man kept a straight face and swung the door wider, 'Inspector Hunt, The Prime Minister will see you now.'

*

It was not surprising, of course, Hunt thought to himself, if one reflected on the man's career, that he would do something like this. A "Peelite" since 1843, he had been Chancellor of the Exchequer several times. Now, as well as being Prime Minister, Gladstone had taken over as Chancellor again that year. Hence the meeting at the Treasury. Hunt ran a tick-list of reforms Gladstone had accomplished. Under him the Irish Church had been disestablished, Irish tenant farmers granted more rights vis-à-vis English landowners, a national elementary education programme set up to which the new Boot Boy at Camberwell New Road was a testimony. Secret Ballots in elections had also been introduced. His popularity with the working-class had earned him several nicknames: "the People's William," and the "Grand Old Man." Disraeli, however, had christened him "God's Only Mistake."

As he walked into the meeting room in the Treasury Hunt wondered how discreet he should be. The hawk-eyed man who turned to greet him, face deeply lined, was not renowned for tact. He could also imagine that a hostility could quickly build up between them if Hunt played it wrongly.

Here they were, the working-class policeman who had spent his child-hood in a school on the Windsor estate for the children of servants of the Queen, and the old Etonian, ex-Oxford University scholar with a double first-class degree in Classics and Mathematics.

To Hunt the most extraordinary event of Gladstone's career was that he had opposed the abolition of slavery. That had never sat right with Hunt. Economics, he had supposed, as the man's father had had nine plantations in the Caribbean. Hunt could not reconcile the stance given the man's commitment on other issues. Gladstone still went out rescuing and rehabilitating Prostitutes even as Prime Minister, much to the chagrin of his party and he had been almost a lone voice opposing violence against China in the Opium Wars after his sister had become an addict.

But Gladstone was speaking.

'I understand we have a common acquaintance.' Gladstone said.

There was no indication of irritation Hunt noted. Nothing to show that he felt cornered into a meeting with Hunt.

'I'm uncertain as to who that would be, sir,' said Hunt.

'Percival, Boot Boy currently to Mr Pendle of the Grove, in your area, I understand. I met him a few days ago as an example of the milestone that the Elementary Education Act has been. I understand he's joining your team, at least that's how Pendle described it to me. So, I assume the elementary education legislation has been a great success. How else would a boy of twelve be able to stand before the Prime Minister and explain that he was joining the Metropolitan Police as a civilian with the view to becoming a Police Inspector in the future. I have less fears for the competitive nature of this country now,' said Gladstone.

Hunt smiled in a friendly fashion. 'Yes, I would agree that Percy is an example of the success of that reform.' He paused, unsure if he should go on. Why not?

'He told us at the New Road Station that his teacher had said becoming a Footman was a thing of the past,' explained Hunt. 'Industry was the future. He decided being a Policeman was better than that. Although I wasn't sure if it wasn't the Sergeant's biscuits that clinched it, rather than any real understanding of the job. However, he made a good deal for pay and board.'

'Yes, sharp with the mathematics, you see. Do you know how many children of primary age are still without access to a school place?'

'I'm afraid I don't,' said Hunt, realising that he soon would.

'Two million. We have still to effect further reform. Sit down, won't you.'

Gladstone also took his seat again. 'I expect you wonder at my part in all this subterfuge,' he said. 'You will know the phrase the best person to recognize a thief is another thief?'

Hunt nodded.

'Do you know the rest of it?' asked Gladstone.

'I believe not,' answered Hunt.

'The best person to recognize a thief is another thief, presumably because they share the same way of thinking. What do you think that says about you and I, Inspector?'

Hunt grimaced.

Gladstone continued, 'As a saying it crops up in various forms. I did a little research for your visit in case you did know it. One thing I have learnt in politics is always to be better informed than the person I am about to meet.'

'Sounds wise,' said Hunt.

'A commentary on Cervantes' work of Don Quixote is one source. 1654 that one. But I found it also in Thomas Fuller's Church-History of Britain, dating from 1655. Two sources undoubtedly means it was a phrase in common usage at that time. However, it appears to be older than that.' Gladstone paused and checked the paper before him. Hunt wondered what the point of this was.

'Callimachus wrote in the second half of the third century B.C. His version was:

"being a thief myself I recognized the tracks of a thief."

'It's a phrase that's been around a long time in other words. Similar to the one about the game keeper:

"a poacher makes the best game-keeper."

Gladstone was enjoying himself at Hunt's expense. 'Yes?' he said. 'In other words we are all capable of being two sides of the same coin. But I will not permit the rule of law to be destroyed by an arbitrary tyranny, whether it be in religion or the law. In that, I suspect, you and I are the same. That is why I wanted you to know who the man is behind your instructions. You and I won't agree on many things and I suspect that you will be more socialist than I. I was at Eton while you were schooled in a stable, isn't that right, Inspector? Somehow or other you got that elementary education though? My point of entering a social problem would be at a different level than I suspect would yours. You will know that I disagree with Government interference with the free action of the individual, whether by taxation or otherwise and believe that it should be kept to a minimum.'

'I think, sir, that your beliefs are very complicated. However, you are right that we are agreed about arbitrary tyranny as you call it. Would I be right that you may know who we are dealing with?' asked Hunt.

'If I did, do you imagine I would have remained silent knowing all you do about what I stand for?'

'No.' Hunt was unsure about how to ask the next question. 'But if you have any inkling, would you confirm it to me?'

'Are you saying that you believe you know who it is?' Gladstone's eyes had become even more piercing.

'I may do,' said Hunt.

'And would you tell me?' asked the Prime Minister.

Hunt met the steely gaze. A saying came into his own mind. Courtesy, he thought wryly, of his elementary education on the Queen's estate. Yes it was true that part of his education was in a stable. But that was because he was supposed to follow his father as Queen's groom. Thanks to Prince Albert a few skills had been honed more than the average boy would have experienced. Why not? Hunt decided.

'I've a couple of sayings for you:

195

"To withdraw is not to run away, and to stay is no wise action when there is more reason to fear than to hope. 'Tis the part of a wise man to keep himself for tomorrow, and not venture all his eggs in one basket. I believe that's the same Spanish author, sir, according to my old teacher. Elementary education for me was just that but I too learnt a few quotes. Prince Albert liked them. Won a prize for recitation as well. There's a difference in having suspicions and evidence. I don't have the latter yet so any accusation won't hold up. So, to quote Oliver Cromwell:

"Trust in God and keep your powder dry." That is what I intend to do.' Hunt had finished.

There was a clear reluctance in Gladstone's body language to take the contact further. Hunt could tell. So, thought Hunt, I have to catch the man, and I'll get no direct help to do so. That confirms the power the suspect has and how well protected he is. Must be if he's got Gladstone on the wrong foot. Well, I will do it my way and no amount of pressure will make me act without solid evidence.

Hunt breathed in slowly and paced how he exhaled. Today meant he was not going to get to his objective easily. However, he potentially had a powerful ally in Gladstone. He must not push too hard. He had clearly surprised the Prime Minister about Prince Albert.

'Although it has seemed before today that we are in a weak position, knowing your involvement now sir, means that we are not.' Hunt said, graciously.

'Perhaps so, Inspector. We will meet in a month's time, and each month, until you place that evidence before me,' said Gladstone. Hunt stood up as the Prime Minister added. 'You are riding as a member of the Prince of Wales's party I understand this afternoon?'

Well informed even to that minor detail, thought Hunt. But the change in subject indicated that the interview was over. Remaining on the same spot Hunt nodded. 'Yes, my background was with horses as you already know, and I shall be there as rider on one of a pair of carriage horses. Some time since I did that but I hope the creatures will be kind.'

196

'I shall think on our exchange, Inspector,' said Gladstone, standing.

'Thank-you, sir, so will I.'

'I will send you a note when we are to meet again.' Gladstone turned to the window and Hunt looked at the back. He started to walk to the door.

The Prime Minister looked out in the direction of a man leaning against the passage wall, staring back at him. The Metropolitan Police Inspector had surprised the Grand Old Man with his knowledge of Cervantes. Gladstone had not foreseen the role of the Prince Consort but if anything it confirmed his stance on elementary education. There was just the glimmer of a smile for a few seconds. Again he felt he was right to fight the grassroot Liberals in their opposition to Church Schools being open to receiving local Rate Payer's money. Reflecting on that he failed to notice how he keenly he was being observed by the man in the alley who was whittling a stick.

*

Hardly predictable thought Hunt as he turned out of the Treasury to cross Horse Guards Parade. He walked towards the Lodge by Green Park. He was late by fifteen minutes for his meeting with Harry. He somehow thought Harry would not mind if he knew. And there was a question. Should Harry know? Hunt did not think he could stand it unless just one of the team knew.

Harry was there and waved an arm and Hunt responded. Walking a respectable distance at the back of the Inspector, Stan put his piece of wood and the knife he carried away and turned off towards Whitehall. Harry's wave had been for two people. Stan responded and gave Harry a thumb's up. He had the dirt on Hunt and Harry would hear it later.

'Sorry to be so late for you,' said Hunt, apologetically. Harry dismissed the comment with a wave of his hand.

'Don't worry, I had a late breakfast. You look a little grey around the gills if you don't mind me saying. I'm not dressed for anything but a Tavern and there's not much around here apart from rich men's clubs. Can I suggest we walk back to Trafalgar Square and go into the National Gallery? The streets are already filling up, Tom, and it will be difficult to find somewhere we can talk quietly. I suggest we go in as its unlikely to be busy today with the Shah being the main attraction in the area. It's open until five o'clock. I don't think we'll be disturbed.'

'Yes, but I do need to eat, as I'm due at Great Scotland Yard shortly,' explained Tom Hunt.

There was a brief silence as the two men walked towards Spring Gardens Mews and then on to the dreary building which was the National Gallery. Hunt made an effort and asked, 'How was your journey up from Brighton?'

'It gave me time to think. Your telegram arrived shortly after seven this morning. I thought this was an interesting location that you'd picked for us to have a briefing. But now I see it as you're due at Scotland Yard.' Harry paused to see if Hunt was ready to disclose anything about the meeting.

'I've had an extraordinary meeting in the last hour,' said Hunt. He had decided he must tell Harry in case something happened to him.

'Tell me about it,' said Harry. Hunt did so. They walked past the entrance to the National Gallery and Hunt talked while Harry Franks listened. The Detective Sergeant did not comment as they completed their circuit around the famous church of St Martin's-in-the-Fields. It was clear that he wanted time to consider all options. Hunt knew he was breaching confidentiality, but clearly needed to.

'Regardless of how I'm dressed, Tom, I think you and I should go and eat at a place where I'm a member in the Strand. '

*

The train from Dover arrived on the Up-Platform on the western side of the station. The train was ten minutes late into Charing Cross much to the chagrin of the company. Harry Franks and his team were distributed amongst the seats that ran the whole length of the station, sitting in pairs. Percy was with Harry and if they leaned forward enough they could just make out where Stan and Alf had taken up position at the end of the railway bridge. Between the signal box and the platform constables Henry and Arthur stood by tall Venetian masts sporting streamers. Arthur turned to Henry and raised his eyes to heaven. Evergreens decorated the lamps.

Stan, always affected by too much fauna and flora, was sneezing into a handkerchief that reminded Alf of a damask tablecloth of his mother's. There were wreaths of evergreens and hanging baskets of fuchsias, sweet peas and roses attached to each lamp-post. Even more flowers added to Stan's purgatory, hanging from the hotel balcony along with flags. They even extended up to the roof.

Someone had decided to add paper roses to real flowers in a canopy to the Strand. Ted muttered to Morris that it was in poor taste.

The Coldstream Guards were mounted and met the train with the Prince of Wales and his party. Tom Hunt, now mounted on a carriage horse, sporting a black top hat and royal livery, was regretting the amount of time he spent behind a desk. Horse Guards escorted the carriage from Charing Cross to Buckingham Palace and the route was lined with her Majesty's Household troops.

Once the Shah had left the station, Harry and his team made their way back to Shadwell for the night. Harry had his orders to be at Buckingham Palace ready for the Shah's departure on the nineteenth.

'Well, lads,' said Harry. 'I doubt anyone will get past that lot guarding tonight. I'm standing dinner if you'd like to join me.'

'I think I'll get off home, thanks, it's been a long day and we're back here early tomorrow,' said Alf.

'Yes, shame the Shah won't take advantage of that off-day he was given by the Lord Chamberlain tomorrow,' said Henry.

'We should know where he's going early so I'll see you all by eight o'clock at the station,' said Stan. The four constables left together and separated on the Commercial Road East to go to their respective homes.

'Are you abandoning me as well, Stan?' asked Harry.

'Nah. Mason's Arms?' asked Stan.

'No, can't stand the food. It has to be at least as good as Rose's, these days. Also I feel the need for something finer than the Commercial Road,' Harry said.

'You've got a little too used to the Royal Hotel, Harry. Bearing in mind how we're dressed we need you out of that waistcoat before we go in anywhere respectable. Any chance you can change back into your travel clothes you had on this morning? Why don't we jump on the train to the end of the Blackwall line, and get a cab from there. Have to be the City I think, now. There's a good place I know off Threadneedle Street.'

'The waistcoat is gone,' said Harry, starting to unbutton it. 'Lead on Stan and I will follow. Then we can get some rest before the performance begins again tomorrow. Ten o'clock at the Palace, Hunt said.'

'How was he?' asked Stan.

'Hunt? Like the rest of us. Wondering what he's got himself into as the Prime Minister's involved.' Harry started for the door, and as he always did, Stan had his back.

*

Twelve

Jack and Mrs Curzon arrived back at the Ship Hotel later than he had intended. It shocked him how little he could do before his energy completely evaporated. By the time they left Arundel Jack was having spasms of coughing which he found hard to control. Back in Brighton he apologised to Mrs Curzon and withdrew to his bedroom. Not wanting to press him on his health but aware that he needed sustenance she approached the reception desk and asked Alice if tea and bread and butter could be taken to Jack's room. Then she went in search of Sam.

The knock on the door came just as Jack had sat down in the armchair by the side of his bed. He had deliberately avoided laying down as he was fighting the urge to sleep. Sitting and reading for a while would no doubt help him feel better, stay awake, and have a better night.

Alice opened the door with a pass key before he could answer, calling out as she did. Slowly her head came round the door and she said, 'May I bring a tray in?'

'That'd be kindness,' said Jack.

'Mrs Curzon mentioned you could do with a little treat so here's the Farmhouse cake for you and a good pot of strong tea. Put you on 'til dinner.' She set the tray down on a side table and from the look of him registered that Mrs Curzon was right. Alice decided to pour the tea, added sugar and placed the cake at his elbow.

'I never could resist cake,' said Jack, picking out a raisin and putting it into his mouth.

'That's the way. You look as if you've worked hard today. Try and get a rest and we've a nice boiled spring chicken and asparagus sauce tonight for dinner, peas from the garden and new potatoes. Will you be here?'

Jack smiled, appreciating the fact that the two women had colluded to sort him out. 'How could I not be, with a dinner like that. Just one question. What's the pudding today?'

'Lemon Jelly and custard,' said Alice.

'Would you know if Sam and Mrs Curzon will be here?' asked Jack.

'They've said so, and anticipated your question as they've arranged a table for three. Now you rest up, and we'll see you for dinner,'

'Thank-you again,' said Jack.

'Charles has the local paper if you'd like it.'

'Perhaps later,' said Jack. 'I'll enjoy the tea and fruit cake.'

Alice smiled at him and pulled the door to behind her as she left the room.

Jack reached across the table and pulled the muslin curtains back to better see the sky. He pushed up the sash window to let the seagull's cry pervade the room. The sky was poor now and the wind had cooled. He wondered if he would ever do a day's work again without this dreadful weariness and hacking cough coming over him.

By seven o'clock that evening, when Jack had not appeared for dinner, Sam found Burgess and explained that Jack had not emerged yet. Burgess let him into Jack's room and as he followed Sam in registered that he could hear the deep breathing of sleep.

'That's fine then, I'll let you wake him,' said Burgess, quietly retreating.

Sam hesitated, wondering if he should let Jack sleep through the night. He saw the plate with the evidence of a rich dark cake half-eaten and an un-finished cup of tea. Mrs Curzon had told Sam how tired Jack had been on the way back from Arundel and they had agreed to make sure he ate a dinner. When Jack had still not appeared, Sam had decided he must check on him.

Sam placed a hand gently on Jack's shoulder and rocked it back and forth, deciding if he did not wake as a result Sam would withdraw and let him sleep.

The eyes opened as Jack came to, at first not knowing it was Sam waking him, or even where he was. He gripped the hand on his shoulder and Sam winced at the strength in the hand clenching his.

———

'Jack, it's Sam, and you're in the Ship. I'm sorry to wake you suddenly like that. Take a few minutes to pull round. I thought I had better wake you as dinner is ready and you won't want to miss it. It smells wonderful. If you'd prefer I can bring a tray to you here?' asked Sam.

Jack looked at his friend. He sat up and took in the surroundings.

'I wasn't certain where I was for a minute. I've slept despite trying not to. I don't even remember closing my eyes. What time is it, Sam?'

'It's seven o'clock and we have a table for us all together. Rose is joining us. There's no rush and we'll wait for you.'

Two hours, thought Jack. 'I'll just change a shirt and splash some water on my face and then I'll join you,' he said.

*

Burgess had given them a table for four people in a recess by a window. Rose was seated next to Sam and Jack's place was next to Mrs Curzon.

'I'm so sorry I'm late,' Jack said, as he came to their table. 'Rose, this is a treat to see you. I didn't know you were with us tonight.'

'It seemed the best way to get time with you and Sam. Mother's having a gentle evening and was going to eat in her room. Harry asked me to see you both today. Sam knows this as we met this morning but Harry was called to London early because the Shah arrived at Dover before travelling to London. He wanted me to let you know that we still don't know when, if at all, the Shah will come to Brighton or when the visit to Portsmouth is. Harry was to meet Hunt today for orders in London for the days ahead. So, he's unlikely to be back before Friday.' She paused while the food was served.

203

Alice was at Mrs Curzon's side serving a mock turtle soup. Conversation changed to an easy and pleasant topic as Sam asked Jack about where the exhibition was tomorrow. A waitress in black offered a basket of bread and they all took freshly baked rolls. As the waitress moved to Mrs Curzon, Alice was serving Jack the soup.

'At the Royal Pavilion,' explained Jack.

'Oh, that should be very pleasant, especially if the weather is good,' said Sam.

'Yes, I was speaking to ... a local, who said that the roses have only just started to bloom this year.' Jack had just stopped himself mentioning Sergeant Field. 'The weather was too bad at the main time, so he didn't think the floral display is likely to rival previous years. Still it will be a pleasant way to see the world as it pours into Brighton.'

'Would you like company?' asked Rose.

'I would love company,' answered Jack, with a smile.

'It's just that Mother and I have been very hotel bound so far with our activities and I rather think we could do with getting out and away from Lady Bruce's companion. What about you Sam, and Mrs Curzon? Why don't we make up a party?' suggested Rose.

There was a general agreement to go together. Sam moved on to mention to Jack the work that he had done.

'I managed to look at those papers you left,' said Sam.

'Any good?' asked Jack.

'Very clear, very helpful.' Sam nodded. 'I think you're right about access from the sea and needing to close the area around Brunswick Terrace.'

They carried on like this for a while, it was pleasurable and not draining for Jack. He took a moment to look around the table at his friends, valuing the relationships and glad that Sam was back in his life. He wondered how optimistic he should allow himself to be for Sam in the future.

'Did you tell Sam he has an invitation for tea?' Jack asked Mrs Curzon with a wink.

There was a chuckle from her. 'I hadn't yet,' she said.

'Tea?' Sam looked enquiringly from one to the other.

'Yes, we met a family who had been into Brighton and were going back to Worthing. A mother and two eligible daughters. One's a music teacher. I thought you'd like her, she's very bright. It's not far, but your mother got on well with them and before they left they gave her their details to let them know when you all are living in Brighton. They have invited you to tea.'

'How very nice. Did you like them, Mother?' asked Sam, seeing this as being potentially another reason for them to move as people were so friendly.

'Yes, I did, and they had a taking for Jack too,' said Mrs Curzon looking at her neighbour.

'Well, you must come and stay and we'll go across together. Seriously, Jack, I've been thinking how easy it would be for you to come down for a few days every so often and stay and get good fresh air. We will have a big enough place and a good income between us, won't we Mother?' said Sam, smiling. She nodded in response at her son, half smiling at his conviction about the future.

'Have you made some plans?' asked Rose.

'More than plans, Rose,' Sam answered firmly. 'I've details of a house, which we can afford to rent, as my work is to continue. Inspector Hunt confirmed it today in a letter. I made enquiries and this afternoon went to see a house in Kemp Town. It's big enough for us to live in and if my young brothers share two to a room leaves us with another two rooms, if we convert the front room, for paying guests. So a respectable way to supplement our income.'

'And have you seen it, Mrs Curzon?' asked Rose.

'Not yet, later tomorrow Sam has arranged for us to go together,' the lady said.

'If you like it I would do it, and quickly,' said Jack. 'I think it's good for you here.'

'Thank-you, Jack,' Sam beamed at him and grasped his hand, giving it an enthusiastic shake. 'Just the encouragement we need.'

The plates were cleared and the chicken in asparagus sauce was placed in the middle of the table. Rose offered to carve and Burgess gladly agreed as they were busy.

Jack asked Sam where Kemp town was in relation to the railway, thinking of Sam's idea about commuting into London.

'There's to be a branch line. So, I can either walk ten minutes to the Brighton Terminus in one direction or ten minutes in another to the Lewes Road Station. That will do me good. The house is just at the back of St. Peter's Church and there's a park nearby. Perfect,' said Sam, in his matter of fact way.

Jack nodded and glanced at the two women who were involved in apportioning the chicken.

'Any chance we could have a chat about our friend Nathan later?' he asked Sam, quietly.

'Yes,' said Sam. 'I'd wanted to raise it with you but was unsure when to.'

After the pudding, Rose suggested that she return to the Royal and it seemed a perfect opportunity for a walk after dinner and to keep Rose company. Mrs Curzon went to get a shawl, and the other three waited by the front door.

The evening was mild although the sky on the horizon still threatened to drive them indoors. The ladies walked on ahead with Sam and Jack following behind.

'How are your brother's doing while you're away?' asked Jack.

'Well by all accounts. They're to take it in turns to write to Mother each day. Grandmother's with them. They have a lot to do with her and it feels normal for them to have her to stay,' said Sam.

'Will she not miss you all if you come here?' Jack asked.

'I plan to ask her to come. She's a good cook and Mother will find her company helpful especially if we take paying visitors. I think the family being together will help my brothers settle. It will be a better life here for Grandmother with us than staying where she is currently.'

'That's good.' Jack paused deciding on mentioning another case to Sam. 'Has Inspector Hunt said anything about the art theft to you on the day of the Alexandra Palace Fire?'

'No. Should he have done?' asked Sam.

'I just wondered. When I saw the Inspector and Ted before I came down to Brighton we discussed two thefts on the same day as the Alexandra Palace fire. I got a good look at one of the thieves for both pf them. Because the items that were stolen were precious and valuable in the art world they seemed to think there might be a link with the man behind the corruption that Hunt has been tracking. It's thought to be a person of influence. Possibly Mrs Berringer's lover or someone behind him. As that links right back to the Faceless Woman case I wondered if he'd asked you to do any work on researching the thief?'

Sam thought momentarily. 'I can do,' he said. 'I can get access to records if you think it's relevant.'

'I thought you might like to, given the effect that case had on your life.'

There was no hesitation. Sam's face was grim: 'Tell me what you know,' said Sam.

*

'I can't see the harm in you looking into this,' said Jack. 'You've got the sort of mind that will piece things together. Shall we talk about this missing woman without spoiling a jolly evening?' said Jack.

'We should, it's the first time you and I have had chance since we met Nathan Long. It's how to take it forward that escapes me,' said Sam, pocketing the details Jack had given him about the West India Dock theft and a fair description of the blonde man. Sam had decided to speak to Harry as well.

'Well I may have the answer to that,' said Jack. 'Burgess has made some enquiries by all accounts. It seems there may be a bit of a pattern in the area with missing women who have found themselves with child. That's bad enough but there's a question mark as well about the welfare of the children.' Jack paused, trying to work out how to explain without disclosing the link with Field.

'Women from Brighton?' asked Sam, looking horrified. 'How many?'

'I believe it's mainly Hastings and St Leonards rather than Brighton, but I don't know how many. Grace may be the only one from around here. No one appears to have found them. I've a thought developing about an old friend helping. I've a visit to make to an old Parson after Sunday, to see if he can help find out if there's any evidence of the children, such as if they were christened. The births might have been registered as well but we don't want to start making enquiries officially. We only know names of one potential mother and that's Grace. If, as you and I suspect, she was carrying Nathan's child when her parents stopped supporting her, we may be able to trace a christening or a registration of birth. The Parson can do it probably, and quietly. He may have a feel about local midwives and any scheme that there is for poor relief in the area.' Jack didn't want to say any more at present.

'Should we tell Nathan?' asked Sam.

'I'm not sure. Perhaps Burgess would be the best judge as he's the one with the contacts. I could have a word with him in the morning.' Jack looked at Sam who nodded. A few minutes went by as they walked in silence. Then Sam asked,

'Where do you go to see the Parson?'

'He's at a church in Simpson, but its spelt differently to how it's said if you're looking for it,' said Jack. 'On a map its Selmeston. It's not far from here and I'll take the branch line to Lewes. There used to be a cart or something going over to Lewes from the station. I've got to send the Parson a note first to make sure he can see me but I plan to go on Monday.' Jack drew a breath, hoping Sam had enough information to understand they were looking at a potential pattern of disappearances. The last thing he wanted was to tell him how he knew.

*

The following morning Jack came down to breakfast early in order to see Burgess before the day's dealings unfolded. He had been awake since five o'clock, his thoughts on what fate awaited Nathan Long on yet another expedition. He wondered what the odds were in the Navy of surviving so many wars.

Standing on the front steps of the Ship Hotel Jack took in the early morning sky, remembering the heavy clouds of the previous summer and how he had hated the grey blanket that had become the norm on the Weald from January 1872. The sky was brighter here on the coast this year and although the clouds were stacked up like nine pins on the horizon the morning light lifted his spirits. He did not regret his decision to leave last year and join the Met. The growing period to harvest had been the wettest he had known and the summer temperatures down. The farm had been near finished and the Squire had been unsure how it would survive. Jack had seen little future there.

The clock in the hall chimed seven and Burgess appeared in the hall beckoning to Jack to join him in the room behind reception. As he walked down the hall the cooking smells taunted Jack's stomach and it registered that this was the first morning since the Alexandra Palace fire that he had an appetite.

Following Burgess into his office Jack took a chair while Burgess picked his pipe up and knocked the old tobacco into the cold grate.

'I think you'll enjoy some fish caught yesterday with eggs from the poultry Alice keeps. She's doing them now for you. You're up early this morning.' Burgess opened his leather pouch ready to prepare his first pipe of the day and offered tobacco to Jack, who shook his head.

'No thanks, it's not something I could afford and now I've no taste for it,' said Jack.

'Very wise with that cough. The papers are full of the Shah. I suppose it's not surprising as he's such a spectacle. He's being honoured because he's rich. But no matter why he's come he's being shown every civility. There's a lot of articles about Persia opening up to trade, but also the railways too and articles about ritualism and Christianity. I'll leave the papers for you if you like?' Burgess nodded to a few copies on his desk.'

Jack picked up the Daily Telegraph and looked at the front page. 'Thanks but I'm not sure when I'll get time to do more than glance at them,' said Jack. He set it back on the desk.

'I'll get your message across to the Parson at Selmeston. What time are you off today to the Exhibition?' asked Burgess.

'As soon as Sam and Mrs Curzon come down. Sam and I wondered if it was time to get information about the enquiries we're making across to Nathan Long? I suggested you were the best judge of that.'

'No, I'd leave it a while. But he's left by the looks of it. Sergeant Field has put a man on his tail for a couple of days. Our sailor has gone over towards Hastings,' Burgess said, while he pressed the tobacco into his pipe.

'Then given what Field said about that area Nathan must know something,' said Jack.

'Yes, that's what I thought. Anyway, Field will keep an eye on him. Hope you enjoy the morning. I'll follow you out as we've to get luggage up to the railway. Quite a few checking out today.'

Jack did not move. 'You'd think he'd go back to the police. Nathan, I mean, if he's got a lead.'

'Why?' said Burgess. 'They gave him no help. As far as he knows they would turn him away again. No, Jack, this is a man who's fought in wars, and managed to survive. He'll go his own way. And there's no reason why he should ever get in touch with us again, either. We're just people who gave him some time one day.'

Jack nodded. 'Perhaps I could help if Field's man can get in touch with me. I'm going across to Lewes on Monday and then Kewhurst and Bexhill next week, to see old friends.'

'I'll let Field know. When will you be there?' Burgess asked.

'Plan is to see the old Parson in Lewes either on Monday or Tuesday. I also hope to visit an old friend of Father's that was a Coastguard. I've a taking to visit my parents' grave at Bexhill at the same time and will go on from Kewhurst to there. The Coastguard and Father were a similar age and I've been told he's still around. Father and he took me fishing at times.'

'I hope you find him. When did you last see these two men?' asked Burgess.

'At the funerals. I was nine, so they wouldn't know me now.'

Burgess let it pass, but hoped that these old friends of Jack's father would be receptive to the young man turning up. He brought the subject back to Sergeant Field.

I'll pass on your willingness to help Field. What are your movements today and over Saturday and Sunday in case he wants to contact you?' asked Burgess.

'Exhibition today and cricket matches Saturday and Sunday afternoons and resting in the mornings to compensate.'

'That's easy enough to find you then. Field will get a message to you somehow if he wants you. I can't press him to use you, but I imagine he will. Dinner tonight?' Burgess asked.

'Definitely. I'll get into breakfast.' Jack opened the door and Burgess followed him out into the reception area. The barking of a Yorkshire Terrier led Burgess to raise his voice in dealing with a guest who wished to settle her account and start her journey.

The smoked fish and eggs lived up to their promise and in his pocket was a small bag of dried apple slices and nuts that Alice had pressed on him in the dining room. He would enjoy them later.

Jack hesitated in order to avoid a woman with a large hat, and started to negotiate his way towards the front door, stopping briefly to acknowledge a child who held a ball up to him.

Sam and Mrs Curzon were waiting in the lounge and were ready to go once Jack appeared. Jack made an effort not to say anything to Sam about Nathan Long. Sam stopped on the front step of the hotel to briefly check he had his notebook and pencil. Patting his pocket he smiled at Jack and said, 'Old habit, but it helps to jot down the odd note as I go.'

The weather was now becoming more pleasant as the morning advanced and held the promise of a fine day. The exhibitors had come from a wide area. The domes rose skywards and in the approach to the Royal Pavilion Mrs Curzon saw Rose waving to get their attention, while Mrs Phillips chatted to a woman next to her in the queue. Pleasantries were exchanged about the night's sleep, breakfast, and Sam asked if Rose had heard from Harry. She had not but did not expect to. They slowly processed towards the entrance and Sam ran his eye down a programme and started to underline names of exhibitors and where they were from: Salisbury, Guildford, Lewes, and Maidstone.

Once inside Rose raised her eyebrows as she and Jack paused at a stand. Looking around her at the Royal Pavilion she said: 'Doesn't it strike you as strange when you look at this place the way the monarchy has changed?'

Jack glanced at where the two older women of their party were, and was glad to see they were enthusiastically chatting to an exhibitor.

'Of course,' he said. 'But would the Queen have wanted this style? I've wondered how much of the way her Majesty is was due to Prince Albert's influence on a young Queen?'

'A great deal I should think. Have you ever thought what might have happened if she'd gone this way, instead of how she and the Prince Consort lived?' Rose inhaled the scent of a flower that was her namesake.

'I'd not but it's a good question. This place with its domes and minarets are another world from London. Brighton owns it now so we'll see what the town does with it. This sort of exhibition is a good idea, lets people in to see how the Palace was. But London, Rose. There's a conundrum for you. So much poverty and hardship, people dying of infection and suffering, the bad air that we breath down at the Docks. And yet it reels me in like a fish hooked. I know there's been changes and people are eating better, we've clean water in parts but it takes time to get the improvements through to everyone. Things still need to change for the majority in the cities and the longer I see conditions on my beat the more I wonder if the Government realise how close the people could come to taking matters into their own hands for change.' Jack blinked at the sunlight pouring through a gap in an awning behind a stand.

Rose looked at him but before she could respond she had noticed a young, smart, woman making her way through the crowds towards them. The walk had a determined pace and somehow her face was familiar. The woman called to Jack as she grew closer.

'Well, Farm Boy, you're a one.'

Then Rose had it. Mary from the Royal Hotel, dressed for a day out, had seen them and not as constrained as she had been at work had decided to pick up the former acquaintance.

Mary's eyes were brilliant, thought Rose, and they were only for Jack. He turned and for the second time while in Brighton said: '*Mary.*'

Rose smiled at the young woman while giving her an appraising look, finally understanding the pull Harry would have experienced as she took in the figure, hair and eyes. Not Jack, though, she thought. He was interested in finding out how she had settled as he fired one question after another at Mary. Did she like Brighton? Were her employers good? Jack finally remembered his manners and included Rose. She smiled and held out her hand.

Mary hesitated, working out the social behaviour she should follow as a waitress with a guest.

'Well there's no-one to observe is there,' Mary said, as she and Rose shook hands. 'I can say it now, ma'am, congratulations on your betrothal to the Sergeant. These two men quite took me in last December at the Mason's Arms, I can tell you, with their costume and behaviour. I didn't want to offend you by the fact I knew them.'

'You haven't. I'm glad we've been able to meet properly now.' Rose had noted the smile which was all going in Jack's direction from the younger woman and concluded that her own man was safe. She laughed a little too loudly with relief, excused herself and walked back to Mrs Curzon and her own mother, who were still involved in a discussion with a stall holder.

Jack fell into step with Mary and they started to progress around the exhibits. They walked together away from his group, a relaxed manner between them as the pretence he had maintained with Mary in London, had gone.

For her part, Mary had liked Jack's looks last December in London but had dismissed him as someone without a future. The rough clothes he had worn in the bar had shown him up as a country labourer and that was not the life that Mary wanted. Now, she reflected, as she walked and looked at him, knowing what he did and his likely prospects, it was different. He could be everything she had ever wanted.

Jack, for his part was enjoying the vivacious company, lonely as he had been for Harriet. Mary and Jack were the same age and they were drawing glances from other visitors as they laughed together. They moved between the exhibits, exchanging opinions on displays of plants and the scent from the roses, walking at a steady pace. Mary told him about her background and determination not to end up in a London Slum. Another woman, Jack thought, who was changing her future. Like Harriet, the ambition registered with him.

Jack bought a rose for Mary from an exhibitor. It was nothing more than sheer enjoyment on his part of being with someone who knew and accepted who he was. But it registered with her. For him her smile and laughter had brought back his own, and this was noted by more than one person in his party. Sam, looking up from his note-taking, watched the couple for a while and was glad to see Jack's transformation. Rose joined him, having been watching them herself. Sam glanced at her.

'Have you ever met Jack's young lady, Rose?' Sam asked.

'No. Have you?' Rose followed the direction of Sam's eyes.

'No. Charlie Banks and Ted did last December. Thing I remember Charlie saying was she seemed very young, even for her age. Seventeen, I think, at the time. From a large family and her mother was widowed a while ago. I gather there's an older sister in London who helped Harriet get work and acts as a buffer to the hardness of the city. Mother's made a success of a dairy farm so there's an ambition in the girl. Jack's keen from what I remember but I sensed in him he's growing tired of the wait. This woman is a different kettle of fish and knows what she's doing don't you think?' asked Sam.

'Yes, but Jack is completely unaware of anything except enjoying the company of a vivacious woman, Sam. Look at him, I haven't seen him laugh like this for months.' Rose smiled and gave a little wave as Jack looked across at them. He waved back and then gave the roses on the next stand his full attention as Mary pointed a few varieties out to him.

'He's bought her a rose,' said Sam.

'Foolish,' answered Mrs Curzon, who had joined Sam and Rose.

'I think it's innocent, Mother, 'said Sam, turning to her.

'Not to a woman, Sam,' Mrs Curzon said quietly. Her sad tone registered with her son the things she would never forget in her own marriage. He took her hand and put it caringly into the crook of his arm.

'Let's walk, Mother,' Sam suggested.

Jack and Mary's progress around the tent was also noted by a member of another couple who was visiting for the day from London. He and his fiancé had arrived early and were now rearranging chairs for their own group of friends. Constable Arscott Ward, who had played go-between with Jack and Harriet at Christmas, was at the Summer Exhibition with his fiancée, Harriet's sister, Georgina.

As it was cooler away from the exhibits Jack and Mary turned to continue their walk in the open air. Coconut cake was on sale from a stall, for a penny a piece. It was proving very popular and a large queue had formed.

'Let's get some,' Jack suggested and joined the queue to buy two pieces.

'Aren't you the rich man,' said Mary, smiling.

'I'm not paying for my keep at present,' said Jack.

'So, money to burn,' Mary replied. 'What are you doing here, you and Harry Franks?'

Jack's answer was to remember his fruit and nuts put up for him by Alice that morning. He pulled the packet from his pocket and grasped Mary's hand to turn it, palm up, while he poured some of the mix into it. She laughed and responded by popping a piece into his mouth.

'You're not going to tell me, are you?' she said, coming close.

'No,' said Jack, aware suddenly of the scent she wore. He paid for the cake.

Arscott, who had followed Jack and his companion out of the tent in order to greet him, watched the interplay for a few moments. He thought better of his idea of making his presence known and turned back to find Georgina.

'What's wrong?' Georgina asked as he sat down.

Arscott relaxed his expression and gave her his attention. 'Nothing's wrong, just thought I saw someone I knew, but I realised I was mistaken.'

'Always the policeman,' said Georgina, smiling.

'Habits,' he answered. After a few minutes thought he decided he would make himself known to Jack. He asked Georgina, 'Would you like lemonade?'

'I would, thank-you. Where do we get some from?' Georgina turned in her chair to look over her shoulder in case there was a stall that Arscott could see.

'It's outside. I won't be long.' Arscott moved into the fresh air and surveyed the crowd. Each vendor was busy and he calculated how long he had before Georgina would probably come and look for him. It seemed that everyone at the Summer Exhibition had decided to retreat into the open air. Several stalls away from where he was standing he looked across the area. Jack's blonde hair stood out. Arscott moved towards them, assessing the behaviour between Jack and Mary. He thought he would give Jack notice.

'Jack, Jack, fancy seeing you here, small world.' Arscott called as he approached.

Jack looked round as he heard the Devon accent and his face broke into a grin. Arscott noted there was no embarrassment, no attempt to move away from the woman. She was attractive, and about twenty herself, he thought. Jack had the body language of being relaxed and Arscott felt he had jumped to conclusions.

'Harriet with you?' Arscott asked although he knew the answer. Jack shook his head. 'No, she was supposed to come down on Tuesday but I wonder now if she ever got my note. I haven't heard from her. But look at my manners, let me introduce you to Mary....' Jack laughed and said to Mary. 'I don't know your surname.'

'Cunliffe,' said Mary, turning to Arscott with a small nod.

'How do you do. Arscott Ward,' Arscott said.

'This is another policeman,' said Jack quietly, leaning towards Mary.

217

'Here for the same reasons?' Mary asked, looking from one to the other man.

Jack laughed and said to Arscott. 'Mary is a friend from London. She knows Harry Franks as well. Sensible girl changed jobs and came to Brighton and we bumped into each other this morning. Look if you're on your own why don't you join our party?'

'That's kind of you but I'm with friends myself. Just wanted to say hello before I joined the queue for the lemonade. Hope to see you in London soon, Jack and good to know Brighton is helping your health.' Arscott turned to Mary. 'Goodbye Miss Cunliffe. Nice to have met you.'

'And you,' replied Mary. As he strode away she watched Arscott go. Turning back to Jack she asked, 'So your ladylove didn't come?'

'No,' and not to be drawn further Jack extended an arm towards a stall. 'Shall we carry on over there?'

Satisfied of Jack's complete lack of involvement with the young woman Arscott had moved quickly away until he melted into the crowd. He pondered on Mary Cunliffe. Possibly she was in a different position to Jack. A young woman without any involvement of her own. Fine eyes and figure, he thought, and no doubt she will come to the notice of the patrons of Brighton soon. Intelligence in those eyes and clearly will have her own ideas of what she wants for her future.

Arscott turned and watched the two friends move among the stalls. Mary had a vivacity, that Jack would not find in Harriet, he thought. And he doubted that she would easily be put off. He took his place with twenty others for two glasses of lemonade. Now Harriet, Arscott thought, what are you playing at not coming down? And why no message to your young man? Georgina had told him earlier in the summer that Jack was eager to meet their mother. Apparently, Harriet had put him off, despite Georgina giving her a talking to. Harriet, perhaps was playing hot and cold? Arscott was not sure, but knew that a meeting with Mrs Fildew in Honiton had not taken place yet. Was there any reason, Arscott mused as he reached the end of the queue, not to mention having seen Jack here to Georgina? Would it matter if Harriet knew Jack was spending time, although clearly innocently, in a young woman's company? After all, it was a public place, and he was with a party of people. He would mention it to Georgina and leave it with her as to whether or not she told Harriet.

*

Some miles away in London the Shah's impact was being felt. Lord Elcho was on his feet in the House of Commons. The Speaker nodded and called, 'The Honourable MP for Haddingtonshire.'

'Mr Speaker, with regard to the Shah and his visit to Woolwich, many honourable Members would desire to see the great review of Artillery. I wished to know whether a part of the ground might not be reserved for the accommodation of Members?'

Viscount Cardwell was on his feet to respond. Some members wondered why the Secretary of State for War was taking the question. Gladstone, eyes everywhere, noted the comments. Cardwell had started his answer.

'There's no doubt of the interest of honourable Members in the Review. And I emphasise that thirteen or fourteen batteries of the Royal Artillery will take part. But there will be no stands, and space for carriages is very limited. If any Members of the House desire a portion of space and will communicate with me, I will endeavour to secure it for them.

There was a general level of conversation. A few comments reached Cardwell's ears which he chose to ignore.

"The Grand Old Man," Gladstone, moved proceedings towards the course of business for the twentieth of June. The House was due to consider the Rating (Liability and Value) Bill. Gladstone suggested that it be postponed.

'The Government was given to understand that tomorrow evening there was to be an entertainment given by the Lord Mayor in the City. It will be difficult to obtain the necessary attendance of Members for the evening session. I propose, therefore, that at the end of the day session, the House should adjourn until Monday.'

The Alderman's Secretary struggled past several ladies in the Gallery as he moved to leave to get word to the Lord Mayor's office. Once out he raced to the gate where a runner was waiting and handed him a quickly scrawled note.

It read: 'Tomorrow, its tomorrow. It's the twentieth.'

*

There was equal interest in another part of the Palace of Westminster. In the Lords the Peers were jostling for a place at both reviews to be attended by the Shah.

Lord Cranmore and Browne was on his feet.

'Is any provision to be made for the accommodation of carriages of Peers at the reviews at Windsor and Woolwich?'

'Hear, Hear,' echoed around the Lords.

The Marquess of Lansdowne, Under Secretary of State for War, had drawn the short straw for the response. Up he got to answer the question.

'There will be space set apart for the carriages of their Lordships at the Windsor review, and his Royal Highness the Ranger of Windsor Forest, in whose hands the arrangements were, had been pleased to forward tickets for distribution to their Lordships.'

'Quite right,' met his ears. He took a sip of water.

'The Review at Woolwich is less formal in character, and at this point in time I am not aware of any special facilities for Members of either House of Parliament.'

General muttering ensued from members:

'Can we get on?'

'You'd think nothing else was happening.'

'Can we move to the Agricultural Children's Bill? Where their Lordships are parking their carriages is of no interest to me!'

*

Thirteen

While Peers and Members of Parliament had made their dutiful opinions known in the Palace of Westminster Harry Franks overslept. It was understandable that he would. Several drinks and a good meal with Stan, debating the political involvement in the duties of the police and comparing it, potentially, to France in the days of the Terror, Harry and Stan had concluded, if they were not careful, they would end up with a political role. Neither would accept that and the early hours had seen discussions from them both of the possibility of emigrating if their work took a certain direction.

Stan, however, was on duty before eight o'clock despite the late hour that he retired. He received word from Harry by nine o'clock that Harry was late and would go straight to Buckingham Palace. Stan, and the four constables, were hard pressed to make it across the city having hung on for Harry at Shadwell Police Station.

'To hell with it, let's get a cab,' Stan declared and Alf cheered.

The other three Constables looked at each other. It was clear to them that the Sergeant was in no mood for the congested Blackwall Railway. Even in plain clothes that meant one thing. He was likely to overreact in a crowd. Percy, who had worked with Stan the longest of the four men, knew it would fall to him in Harry's absence to keep an eye on the Sergeant.

Stan looked out of the window of the cab as they rolled out from the Police Station yard. As he did most days, he stared past the tortuous lives of the inhabitants of the area, being unable to change them. His was a reactive role.

Stan and his men rode up Sutton Street East on the uneven road and then made a left turn onto the Commercial Road East. Most of the paint on the dwellings had peeled off long ago and the few residents who caught sight of Stan as he leaned against the carriage window noted the Sergeant was about unusual business. The shirt was threadbare in parts and he was not in uniform. Those on the street who knew what this implied muttered remarks to one another as the coach swayed past.

Stan's mood was triggered by the discussion with Harry the previous evening. He thought that he had a few things he would like to say to Tom Hunt about the connection with Gladstone. The Prime Minister was a dogmatic man, un-bending and, in Stan's opinion, likely to drop them in the proverbial.

There was more though. Stan wanted to make the point about the tendency the Prime Minister had to tracking prostitutes and getting them to repent of their ways. This bothered Stan. He was sceptical, he had to admit, of Gladstone's activities. It was rumoured Gladstone scourged himself to avoid temptation. But what added to his dark mood that day was the fact that in all his years of policing he had never met a woman who had chosen that life. He believed in repentance but he would have liked to get the men who had brought these women down. Landlords, fathers, lovers and husbands, definitely the pimps but usually there were others in there first. From the women he had moved on when the trade became too obvious most had been very young when they were put out to work in the trade. This sickened him as many were little older than his daughters. I'd make the men repent, thought Stan.

Another point bothered him. Harry said Hunt had told him there were still two million children without access to a school place since the Education Reform Act. Gladstone had mentioned it for some reason. Harry and Stan had both disliked the fact last night and Stan liked it less in the morning light. They had both gone quiet at first, taking in the impact on the current generation. Stan had to admit that he had hoped for better after the reforms. Then the impact on policing of a lost generation in the burgeoning cities, un-schooled had dawned on them both.

'How long's it going to take then before every child has a school place for an elementary education?' Harry had posed it as a question but Stan's impulsive response was to slam his fist down on the bar.

Stan had thought about what Harry had told him through the early hours and it had influenced his mood as he woke. He regretted having too much to drink. As he was getting older it always stopped him sleeping. Perhaps he had had about four hours but had seemed to wake every hour. By six he had given up the hope of getting another hour and had quietly moved from his wife's side so as not to wake her. She had known he was going though, and had put her hand out to him. His face softened at the memory.

Stan disliked the Prime Minister. He concluded that he disliked Disraeli more. Yes, there were quite a few things he would like to say to Tom Hunt about getting them involved with the Prime Minister in his efforts to unearth corruption. Then he would like to say them to the Prime Minister. He also wanted to tell Gladstone to get on with building the schools. The phrase he had in mind was not overly polite but he might water it down if he got the chance.

But of course he would not say any of this to Gladstone, nor to Hunt, because he was not supposed to know anything. Harry had shared it with him, as he shared everything. The men had the right to know the implications, Harry believed. Stan had cautioned him about telling them, however. It was hard to know how to do it discreetly. He and Harry would protect them as much as they could if something went wrong.

Stan smirked as he thought back to Hunt's meeting with Gladstone, while he sat on his haunches in the passage opposite the Treasury windows, whittling a stick with the knife that he always carried on these duties. Although he had not heard the exchange he had seen that neither cared too much for the other's opinion. Indeed both had eyed the other without much esteem.

'Where will we get provisions, today?' this question was from Henry and it brought Stan out of his reverie.

'You know you're so predictable, Henry,' Percy cut in.

'What do you mean?' Henry frowned.

'It's always the first thing you want to know. Where do we get the food from?' Percy pointed out. The other men grinned at each other.

Stan ran the area from Buckingham Gate to Victoria through his memory. It had changed somewhat from his days around Victoria but he remembered the Baptist Chapel in Princes Row and its soup kitchen.

'If the place I remember is still there we can get some sustenance at midday. After that it will depend how long we're around,' Stan answered.

'What's happening at the Palace anyway?' asked Henry.

'Some shin-dig at half-past two,' said Stan. 'I've no idea yet what the Shah's other movements will be today. Hunt will tell us when we meet him. But loving the general public as we do, lads, we are to mingle around the area of the Palace after we've linked up with Hunt and Harry, and keep our eyes open for any trouble.'

'Where are we meeting Sergeant Franks?' asked Alf.

'Buckingham Palace Mews. Inspector Hunt will be there as well, but not as you know and love him. He'll be dressed in the livery of the Queen, as a rider,' explained Stan.

'How come?' asked Percy.

'Background and character. Something none of us have,' Stan smirked, and the men laughed. Except for Arthur. Stan glanced across at him and it registered that Arthur had been unusually quiet that morning. Heart sick, Stan would call it from the expression in the eyes. What was going on there?

He logged it away as a potential problem if the man did not engage with the team today and made a decision to get Arthur on his own later.

'Seriously Stan, how come Tom Hunt's involved? He's usually desk bound.' Henry again.

'Not always. He's involved because he was asked. He grew up on the Windsor Royal Estate, didn't he? His father was the Queen's Groom so Hunt was being prepared to follow in his father's footsteps. He's riding to keep an eye on the royals, step in if need be as he'll be armed. Main order is to protect the Prince of Wales.'

'Why?' asked Henry, incredulous.

'Because it gives the Queen comfort to know Hunt's there. She's known him since he was a child,' said Stan.

'Blimey, I didn't know anything like that,' said Percy.

'Right, well now you do. Keep it to yourselves and give the man some respect when he briefs us. No laughing at the way he'll be dressed.' Stan sat back and closed his eyes. A sardonic smile played about the corners of his mouth. He thought he could safely bet that Gladstone didn't know it either. Better watch your step with Inspector Tom Hunt, Mr Prime Minister, Stan thought.

The cab pulled past Victoria Station and turned into Buckingham Palace Road. It drew to a halt outside the Royal Mews and Stan spotted a disreputable character by a lamp post. The man wore a stained waistcoat. He grinned at Harry's alter ego and paid the cabbie as the other men got down.

Stan looked at the crowds that had spread into Buckingham Palace Road already. He didn't like it. If this kept building in numbers there would be thousands on the street by midday. If something went wrong....

Uniformed officers were already in evidence attempting to keep the crowds in lines, especially near the gates of the Palace. The Shah had apparently already been out from what he could hear from a couple of the men.

'Where did you pick up the cab?' called Harry, as the team walked towards him.

'Shadwell,' said Percy, watching Harry flinch at the cost. 'Stan's got one of his moods on,' Percy added as a way of explanation.

Harry acknowledged the fact with raised eyebrows. He knew that mood and had seen it develop last night as they had chewed the fat about Gladstone. He waited for Stan to catch up with the others but the man had fallen into step with Arthur.

'You look tired, bad night?' Stan asked.

'Yes, our youngest isn't well. It's been like this for days now and she's not picking up,' replied Arthur.

'We'll see what we can do. I'm sure Ann Black would have a look at her. Get her up there today.'

'It's not that easy. We've others, Stan, and no one at home for them if Elisabeth isn't there when they finish school,' Arthur said.

'They have got school places then? That's good.' The effect on Stan of his discussion with Harry last night and the inadequate facilities for children now helped him decide.

'Right then you'd better get off and take the child yourself, hadn't you,' Stan quickened his pace to catch up with the other three. Arthur had stopped in his tracks with the shock but then ran after him.

'But, Sergeant......'

'Don't argue with me, it's an order. We don't need you until half past two. Get back home now and take her across to the station at Leman Street, as that's Ann Black's base before twelve noon with Doctor Brown away. When you've seen her and got the child back home, come back to the Palace and we'll be in the crowd. If you make it before one o'clock come to the Baptist Chapel in Princes Row for a bowl of soup.'

Stan walked after the others and Arthur stood, watching him go. As Stan put distance between them Arthur shouted, 'Thank-you, Stan,' and melted into the crowd in the opposite direction.

'Where's Arthur off to?' asked Percy, as Stan caught up with them.

'Special duty,' said Stan.

———

Harry Franks gave Stan a look. Stan generally ignored such looks from Harry and this was no exception. Harry sighed and glanced at the sky and decided the afternoon was likely to be miserable, especially if a breeze got up. He heard his name called and realised that Tom Hunt was walking towards them from the Royal Mews, having slipped out to meet them.

Hunt half expected to get a ribbing, given his dress. Walking up to the group the humour they generally expressed was absent and Percy just stopped himself saluting. Hunt assessed them trying to work out what was wrong with them.

'Had a good morning?' he asked.

There was a general response that they had, things had gone well with the journey across, they were ready for orders. Hunt looked at them warily.

'Aren't you one man short?'

''Oh ... he'll be back before half past two. A special duty came up apparently,' Harry responded, staring at Stan.

'That's right,' said Stan.

'Will he find you?' asked Hunt.

'Arthur's a cunning bastard, sir, he'd find a forged bank note in Threadneedle Street if he had to,' explained Percy with a grin.

'Good to work with you, sir,' said Alf, politely, touching his forehead with a finger. The others concurred.

Hunt looked round the five men expecting a joke, but they actually looked as if they were seriously pleased.

'It's good to be working with you men as well,' said Hunt.

Harry peered round at his team wondering what was wrong with them. Then a thought occurred to him. What had Stan done to them?

There was a moment's silence before Hunt said, 'The news I've had today about the Shah's movements are that he's going out earlier than we thought. At one o'clock There will be a group of them leaving the Palace, three carriages with the Shah's people and the Queen's. The crowds won't go as they know he's coming back for the Diplomatic reception later. Harry, regarding Brighton, we know he will go to Portsmouth on Monday. He's sailing there apparently for a naval review and I would expect if Brighton is to come up for a visit it's likely to be on the way back.'

'We won't get our lunch then,' said Henry.

'We'll go at twelve instead,' Stan muttered.

'Right,' said Harry, after staring at Henry and Stan. He turned back to Hunt. 'I'll get back to Brighton tonight then and see what Sam and Jack have come up with between them. You're going to be busy Inspector by the looks of it today.'

' Yes a lot of back and forwarding for me. The Shah will be out tonight, so we need the rest of you on the street quite late I'm afraid. I'll be at the Duchess of Sutherland's ball myself and then as escort back,' Hunt explained.

'Will you get to do a bit of dancing, Sir?' asked Henry.

Hunt glanced round at the men again, trying to read them. Stan spat to the side. Henry took the hint from his Sergeant.

Hunt smiled knowing Stan had methods of control with this team. He glanced at Harry who was also looking round at the men and Hunt knew he was also trying to work out what was going on. Whatever concern Stan had had for him had been explained in some way that would have registered with the team. Harry was clearly as much in the dark as he was. Hunt smiled and the men visibly relaxed.

'I'll be a wall-flower in the ball room.' Hunt said.

'Full evening dress, sir?' asked Alf.

'Queen's livery, holding a tray,' Hunt smiled at him.

'Hope you get to sample what's on it, sir. I mean it's a long day and a man needs to keep his strength up,' said Henry.

'They generally look after me. I'll look for you all in the crowd later,' Hunt said.

The men paused for a few moments and a couple of them nodded. Henry couldn't help himself.

'You've done this sort of thing before then, sir?'

Hunt nodded, but Henry had not finished:

'The Prince will be safe with you there,' Henry said, firmly.

Hunt's eyes narrowed and he looked at Harry. No, there was no recognition there of what was going on. Perhaps it was a genuine coincidence and Henry really did think the Prince of Wales was safer as the Inspector was there.

'I mean, sir,' continued Henry, 'as you're one of us that you'll do a proper job.'

*

At one o'clock that afternoon the Shah's party drove out with the Queen's Equerry, the Queen's Groom and the Lord-in-Waiting, in three plain town carriages. Tom Hunt was with the second carriage and he could see Stan by the gates. Good man, thought Hunt, positions himself well every-time although he's a bit unpredictable.

The Shah's visit to Marlborough House, the Prince and Princess of Wales home was first. After that it was onto Clarence House to visit the Duke of Edinburgh, followed by Kensington Palace for the Duke of Teck and finally to Gloucester House to see the Duke of Cambridge. Formalities over, the Shah returned to Buckingham Palace in time for half-past two and the diplomatic and official reception began with members of the Royal Family and principal members of both the English and Persian Courts meeting each other.

At three o'clock the Queen's Ministers arrived at the Palace and were presented to the Shah in a record time of ten minutes. Tom Hunt breathed a sigh of relief and went to put his feet up to get some sleep.

*

In Windsor, Queen Victoria considered herself well out of it all as she drove out in a carriage to survey the Great Park. The issue for her was where should she witness the Windsor military review on Tuesday? All those people and she supposed she would have to meet the Shah? Apparently, he'd had a whole sheep prepared last night for his entourage and they had sat around picking at it all evening. She made a mental note to speak to Mr Gladstone about having the carpets replaced at Buckingham Palace.

All the arrangements had started in April. She remembered clearly seeing Mr Gladstone and talking, amongst other things, about the details of the Shah's visit. She had agreed to entertain him in the Oak Room for luncheon, give him the Garter and Diamond Star and Badge, providing Arthur and Leopold helped her put it on. Gladstone had said she was to receive two orders from the Shah. It was not as though one needed anymore, thought the Queen. Mr Gladstone had said it was important as the Sovereign's order had never been given to a woman before.

'Where's it worn?' the Queen had asked.

'Around the neck,' Gladstone replied. 'The second order has been created especially for ladies and is worn across the shoulder.'

'Well Louise can help me with that. I don't want the Shah knocking my cap off.'

*

In the evening the Shah's party left Buckingham Palace to dine with the Prince and Princess of Wales at Marlborough House and from there he went on to attend the Duchess of Sutherland's Ball at Stafford House. He had met the cheers of the crowds that afternoon with the same kind of military salute used by the Duke of Wellington. The warm welcome from the crowd made up for the perverse weather.

In all of this, back and forth went Tom Hunt, charged with his mission from a lady who had always taken an interest in him. Stan watched Hunt's top hat, visible above the crowd, moving up and down as he rode on one of a carriage pair of greys.

The Prince of Wales had an intense dislike of the Inspector. Tom made sure he was out of his view but the Prince was well within Hunt's. He was armed and ready to protect the Prince for the sake of the mother. As Stan said, in a tone his men never questioned, and protect him he would.

Stafford House was a grand affair that evening with the great and the good gathered to honour the Shah's visit. Quite a shin-dig, thought Hunt, as he stood by a pillar with a tray in one hand, a gun in an inner pocket and the Prince of Wales in clear view.

Lady Anne Hay-Mackenzie, Duchess of Sutherland, had done the occasion proud. No doubt she would take a dim view of an armed policeman posing as a servant, even if he was there at the Queen's request. A journalist sketch artist on Hunt's right worked hard to capture the occasion for the London Illustrated News. Hunt asked him not to include him and the man turned to face a slightly different angle. Hunt offered him the tray and the man gladly took some of the delicacies.

Hunt, for his part, had an excellent view of the proceedings. Standing half-way up the grand staircase the Shah received those presented to him, jewels glittering. An array of British aristocracy lined the stairs, and the lights blazed. Evening gowns rustled and shoulders glistened as wealth and beauty was displayed.

It had been some time since Hunt had done this sort of thing. In fact the last time was while still a Sergeant and with Matthew Doyle. He thought with sadness of what Matthew had become, now in Canada trying to forge a new life for the sake of his tiny daughter Sarah, following the suicide of his wife Emily.

Hunt had written, of course, but there had been no response. A broken man he had heard, ruined by her involvement in the attempted murder of the Diplomat's wife and also of Sam Curzon. There was talk that Matthew had changed his name. If that was the case Hunt was unlikely to hear from him.

Sam, Hunt could help but unless Matthew responded …. But he must shake off the ghosts and remain fixed on the Queen's request that he protect the heir to the throne.

Standing as he was on the periphery Hunt watched the Prince and Princess of Wales. She, brilliant at twenty-eight and long-suffering, no doubt facing a life-time of infidelity with this future monarch. May the Queen live long, Hunt thought, and may she surface soon from her extended sorrow. It always struck him as odd that the Prince did not bother to read, but seemed only capable of socialising. And on that subject Hunt had been put in a funny position on the last time he had visited his own mother at Windsor.

Hunt's mother had remained in a cottage after her husband's death on the Windsor estate. Her garden was visible from a particular window of the castle and for some years it had seemed to give the Queen comfort to see the other widow of Windsor tending her garden. Hunt had been called in to see Her Majesty after working in his mother's garden on a visit.

Tom Hunt had once been destined to take his father's position, only as a young man he had disappeared one day and joined the police.

Mr Hunt senior had driven the Queen out through Windsor Great Park on the occasions of the Royal Family's visits. His father had claimed that the Queen was a past master in using clothes to promote herself and was obsessed with the image she could portray with them.

He told Tom of the time in Scotland in 1842 when everyone else wore tartan and the Queen, who had been in tartan all day, chose that evening to appear in pink. Everyone else had been her backdrop and she was the one who stood out.

There had also been the story of the Royals at Princess Vicky's christening. The Queen had stage-managed her family and friends to all dress in a uniform fashion, ladies in silver, gold and white and men in uniform. Hunt senior had told his son that she micro-managed the dress of her family to win the British people over after the excesses of George IV.

His father had been trusted and he heard many a discussion. Thinking that his son would enter the service of the Queen he had told him of some of them so that he was prepared. As a result Hunt did not think the portrayal of the grieving widow was solely due to despair.

His father had told him of a letter the Queen had sent to her eldest son the Prince of Wales about her belief that dress was the one outward sign that people judge the inward state of mind. The Prince had been told to avoid "slang," or casual dress, as it would be an affront against decency. If that was right, Tom Hunt thought, then the assumption and prolongation of mourning dress was deliberate and she was far from being the disconnected monarch everyone assumed that she was. His father too, had had no doubt that she understood the power of the press with their expanding numbers of readers and managed closely the way she would be viewed by the people through the newspaper reports and development of photography.

After her bereavement Mr Hunt senior had continued to drive the Queen, although the visits had grown less frequent to Windsor. But he had listened to the tears and the reminiscences of the royal widow.

So, on the day he was summoned to see Queen Victoria he had found her in something of a reverie about Prince Albert. He was convinced that Her Majesty had mistaken him for his father, long dead. It was as if she was talking to him instead of to Tom. She had commented that she had never understood how the Prince of Wales, with such a father, could be so loth to read. Tom Hunt found himself in the embarrassing position of being on the receiving end of a confidence.

'Newspapers and rarely a novel. I've tried endlessly and boldly to point him to intellectual activities but with less and less success. Not like your boy Tom. He devours the books, doesn't he. Mr Gladstone spoke to me about urging the Prince to read. I said it was all well and good for him to suggest this but I have *tried*. Go and talk to him, I said, go to Sandringham and talk to him. He did but neither of them faced the real issue of what the Prince should do to occupy himself. You know we can do without another George IV,' she said emphatically.

Hunt had stood quietly staring at the wall, briefly glancing at Her Majesty when she shared this private detail about her son and heir. She had walked to the window afterwards and called him across the room to join her. He had done so and she had returned to the present, realising that she may have said too much.

'Your father was always so discreet,' she had said. 'I hope it's a family trait. We get to know each other over many years. Quite a curious set of friendships that we have. I value your help because you remember.... you know. Prince Albert was always so interested in all you children.' The control was returning. 'How is your family?'

They were back on more formal grounds now.

'Well, thank-you, Ma'am,' Hunt had said. He took the risk of adding, 'We were all grateful for the Prince Consort's concern.'

A small nod of acknowledgement and a look of satisfaction in the widow's eyes and then another question.

'And your work? Do you see improvement in London?'

'Demanding,' said Hunt to her first question. 'Some improvement, Ma'am, but slow. Conditions don't create much hope for many.'

'I understand there are a great many bills going through to make things better. They will surely help.'

Gladstone in his weekly briefings, thought Hunt.

'Yes Ma'am,' said Hunt. 'Eventually, but I fear for many it will not come soon enough. There are too many in a sorry plight.'

'When do you come again?' the Queen had asked. Hunt explained that he would try and come in a month. She had looked shocked and wheeled round on him.

'*A month.* That is too long for a mother alone. Badly done, Tom.'

Hunt repressed a smile at the reproof, remembering the similar situation when he refused to take his father's position. There had been the use of his first name as if he was still a small child. The children from the Great Windsor estate had given recitations to the Queen and Prince Consort at times. The Prince had told the young Tom Hunt always to look each member of his audience in the eye. It had been good advice for his current work and, feeling he had the Prince Consort's permission to face down the Monarch, he did it now. Meeting her eyes he said:

'I agree, Ma'am. It would be much better if Mother were to move and live with us, but she won't leave.'

'Of course not, we are a comfort to each other. We share much the same sorrow. And Windsor is her home. No you must try harder,' and with a flutter of her hand she dismissed him. Hunt had made it as far as the door, first five steps backwards, of course, reflecting how different his mother's life was as a widow to the Queen. He had left his mother blackening the kitchen grate as he came up to the Castle. As the door was opened for him the Queen half-turned and said, 'Come and see me when you next visit. I'll know you're here, I can see the garden.'

'Yes, Ma'am.' The Tyranny of old age? Hunt had thought. Or was it just of monarchy?

*

For their part after the meeting with Hunt, Harry, Stan and the team, mixed with, and were jostled by, the crowd in the narrow spaces available to them. At twelve, Stan had proved true to his word and taken the team to Princes Row. They had enjoyed their soup and a chunk of bread from the Baptist Chapel, flavoured with an evangelical theme. But the men never minded saying grace, or someone offering to pray for them. The people at the Chapel worked hard, having shunned drinking and most of the other activities that went along with it. Their time was spent at work or at the Chapel and many of them were doing well as a result. These people were not going to give Stan a problem.

Arthur had returned by two o'clock and found Stan and Percy outside the Palace by the Gates. Alf and Henry were in the Mall and Stan sent Arthur to join Harry by the post office on the corner of Buckingham Gate. No word had passed between them about the child but Arthur looked relaxed and had given Stan a thumb's up. A barely perceptible smile was witnessed on the Sergeant's face but Percy saw it. Arthur's return appeared to have the desired effect on Stan. He was positively euphoric with a member of the public who had taken his life in his hands when he bumped into the Sergeant.

By ten o'clock that night, a Detective Sergeant in a stained waistcoat made his weary way to catch a train to Brighton from London Bridge. He collected his bag from the luggage store and sent a telegram to the woman he loved. This should ensure that she would wait for him in the lounge of the Royal, regardless of how late he arrived. He had need of something fine after the last two days and Rose at the Royal was the balm the drained Detective Sergeant from Shadwell needed.

With Harry gone Stan and the other men hung around until the crowds dispersed and then travelled back together in the early hours of the morning. Stan had dug deep into his own pocket and paid for another cab to get them back to the Commercial Road East.

At the corner of Dean Street the cab stopped and the four constables climbed down. A cool night, the sort that had can come still in June. Between Christ Church and the Primitive Methodist Chapel four tired but jovial men bid each other and their Sergeant, goodnight. From there they all went their separate ways and Stan settled an extra coin with the Cabbie to turn towards Shadwell New Basin, calling goodnight to his men.

Familiar with the area from walking their beats each man made his way home. Stan told the Cabbie to turn for the Police Station once they were in Back Lane. The cab dropped him in David Lane, between the Sailor's Rest and the Police Station. No point in disturbing the family at this unearthly hour, he thought. He stared out of the window at the women on the street who were more sinned against than sinning. No sign of Gladstone, he thought, with a chuckle.

'We're here,' called the Cabbie.

'Thank-you,' answered Stan, swinging the door of the cab wide open. He'd sleep at the station for what was left of the hours of darkness.

*

Jack had had an entertaining morning. For Mary as they had walked between the exhibits of the Royal Pavilion throughout the morning everything seemed just as she would want it to be. The conversation between herself and Jack had flowed easily without any awkward silences. At times Jack had seemed pre-occupied with who was around but she put that down to the work he had to do.

By midday Jack pulled out his watch to check the time and gave a rueful smile.

'I'm afraid I will have to neglact you and go. I'm under orders to rest in the afternoons.'

'Why, what's wrong?' asked Mary, gently.

───

238

'Oh, nothing serious, just the effects of the smoke from the Alexandra Palace fire. Doctor said I was to spend three weeks here and I could do some work if I rested every afternoon. I didn't yesterday and kept going too long and was in a rare state by late on. Mustn't make the same mistake.'

'Well I should be going soon as well as I must be back at the Royal for the Afternoon Tea. It was a half day for me, you see. We could walk together to the front?' Mary paused, and drew a breath, wondering if she should risk the idea that had come to her.

'We could walk to the Marine Parade together certainly but then you go right and I will go left,' said Jack.

'Where is it that you're staying?' asked Mary.

'The Ship Hotel,' said Jack. He glanced back towards the last area that he had seen Sam. 'I must just let my friend know where I'm going. If you wait here I'll find you again?'

Jack disappeared but was soon back. He had found Sam and mentioned he was leaving to return to the Ship for the afternoon. The two men agreed to meet for dinner later and compare notes.

Jack and Mary set off from the Royal Pavilion, past Castle Square and the Old Steine. Rose and her mother watched them leave the grounds.

'They're both going in the same direction,' said Mrs Phillips, raising an eyebrow.

'I think, Mother, we should go and get a cup of tea. They're not likely to meet again, are they, with her work pattern and Jack is only here for another few weeks.'

Rose linked arms with Mrs Phillips and they walked towards a tea tent. 'Does Jack ever mention his young lady to you?' she asked.

'Not to me,' said Mrs Phillips. 'There was a time when he always seemed to mention her, when he first came to live with us, but not in recent months now I come to think of it.'

As Jack and Mary reached the Marine Parade there was a natural comfortable quietness between them. Mary broke it as they reached the point for her to walk in the direction of the Royal Hotel.

'I expect you may come for tea again before you return to London?' said Mary.

'I've no idea. Tomorrow and Sunday I'm playing in cricket matches,' Jack said.

'Here? Who for?'

Jack hesitated and Mary understood and nodded.

'Of course, it's part of the work you're here for. You can't tell me. How strange an activity for a Policeman, though?' Mary caught a ribbon that blew across her face and it mingled with a tendril of her hair that had come loose in the wind.

'Not really, if you're checking who's around a public game is a good way to do it,' Jack explained. He leaned against a railing and looked down to the shoreline on the right towards the fish market, straining to search amongst the boats for the fisherman who had taken him and Mrs Curzon out the other day. He could make out the boat but it was hauled up onto the beach and unattended. A thought had occurred to Jack that if the fisherman was there he could make an arrangement with the man to sail to Kewhurst on Tuesday next week.

'Well, I must go,' said Mary. 'No further for us both so I'm not seen with you by anyone at the Royal.'

Jack straightened up and hesitated. 'Why does it matter? I'm not a guest there. Are they that strict?'

Mary moistened her lips. 'Yes, with the women they are. And you have been a guest and you're very memorable with that colour hair you have.' She walked past him giving a small wave and then called experimentally, 'I may come to see the cricket tomorrow.'

'That would be grand,' Jack called back, with a smile. And then Mary turned and walked on. She had all the encouragement she needed at this point. She was accepted as a friend. How to move the relationship on from this point would take some thought.

*

———

Fourteen

Jack had looked the part, in his cricket whites, of that he was sure. He knew it was his accent, that broad and drawling way of speaking he had on some words that had shown he was of the labouring class in Sussex. Still the point of the afternoon match for him was to survey the crowd.

The men of the Sussex rifles were locals as well, except there were different definitions of "local" for officers. Born into Sussex landed families they had been educated to have the accent accepted at court. They were all from well-heeled backgrounds, knew more about handling a horse than he ever would but would never groom one, or bale the hay for their animal's feed. Hunt should not have sent him he was sure. It was obvious he could not be Captain Knox's cousin. The story in the changing room was that he was from the wrong side of the blanket and Jack grimaced at the thought. Captain Knox would not thank Inspector Tom Hunt for that story.

He was tolerated in the changing room, but several of the men moved their things away from his. There had been a ripple of muted laughter when he had been introduced. A few caustic comments under a breath, still audible, had been made. If he was to survive the afternoon something had to overcome the class game these men were playing. He pushed his bag under a bench and picked up a ball and prayed he would not disintegrate into a spasm of coughing. He knew he was about to disobey Doctor Brown and Tom Hunt but as a fast bowler, renowned in Battle for getting the most swing and bounce with a new ball, he walked out to the practice net. If this paid off they would not be bothered about his background.

Jack bowled the kind of action that would make it hard to bat without an error. He collected the ball and looked around as he walked back to go again.

It had been noticed.

Three of the team's players were watching him. He delivered another of the most difficult balls to hit. The pitch should be moist after a poor spring and early summer. That would help. He hoped more were now paying attention.

Five watching him now. Two of them having a discussion. One of them was the Captain of the team. Jack controlled the desire to smile.

'Look, Sargent, isn't it?' A voice called to him from behind the net. Jack stopped his action and turned, looking friendly.

'Yes,' he answered.

It was the Captain of the Sussex Rifles cricket team. He had been introduced as the Honourable Richard something or other and a Lieutenant. Jack had not caught the full name as the introduction had been swallowed in one of those accents he generally did not mix with.

'Brighton's into bat first and they're under pressure. We need to bowl them out and finish the game. I know you're down to field but we could do with you as a bowler. What do you say?'

'Of course,' Jack coughed but it was more because of a restriction in the throat.

'Get some tea before we start.' The Captain waved a hand towards the left and Jack looked across to the ladies behind a table. He walked over and collected hot, sweet, tea and wondered where Sergeant Field's man would be. Having just negotiated his way into being accepted by the sons of the landed gentry in the 6th Sussex Rifles to bowl he had effectively made it more difficult for contact to be made. Standing with a cup of tea would make it easier if the man was watching out for him. Jack turned a slow circle, taking his time while he sipped the tea, making sure anyone looking for him in the County Ground in Eaton Road would see him.

'Jack,' called a familiar voice. It was Rose. Surprised and a little irritated as this would deter an approach, he strained his eyes and put his hand over his eyebrows to provide a shadow from the sun so that he could see her better.

'Rose,' he responded, and made an effort to wave a hand. Carrying the cup and saucer carefully to stop the tea from spilling he walked across to her.

'Nice of you to come and cheer me on,' said Jack.

'I have a friend of yours with me, which is how she is describing herself. Mary from the Royal. She mentioned that she was coming and wondered if I was. I thought I should after such an approach. Mother's here as well. Was that you demolishing the net a few moments ago?' asked Rose.

'Yes, and I'll do some bowling later. It's a long story but at least the team will accept me and not question how I could be a rich man's cousin. Problem is it will make it harder to focus on the crowd. Can you keep an eye open as well, as you're here?'

'Yes, I'll do some sketching so anyone interesting gets a record on paper,' said Rose.

'Thank-you. Nice you've made a friend of Mary,' said Jack. Rose looked at him with raised eyebrows.

'I think it's you that's the friend, Jack. I'm just keeping things respectable,' said Rose.

'I hope you don't mean anything,' Jack said flatly. 'There's nothing like that, just a lonely girl in a strange town with working hours that don't mean she can make too many friends I expect. Where is Mary, anyway?' Jack asked, looking around the crowd that were taking their seats.

'I'm sorry, you'll have to forgive me. She was chatting to another employee from the Royal. You'll have a following with quite a few of the ladies if you're a bowler. Shame Harriet can't see you,' said Mary.

Jack laughed and took a swig of his tea. He nodded at the tea table. 'I should get going and take this back and join the men. Did Harry get back alright last night?'

'Yes, terribly late and very tired. I waited for him 'til one o'clock this morning. The word from Inspector Hunt was that if the Shah is coming to Brighton it is likely to be Monday afternoon after a naval review at Portsmouth. Earlier than we thought. Harry will join you and Sam for dinner tonight. He spent this morning going over the background from you both. I've encouraged him to go and have a sleep this afternoon,' said Rose.

'Ah, the shape of things to come, Rose, as a policeman's wife. You'll not feel like running your café if you're waiting up for Harry,' said Jack.

'It's important work he does, Jack. I'm starting to realise how keeping him well and happy will affect his work. He's starting to tell me things as well, as if he values my perspective. He's treating me more like a partner and values my thoughts. I think he's had years of being very alone in the work. We sat up in the lounge until two o'clock this morning, with hot chocolate and delicious little cakes. We laughed together but there was a hint of exhaustion and sadness about him of the things he had seen and heard over the last two days.' Rose explained.

'So, Ted will lose his eyes and ears at the docks after all. And I will starve. Who will feed me now, Rose?' Jack asked with something of a poignant tone.

'Oh, you'd better come and be our lodger, Jack. Mother's given in and is coming to have a look at where Harry's new house is when we get back to London. You know there's a room for you. So, yes there will be a few changes. I think Mother and Mrs Curzon will see a bit of each other as well, once Sam moves the family to Brighton. Mother and she have been making plans to make the furnishings for a house for Sam and the boys. Curtains, that sort of thing. A little upholstery. It's good a friendship has come out of this work for the two mothers,' Rose said.

'Sounds like a done deal. I'm glad it's so clear for you what you want. I'll find you at tea. I must re-join the team. Look for me on the pitch,' said Jack.

'You are the reason we're here. That and keeping an eye on your friend Mary when she's with you, for Harriet's sake,' said Rose, tartly.

Jack stood his ground: 'Rose, we should change the subject. You know Harriet and I are to be married. Why do you think I would look at another girl? I'm fixed on wedding Harriet.'

'Yes.' Rose bit her lip. 'Frankly, I thought there was rather a gap in time developing in you seeing each other. Forgive me, I was obviously wrong to say anything. A word of advice though, you will be thought of as available as Harriet isn't here. You're not engaged Jack, you know that. You cannot say that you are. You have an understanding.' Rose looked across at a female figure walking towards them. 'Here's Mary now.' Rose smiled a welcome and Mary held out her hand to shake Jack's.

Jack had a pleasant sense of a friend being present. A persistent bee hovered around Mary's hair. Jack wafted it away, making contact with the back of his hand against a stray curl. She moved with a little jump and he laughed at the way she had reacted. Mary's laugh joined his.

'How is that cough, today?' she enquired.

'It's fine. How was your shift?' asked Jack.

'Long and boring,' said Mary.

How natural they are, thought Rose. 'Jack you must go or you'll miss the team coming out. Give me your cup,' she held out her hand and he passed the cup and saucer to her and nodded. 'Before you go, good luck.'

'Thanks. I'll see you both later,' said Jack and then strode off with a backward wave of his hand.

'Come Mary, you and I have to lead the clapping,' Rose said.

'Where are we sitting?' asked Mary. Rose pointed over to the side where her mother was keeping three seats. Together she and Mary walked towards Mrs Phillips. Mary glanced back a few times to see where Jack was being positioned.

Rose considered the role of obstructing the development of any relationship that could form between Jack and this woman more out of respect for Harriet Fildew. She looked at Mary to see what effect contact with Jack had had. She realised that the ember had already ignited, on the woman's part at least. Now she might need to be able to contrive arrangements to stop a fire from blazing.

Jack focused on his position with the Sussex Rifles team ready to walk onto the field. He looked at the sky, weighing up how the sun would affect his view. After the strange conversation with Rose he thought it a shame that Harriet could not enjoy the afternoon with him. It was an activity he had always loved and he had been on and off a cricket pitch every season in Battle since he had joined the Squire's labourers. Last year had been different as play had generally been rained off due to the poor growing to harvest period of May to September. The usual warmth of the summer had not been evident either but village cricketers had still turned out with that element of optimism as persistent as was the guaranteed changeability of the weather.

Jack scanned the men in the team. They were well-schooled in the game. The Squire's team had had skills and knowledge but the village against village cricket in those endless summer days were no comparison to the Sussex Rifle players. The only difference in enthusiasm, Jack thought, as he joined them to walk out onto the pitch, was that these sons of the well-heeled would have played the best from their schools and been coached, whereas he had relied on the Squire to explain the tactics to him. It had been an activity for men and had certainly cut across the class divide once a skill had developed in a player. That had been his experience both then and now.

Jack took his position as Long-off until they called him to come and bowl. The Lieutenant had opened and in the interim of a run being scored Jack took time to glance around at the crowd.

'Better keep your eyes on the ball, or you'll not catch them out,' said a burly man in the crowd.

'It's not likely to come my way,' Jack said with a grin.

'You should see Hastings play,' the man replied.

'Why, are they good?'

'The best. Better than either of these two teams, although as a Brighton man I shouldn't say so. I'll be there on Tuesday, and have a spare ticket. Perhaps you'd like it?' The man was reaching into the inner pocket of his jacket and pulled out an envelope which he held out to Jack.

'That's kind, but ....'Jack stopped as the eyes had changed expression. Jack looked at the envelope and on it read P.C Sargent. This was Field's man. He took the envelope and pocketed it.

'I'll look later at it. What time is the match?'

'Two o'clock. The location's on the ticket. See you at the tea stand before the match,' the man was already returning to his seat.

'Many thanks,' Jack called after him. He focused on the game but he had been correct. The ball would not come his way but he had made contact with Field's man anyway and would learn what they had discovered about Nathan Lane's movements on Tuesday afternoon. He was now doubly determined to get to Kewhurst, find the Coastguard and from there he could move up the railway line from Bexhill to Hastings and meet Field's man before the match at two o'clock. It was convenient that the location tied in.

Monday would be a different kettle of fish though. Jack thought of the note he had already sent to the Parson. He would have to delay the visit to later in the week. If the Shah came to Brighton there would be a part for him to play in the surveillance and he must leave Monday free.

Ensign Williams was running towards him. As he approached Jack he called to him, 'The Captain wants you in Slip to catch balls that just edge off the bat.'

'Which one?' called Jack starting to walk after him.

'He'll tell you. He just wants you to take catches, 'Williams called back. 'Get a move on, man.'

Jack wondered if he could risk a jog without collapsing into coughing. He started to move and felt the stiffness of over a week without anything other than walking. As he approached the Captain the man pointed to the off-side of the wicket keeper. Jack coughed and felt flem in his mouth. He pulled out his handkerchief and spat into it. The colour at least was no longer black. He joined another slip, smiled and nodded at the man, and hoped for little movement his way. The Captain obviously intended to make a spinning delivery to catch the outside edge of the bat. Five minutes went by with nothing his way and then it was made and Jack dived forward and made the catch. He was mobbed by men who had earlier ignored him.

Jack stood up feeling waves of sickness, stumbled and steadied himself. He had to get a grip of himself. He must not shake. Jack stared at the now friendly faces. Tea would not come a moment too soon.

*

Twenty minutes later Jack sat in the team room and sweated. He could feel the shaking starting and found it difficult to concentrate. To the side of the ground he could hear the usual hubbub as spectators moved around.

Mary ignored the conventions as Jack had not reappeared and knocked on the team room door. There was no response as the rest of the team had gone straight to tea. After a respectable period she heard the coughing and pushed the door open and went in.

Jack got up and Mary looked at the grey face.

'What's wrong?' she asked.

'Just effects of smoke after the Alexandra Palace fire as I told you. But I wasn't supposed to do as much this early as I have done.'

248

'Let me help you. If I link my arm through yours you can put some of your weight on me. Let's get you to tea and get something inside you.' She thought how much he needed help but had been constrained by male pride not to show how affected he was.

'I don't want to be a burden to anyone. I'm heavy, you'll not take my weight.'

'If I can roll a drum of beer down the ramp in the Mason's Arms and stand on my feet for hours with silver trays loaded with tea I can help a sick policeman walk a few feet. Come on, let me help you. We can do it in a way people won't guess you're not right. They'll think we're a couple that's all.'

'Your reputation ....' Jack started.

'You and I know the truth, that's all that matters. Come on now, the quicker we get something inside you the better you'll be.' Mary said.

Rose and Mrs Phillips saw Jack and Mary emerge for tea. Rose hesitated but Mrs Phillips saw past the geniality Mary was presenting and looked at the state Jack was in.

'Come on, Rose, he's not well and needs our help,' said Mrs Phillips.

'It's so overt,' said Rose.

'It's nothing. She's trying to help him cover up the state that he's in, that's all. We should go over.'

By the time they reached Jack he had sat again and was in the process of swallowing most of a large tea. Mary had retrieved a plate of food from amongst the other players and encouraged him to devour it until the shaking stopped. The attractive and attentive woman with Jack did not go unnoticed by the other players. Rose realised she was also drawing interest from the other men but her mother's presence deflected it by her expression. The young men soon stopped staring after the sternness of the matron.

Jack had grimaced as Rose arrived. 'No fuss now,' he had said.

'Fuss?' Rose's eyebrows arched. 'You've done too much. You should go back to the hotel.'

'No, if I finish the match you will make the observations. If we leave now any potential findings are gone. I'm up to bowl,' said Jack.

Rose shrugged, 'Ridiculous. Half the people have already gone. This game goes on for ever. I've not seen anything of any interest in the crowd and we're saying far too much in front of Mary.'

'Without Mary I'd be on the floor in the changing room. It doesn't matter what she knows. What the Shah does or does not do will be well known in the area by Monday,' said Jack.

'Oh, is that it? That's why you're here?' Mary looked at them one by one. 'I see things in the hotel which I know how to keep to myself. Jack is unwell and I've helped him, that's all. I shan't say anything. Perhaps I should go now, and leave you with your friends.'

'No, I prefer it if you stay. You are also my friend. Now I need to re-join the team. The shaking has stopped. One over and Brighton should be out. I'll go back onto the field and I'll try and be the entertainment long enough for you to check who's still around, Rose,' said Jack, standing.

Rose had to be content with that. At the back of her mind was the young maid in Camberwell that she suspected she could not help. In addition Jack had blown his own cover to someone he hardly knew. What Harry would say she could only imagine.

'Let it be, dear,' said Mrs Phillips, quietly as Jack left them. 'Raising his stubbornness about the girl will do more damage as it will give him a cause to fight. Harriet has not been heard of since he left London. We don't know why. And, give Mary her due, she has looked after him this afternoon. Let it all take its course.'

'But he's *told* her, Mother. He's told her why we're here.'

———

250

'Yes, I know. That's because he trusts her. She's earned that trust this afternoon, Rose. I don't think he should have said anything but I rather think we caused it by pushing him. Anyway, it's done now. We should withdraw or we may push it deeper and the next thing maybe … love. Come on, let's go back to the seats and leave them. Harry will be over later and I would let Jack tell him what he said. I think he will. You should certainly not do so.'

There was indeed one more over and Jack's fast bowling brought an outcome faster than hoped. Pale, and coughing every few minutes, he excused himself to the Captain, who nodded as he could see Jack was unwell. Rose sent a boy to get a cab and, despite her mother's advice, scrawled a quick note for Harry. With Mary in attendance still, they all four left for the Ship Hotel.

*

About the time that Jack and his friends arrived at the Ship Harry Franks was leaving the Royal. Rose's note was in his pocket and it had surprised him:

Harry, (said the note),

You should know that Jack is unwell and has overreached himself this afternoon in the cricket match. That is not all. Unfortunately he has struck up what is becoming a close friendship with Mary from the Royal. He has confided in her the reason for our visit to Brighton. I think you should come to the Ship Hotel. We are on our way.

Rose.

Odd of Rose, Harry had thought, stiff in tone. But it was asking for help and he would of course go. Jack's disclosure of confidential information was a worry.

He arrived as Mary was leaving the Ship Hotel. Harry paused on the first step and Mary briefly smiled at him.

251

There had been a number of times when he had almost fallen into unfolding all the secrets of his work to Mary across a bar. Those were brilliant eyes, Harry had to acknowledge that. Now he had to decide if Jack should continue with them.

'I must get to work,' she said and Harry nodded.

'Where are they?' he asked.

'In the lounge,' Mary answered as she went past him.

Harry stood, assessing for a short while, at the corner of a partition quickly put up to give Jack some privacy. He could see Jack with Burgess in attendance. Rose and her mother were quiet, having become alarmed at Jack's state, and were standing to one side. Burgess had silently and efficiently closed off half the lounge area and was equally as quietly plying Jack with some hot concoction that had been produced from Alice's kitchen. He looked up and Harry beckoned to Burgess, who passed the dish to Mrs Phillips. Burgess got up, shifting his ample weight from one knee to his two feet. Harry retreated out of the area into the hall. When Burgess joined him he asked, 'How is he doing?'

'Better, the sweating and coughing has subsided.'

'Better enough to listen to me?' asked Harry.

Burgess's brow furrowed at the tone. 'I would say that depends on what you are about to do. However I should wait until we can move him into his room. From your tone it should be you and him alone.'

*

The shaking had stopped and Jack was debating about moving when Burgess returned.

Jack stared at him after he had whispered that the Detective Sergeant was in Jack's room and wanted a word.

'We'll help you, Jack,' said Rose, but Burgess held up a hand.

'I'll assist if he needs it ladies. The Detective Sergeant wanted a word alone.' Then to Jack he said, 'Do you want help or can you manage?'

'Just to the door,' said Jack, pushing himself up from the couch.

252

Burgess steadied Jack and placed a firm hand on the young man's elbow. They went down the corridor together and Jack entered his room. Burgess pulled the door behind his guest and turned away.

*

Harry had placed himself by the fire-grate. They got on well, this constable and himself. He may have handled it differently but Rose had left him no choice. There was the possibility as Ted's sister that she would contact her brother if Harry ignored Jack's behaviour. She had also written the problem down and, in Harry's experience, notes had a tendency to turn up as evidence. Admittedly something about Jack's activities all week had started to worry him but the lad had been acting on his initiative and was so used to being strong that Harry had thought he was having problems adjusting to the physical weakness he was experiencing. Disclosing information to Mary was another issue.

'You're early, Harry,' said Jack attempting to stand.

That was the irritating thing about this man, Harry thought, he always had the right amount of respect.

'Don't get up. You look rough, Jack,' said Harry, remaining standing himself.

'Overdid it at the cricket.'

'And why was that?' asked Harry.

'The story that they'd had. The story about me being the cousin of Captain Knox out of wedlock was daft. That wouldn't have held up when he got back. The only way to get past that was for me to show the skills I have so I went for what I can do. Fast bowling. It distracted their attention and made the other story irrelevant. Only it got the better of me and by tea I was in a mess.' Jack paused and coughed. 'Then I realised that if I was bowling I couldn't watch the crowd. So I asked Rose to. We needed more time so one over would do it. But I got worse.' He coughed again and this time could barely stop.

Harry listened and waited for the spasm to die down. He had the point he must make although he could imply that Jack had acted in the interests of protecting the team.

The issue was not isolated, that was the problem. The unpredictability had begun before Jack had arrived. Hunt had got to hear that Jack had disobeyed an order and he had passed the information onto Harry. Nothing heavy, just so Harry was aware and to watch the behaviour. Hunt said Jack had invited Harriet to Brighton but that Ted had headed that one off. In one way or another Jack had daily disobeyed orders, particularly to rest, deciding he could 'get round things.' The lad had been still trying to stay on the job regardless of the state he was in. Harry could understand it. He could understand the desire to share the problems of the job with a wife or fiancé but Mary was neither. That disclosure had been the final issue. Plus the man's health was in tatters.

'You've been getting worse daily, by all accounts. Maybe, with the exception of yesterday when you did rest in the afternoon, you've gradually got worse because you won't actually do what the doctor told you to do. That's going to have serious consequences for your health if you don't beat it now,' Harry paused.

Jack's brow was furrowed and he nodded. 'I know, Harry.'

'But there's another issue. You disobeyed the basic principal on under-cover work and disclosed why we're here to a civilian. So, as you are technically supposed to be recuperating from your injuries I have no option but to take you off any further involvement in the security details for the Shah's visit. What I tell Tom Hunt is another thing. I've no desire to damage your career, lad. I'll speak to Rose and ensure Ted isn't told too much as well. You will obey the doctor's orders for the rest of the time here. Your objective now is to rest and recover. I ask you also not to have any further contact with Mary.'

*

At Windsor, June the twentieth for her Majesty had also involved an appearance and what seemed like a game. It was the thirty-sixth anniversary of her accession to the throne. It was not meant to be a game but she viewed it as if it were because things regarding the Shah's visit on that day did not go to plan and some improvisation was necessary at Windsor.

In the corner of the room she had noticed that Tom Hunt was there again. So soon after their previous chat! The Queen smiled her approval, but then frowned when she took in his appearance.

'Tom, why are you dressed like that?' The Queen called over to him. All eyes turned. 'The man's a Police Inspector not a servant. For heaven's sake put him in something else. Why all this nonsense about the visit of the Shah? It's not as if he's *important* is it. It's because he's spectacular that the people are reacting. Today is a celebration, I know, but then there are so many! Ah, the guns are firing now and the bells ringing.'

One of her daughters said something quietly into the Queen's ear.

'What? What do you mean we can't go out at present? Oh I see, the troops that are supposed to line the hill at Windsor aren't in place. And there's a dozen carriages coming! Someone's mismanaged that. Well, clearly, we should move to the Sovereign's Entrance to greet the man. Tom, as the army isn't here, it's all up to the Metropolitan Police!'

*

255

Fifteen

Saturday night came and went for Jack with no further involvement with the team except for one visitor. Sam was told that Jack was too unwell and would play no further part in the security arrangements. Nothing else was said. Sam had thought to leave Jack alone but his nature got the better of him and by seven in the evening he knocked at Jack's door. Harry and Rose were at the Royal and there was no reason why Jack would see them unless arrangements were made.

Jack was about to take his meal in his room. His appetite had continued to return in the last few days and Alice had produced suet puddings.

'Come in,' Jack called, putting his tray to one side.

Sam poked his head round the door and at Jack's grin brought the rest of himself into the room.

'You'll get sacked if they know you're here,' said Jack.

'No, I wouldn't worry, Inspector Hunt isn't available for anyone to tell him what you've been up to and I don't think for one minute that Harry has any intentions of reporting this afternoon to him either. How are you feeling now?' asked Sam.

'Really tired. But the food is helping. What are you up to?'

'I'm off to the Royal to meet Harry,' explained Sam. 'Planning his presence on a yacht at Portsmouth on Monday when the Shah reviews the fleet. Harry says you're off the case because the main reason for you being here was to recover. He's quite relaxed about what you said to that young woman and actually told me he could have opened up to her himself a few times in the past, if she'd been interested. So, you may be off the security for the Shah's visit but we've still got the disappearance of Grace to sort out for Nathan. Will you go to see your Parson?'

'Yes. I should try and get to see him and the coastguard. I've questions about the intervening years between now and when my parents died. I need to try and understand things. The Parson is likely to be able to help on Grace's case as well,' said Jack.

'Good. Keep me posted, won't you? And there's some movement on the blonde man you told me about,' said Sam. 'I used Tom Hunt's name to contact the police artist at Scotland Yard. Tom Hunt had just been in apparently. Anyway, there was no problem. I've got them to send three sketches they have of known blonde, international jewel and fine art thieves, to Burgess. They should be here next week, so you and I can have a look at them and see if any of them are our man. When are you back here?'

'Not until Wednesday or Thursday. I haven't decided. Partly because I'm hoping that there will be a real welcome for me from the two men I'm going to see. That might mean I'm back on Thursday if it goes well. Wednesday if it goes badly,' said Jack.

'Alright. I should have the sketches by then. If you do make an identification we can inform the ports. I'd better get off. I know it's frustrating what's happened, I really do know as I had months of feeling I was making advances only to be set back again. What I'm trying to say is rest up. It's worth it in the long run.'

'I do know it is Sam. You get off and see Harry and I'll go in the lounge when I've finished this meal,' said Jack.

By the time the sky clouded over it was like the drawing of a curtain in the room and Jack, sick of the four walls of his bedroom, moved to the lounge. He instinctively knew it was a change of the tide as he felt the air through an open window. He closed it, nodding to other residents as they watched him and took a seat by the window. After that he avoided eye contact and remained reserved, picking up a novel which he did not read, merely tuning the pages of Anthony Trollop's, 'The Eustace Diamonds.'

From his position he could see the front and the entrance of the hotel. At dusk he watched as Sam and Harry came into the hotel and walked towards the stairs. They were going to Sam's room, Jack thought. He glanced at the clock on the mantelpiece to note the time. It was almost ten o'clock. The minutes ticked by.

Harry left as darkness started to descend.

Sometimes in his life Jack had been very alone. This felt like one of the worst. He should sleep but could not bear the thought of returning to his bedroom.

At close to eleven o'clock the lounge had emptied with the exception of Jack. Burgess appeared in the doorway with an enquiring look. The hotelier held up a bottle and two glasses and then walked back towards his office. Jack dutifully followed him down the corridor, closing the door of the office behind him. Burgess glanced up as he poured brandy for them both.

'Not sure I'll do it credit,' said Jack.

'Do your chest good,' replied Burgess, passing a glass to Jack.

Jack hesitated, sniffed the liquor and then took a taste. Burgess pulled a kettle off the range and offered it to Jack.

'Try some hot water in it if you prefer, and there's sugar here. Makes a nice drink.'

Jack added the hot water and spooned in the sugar. As he sipped he felt the warming liquid slowly seep into his system. He patted his lips with his handkerchief to remove the sugar granules that had stuck to the rim of the glass. Burgess topped up Jack's brandy before he could refuse. At first, they sat and stared at the wall, Jack running through the events of the last few days. Burgess thinking, he knew not what of. Then they talked of general things, the weather and Jack's potential trips next week. Finally Burgess broached the subject on both minds.

'This discussion with Detective Sergeant Franks that you had.'

'Yes?' said Jack.

'I take it, as you were not at dinner and part of the planning obviously going on, that they've removed you from the surveillance?' Burgess asked.

'You take it right. I'm here to rest only now.' Jack paused and added, 'Also I made a couple of mistakes. The worst thing was I thought Harry didn't trust me anymore but it seems that isn't the case.'

Burgess said slowly, 'You're talking to a man who is a past master at mistakes. The worst one was to let it affect me. So, you will still go and see your old Parson? And the Coastguard up at Kewhurst? I ask because if you're off the planning and surveillance you've more time for proper police work and solving a murder.'

Jack stopped sipping and put his glass down. 'Is it a woman? Do you think its Grace?' he asked.

'No. It's a local man. Well known. Field thinks its connected with the number of women that have disappeared though. I agree with him,' said Burgess.

'Why?' asked Jack, his eyes narrowing.

'Because the corpse is the Doctor we mentioned that certified the child deaths. Doctor Elm. Field mentioned him at lunch that day you met him.'

Jack nodded. Burgess watched him and waited.

'Where was he found?' asked Jack.

'Hastings. Bit of a coincidence, eh? It's interesting as Nathan Long is up there. He must have found out some connection between Grace and Hastings. So, as you're likely to have some time on your hands now and were going up the coast anyway, I thought you might like to help the investigation. You have a good cover story of why you're in the area. As you've already met Nathan it might be good to try and find him, speak with him, find out if he's uncovered any information.'

'That would be like jumping out of the frying pan into the fire, given I'm ordered to rest. I was also told by Tom Hunt not to get involved with the Brighton Force. The last thing I want is a message to resign before Monday,' said Jack.

Burgess moved the liquid in his glass round and round. 'You're forgetting one thing, Jack. Tom Hunt is my friend and I rather think he has enough on his plate at the moment without giving you too much attention. I also doubt that Detective Sergeant Franks will pass on any information other than that you've overdone things and need to rest. He doesn't strike me as that sort of man. Let me top your glass up.'

'No, this is enough, thank-you. I've not had much call to drink brandy in my life,' said Jack.

Burgess added a few drops into his own glass and put the bottle away in a cabinet. He said:

'You would still be resting and we can make sure you do by you having breakfast late in your room. You would be working with me not the Brighton force. Field is my contact. Should you happen to come across a situation how can you, as a constable, ignore it?'

There was a long pause while Jack weighed up his dilemma. Harry may say nothing of his disclosure to Mary but Rose was another issue. Harry would have to convince her not to share details with Ted.

Burgess continued:

'You saw Field's contact, I hear. So will you still go on Tuesday up to Hastings and meet him?' asked Burgess.

Seeing Jack's concern he added, 'I saw Field after the match. His constable had reported back to him. Don't worry, no-one else knows.'

Jack felt a warning within his innermost being but dismissed it. He stared, almost dazed at Burgess, not really seeing him, and thought about the plans he had formulated in his mind. He must find that fisherman and make arrangements to sail to Kewhurst on Tuesday and see the old Coastguard. From there he could get to Bexhill somehow and find his parent's grave. Hastings was supposed to be all part of that day. He had until two o'clock before he had to meet Field's man at the cricket match. Now he was not involved in working with Harry his time was his own. So long as he built in rest there could be no criticism. If he found himself in a position of a crime being committed anyone would expect him to act. Harry would not enquire what he was doing as long as he was resting from the surveillance work. Monday could go ahead as he had planned and he would get to Selmeston and see the Parson. Thank goodness he had not had time to send another letter and cancel the visit.

'If I happen to come across a crime it would be my duty as a Policeman to act, wouldn't it?' asked Jack, moving his glass backwards and forwards on the table.

'Exactly,' said Burgess as he offered a wheel of cheddar cheese to Jack, who cut himself a piece.

'So, you'll go and meet Field's man?' Burgess asked with raised eyebrows.

Jack realised he was sweating. He smiled gloomily at Burgess.

'He'll make himself known to you,'

'Yes, I'll go. I might as well sink as swim.' Jack said.

Burgess looked at him and perceived there was rebellion in the young man's spirit. He would obey orders to a certain extent but would still follow his own instinct if he came across something. Burgess was satisfied that they would get a result on the missing women case with this young constable.

So they continued until the early hours. The bottle was produced again and went back and forth for some time. Burgess talked about his past and Jack listened. Little more was said about Jack's situation with his own team. There was no need. Of all people Jack knew Burgess understood.

By ten o'clock on Sunday morning Jack had slept long and was woken when his breakfast arrived. He had slept fitfully, waking often, which he knew was the drink. His dreams were incoherent and for once he was glad that he could not recall them. He briefly wondered how Harry would handle the cricket team involvement for that day. Pouring water over his head he reached for a towel and stared at himself in the mirror. Drinking brandy had not helped his mood, nor his looks. He had rarely wanted it and seldom felt the need to get drunk. Last night it had been the activity with a fellow sufferer, like a ritual for both men. Now on waking the effect of the drink had left him depressed.

Jack lifted the cover off the plate and picked up a sausage and bit into it. He felt his stomach turn at the thought of the eggs and covered them over again. Slipping the rest of the sausage between two pieces of bread he walked to the window and lifted it fully open. The air was refreshing.

Thinking through his conversation with Burgess he felt he was in a wilderness. Potentially he could make things worse for himself by working with Field and the police detective at the cricket match. He knew he did not understand compromise. It had been the same in his decision to join the police and it was the same in his relationships. He thought briefly of Harriet but it gave him no comfort. Not long now before she went back to Honiton for her sister's wedding. Would she have gone when he returned to London? Somehow, he knew she would not be there and the summer would be into mid-July before he saw her again. His sense of frustration at not being able to contact Harriet made him want to smash something.

He put the half-eaten sausage and bread down and changed his clothes, having not bothered to undress before he slept. The day was fine and he knew he had the need to stand and stare at the sea. He also needed to make arrangements with the fisherman for Tuesday.

Burgess was at the desk dealing with guests as Jack entered the hall. He caught Jack's attention as he approached and handed Jack an envelope.

'It came this morning,' said Burgess.

Jack glanced at the hand writing once he was outside on the front step. He did not know it. He had briefly thought it might be Harriet but dismissed it as she could not possibly know where he was. It said:

Jack,
I will always be your friend.
Mary.

When he had read the few words it struck him that Rose and Harry had sorted Mary as well. Or perhaps not as she had still communicated with him. He smiled at the note and pocketed it. No reply was needed. She had given him all the information he needed.

From the lounge Mrs Curzon had seen Jack stand in front of the hotel. She had been concerned for her son's friend when Sam told her he was taken ill at the cricket match. Now she stood up determined to join him. This morning, though, he seemed lost in reflection, at times with a face like thunder, and now a smile. If one could only see inside that mind, she thought. She wondered about suggesting a walk but before she could join him Jack went down the steps and turned for the sea front.

*

By Monday morning Jack had realised Burgess was right and Tom Hunt would not have received any word from Harry. Jack had decided that he must focus on his health if he was ever to play the role he wanted again. The hard lesson he was learning was that if he did not rest his body would not respond when he needed it to.

Jack left the expanse of sea for the town and the Brighton Railway. His destination was Lewes and he had packed a small bag having decided not to return for a few nights. No-one seemed to need him and Burgess had agreed to let Harry know that he would be staying with friends of his parents. Jack had been told there was the White Hart in Lewes where he could get a room if he decided to stay in the area. There had been no sign of Sam and no message about the sketches. It would be a busy day for the team with the Shah arriving at Portsmouth. Harry's movements remained a mystery.

*

About the time that Jack was travelling through the seven miles of undulating country-side from Brighton the Shah continued to be entertained in a manner without precedent. The Naval Review at Spithead was being held in his honour and he was present on the Royal Yacht, 'Victoria and Albert.'

Harry Franks was on board a private yacht, moving up the coast towards Portsmouth and the Isle of Wight. He was armed in case of problems.

The Naval review was due to get underway and the Shah and the Royal Party had left London that morning. Jack's assessment that Portsmouth was not a problem given the naval presence but that an attack could still come by sea was right. Harry was on his way to help prevent that.

Jack enquired about the walk to the White Hart in the booking office at Lewes and was told it was roughly half a mile. That was fine and he enjoyed a walk until he reached the River Ouse. The castle walls were still there giving testimony to their builders and he walked past several elegant buildings in the town. If they had a room for him at the White Hart he would stay the night and travel onto Bexhill from Lewes early on Tuesday. He had not found the fisherman he and Mrs Curzon had sailed with and no-one at the shore wanted to take a stranger as far as Kewhurst. He had resigned himself to going eastward on Tuesday to Lewes by train, and then on around the foot of Mount Caburn and through a valley in the South Downs. It was all somehow strangely familiar from past days.

He paid for a room and breakfast at the White Hart in order to assuage the proprietor's suspicions that he would ever see the money. There had been no time to write to them but Jack was dressed smartly, carrying an overnight bag that spoke of quality, and his direct gaze reassured the man at the desk. The money was on the table and this went a long way to make the man friendly. Jack was shown to a pleasant enough room and he left his bag under the bed. On his way out he accepted the offer of a broth and bread for lunch but declined an evening meal later in the day, explaining that he was visiting old friends and would eat a dinner with them. He hoped he was right.

Jack enquired back at Lewes station about the best way to get to Selmeston and was advised to take the train for the next three miles towards Glynde. After that Selmeston had a halt but not a station and he could alight there if he advised the guard. As the train pulled out of Lewes past strong fortifications, he could see Firle Beacon in the distance, rising to a height, with cloud darkening the incline. They were at the halt before he knew it and with a wave to the guard he left the train to go on its way to Berwick and Polegate.

As Jack walked up to the garden gate of the small cottage at the side of the church the first thing to be seen of the Parson was his elegant shock of white hair and a ruddy complexion, forged in his face by the wind on the Weald. Older than Jack had expected, the stooped figure of an elderly clergyman who still wore a dog collar, was bent pulling up weeds from around a rose bush. At the kitchen window was a middle aged woman, her hair tucked up in a mop cap, a grey strand or two flopping over her eyes. Doing a parishioner a favour in helping with the garden, Jack thought.

In his memory the Parson, Reverend Peter Fisher that is, had dark hair speckled with grey. He recalled Father laughing with this man who was now glancing at Jack, still standing at the gate. Fisher shaded his eyes as the sun was in front of him. Jack lifted the latch and came in. His note, sent to the Vicarage had explained he was in the area briefly. The present incumbent had sent it on to the cottage which the old Parson occupied. Jack had mentioned he had been labouring in Sussex for some years, making a change in 1872. Fisher had busied himself that morning, remaining in the garden so that he had the vantage point of seeing anyone walking up towards the church. A young man was now before him, not someone he knew, quite well dressed, therefore not the labourer he had been anticipating and not really dressed for walking. And yet there was a look about the man that tweaked a memory and pulled him back in time.

'I'll be with you in a minute. Let me dispose of the weeds and remove my gloves,' Reverend Fisher called.

It was eleven years since Jack had last seen the Parson, as his father had always called this vicar. Memory had made Jack forget that no-one stayed the same and just as he had changed from a small nine-your old child so the Parson had aged. He had rehearsed his father's greeting that he recalled. A momentary hesitation as he had felt wrong-footed but he went ahead and called out:

'Marning, Parson, I was abouten going and afraid I'll ache waiting so long.' The effect was ruined by a coughing spasm that Jack could not control. The woman in the kitchen was called to bring water and a chair brought while the Parson stood by Jack. Once seated and his cough under control, Reverend Fisher brought another chair across from a set of glass houses and sat opposite his young visitor.

'Jack Sargent, I see your father's eyes and note you have his sense of humour,' said Reverend Fisher in a friendly way as he gripped Jack's hand in a welcome handshake. Still a strong grip, Jack noted and a direct eye. Reverend Fisher was running an eye over Jack's appearance.

'You're better dressed than I expected, having told me that you were labouring. Where have you sprung from after all this time with that Sussex way of speaking?'

'From London, in the Police since last November. Before that I was over at Battle,' Jack explained.

'But your note said you had been working as a labourer up to last Autumn. How did that come about?' asked Reverend Fisher, sitting back.

'I was of an age, Parson and had to be placed, but I think I was fortunate with the Squire.' Jack smiled. The old Parson looked at Jack for some moments, took a handkerchief from his pocket and dabbed his brow.

'Hot work. Tell me where you went to live with your aunt. I remember she was to marry.' The Parson asked.

For the first time Jack made an assumption that age had confused the man. He said slowly: 'There was no aunt. As to the business I assume it was sold off. I knew nothing more of it.'

———

Reverend Fisher sniffed and looked away. 'Irritating thing old age. People assume you're becoming addled, when you're not.' He looked back at Jack, eyes piercing and then leant forward, resting his forearm on his knee and staring into Jack's face. 'Young man, I clearly remember a woman holding your hand at your parents' joint funeral, at which I presided. Was she not an aunt?'

It was Jack's turn to sit back. 'No, Parson, she was from the orphanage,' he replied, quietly. 'There was no aunt, there wasn't anyone left.'

Reverend Fisher took out a pair of spectacles. Several sparrows caused a commotion in a bush nearby. Time went by audibly from the clock on the mantlepiece. Jack thought the elderly man must have lost his thread.

Reverend Fisher asked, 'Why did you think she was from an orphanage. What happened in the last eleven years?'

'Because that was where we went. I was there for four years, and then to the Squires and the farm. Last year I answered an advertisement for the Metropolitan Police and joined Camberwell division. Now I'm based in Stepney.'

There was a longer silence while tea was brought on a tray. Adopting his father's name for the Reverend, Jack called him Parson and Peter Fisher accepted that so he would forever be from this young man. He searched Jack's face for traces of the boy and found the father the more he looked at him.

The reference to the orphanage appeared to have upset the elderly minister and Jack realised that he had not known about it. Jack stood to greet the woman he thought was the Parson's wife as she entered from the kitchen with a tea tray. General hilarity broke the silence at Jack's mistake. Reverend Fisher introduced her as Mrs Simcock, "a treasure."

'Goodness, no, bless you,' said Mrs Simcock, laughing. 'I come in each morning to prepare lunch and an evening meal and do a general tidy for the Reverend. Have done all these years since his good lady passed away and he retired.' Turning to the Reverend Fisher, she asked, 'Will there be two for dinner today?'

Reverend Fisher looked at Jack:

'Well, can you stay?' he asked.

'I would like to,' said Jack accepting gladly as it was what he had hoped.

Over the tea Jack asked: 'Are you retired, Parson?'

'In a manner of speaking, yes. Although I do not see that a Christian minister ever takes his boots off. The new Vicar was kind enough to make a cottage available to me on a low rental, and also to involve me in his own work on the Sussex Dialect. He labours on with it and I shall get some acknowledgement when it's published. Your father's input will be there too, you know.'

Reverend Fisher paused, looking at Jack from under bushy eyebrows.

'Jack, you said in your note that you had some things to ask my help on. Before you explain let me say that I will gladly help you. I would have tried to do so anyway but I am eleven years late. I made an assumption all those years ago at your parent's funeral, which I should not have done. As a result you have had the sort of life as a child your parents would have looked to me to prevent, such was our relationship. It is possible that you might have had a very different life had I have acted. It is late to ask your forgiveness, but I do.'

'I don't see I have anything to forgive you for, Parson. It has never occurred to me once my parents were gone that it could be any different. I think your creed would say it was never too late and if it helps then of course I forgive you, although I still don't see what it is that you're asking forgiveness for.'

'Thank-you for your generous heart. We, that is those of us who were charged with keeping an eye on the material side of your parent's treasures have worked for you, despite not knowing where you were. My regret is that we did not know where you were. I will endeavour to put that right if you can return next week. Now, tell me what specifically it is that you want my help for,' said the Parson.

Jack told him of the German Tract, pulling the copy sent to him from Miss Cohen out of his bag. Reverend Fisher accepted it and took Jack into a small room which doubled as study and sitting room. He looked at it briefly and deposited the work on a small mahogany bureau. Jack suggested that he could return in a week's time as the Parson suggested and would collect the copy then.

'If you have time to look at and summarise it I'll pass it onto my Inspector in London,' said Jack.

'Yes, leave it with me and you shall have it on your return. Could you stay a night when you come back?' asked the Parson.

'Thank-you, that's kind,' said Jack.

That part of the reason for his visit dealt with Jack turned to the issue of Grace's disappearance and explained what he knew from the Brighton force. The old vicar listened.

'And you want my help in sleuthing?' The Parson asked. His expression had become more sombre as Jack explained about the number of missing women and the death of the Doctor who was the signatory on the baby death certificates. He listened to the suspicions that Burgess had recounted to Jack.

'Yes, Parson. I hoped you could tell me what arrangements in the area of Brighton there are for Poor Relief, and if there was any way we can find out if the dead babies had been christened, as that way we may link the children up with their mother's names. If births were registered the fathers may be named on registration. I can't be seen to be making enquiries, you see. It's not what I was sent down here to do. The Brighton force has men there who are working quietly on the issues but undercover, so to speak,' explained Jack.

'And you, Jack, why are you here?' asked Reverend Fisher.

'Mainly to recover from the effects of the Alexandra Palace Fire. You heard the cough. There was other work as well but I can't go into that as I'm off it now due to the need for rest. It will be over by the time I get back to Brighton anyway.'

'We should have more tea before you tell me the rest,' said the Parson. He called, 'Mrs Simcock, top the kettle up, please.'

Jack continued: 'I've become involved with the investigation into the missing women as I met a young sailor, a navy man, trying to find his sweetheart. I suspect she's had his child and I don't have good feelings about what has happened to either of them. I only know of her as Grace. Tomorrow I'm to meet a Police Constable from Brighton at a cricket match in Hastings. The young sailor has been sighted there, which may imply he's found a few things out. In addition the Doctor who is dead may have been murdered. There may be a link of some sort with the missing women.'

'Let me get some sort of a time frame to this. When would the young woman Grace have had a baby, if indeed she has?'

'It's a bit unclear. The sailor, Nathan Long is his name, would have gone away about a year ago. There was something that brought the parents of Grace to disown her. They refused permission for them to marry, you see, before the sailor returned to duty. Afraid he'd be killed in action, probably. I'm sure he said that he had expected to return earlier but the ship was delayed.'

Reverend Fisher was making notes. He looked up at the clock, and then at Jack.

'Well, that will keep me busy for the next week until you return. We'll get some fishing done when you come back. Now, I dine early these days young man. Shall we take a Sherry in the garden? It faces south-west and the sun will be a pleasant companion after the dire things you have shared with me this afternoon.'

'Gladly, but I'll leave off Sherry, if you don't mind. Sleep gets affected, you see, and the dreams,' Jack explained.

'A cordial then? I have some Elderflower cordial put up by Mrs Simcock.' The elderly vicar pottered about in a cupboard and put two glasses ready and uncorking two bottles. Jack moved into the garden glad to be in the air again.

'Here we are,' Reverend Fisher set the two glasses on the unsteady table. Jack bent down and slipped a flat piece of flint under one of the legs. The Reverend lifted his glass in thanks and said:

'Now tell me, how are you really after the fire?'

'Lacking in physical strength. A strange experience and worrying for the future as I need it for the policing. The Police Surgeon packed me off to the sea for three weeks, said he's had some success with that treatment with London Firemen. I've been in Brighton a week, walking, but I've over-done it on a few occasions and it leaves me with the cough, as you saw when I arrived. Then there's the dreams,' Jack took a sip of the cordial and nodded his appreciation.

'Natural after something like a fire,' suggested the vicar.

'Bad dreams generally, one case in particular seems to have affected me, a woman's involvement in a murder and her own suicide. At times I'm afraid to sleep,' Jack said.

Reverend Fisher nodded and stared into the distance.

'The cords of the grave coil around me. King David threatened with death by his enemies. Dangerous situations can sometimes seem to be pulling us into the grave, Jack. If you can, tell me more.'

*

The first battleship to be built without sails for the Royal Navy, 'The Devastation,' was present for the Naval Review at Spithead. It was clear that the Shah was extremely interested as it was the latest product of the Dockyard at Portsmouth. The Prince and Princess of Wales with their children were also present. Soon after starting, The Vigilant, with a large number of visitors including members of the Persian party, was disabled.

Harry Franks felt that their yacht was very low in the water. This enhanced the drama when the battleship fired a salute. The sea was choppy and with the smoke and the dark form of the iron-clad bearing down Harry had a sense that he wanted to be anywhere but there.

It was argued later in the House of Lords that there had been some mismanagement at Spithead. Pebble powder had been used without shot and some damage was incurred by the yacht. There were only two people in the gunboat who might have been responsible. The Warrant Officer was one and the Captain of the Gun. Of course, to them the yacht should not have been there and the Peer that had been prevailed upon to allow a team on board should have known better than to get so close.

After all, an official notice had been placed in The Times, and other newspapers, and was also put up at Portsmouth. It particularly requested that all yachts and steamers visiting Spithead on the 23rd inst. would refrain from passing between the lines of the iron-clad fleet during the inspection of His Majesty the Shah of Persia; and it also requested that all vessels refrain from closing round her Majesty's yacht and other vessels in attendance. Yachts and other vessels should occupy positions north of the gunboat line, and south of the southern line of the Isle of Wight.

The Warrant Officer was aft, watching the gunboat astern of his. He was there to take the time, six seconds, which was to elapse between the firing of each boat. The funnel and the casing were between him and the yacht; therefore he did not see the yacht Harry and the rest of the protection were on.

The gun's Captain had his view blocked as the high rifle proof shielding was around all the forward part of the boat except where the gun protruded. The Captain was given the order to fire and carried it out as he could see nothing in front of the gun.

Two men on the gunboat signalled to the yacht when it was fifty yards off. They did this by holding up their hands. This was supposed to mean to keep out of the way. They received a similar gesture from a man on the yacht. As to what each thought was being communicated was a mystery.

The yacht, on which Harry Franks, landlubber, sailed, was only about fifteen yards from the mouth of the gun. Fortunately the gun pointed upwards not at the yacht. Harry stood back, putting his future first for once, his head pounding, or was it his heart. He no longer knew. There was the smell of smoke and somewhere in the distance he could hear shouting. Something at the back of his mind told him that this would not be happening if Jack was here.

It really did not matter what was fired. The debate on pebble powder was irrelevant. The yacht was so close to the gun that it was scorched. Harry crumpled with the shock of the searing pain to his right forearm. Five people were injured. Surgeons and officers boarded and arrests followed.

*

Sixteen

The following morning Jack woke to the sound of barrels being rolled into the White Hart's cellar. He waited until the last one was in and then listened to the silence. It did not last long as the early morning birdsong interrupted the serene quiet, particularly as the starlings copied the other birds. He waited for the one call he always had woken to. It eluded him as the sparrows continued with their frenetic chase along the half open shutters. And then the sound was there. A lone wood-pigeon's call that spoke to him of hot summers in Sussex, now it seemed long-gone, like his childhood.

By nine o'clock Jack was walking back to Lewes station to catch a train eastwards as he had done yesterday. He had lain in bed until eight-thirty, a complete luxury, enjoying the scent of the white cotton sheets. In his book that was a rest. Breakfasting briefly he left with a thickly buttered piece of bread wrapped in a piece of soft muslin.

This time he stayed on the train past the halt at Selmeston. At Polegate the line branched off towards the Pevensey level and Hastings. Like every local child he had been taught the history, both Saxon and Norman, of the area and the importance of defending the coast. Pevensey and the Marsh, or "Mesh," as his father would have called it, had become little more than a village and the sea, which Jack knew had at one time washed up against the castle walls, had receded by two miles. On the train went, past rich grazing, until he felt it slow ready for the stop at Bexhill.

He took a cup of water and grimaced at the taste like iron while he waited for information on transport out to Kewhurst. The railwayman promised to do his best if Jack could return in an hour. Jack said he would be back by twelve and then turned to walk to the church.

The Parson had said that the verger could check the exact location of the grave in the records, but he recalled from his memory of the joint funeral for Jack's parents that the position in the graveyard was opposite the gnarled old tree next to the path leading to the church. The sky was overcast as Jack reached the church and he walked into the porch and tried the door. The verger had left a spade propped up against a wooden seat. The door was unlocked and he went in, calling out a greeting as he entered in case the verger was there. Instead he was met by silence as the only response broken suddenly by the fluttering of a bird's wings up in the rafters. He went in and took a seat in the east end of the church, remembering how the sun had streamed in through the stained glass windows on the day of his parent's funeral. Not today though.

He bowed his head as he had been taught. Then he looked up at the gallery and wondered as he had done as a child what had possessed the church to add the seating up there.

He stepped out into the churchyard and walked towards the tree. Standing in front of it, facing the gravestones, he tried to remember the small boy holding the hand of the woman from the orphanage, the Parson holding a prayer book and Father's friends taking their hats off. Edward Croft and his wife, newly-wed, had been there. Jack remembered him in his Coastguard's uniform and the way the reflection from the sun bounced off the buttons. He realised that he had little to do with that nine year old child today. The sense of distance shocked him. How had he changed in the last year? Was it London that was helping him put a distance between himself and the past? Shrugging the sentiment off he walked forward and started to read the gravestones to find the right one.

When he found it he was struck by the simple headstone that fronted his parent's grave. It was rain lashed and soil partially obscured the words. He could see the engraving, which announced that William and Jane Sargent had quitted this life in February 1861. Jack felt a frisson of irritation. It sounded as if they had made a decision to do so whereas the reality was the opposite.

His mother's fevered eyes came back into his memory and her hand touching his hair. Then she had lain still forever. Who had chosen this headstone and the inscription? The stone needed cleaning and it was leaning to one side as a bank of earth had been driven against it by the rain. Once again, as he had done at various stages of his earlier life when the sense of isolation consumed him, he wept.

The emotion eventually subsided, leaving him able to control it again with a dull ache in his being. The coughing had begun during the sobbing and the uncontrollable nature of the spasms had given the second shock that morning. Slowly he controlled the grief to deal with the cough and enable him to complete the task ahead.

Jack walked back to the porch and picked up the verger's spade. Looking around at the beds of evergreen near the church he drove the spade into the soil to cut a piece. He dug under the root of the plant with a yellow flower. He knew it as Rose of Sharon but could not recall the botanical name. It was a spreader and it would do to keep flowering until September and then he would be back to plant holly for the winter. Perhaps Sam would let him stay in Brighton and he could call in and see the Parson as well. Everything would have died down about Mary by then and there was no reason why he should not also see her as a friend.

Shovelling the clump of the plant onto the spade he carried it back and put the spade with its contents down, lining it up to be parallel with the grave. Taking his damp handkerchief he rubbed the soil away from the headstone, and by the time he had finished his nails were black. He scraped the mound of soil away from the back of the headstone with the spade and applied his weight to level it, starting to cough more as he exerted himself. Ignoring the warnings of his body he kept on until it was straight, piling up the displaced soil to fill the gap he had created on one side of the headstone. At least their span of life now showed. He would talk to the Parson next week about how to get a better headstone and replace it.

Spasms of coughing were coming every few minutes by the time he had finished tending the grave to his liking. Instead of resting he kept on, pulling up cooch grass, working at smoothing out the soil he had scraped from the engraved words. He could have written a history of them if it had been left to him not just their names and span of years. Loving parents to John William, Market Gardener for his father and Book-keeper for his mother.

His mother would have flowers now and his father would like it tidy. The plant was trimmed as well as he could with a spade, to give it the potential for health and growth. It should be watered but Jack had no idea where in the church he would find a supply. He would have to trust the Almighty to provide on that one. At the end of his labours he almost retched with the coughing. He waited ten minutes, eating the thick bread and butter he had brought with him, leaning against the spade until the coughing subsided.

He carried the spade back to the porch and unlatched the door into the church. Jack had nothing to wipe his face and hands now as his handkerchief was filthy. Again he called out in case anyone was in the back of the church. Silence and dust particles in a thin shaft of sunlight was all the response he had. He sat in a pew and waited five more minutes to ensure he would not cough again. His stomach muscles ached with each bout. Concerned for the time Jack pulled out his pocket watch to find it was already eleven o'clock. He could not make his way back to the station yet. Laying down in the pew he slipped his boots off and closed his eyes.

He was dreaming again of a woman screaming.

Except it was not a dream. He had been asleep for ten minutes when a woman had come into the church to change the flowers. She heard his regular breathing and stepped softly towards the pew. In shock at finding a man asleep she had screamed. Jack sat bolt upright, unsure of his surroundings and then, recalling where he was, tried to apologise. The woman screamed again as he stood up and then her voice found the acoustic. The verger came running from the back of the church and Jack momentarily wondered where the man had been.

'Who are you?' shouted the verger in order to be heard, taking in Jack's clothes but also the dirty hands. The clothes and the travel bag were a comfort though, the man was not a vagrant. He repeated his question more quietly, adding the word, sir, at the end.

'I'm very sorry to give you such a shock. I'm Jack Sargent, a policeman. I came to look at my parent's grave. I had a coughing fit and lay down with exhaustion after clearing the weeds away from the grave. If there's somewhere I could wash my hands I'll be on my way.'

The woman was not to be placated and the verger looked from her to Jack.

'I'll go,' said Jack, making a decision. He moved a few steps away and held up his grubby hands in defeat. At least the cough had stopped and he thought he could probably now make the station for his transport.

After a last look at his handiwork and a spoken commitment, which his parents could not hear but which he had to trust about, he joined the path running at the side of the graveyard and started the walk towards Kewhurst and the coast.

He reached Cheeseman's Farm and felt he could go no further on foot. The extra weight of his bag added to a sense of weariness.

There was a bell by the kitchen door of the farm house and he pulled the rope to bring someone out.

A man and a young boy appeared from a sheep pen to the side and Jack was able to negotiate for water and soap to wash his hands explaining that he had been tending his parent's grave. He asked for a cart to take him to the Coastguard's cottages at Kewhurst, holding out a florin. If his father's old friend was still working as Coastguard Jack did not want to meet him in this state.

Drying his face and hands on a piece of sacking held out to him by the farmer's boy, Jack was ready. He climbed up on the seat next to the boy and glanced into the back of the cart. Milk Churns for the station. At this time of the day they would be empty.

'How old are you?' Jack asked.

'Twelve, next month,' said the boy.

'A happy birthday for next month. Where does your milk go to?'

'London. We take them down for the milk train each morning and they'll be full for tomorrow's train. We're here now, sir.'

Deposited by the boy at the Kewhurst Coastguard station Jack looked up at a watery sun just visible through lead coloured clouds above a grey, rolling sea. Several of the fisherman at Brighton had been right in refusing to make the journey. The visibility was poor and he stood on the pebbles, his back to the sea and stared at the Coastguard cottages, fighting the memories. Slowly, Jack turned and strained his eyes through the poor visibility to the left where Hastings should be, then to the right, towards Eastbourne. Like an act of faith he knew they were there but the visibility was poor and he could only see a couple of hundred yards in either direction. Could there be too much grief in one day?

Time passes, he thought, as he heard a movement behind him. Young men grow old. Jack turned as the slight movement became the crunch of boots on the pebbles and a middle aged man in uniform walked across to him.

'Marning,' called Jack. The man nodded a welcome.

'Would it be Edward Croft?' Jack asked.

'You're looking in the wrong station, it's been some years since he was here. Friend of his, are you?' The coastguard uniform was distinctive.

'My father was. Would you be able to tell me where I can find him? It's some years since I last saw him and I'm in the area just for today,' Jack smiled but it was wasted.

Although smuggling had declined years ago after the government had slashed the import duties there were, no doubt, still those from families once involved in the "Trade" who would bear a grudge. Jack's father and Edward Croft had told him tales of dramatic scenes of fighting and "running" as traders unloaded goods and battled with the Coastguards. It was forty years ago but the man in front of him was wary in case he was from one of the smuggling families and sought revenge. The coastguards had rescued many as well, some losing their own lives putting to sea and capsizing. Jack remembered being told that by the time he was born, their role had become that of a naval reserve and defence of the realm, although protection of the Revenue against smuggling was still in the job description. Edward Croft, and his father as a volunteer, had saved lives. His father had taken him to see the wreckage strewn along the coast when he was quite small, hauling Jack onto his shoulders so that he could see the waves crashing below and the wreckage piling up.

'Have respect for the sea,' his father had said.

The coastguard in front of him was speaking and Jack's attention was hauled out of the past.

'Mr Croft is up at Fairlight Coastguard Station usually. But he'll not be there now. Could I ask your name?' Still the suspicion, Jack thought.

'Jack Sargent. I'm on - visiting from London but I grew up in Bexhill and my father was a volunteer life saver. Mr Croft and he taught me to swim here. It's years since I've seen him.'

'Yes, must be, as he's been gone from here a few.'

'Could you tell me how I can get to Fairlight?' asked Jack.

'Won't do you any good. He's at Pett Level today not at the Coastguard Station. You can leave him a letter, if you like and I'll telegram it across.'

This was something. Irritating as it was Jack could tell he would get nowhere with this man. He had no idea of the exact location of Fairlight or the place called Pett Level. Time was short if he was to meet Sergeant Field's man at two o'clock.

'Alright, wait a minute while I write something,' Jack said. He pulled his notebook and pencil from his pocket and started to write a brief note:

Mr Croft, (it said),
I am Jack Sargent and you may remember me as your friend William Sargent's son. I am staying at the Ship Hotel in Brighton and can meet you next week if you have the time.
Yours sincerely,
Jack.

It was more formal than he felt but years had gone by. Jack tore the page out and gave the paper to the Coastguard. The man took it without reading it, folded it and pocketed it. However his face assured Jack that he would send it. As there was nothing else to do Jack took his leave of the man and walked back to the lane. What he most needed now was food and drink. The wind had grown stronger while he had stood talking to the Coastguard. Now, as he walked, the lane that ran up to the station was sheltered by tall hedging and he felt stifled after the freshness of the beach.

He bought bread and cheese from the clerk at the station and paid over the odds to ensure he got enough. Water was only available in a cup and Jack drank it quickly. It would do. The train to Hastings could be heard coming along the coast to the station.

There were three people in the carriage as Jack climbed in. He glanced at them and settled into a corner seat, indulging in the Policeman's occupational hazard of assessing his fellow travellers. One of the passengers was older than Jack by at least thirty years and lost in a book which was a "yellow back" that he must have collected from a W.H. Smith stall on a station. The two other travellers were also men and a similar age to Jack.

The train passed through St Leonards with its eastern looking hotels. Jack caught sight of a billboard on the station advertising a debate on women's suffrage on October the fourth, with the main speaker to be Miss Millicent Fawcett. Hastings was only a few minutes away and the train slowed as it pulled into station.

Jack stood to reach for his bag on the luggage rack and the man reading the book snapped it to and stood up for the door. As the train stopped Jack waited for the other two men to clear their luggage from the rack and then pulled his own bag down. It had moved to the back of the rack with the jolting.

He climbed down, waved away a friendly porter who offered help with his luggage and started to check the destinations of the omnibuses at the station which met every train. It was not clear which one he needed and he eventually asked a driver if he knew where any cricket would be played that afternoon. The man gave him a pitying look and pointed to a vehicle going to the Central Recreation Ground.

'Not "any" cricket,' said the driver pointedly. 'First class and List A cricket. The county team is using out-grounds to host the match.'

Jack climbed onto the omnibus that the driver had indicated and selected a seat. He looked around at the other passengers and nodded to an older couple. He sat and closed his eyes, momentarily nodding off. He must have slept for five minutes when he was brought out of his slumber as the omnibus jolted. He viewed the area they drove through and the sea as it cut into the high cliffs. The wide bay and its heaving waves gave a crashing music onto the shingle. By then the visibility out at sea was also improving and he sniffed the air. It felt milder and cleaner than it had at Kewhurst. Jack strained his eyes towards the shadow on the horizon, which announced the opposite coast of France. There was a different feel to Hastings.

The town had the reputation of being sheltered from the north and north east winds in the worst months of winter with less fog than any-where else along the coast. Hastings and St Leonards together had had the reputation of being good for invalids with poor chests in winter due to the reputed dry and absorbent soil. Jack logged away the fact with the intention of mentioning the benefits of the town to Dr Brown for his firemen, on his own return to London.

The journey took him past the ruins of the castle, a flower garden and shrubbery, meticulously laid out with seats and refreshments. Although it was only six miles from Battle Jack had never had the time, nor the reason, to visit. He could see a strong fence had started to be erected to eventually go all the way around the walls of the castle to stop the souvenir hunters.

Ahead of him the Central Recreation Ground came into view.

Jack alighted from the omnibus and walked straight across to the tea tent both to be seen and in order to satisfy his age old problem of hunger and thirst. The world seemed to be there and he joined a long queue, sure that Field's man would be scouting around to find him. He did not have long to wait.

'It seems we are to have a short stay here,' Field's man was on his left, joining him in the queue.

'Do we need to go now?' asked Jack.

'After you've had some tea and before the match starts. I saw you were unwell at Brighton. Damn shame given the way you bowled that over. We've time for me to brief you while we eat. Pork pie I see and little sausages, sandwiches and sweet tarts, I think that will do to keep us going constable, don't you?' smiled Field's man, holding out his hand to shake Jack's.

Jack responded, liking his companion's attention to just what he needed after the day.

'Jack,' he said with a slow smile and they shook hands.

'I can be Constable Hockham, or plain Shaw, which ever you prefer. Let's load up a couple of plates and find a shaded spot and I will fill you in, so to speak. We have a long evening ahead of us I'm afraid as there have been some developments since we spoke yesterday.'

They chose two chairs as far from company as they could and Shaw Hockham and Jack ate. As the appetite started to be satisfied Jack felt his concentration starting to return and he asked, 'You mentioned a long evening ahead?'

'Yes, I'm afraid so. A body's been found and an arrest made. The body is of a young woman, found at a local beauty spot called "Lovers Seat." Do you know that side of Hastings?' Shaw asked.

'No, only the town where the castle is and that's from when I was a boy. We lived at Bexhill so it's really that side of the coast that's known to me. When was she found?'

'This morning. Under some subsidence which may have been helped along to hide the body. It's clay and sandstone you see, and gets worn away with rain and tide. The other news is the person arrested is known to us both. It's our friend, Nathan Long, I'm sorry to say. He found her, from what I've been able to gather and identified her as his love, Grace.' Shaw stopped to bite into a small pork pie. In the top of it was Stilton cheese. Jack had seen these before and liked them. He waited while Shaw chewed. Shaw nodded to him to eat himself.

'Can I encourage you to eat. Sad news as it is you and I will need to have this sustenance before we start our enquiries. There's not much up there in the way of hospitality.' Another bite into his pie.

Jack followed Shaw's example and was struck again by how good the pies were. Shaw wiped his mouth and resumed his story.

'Nathan Long went to the Coastguard Station at Fairlight.' Shaw continued. 'They, and the local constabulary are still there now. Lover's Seat is near the Coastguard cottages. Our Nathan is a navy man and the coastguard are reserves, of course. Natural he would go for them, I suspect. They would be likely to be more understanding of his plight. When we've had this little repast, Jack, we'll get along to Fairlight and see if we can speak to the Coastguard.'

Jack put his plate down and said: 'That Lover's Seat must have been the place Nathan and Grace went to together. That's why he went there. He must have found out something to make him go back and look for her. It's a long way from Brighton to here. I suppose there's no sign of a baby? Any likelihood it was suicide?'

'I don't give much for the local Coroner. You recall the Doctor who was certifying the deaths of the babies? The one who died? The Coroner decided that Doctor Elm's death was accidental. I ask you, a doctor dying of a knife wound that was accidentally self-inflicted. Ridiculous! Supposed to have fallen against, just in the right place to bleed to death quickly. How is that likely to be accidental? As you'll imagine it's not being investigated as a result,' Shaw moved onto the fruit tart.

'Where is Nathan now?' asked Jack, reaching for one himself.

'In custody in Hastings. We won't get to see him. Sergeant Field wants us to go over to Lover's Seat and Fairlight Coastguard Station. Personally, I doubt the Coastguard will talk to us. Still, we can have a look at the area. Why do you think there's likely to be a baby?'

'Something Nathan Long said about the circumstances. It's what happened to the child that's the mystery. A local Parson I know is going to check registry records and Christenings for me in the coming week. I'll see him next week for the answers.'

Jack took a moment to chew before continuing.

' I don't know if the baby died but most mothers register their children and name the father. She's likely to have wanted a Christening. I think Grace would know that Nathan would eventually return and come looking for her. Perhaps they always meant to meet again at Lovers Seat. It might have been something they vowed to do if things went wrong. Maybe she knew that she just had to hang on, keep the baby safe, if it was alive and when Nathan came back everything would be alright. Poor girl may have hoped that they'd get married and bring up their baby. Anyway, the Parson's going to check the Poor records as well. I wonder if she despaired because it was so long a time since he left. Perhaps she shared the location with someone who meant her harm.' Jack thought for some moments, staring into the crowd across the field. 'Poor girl,' said Jack again.

'Indeed,' said Shaw, quietly.

Jack reflected for a few moments more while he ate.

'Look, there's a chance the Coastguard might see us if it's Fairlight Coastguard station. If the Coastguard is Edward Croft I think he will see me. I tried to contact him earlier today but I didn't know he had moved stations. He was my father's great friend and if he has received my telegram I'm sure he'll talk to us,' Jack explained. 'The Coastguard at Kewhurst said he'd gone to Pett Level today, though.'

'Really? Interesting. There's been another body found there which might imply there's a connection. Local woman this time. Someone we've had our eye on for a while but that's a different story, of course. I won't muddy the waters but something you've said has made me wonder if Grace might have known the other victim.' Shaw stood up and peered into the distance towards the Albert Memorial Clocktower.

'Time we moved,' said Shaw. 'Well, let's set up supplies and go across. If the Coastguard is hospitable we may also get dinner. How fortuitous, Jack, that he's a friend. What are you thinking of now?' Shaw smiled at the furrowed brow.

'Just an idea. Is there a telegraph station fairly close?' Jack asked.

'At the railway station. Why?'

'I've a colleague, a doctor, or near enough. I'm sure she'd come down and have a look at the area where the body was found. I suppose there's no way we can get at Dr Elm's body and that of Grace?' suggested Jack.

'Not unless you want to face dismissal. Wrong team, lad. Hastings aren't too inclined to be friendly to Brighton pushing in, despite the fact that Grace is a Brighton woman. No, if this lady would come down, say tomorrow, we can get a look at the sight where the body was found once it's clear of the local constabulary. That's as close as we'll get.'

'As Grace is a Brighton woman can't Field exercise some authority? The case could get neglected. I doubt Nathan killed her. I saw what state he was in because she was missing and we don't know when she died, or why. Ann will get close to how if there's still evidence at the scene but as to why I'm not sure of that answer,' Jack started to roll out the napkin Shaw had collected and piled the remains of his afternoon tea into it.

'Ann?' asked Shaw.

'My doctor. Or rather she will be, should be, one day. I think she might be considered qualified in France. Not sure. We're going to need somewhere to stay. It's a waste of time going back to Brighton tonight, and as you saw at the cricket match in Brighton, I'm supposed to rest,' said Jack.

'Why not stay the night here?' asked Shaw.

Jack shook his head. 'No, I can't do it, no money for hotels in Hastings. I used what I had last night. There's just a chance the Coastguard might let us bed down, or there's the Parson at Selmeston. At a push we could get up to Battle and ask the Squire I used to work for if we could bed down. We also need to have somewhere respectable for Ann to stay tomorrow. Let's get back to the railway station and I'll get a telegram to her to come tomorrow, and then we can get across to Fairlight Coastguard. Do you have a map of where we're going?'

'Here,' said Shaw, passing an Ordnance Survey Map to Jack. 'It's recent,' He delved into his jacket pocket and produced another sheet of paper. 'There's an old plate picture as well, dated 1849, of Lover's Seat.' He passed Jack a small copy of an old print. It showed a couple sitting on a seat by a landslip with the title "Lovers Seat" underneath it. The area was clothed in dense woodland and tall cliffs with near vertical faces.

Jack nodded and handed it back. 'Looks difficult to get to,' he said.

Shaw sighed and struggled up.

'We can get there from Hastings alright.' Shaw pulled the Ordnance Survey map back towards himself and traced a route with his finger. 'It looks like the area has some paths on the top but it's not an area known to me. We can get to it from either Hastings or Fairlight by the looks of the map. Let's pick up a cab and get back to the station.'

Jack looked at the area on the map, tracing the paths back to Hastings. 'It would be easy for someone to have followed her,' he said.

Shaw stood up and folded the map along its creases. 'If someone was that determined it would not be hard. Look don't worry about where we stay. Field and Burgess have contacts in the town. They'll probably fix us up. I'll get a message to Field while you deal with your telegram to Doctor Ann. Let's get off.'

*

'The local advertising around here has it these are "fairy like nooks," explained Shaw, as he and Jack made their way on foot from where the cab had set them down on the headland. 'Sweet, umbrageous spot,' continued Shaw.

'I don't know what that means,' said Jack.

'No, neither do I. It's on an advertisement in the town. We need to go down one at a time. I'll go ahead if you like?' Jack nodded and Shaw started down the narrow steps which wound around the rock, hewn out of it by some workman. In the distance the roar of a waterfall could be heard.

Jack followed, examining the water seeping out of the rock. For a moment he thought it appeared as if the rock was crying. The water dripped incessantly through pores but no trace of it was left below. It was fanciful but he thought there was something supernatural about it. Tears shed for Grace and a potential miscarriage of justice in the arrest of Nathan Long. Bending down he found the soil was sandy on top of a beach stone, giving a subsurface flow of water.

'It comes out over there,' said Shaw, pointing to a defiant stream about a hundred yards away. From there the water disappeared again just as mysteriously as it had appeared. Jack found himself praying.

'The locals say its spiritual. Science says it's the type of soil,' Shaw called over his shoulder.

'Both are right,' said Jack, quietly. 'In such a place a murder like this should not happen.'

'Should it ever, anywhere,' Shaw said, grimly. Jack grunted his agreement.

'There are fish ponds over there. It's quite a romantic beauty spot apparently. I doubt it will be from now on for a while. If there's a killer loose, that is, there won't be much kissing and cuddling going on here.' Shaw had reached the bottom of his descent. He stepped to one side to allow Jack space to join him.

'Is that a sign over at that farm house?' Jack pointed to a building near a well a short walk from where they stood.

'My word, it is, we might have fallen on our feet, Jack. More tea I think and a little enquiry about some accommodation. They may be glad of the business as visitors will be a little sparse for a while. Are you up to sharing?' asked Shaw starting to quicken his pace towards the dwelling.

'Provided you don't snore,' Jack said with a grin.

'Good afternoon, miss,' Shaw called to a young woman carrying a pale of some type of liquid towards the kitchen door. 'Would you be providing tea today?' Shaw added.

'You must speak to Mother, sir,' she replied. 'The police seem to be putting everyone off today and we thought there would be no call for it.' She turned into the farmhouse and reappeared moments later with an older, worn version of herself, indicating that this was her mother. The older woman wiped her hands down her apron. There was flour on her sleeve which Jack took as an encouraging sign.

'Good day gentlemen, Emma said you were wanting tea?'

'We wondered if you had rooms also for the night with a dinner and breakfast available?' Jack asked before Shaw could.

'I do, although its simpler accommodation than you gentlemen look as though you are used to, but its clean and a comfortable bed in the rooms.' The woman weighed up Jack's manner of dress and the leather bag he was carrying. 'Looking at your suit, sir, I would think it may not be fine enough for you. Down from London are you?'

'My friend is,' interposed Shaw, 'and I'm from the other side of Eastbourne. Clean and comfortable is what we are after, madam, eh Jack?'

'Yes, this is an absolute Godsend as we were not expecting to come across any accommodation. We'd set our minds on finding the well and seeing the beauty today. Has something happened as you mention police?' Jack asked as innocently as he could manage. Shaw glanced at him.

'Oh, lord, yes, poor child, not much older than my Emma I would think. We saw the young man that's been arrested. He looked nice but funny how looks can be deceiving. Murder at Lover's Seat, sir. The body was covered over, the constable said. His opinion was it had been there for a while. The local force are all over the area. Tramping with their big boots. I shouldn't think there will be any evidence left to find after they've all been in there.'

'How perceptive you are, madam. The big boots of the average constable, eh,' Shaw laughed and the woman joined him. 'Well good to know an arrest has been made. Did the constable say how long the body had been there? I only ask because if it's a few days the killer is probably long gone and we can start our examination of the beach tomorrow, safely.'

'Oh are you here on a scientific enquiry? We can see the area from the bottom of our field if you're interested?' she asked.

'Marvellous,' said Jack. 'Yes we are and some colleagues may join us tomorrow. Shall we settle up with you now for two rooms, breakfast and dinner?'

'I've only two rooms but Emma could share with me if it's a third room you're wanting?' said the woman.

'For a female colleague, a Doctor of French Science,' Shaw nodded, raised his eyebrows to meet the expression of their new landlady whose own had met her hairline.

'Well goodness, what goes on these days. How clever she must be. From London is she?' asked the woman.

'London and Paris. A married lady, works with the children and women's hospital, and has been of great use in many scientific enquiries,' added Jack.

'Well we must make her comfortable, eh, Emma. You can move in with me in the morning and we'll get your room ready for her. It's a simple dinner, gentlemen, just a stew with bread today as I wasn't expecting many folk after what's happened. I can do a cake and there's local Sussex cheese. Simple but good food but though I say it myself I'm known as a good cook. Breakfast in the morning will be with our own cured bacon and we've our own dairy herd and eggs from our own chickens,' she looked at the wallet Shaw had produced.

'Let me get this, my friend,' said Shaw to Jack. He opened the wallet to invite her interest.

It worked.

'As we're here on business in the area I can make a claim from my employer. Could I trouble you for a receipt Mrs -?' asked Shaw.

'Crowhurst, like the place. Yes of course I'll give you one when you step into the hall. What kind of scientific business are you in?'

'Excavation,' said Shaw, 'the unearthing of dark and hidden secrets, history that would otherwise remain hidden and, of course, the truth.'

'Oh, you're like those gentlemen who came last year. Arch, something. What was it, Emma?' Mrs Crowhurst turned to her daughter.

'Archaeologists, Mother, from the university,' Emma answered shyly. She glanced at Jack, who controlled his expression, and then dropped her eyes.

'That's right. They said the truth is hidden often under-ground and often different from the accepted story,' added Mrs Crowhurst.

'Yes, I would say that's our trade, wouldn't you, Jack?' said Shaw.

'Exactly,' said Jack, starting to smile. It dissolved into a cough. Shaw gave him an assessing look.

'Well more scientific gentlemen is very interesting. We just have the two rooms and the bathroom is down here I'm afraid, just off the foot of the stairs. Only place we could put the pipes, you see. You'll be quite private though gentlemen, as we are at the back of the farmhouse. Emma's room for your Doctor is away from yours so all is respectable, as it should be. I'll take you up to your rooms and then Emma, show the gentlemen the view from the edge of the field. I haven't discussed terms with you, have I? It will be five shillings for the room each and half a crown for dinner and breakfast. I'll do a reduction for the lady tomorrow as it's not actually a guest room. That's each, mind,' added Mrs Crowhurst, for emphasis, as she looked into the wallet.

Shaw pulled out a pound note from his wallet and placed it into her hand. 'If we may trouble you for hot water tonight and also in the morning, Mrs Crowhurst, and a bill before we leave with any extras. My young colleague needs to rest, just for a short while as he's been a little unwell, you know. I wonder if we could prevail upon you for some tea? Thank-you. I would like to look at the activity from the edge of the field, however and perhaps you can point the way for me, Miss Emma. No need to take me down. Jack, I will report back to you after you've rested.'

Mrs Crowhurst led Jack upstairs to the two bedrooms while Shaw made his way around to the back of the farmhouse, following Emma's directions.

Upstairs there were two simple rooms, but as promised clean, with handmade patchwork quilts on the beds. These leant warmth and colour to the rooms. Handmade curtains of a brown cloth, hung from simple poles at the small windows and privacy was provided across the windows themselves by muslin drapes.

Emma was soon in and on her knees quickly laying a fire for later, as the stone building with its small windows was cool. She did so first in Jack's room while her mother showed him the outhouse which fronted as a bathroom.

There was a stone sink and a free standing tin bath with a separate lavatory next door. Jack wondered where the waste would go out to and assumed there would be a pit somewhere nearby. As with most old farmhouses the building was inclined to be warm in the winter and cool in the summer and a fire could well be needed later that night.

He retired to his room and picked up a book from the few on a shelf, "Smugglers and Smuggling," by John Banks. Jack lay down on the bed, drawing the quilt across the lower half of his body to provide some semblance of comfort. He read half way down the first page and then knew no more until he woke forty minutes later. He was shocked to find he had slept and that it had been so deep.

293

He could tell there was a difference from resting and the cough was more controlled. Dr Brown was right about resting. He could see that now. Well, he would do it each day as advised. Jack felt the most positive he had done since the Alexandra Palace fire because it was the first time his body had responded to a simple rest.

He swung his legs over the side of the bed and slipped his boots back on. Tea would have been nice, he thought, but he assumed that he had missed that. Lifting the latch on his bedroom door he looked round the landing and saw the tray of tea on a small bureau in the corner. Jack smiled and carried it into his room. Thick slices of farmhouse bread, strawberry jam, with wild fruit from their own grounds he assumed. It had been freshly and hastily made by just adding sugar and boiling the fruit. Its flavour had flavour. Butter from their own dairy, no doubt. Perfect, he thought. He lathered on the butter and jam and took a bite while he poured his tea. Five minutes and then he would go and join Shaw.

Emma pointed the way for Jack that Shaw had taken. He politely declined her mother's suggestion that her daughter accompany him to make sure he found his colleague. After the trouble over Mary he had no desire for the complications of another situation. For his own part he had no worries that he would become involved with another woman it was just the expectations of others that needed to be managed.

Shaw was busy sketching out the lay of the land in his notebook. The early evening was cool and Jack realised the wisdom of the laid fire in his room. He smiled at the sight of the sea as it cut into the cliffs and then receded and thought how he still would like to sail the coast, weather permitting. Jack called to Shaw to give him warning he was on his way and Shaw glanced up and raised a hand in greeting before returning to the task.

'How are you feeling?' said Shaw, as Jack drew level with him.

'Better, I had a sleep. How are you getting on?' asked Jack.

'Quite well. Come and see our friends spreading out. Mrs Crowhurst was right, we have a ring side seat here. Look, they're all over the site with their big boots. I doubt there will be anything for your Doctor to look at tomorrow by the time they've finished,' Shaw went back to his sketching.

'What are you drawing?' asked Jack.

'The layout of the coast from Hastings to Pett Level. The coast flattens out considerably to the east. If my instinct is right Sergeant Field will come over tomorrow to have a look. Hopefully our friends below will have finished and disappeared by tonight so we can get in there. I don't want someone recognising the Sergeant either tomorrow. What time did you suggest to your Doctor that she comes?' asked Shaw.

'About eleven o'clock as I think she's still covering for the Police Surgeon at the moment. I said I'd meet Ann at Hastings Railway Station. I'll check with Mrs Crowhurst if there's a cart I can borrow or a carrier, locally, that will be going in,' said Jack.

Shaw turned his notebook round to show Jack the layout.

'See how tall the cliffs are, about five hundred feet I would think. The sea cuts back into the cliffs here at Fairlight Coastguard Station, and look, Jack, how vertical they are.' Shaw prodded his drawing. 'They're not a hard rock either so they're eroding and quite hard to climb up. Makes it difficult to think that someone could have approached Grace from the sea up those.'

'Yes, I see. I expect she was followed over land. Or brought here and dumped after the death. But I can't see why someone would bring her here after she was dead. They'd be taking a terrible risk of being seen,' said Jack.

'They might if they knew it was a place she came hoping that Nathan Long would return to it. Frames him nicely, especially if he's been going around the area making enquiries about Grace,' mused Shaw.

Jack nodded, staring at the sea, thinking how different it always looked. 'Anyone approaching from the sea would risk the Coastguard seeing them,' he said.

'Right. So we're ruling out an approach by sea?' Shaw asked.

'Not sure. We could do with going down, over there,' Jack pointed. At the foot of Lover's Seat was a glen and it looked as if there was access from the beach.'

'Perhaps later, when our friends have gone.'

'Won't they leave someone on duty at the site?' asked Jack.

Shaw chuckled. 'Doubt it,' he said. 'I should think by nine o'clock they'll all be gone. We could try a late evening stroll and see if we can get down easily.'

Jack peered over and then looked around the area in which he and Shaw stood. He saw a rock, big enough to cause some movement down the cliff but not too heavy to lift. He picked it up and threw it. A rock fall began as the sandstone fell down the clay slopes.

'No-one's come up that way safely,' he said to Shaw. 'Not carrying a body anyway. I think that confirms there wasn't a sea approach.'

'Let's ask Mrs Crowhurst over dinner if there's a safe way down which we can't see from here.'

Mrs Crowhurst confirmed that there were access steps up from the glen. More than one set but some of them were worn away or crumbling. Care would be needed if Jack and Shaw were going to use them.

'How would you approach the Lovers Seat, Mrs Crowhurst?' asked Jack, as she dished up a fair portion of stew onto his plate.

'Oh from the paths and trails from Hastings and Fairlight. I wouldn't bother trying to get at it from the beach. You can do it but you'd have to come at it from Hastings in the west and Cliff End in the east. It's exhausting walking mind, and slow because there's too many boulders. I'd use the cliff path. You'd have to be careful not to go too close to the edge though because it isn't stable.'

'Always trust local knowledge,' said Shaw quietly.

Jack spooned stew into his mouth, smiled at Mrs Crowhurst and nodded.

'S'good,' he said. For which he received a smile.

*

By eight o'clock the tide had turned and the sea had calmed as the two men negotiated their way down the access steps to the glen. As correctly predicted the local constabulary had vanished.

'At least it won't be dark 'til late being so close to the longest day,' said Shaw.

Jack gave a wary look to his footing which he could see crumbled as he applied pressure. He would not want to do this alone in case of a fall. He could imagine Grace alone, slipping and dying, no one hearing her scream. Was that what had happened? Had someone followed her, frightened her and she'd fallen, perhaps breaking her neck? Then they'd hidden the body and covered it over to delay discovery not knowing that Nathan was back and looking for her. By the time he had found her it was too late. Jack thought of the brave young sailor, a veteran of so much action, finding his love. He must have been distraught.

Nathan would be used to death. How would it have affected him? Jack ran the questions, one after another through his mind. Had he run for help to the Coastguard refusing to accept that she was dead? Had it been Edward Croft that had come to find the body and sent for the police? She had been on a missing person list and Hastings had been told about her by the Brighton force. What had made the Hastings force arrest Nathan? Were there signs of a struggle at Lovers Seat, or other evidence that it was not accidental. Had someone followed her and killed her and left signs of violence there? If that was the case how could this young woman have become a threat to anyone? Or was there another reason? Situations came back to him that he had seen occasionally in London where a woman was violently murdered on the street for no apparent reason.

They were down at the glen at last. 'We shouldn't be too long in case we have problems getting back up,' said Jack.

Shaw looked past him towards an area of ground water in the sandstone above.

'I'm afraid, Jack that we are not alone after all.'

297

Jack followed Shaw's line of sight to see a uniform coming down the access steps towards them. It was then lost in the shadows created by the copse near the Lovers Seat.

'Police?' asked Jack.

'Not sure. Better get our story straight. What are we after down here?'

'Fossils,' said Jack, quickly. 'There's loads of them on the beaches further up the coast. Father would show me in the rocks and pebbles. Probably the same here. If we're fronting this as Archaeologists I think this is our best story.'

'Alright, I'll let you lead,' said Shaw.

Jack turned away as the uniform came into view again. He squatted down and turned over pebbles until he did find evidence of a plant in one in fossilised form. He passed it to Shaw who made a studied effort to get his notebook out and make a record of the find. Again Jack showed Shaw another example.

'You're good at this,' said Shaw.

'Used to do it on the beaches. Father would say he'd buy me a boat if I found a crocodile tooth.'

'Did you?' asked Shaw.

Jack grinned and glanced up. 'No, not where we were looking. Father knew he was on a safe bet. Although there are stories of finds by folk further east.'

The man in the uniform had stopped. His hands were on his hips and he was standing in the shadows. Jack stood up so that he could be clearly seen and looked over in the man's direction and waved a welcome. It was a Coastguard uniform. Jack smiled and nodded, about to resume his hunt on the beach. The Coastguard had recognised the similarity to the volunteer he had worked with so many years ago. He cupped his hands to his mouth.

'Ah, Jack,' called the Coastguard, 'still looking for treasure, eh?'

*

298

Seventeen

'I received your telegram,' called the Coastguard as he emerged from the shadows against the cliff.

Jack let out a bellow.

'Mr Croft,' he exclaimed. Shaw looked from one to the other and finally gave Jack a hard stare.

'You used to say Uncle Edward,' called back Edward Croft, as he picked his way across the boulders and pebbles until he was three feet away from Jack and Shaw.

Edward Croft stood square on, grey speckling the black hair, a much sturdier build than Jack remembered. He had a confidence that skill and promotion had brought to him. Edward turned to Shaw and held out his hand, his eyes twinkling.

'I had a telegram from a colleague at Kewhurst today,' he explained. 'Following a visit from a young man who was my dear friend's son. It arrived before murder was discovered, when the midday sun still had a purity to it that later felt tainted. The telegram told me that this young man here had become a policeman. I doubt you're really here as a fossil hunter. Are you a policeman as well?'

Shaw lifted his eyes warily but caught the humour in Edward's expression. He laughed and nodded, and shook hands with Edward Croft.

'Brighton Police,' Shaw said. 'Here on a missing person's case.'

Croft nodded and Jack knew that the coastguard understood there was some connection with the dead woman found at Lovers Seat.

'And you, young Jack?' asked Croft.

'Metropolitan Police,' Jack answered and held out his hand and smiled, unable to speak further with the emotion sparked by the reunion.

It could have been the wind off the sea that made the young man's eyes water but the coastguard doubted it. Edward paused and assessed how he should greet a young man that, as a boy, he would have swung up onto his shoulders. The day had brought tragedy in two places which he thought he knew well. Human action at both Lovers Seat and Pett Level had moved him to a mood he disliked. Both situations had made him despair. Despite the sense which Edward Croft felt that the day had been fouled by murder he took Jack's hand and pumped it up and down. His wind-tanned face relaxed into sheer pleasure at a reunion he had long ago dismissed as ever likely to happen.

'You've come on a strange day,' said Edward. 'I've spent most of it dealing with police. I was not expecting two of their number almost at my front door this evening. You won't have much credibility here hunting for fossils at Fairlight only. Pett Level is better and I can tell you there's a good reason for you to go there tomorrow. What story are you giving people around here?'

'The assumption at the farm was we were Archaeologists from London, like the last group that visited. We've gone with that as digging up the truth seems to fit with being police,' Jack explained.

'I hope so. How like William you've become,' said Edward, assessing the build and features of the young man. Feeling he should say more he added, 'I feel as if he's here with me. It's so clear in your stance and that smile of yours. He'd be proud if he could see you. And your mother. Come back with me and see Lucy. We have children now and you must meet them tomorrow, Martha and Andrew. Too many years Jack, without any word of you, and we have so much to tell. There's time for that now, but first let me get you both to a comfortable chair and put a glass in your hands. Then you can tell me how you both come to be involved in death here.'

As they walked towards the Coastguard Station Shaw quickly told Edward Croft that there had been a missing woman from Brighton reported and they believed it was Grace that had died at Lovers Seat. They had come after reports of Nathan Long being in the Hastings area. Jack confessed to having met Nathan and to having been drafted into the case by Shaw's superior.

Edward listened as he led the two men back up the steps towards the coastguard cottages at the top of the cliff. He pause as he put his hand on the latch of the door and said, 'Nathan has been arrested for the murder of Grace.'

Edward had understood the nature of the relationship between the sailor and the dead woman but on this he remained silent for the time being. In the walk from the beach back to his coastguard's cottage he had reached a conclusion that he could tell Jack and Shaw about the other body that had been found in Pett Level. But first another reunion was needed.

They reached the Fairlight coastguard station after a good climb. These were still fairly new after their rebuild and they were generous buildings of brick instead of wood, with a yard in the front and rainwater being collected in an underground tank. The gardens stretched up the hill as far as the rock-face and provided a good opportunity for vegetable growing to expand the diet.

Lucy Croft had jumped up as her husband walked in with two strangers. He quickly explained that William's son had come at last. Jack registered they had long expected him with some surprise. At first she did not say anything but looked and looked at Jack and then at her husband. Lucy did not speak at first but held out her hand and then spoke:

'It's the best night for some time and makes my heart happy after the sadness earlier today. But Edward, you must not let me rattle on in my excitement.'

Jack's memory of her was of a young, pretty woman, quiet but with kind eyes, standing next to her new husband, Edward, in the churchyard. He remembered the soft smile and the little wave she had given him as he had stood, holding the hand of the woman from the orphanage, trying to take in how his parents could be in the grave. In meeting her properly now she gave the overwhelming impression of contentment with her life.

'The children are asleep,' said Lucy. 'But here is the little boy I know mattered so much to Edward, now become a man, and a success by the careful way you have dressed. Even though we watched you leave the funeral with your aunt all those years ago, with some heart ache I can tell you, and have had no word for years, we've never forgotten Edward's promise to your father. We've prayed for you daily along with the prayers for our own children. And now you're with us again. I won't take no for an answer. Jack, you must stay here with us for the few nights that you're in the area and tell us about yourself. '

'That's a wonderful idea Jack and it sorts the problem of where your colleague who is arriving tomorrow will stay if you vacate the room at the farmhouse,' said Shaw.

Jack gladly accepted despite the confusion he felt at what had been said.

For the supper she put before them Lucy had brought out wine and cake and Jack joked about how Edward might have obtained the array of bottles in the store. Once the wine was open all reservations vanished. Jack felt memories coming back in being with this old family friend as he sipped wine and served himself a respectable slice of cake. After the events of the day being with Edward in his home felt like it was a normality in some strange way.

Lucy had produced fine crystal, four dainty petal cut glasses which generally only saw the light of day on birthdays and at Christmas. Shaw chattered to her about his own young family, while he obediently set out plates and knives which Lucy handed to him. Jack learnt more about him in that exchange than he had all day.

Jack had also noted, with some surprise, the level of commitment to him from the Crofts. It was, however, the reference to the woman as an aunt again that stung like a barb into his mind. He let it go for the time being as there was other business but made a decision to talk to Edward alone before he and Shaw left him that night.

'The body at Pett Level,' Jack said, 'What do you know about it?'

To his surprise it was Lucy who answered.

'It's a local woman, Mabel Walters. She ran some sort of business putting babies born out of wedlock up for adoption. Local folk called her a "baby farmer," which was not meant as a compliment.'

Edward picked up the tale. 'There was some sort of connection with that Doctor who died recently, Doctor Elm. As I understand it he was on a retainer to check the babies over before they were adopted, issue death certificates if they died, that sort of thing. Suspicion abounds as to what happened to some of those little mites if they weren't adopted.'

'We think Grace may have had a child by Nathan Long,' said Jack. 'It might explain why she was here if she'd put the child up for adoption with this Mabel Walters,' said Jack.

'Perhaps she'd changed her mind?' Shaw suggested.

'And wanted the child back?' asked Jack. 'Lucy, would you know how the woman operated her business?'

Lucy sighed. She paused from polishing her glass and stared at Jack, before dropping her eyes to the table.

'Mabel Walters charged a fee to take the babies and find adoptive parents for them,' answered Lucy. 'I assume she was then paid for providing the child by the prospective new parents. Apparently a lot of them went abroad so we wouldn't have any way of tracing the child. She must have tried to do this quickly, mind, because you wouldn't want a baby for too long, needing nursing and feeding. It was a flat fee, you see, from the mother so I doubt if she would be benevolent once the money ran out.'

'Sounds horrendous,' said Jack.

'Well yes, but, by all intents and purposes, she appeared to run a successful business as the children were moved out quite fast. Certainly there seemed to be quite a turnover,' said Lucy.

'How would you know all this, Mrs Edwards?' asked Shaw.

Lucy looked at Edward before she answered. 'Women talk, that's all I can say,' she said.

'Lucy does some work locally helping young women in distress,' said Edward. 'But she won't tell you anymore, gentlemen, as she would see it as a breach of a confidence.'

'The fathers are long gone in these cases are they?' asked Jack.

'What can I say, Jack? You're a young man, how would you be?' asked Lucy.

'You forget, I grew up in an orphanage. It's not something I want for any children I will have,' said Jack. 'I made a decision that it won't happen.'

Realms of imagination ran wild in Lucy's eyes.

So, they didn't know, thought Jack. Edward's eyes remained fixed on him. Jack looked away unable to cope with the emotion there. But Edward's stare was unrelenting.

Lucy drew a breath. 'You're unusual as a man that you've thought about a child out of wedlock,' she said.

Shaw had been watching the impact of Jack's explanation and sat forward. His movement had the effect of bringing them back to the subject. 'Might you have met a lady called Grace?' he asked the Crofts.

'Possibly, but few give their real name,' said Lucy.

'If you could see the body?' asked Jack.

'That's not likely to happen,' Edward answered. 'The dead woman has already been identified as Grace by Nathan Long. I'm not sure I want Lucy exposed to that.'

'Did you see the body?' Jack asked Edward.

'I did,' Edward answered, briefly.

'How did you think she died?' Shaw asked.

'Frankly? I think she was hit with something sharp from behind. You need a doctor to tell you, really,' said Edward, slowly.

'You'll do from all the stories you and Father told me,' Jack said.

Edward hesitated, recalling a memory. He nodded and drained his glass. Lucy placed her hand on his arm and Jack realised the state in which Grace had been found had upset him.

'Had she been dead long?' Jack persevered.

Edward indicated anguish. 'Gentlemen, you must talk to a doctor. What I can tell you is there was no rigor mortis. Over the years I've heard and seen enough to know if the body's not stiff they've been dead a couple of days or more.'

'And you don't think she died in an accident? asked Jack.

'Who knows. Nathan ran ahead of me. He'd moved her when I got there, half out of his mind with the distress. When I got to the spot he was cradling her in his arms and talking to her as if she was asleep. Broke your heart to hear it.' Edward said.

They were quiet for a while. Edward spoke again:

'There are too many people go to that spot for Grace's body to have been there for two days. I would say she'd been placed there recently when Nathan found her. Why? I don't know.'

Shaw stood to stretch out a back problem he had and Jack finished the small cake pieces he had left on his plate. An obvious check on the conversation had developed. Edward stared at his young friend, so newly restored to them, yet different to when they had last met. Jack finished the last crumbs and saw the expression on Edwards face.

'Tell us,' Edward began with an effort, 'Tell us how your life in the orphanage was?'

Jack told them of it. He excluded most of the detail and stopped the topic quickly. To fill them in completely on the remaining years from the age of nine, he explained his work as a labourer at Battle, the effect of the weather last year on the harvests and the decision to answer the national advert placed by the Metropolitan police in the newspapers.

Shaw moved his position further away from the group to allow the privacy. The silence at the table was heavy. Jack made a half-jolly comment and an attempt to return to small talk but the Crofts held the facts heavily.

'There was a will,' said Edward.

'Perhaps,' said Jack. 'They probably owed money. Most people do.'

'No, no, your mother had too good a business head for that. I know this because your father specifically told me he wanted me as one of the trustees and I've been consulted once a year by the solicitors. What your parents left has been managed well, I would say. The solicitors assumed.... No, we all assumed, that you were safe and cared for and that on your twenty-first birthday you'd come into the trust. Had your aunt submitted bills for your care they were to be paid. Nothing was received and we wrongly assumed she was caring for you and had married as she intended to do.'

Jack shrugged this off. 'I know nothing of an aunt. Well, too many years have gone by now. I've a new life and will make my career in the police.'

Lucy left the table saying she would check on Martha and Andrew as noises were heard upstairs. In the natural break her movement created Edward collected the cheese from the larder and poured more wine for them all. His face, however, showed some unease at what had happened to Jack. He said:

'I realise you're making your own way. I'm sorry.'

Jack nodded.

After a respectable silence Shaw emerged from the shadows in the room and asked:

'You mentioned that Pett Level was good for fossils. As we're masquerading as Archaeologists could we quite legitimately go there tomorrow, perhaps with the excuse that nothing has been damaged?'

'Yes, I'll take you,' said Edward, placing the cheese at Jack's elbow. 'I was going to suggest it to you.'

Jack cut himself a chunk and bit into it. 'This is good,' he said.

'It's from the farm where you're staying,' Edward explained.

'Shaw mentioned earlier if I stayed here it would leave a room free at the farm for a colleague arriving in the morning. I'll meet her at Hastings and bring her out here,' explained Jack.

'Is she a nurse or have some experience of these situations?' asked Edward.

'She has a medical degree from Paris and works with the Police Surgeon in Stepney. She will qualify as an English doctor when it's allowed but, yes, at the moment she would describe herself as a nurse. To me she's much better than most male doctors I've had the misfortune to encounter. Apart from Doctor Brown the Police Surgeon, that is,' said Jack.

'I can take you to Pett Level. From what I heard the Sergeant say tonight about Lovers Seat they've finished there so you've both got free reign in the beauty spot tomorrow.' Edward cut himself a piece of cheese and offered the knife to Shaw. It prompted a question.

'Did they find the knife that killed Doctor Elm?' Jack asked Shaw.

'No, not that I've heard. As I said to you the verdict of the Coroner was it was accidental so I doubt they've tried,' answered Shaw. A thought occurred to him and he looked at Edward. 'How did Mabel Walters die?' he asked.

'That's to be decided,' said Edward as he cut cheese for Lucy and placed it on her plate next to her uneaten cake. 'In my opinion, as I attended after she was found, she had been bleeding from a wound. Her body was dumped in low water at Pett Level, face down. She either bled to death or drowned. You'd need an autopsy to decide what caused her death. She'd certainly been attacked.'

'Why were you called to be there instead of the police?' asked Shaw, raising his eyebrows.

Edward grimaced.

'Sea matters tend to register in people's minds as the duty of the Coastguard Service. Bodies in water, or beached, count as that for locals. Some of the history locally means we go way back in our connections with local families, especially where there's a family member we may have had a hand in saving. We were here before the police were set up, if you don't mind me saying that, gentlemen.'

Shaw nodded, understanding the local connections the coastguard would have.

Edward Croft reached towards a rack of clay pipes and a leather tobacco pouch next to them. He offered Jack and Shaw a pipe and dropped the pouch on the table. Jack refused but Shaw took a pipe and helped himself to the ample tobacco, pressing it into the bowl. Edward continued in his explanation.

'Yes, those times before the police it was called the Coast Blockade Service. We were viewed as the Navy on shore. Hastings commanded the Sussex Eastern Division and we were tough, efficient, and disliked. Fairlight was a Watch House and then a Coastguard Station and the service had bloody years in its history. After the 1840's, when I was a child, the service became known for helping people in distress, and vessels too, plus stopping the plundering of wrecks. I joined as a young man while England was involved in the Crimean War. The service was drafted into the Navy and became a defence force on the coast. We started developing volunteer life savers, which is how I met Jack's father.' Edward took a sip of his wine and held the glass up against the candle to look at the rich colour.

'So you see, here it's about who does someone go to first?' Edward continued. 'In Nathan's case, I think he would turn to us because he thought of us as Navy. There's also some difficult terrain where there's an abandoned cliff line east of Cliff End, behind Pett Level and Romney Marsh, with landslips, mud and earthflows. We'd know our way around there. It's quite a frequent occurrence when a dead body is found, or someone has gone missing who frequented the area, for people to call on us because we're nearby.'

Jack nodded. 'Nathan probably told you he'd had no success with the police in Brighton as well?'

Edward glanced at Shaw, not wishing to cause embarrassment. Shaw raised his eyebrows again and grimaced.

'He did, yes,' Edward said.

'Who found the other body, the baby farmer?' asked Shaw.

'Local historian, interested in the Sunken Forest,' explained Edward.

'What's that?' asked Shaw.

'It's thought to be sunken woodland, goes back thousands of years. The sea levels rose, according to local people, sand piled up and the forest is under the sand. The coastline was much further out than it is now, you see. There's the odd cave in the cliffs as well. People round here take it for granted but some feel it's a bad place. Most of the time you can't see it but after a storm the sediment gets washed away. Whoever left Mabel Walters there was probably banking on her not being discovered.'

'Are there actually trees under the sea there?' asked Jack.

'Sometimes a sapling still grows, but the trees under the sand are soft enough to break as the wood is spongy. The changes make it interesting to local historians and we get many a number coming down from London quite frequently. There's an old wreck too, dating back to the 1690's and at one point there was a whole line of Martello Towers. Those Archaeologists that you referred to who stayed at the farm found fossils. Part of the sandstone cliff crumbled while they were here, increasing their interest. Certainly you men going there tomorrow will be just part of a continuous stream of people. I'll accompany you, if I may, and can show the exact location of where the body was found today. It's not there now, of course.'

'Where exactly was it?' asked Jack pulling out Shaw's map.

'The location is between Hastings and Cliff End, if you're looking at the map. Here.' Edward traced the area with a finger.

'We should go and all get some rest,' said Jack, folding the map up and handing it back to Shaw. 'You must be tired Edward with everything you've had to deal with today. I'm also on doctor's orders to get "rest," so, I must certainly go.'

Lucy returned to the room and took her seat again. She picked at her cake and watched Jack. He smiled at her and lifted his hand in a small wave, as he had done the last day he had seen her.

'You remember,' she said, softly.

Jack nodded.

Edward gave Lucy a meaningful look. She turned and took his hand. He patted it, stood up and said to her.

'We'll escape for the walk back to the Farmhouse and in case you are asleep when I get back I won't disturb you.'

'And you will come, tomorrow Jack?' asked Lucy, as he also rose to go.

'I will, of course,' Jack said. 'Thank-you both. I didn't know there were people still waiting for me, caring, the way you obviously have done, while I was growing up.'

Edward Croft searched the horizon as he did always on leaving his front door. Jack and Shaw followed his line of sight. There was traffic towards the horizon but no reason for concern. The weather was settled and there would be no risk of storm tonight.

The walk back to the Farmhouse in the dusk showed a bright moon bestowing a pathway of light across the sea. Edward Croft pointed out the sandstones to the west of the Coastguard station in the upper parts of the cliff.

As they walked Edward broached the reason he thought Jack was in Brighton.

'I heard of the success of the Shah's visit to Portsmouth from my colleagues there. That is why you're back in Sussex isn't it, to do with the Shah? The Coastguard officers at Brighton and Shoreham were mightily disappointed that he didn't come afterwards. There are eleven officers and their families in Shoreham Coastguard station and they were to be at the presentation. I gather the Mayor of Brighton had to placate quite a few of the dignitaries staying in the town.'

Jack stopped and placed a hand on Croft's arm. 'He didn't come? Are you sure? After all that preparation? I didn't know. I left Brighton on Monday and assumed the visit had gone ahead.'

'No, apparently he had to get back to London. Some function he was due at.'

'I didn't realise that you didn't know,' Shaw said.

Jack started to move a pebble out of the way with his foot, giving it some consideration as he did so.

'I assumed that was why you were there, in Brighton? asked Edward.

Jack nodded.

'When I read about the arrests at Portsmouth and the injuries and I got your message this morning saying you'd be back next week to see me but were staying in Brighton I thought you must be part of the police team that had been there. I hope your colleague is on the mend?' Edward added.

Jack stared at Edward, confused. The moonlight seemed to highlight the starkness of this news. Familiar noises in the undergrowth drew Jack's attention to the small creatures that inhabited it. He was aware of bitterness in his soul. More than that, an anxiety at his exclusion by his colleagues had mixed with a sickness that had grown at the news of a relative he did not know about. He felt sour and tired of it all.

'Damn me, but you're right. That was part of the reason I was there.' Jack placed his foot against a boulder and it moved slightly. 'The other reason was for the clean sea air,' said Jack.

He tried to supress his annoyance but managed to increase the movement of the boulder until he could feel it give. Back and forth it moved, more and more, as he loosened it considerably.

Edward had some recognition of the small boy within the man, resentful of being unable to do an activity. He remembered Jack would keep on until he could master something and at times his father had carried the small child away, angry and tearful at not being allowed to exhaust himself and accomplish what he had set his heart to complete.

The strength of the father at that point could overcome the small child. Edward doubted many would be able to stop Jack physically now never mind when he was completely well.

With a final push the boulder gathered pace and a small landslip started. Jack grimaced at his handiwork but the conflict inside was still there. He kicked several smaller rocks towards the cliff edge and then stood staring after them.

Was there an Aunt? he wondered. If there was why had he been left, forgotten, in the orphanage? What might his life have been? He had not wanted to know this information about a relative. There was no resentment against Edward telling him as Jack knew they were completely in the dark about his life before today. He had been resigned to his lot as long as he had his strength. He had never believed he would remain as a farm labourer. Now the staying power of strength which he always remembered having as he reached manhood was gone, burnt up in the Alexandra Palace fire, perhaps not forever but certainly gone at present.

The thoughts mixed with the irritation at incomplete information. Someone was injured on the team. That could only mean Harry. It certainly could not be Sam who would have remained in the background. Doubts came to him. The policeman injured may not be from his team. Could he have changed the situation if he had been there? Edward had said arrests had been made. Of whom and why? Surely not the police officers involved?

'Field may know who was involved when he comes tomorrow,' said Shaw. 'I'll bid you both goodnight, and get away to my bed.' Shaw did not want to hear the breach of confidence that was no doubt about to happen as Jack disclosed the reasons for his presence in Brighton to his old friend. 'I'll see you at breakfast, Jack,' he added and turned to go.

Jack nodded briefly. Shaw's footsteps crunched as he walked away, the sound fading as he put the distance between himself and the other two men. Edward stood watching Shaw disappear up to the Farmhouse. This was not necessarily a comfortable position to be in but he would do what he had to.

———

'Are you happy with your life?' he asked Jack.

'My life? Until recently I was.' Jack was sweating with the effort he had expended. He coughed. The silence afterwards was dispiriting. Edward waited and looked at Jack's face, and thought it was grey. Perhaps it was the moonlight.

'Look,' said Jack. 'This aunt you mention did not exist for me. I've had no family sen I was nine except for kindness from the Squire I worked for. Then there has been the police. Do you understand how I feel part of them?'

Edward nodded. 'I understand that. I've always felt like that about the Coastguard Service. Has that changed?'

'I hope not, because I've nothing if it has. Look, I need to sit down.' Jack sat on a rocky outcrop at the side of the grass. Edward sat a few feet away.

'If I don't have the police I'll be lost. They're my future. It's how I get back to the position I imagine I would have had if Mother and Father had lived. Look, Edward, I was sent to Brighton to recover from injuries in the Alexandra Palace fire. My Inspector agreed with the doctor that I could do certain small duties but I over-reached myself because I didn't accept that my body wouldn't recover quickly. My Sergeant took me off the small work I had been doing and excluded me from any briefing about Portsmouth. That's why I'm surprised to hear from you what has happened.' Jack paused, wondering how much more to explain.

Jack added: 'I also disclosed information to a civilian, a woman who is a friend, like I'm doing with you now.'

Edward nodded.

'I'm not up to strength after the fire and won't be unless I rest as I've been told to. I was taken out of active duty in the team but, you know the worst thing was that they didn't include me in the planning for Portsmouth at all. They didn't trust me. That's what makes me angry and that's why I don't know what happened.' Jack met Edward's eyes and then looked away as there was pain in Edward's expression for him and Jack did not want to see it.

313

'It may be that they thought you would rest more if they didn't include you,' suggested Edward. 'All I know is there was an accident at Spithead and there were injuries and arrests. It's not in the papers,' said Edward.

'I wonder if the team's still in Brighton or they've gone?' mused Jack.

'Perhaps these colleagues that're coming tomorrow will know?' suggested Edward.

'Yes, maybe.'

'I'll see what I can find out for you as I can telegraph the station there. Jack, tell me, have you been disciplined in any way?' Edward asked.

'No,' said Jack. He stifled a tendency to cough and minutes went by as the choking cough consumed him as a result.

'Let's get you inside,' said Edward. The two men followed the path that Shaw had taken. '

'I ask because I want to know and because I think I have the right to,' continued Edward. 'You see, I made a promise, to your parents when you were born, to you and to God. You really don't remember that I'm your Godfather, do you? Lucy, and I, watched you led away at the funeral by a woman who we were told was your aunt. The Parson also was quite clear about who she was.'

'Yes, he mentioned an aunt as well as you.'

Edward continued: 'We wrote every month for a year to the address we had and nothing came back. I even went to the property. It was rented and I was told that she'd left it, married, and had gone. We thought that she'd taken you with her. If we'd known where you were I would have come and got you. Just a few miles away, Jack, that's all its been but it might as well have been across the sea.'

Edward placed a hand on Jack's shoulder. Jack glanced at him and then looked out to sea, struggling with emotions which he thought he had under control years ago. The two men sat a few feet away from each other as time went on. There was silence between them. The sea was the third companion and the only one that spoke for some time.

Jack coughed. 'I have to look forward, Edward. I just don't seem to have control of things anymore. The one thing I've always been is physically strong and without that I can't do the job. There's bad in the past but there's also been great things, good people and I know nothing of this woman you think was my aunt. All I remember after the funeral is that we went somewhere to a building. She went into a room with a small man with spectacles on the end of his nose, and I sat on a bench with a glass of water, in a waiting area with dark wooden panels and stained glass windows. She seemed to be in there for ever. At one point I heard her shout. She came out, took me by the hand and then I was at the orphanage. I thought that was where she was from and the word "aunty" was just a title she had from them. I understood there was no one.'

Jack shook his head and moved his hand irritably and said:

'As far as I'm concerned my life will be with the police. That's been my family for the last year and now health and a mistake has meant I'm not playing a full role.'

Jack disintegrated into a spasm of coughing. Edward made to move towards him, but Jack put up a hand to stop him.

Edward watched him anxiously but said nothing. The coughing slowly subsided and Jack grimaced at his pulled stomach muscles.

'Let me help you back to your room, and we can meet tomorrow. I'll get you information about the policeman at Spithead, I promise. Jack?'

'Yes?' Jack waited.

'Don't disappear,' Edward said.

*

Eighteen

On the afternoon that Jack and Shaw started their investigation at Fairlight and Lovers Seat, Inspector Tom Hunt was at the Windsor review. There, he seized an opportunity with an old friend from his childhood to get the release of an injured detective sergeant, languishing in custody in Portsmouth.

Hunt did so while the band played a few bars of the National Anthem during which time the Queen was standing in her carriage, looking at a long line of soldiers on the review ground at Windsor.

'Seven thousand, one hundred and forty in fact, Tom,' she said, liking that he was surprised she knew.

He kicked himself for letting it show. He and others should really not underestimate the woman.

The area between the Long Walk and Queen Anne's Ride was the spot chosen for the manoeuvres and the flags of England and Persia floated between them. Eton boys were in an enclosure in front of the stands, with the children of several charity schools in the neighbourhood. With them were officers in uniform.

For a mile or so, carriages in reserved places seemed to stretch endlessly. Hunt glanced around and wondered how long it would take for them all to move off once the review was over. He thought it would be easy for a stray bullet to finish the Shah, sitting there on his white Arab charger with a magenta tail. The bridle was studded with jewels, as was the Shah's outfit. Hunt thought it would be difficult to miss him if someone was of a mind to polish him off.

The Shah moved off suddenly and rode inspecting the line with the Duke of Cambridge. Hunt compared his own costume. Dressed in a dark uniform, as was the man he was there to protect, the Prince of Wales, it could not be more different.

Hunt had hoped for time to speak to the Prime Minister about Harry's arrest but this was not to be as Gladstone had not come. However, an opportunity came for him when a bored monarch, with two princesses, had detained him to stay near their open carriage. Her Majesty felt they had hung around waiting all afternoon for the Shah.

'Of course, he was late, Tom,' the Queen said. 'Now it's five o'clock and we've put back tea. He isn't going to look at everyone, surely. He's far too spectacular isn't he? That's the appeal, of course. I imagine the man is probably driven mad with all the toadying that's going on. A policeman's nightmare I would imagine, with such a show. I believe at Covent Garden he had on a black felt cap rather like those worn by plumbers. However, there was the large diamond aigrette on it, which made it different, of course. His epaulettes, apparently, were all diamonds and on the top was a huge emerald. All the facings of his coat were diamonds and the sword belt was the same, as was the scabbard. Most of our men were in uniform but I gather every display of diamonds on the women was made. One lady, I'm told was almost hidden by diamonds and had a jewelled stomacher, diamonds at her throat, on her head, at her wrists. Really, as if we have to compete.'

The cheering had started and Hunt nodded and made a response of, 'Ma'am.' His mother had taught him not to ask the Queen questions.

'Have you any idea what time I was at the scene this morning? Earlier than any of you. Nine o'clock watching the throwing of a pontoon bridge across the river at Datchet. And they have the audacity to say I've withdrawn! I doubt they'll put that in the papers. Were you at Portsmouth?'

'Yes, Ma'am,' answered Tom Hunt.

'Did you get luncheon at Admiralty House?' asked the Queen.

'No, Ma'am, I went straight to the special train,' said Hunt, meaning they had excluded him.

'Too bad,' said the Queen, knowing that they would have done so. 'I believe the Shah has no interest in music and was more interested in having a look at the women in the boxes apparently, at Covent Garden. They say he roared with laughter at the chorus. Still it got them an encore. I would have liked to see the boxes hung with roses. Apart from that I'm glad to be out of it. What did you do for luncheon at Portsmouth?'

Hunt managed to briefly explain about the problem with the yacht at Portsmouth and an arrest of one of his men, who had been injured. There was no time for any response from Queen Victoria.

'Oh goodness, he's coming over,' the Queen looked away. Hunt positioned his horse between the Shah and the Queen. No stray bullets meant for their visitor would hit her while Hunt was present.

The Shah had deftly wheeled his horse around and rode towards the Queen's carriage. The Shah bent low in his saddle and said a few words, which were lost to Hunt in the noise from the crowd. The Queen smiled a response.

The Shah moved away and placed himself in front of the Royal Standard and apart from once saying something to the Queen over his shoulder, which she didn't catch, he never spoke a word.

Bodies of rifles were being thrust out in a mock skirmish and the field artillery were brought into action. The ranks spread the full length of the review ground with the cavalry charging in brigades.

The Shah presented a sword with a jewelled hilt to the Duke of Cambridge and the Queen's carriage at last turned for the castle. The royal party followed and Hunt followed at a distance. As the Queen's carriage drew level with a Lieutenant Colonel she spoke to him.

The soldier rode to join Tom Hunt, an aide trotting at his side.

Lieutenant-Colonel Hardinge, who had been Prince Albert's equerry in 1858 and then the Queen's after Albert's death, had been delegated to duties with the Shah. The Queen had sent him across to see what help he could give the Inspector in return for a little problem solving of a situation that had developed at the Woolwich review. He was quite blunt with Tom Hunt on the ride back.

'Of course the Queen has been nervous because we don't know enough about the man. It's a bit like a bottomless pit and he's a sovereign from the wrong side of the planet. We'd hoped to get through everything without a problem. But after the review at Woolwich on Saturday six of the diamonds adorning the trappings of the Shah's horse were missing. Embarrassing, of course, but frankly there are so many people coming and going I'm surprised more hasn't got pinched. I doubt he'll miss them, but it's happened on our watch so we need to take action.'

'Did anyone see anything unusual?' asked Hunt.

'We've got a description of a blonde man we're pretty sure is not on the staff. Everyone thought he was part of the Shah's entourage but apparently he wasn't. We've got a sketch of him from a reporter, the hair was so striking. We've held off from that going in the papers at present in case the man disappears as a result. See what you can do, will you? The diamonds are worth about three hundred pounds. How the man got in is a conundrum. Apart from that I suppose it's gone quite well. Need to spruce up the Palace when he and his entourage leave. The Queen heard the Shah engaged professional fighters to spar at the Palace. That and secreting a chicken thigh bone under the table at lunch. No wonder she's felt nervous. Now what did you say had happened to your Detective Sergeant?'

'His arm was damaged in the review at Spithead. He was on the yacht that got too close, there under my orders, but of course he had no say in what the owner would get his crew to do. His right arm was injured but he was one of the men arrested.'

'I hadn't heard about this,' said Hardinge.

'All that's been reported was that the Shah had "assisted" the naval inspection, visiting several ships and showing a great interest in them. The papers commented that the Prince and Princess of Wales were there on the royal Yacht, with their children and the Russian heir to the throne and his wife. They merely said a boat had been disabled but no personal injury was reported. But questions are being tabled in both Houses,' said Tom Hunt.

'Are they indeed? Can't have that,' said Hardinge.

'I'd like to get him released and into the care of the Police Surgeon. No-one wants the publicity but I'm concerned charges have been brought as well as the arm being under threat. I'd like to make him disappear if you understand me?' Hunt waited.

'I'll have a chat with the right people. Where exactly is he being held?' said Hardinge.

'Portsmouth prison,' replied Hunt.

'Get someone across there to pick him up will you? I'll get word to you. And you'll look into the loss of the diamonds? Her Majesty has taken the theft personally, you know,' explained Hardinge.

'Let me have the sketch of the blonde man as I think it may be the same one we're interested in for a few other thefts. I'll get on to it,' said Hunt.

'Good man. The Shah's got three visits here, don't you know. Terrible disruption to the area. Only thing he said to me was that he'd heard about the London fogs but he now knew they hid the gates of paradise. Meant the rhododendron walk here. How we get everyone away that's in the town I don't know. The stations will be overcrowded but that's your lot's problem, isn't it?'

'It is,' said Hunt, wondering what would happen when the crowds became hungry.

'Lucky for Gladstone it's created so much excitement. The attention's been diverted from politics,' said Hardinge's aide.

Hardinge and Hunt remained silent and rode on.

*

It was seven o'clock on Wednesday morning as Jack and Shaw rose for breakfast. A long day stretched ahead and they were both determined to eat well. They left for Hastings Railway Station to meet their colleagues, Ann Black from London and Burgess and Sergeant Field travelling across from Brighton.

In London Sergeant Stan Green and his men were about to experience chaos.

The first incident was caused after a letter from Hardinge reached the Governor of the Bank of England. This explained that the Shah was too fatigued to visit today. Disappointing, yes, so it was to the large company gathered there.

 However that was not the end of it.

From a Police team's view the worst part was that the Lord Mayor addressed the vast crowds from the Mansion House Balcony. He repeated the contents of the letter with the intention of dispersing the crowd and clearing the streets. Initially there was a hush as the people outside stared up at the Palladian front. A policing nightmare ensued as the masses poured into Victoria Street, Poultry and Cheapside and in the other direction, up Threadneedle Street.

The second incident occurred as Stan and Arthur were on their way to link up with Constables Percy and Alf. They had reached the Royal Exchange and were quite visible on the steps. Sergeants Ted Phillips and Morris had also received instructions from Hunt to muster as many of those in plain clothes as they could gather and go towards West India Dock. Masses of people there were everywhere around boats and structures in anticipation of the Shah's arrival in the dock on the Princess Alice.

Hunt had sent a separate telegram for Stan's eyes only and Ted duly delivered it. Ted and Morris had no idea of the contents of Hunt's telegram and simply waited for Stan to re-assign his team to them.

'You'll have to find them first,' said Stan, with a smirk as he took the telegram.

'Where did you arrange to meet?' asked Morris.

But Stan was busy reading the message he had just been given from Hunt. It included a direction for Stan to leave for Portsmouth immediately to help Harry Franks on release from custody.

'Bit confused this,' said Stan, holding out the telegram to Ted.

'I don't think I'm supposed to see it,' said Ted, deliberately not looking at it. Stan gave him a dismissive look. He passed it to Arthur.

'Arthur, looks like you and me are having a day out at Portsmouth. Have a look at this and see what you make of it.'

Arthur stared at the message and shook his head.

'They've missed a bit out. Harry's got to escort someone being released from Portsmouth Prison. That's how I read it,' said Arthur.

'Well, we'd better get going then. The lads will be back at the White Lion at Birchin Lane, off Cornhill. Where's your order? Let me sign it so they know I've agreed,' said Stan, holding out his hand for the order.

'It's an order,' said Morris.

'They still won't go with you unless I sign it.' Stan shrugged. 'That's how it is.'

Morris handed the order across with a look at Ted.

'Do you know where we're going, Stan?' asked Arthur frowning, as he and Stan walked past St. Mary's and turned into the narrow St. Swithin's Lane.

'Cannon Street to pick up the branch line to Waterloo. It's midday now. We'd better pick up some provisions Arthur. But first I need to find somewhere to send my own message. I want more information than we've been given. The telegram says we'll be met but not by who and then to Portsmouth prison. I've got a tongue in my head so I can ask directions when we get off the train. London and South Western I think it will be.'

'Why all the secrecy?' asked Arthur.

'No idea.' Stan said. 'Perhaps to stop something getting out.'

*

It was after one o'clock and the Shah had ignored the potential visit to the Armoury and the Regalia. The party had crossed over the drawbridge at the Tower and walked directly to the Wharf. The Shah boarded the Princess Alice and Tom Hunt and the Prince of Wales, with the rest of the royal party, were on board the Cupid. The National Anthem was underway, played by a regiment of Guards as the Shah and the royal Princes saluted each other.

Tom Hunt blended with the Prince of Wales party in civilian clothes. He was dressed to the Queen's order and he sensed she took pleasure in annoying her heir. The Prince ignored Hunt as usual and watched the Artillerymen on the river's edge with matches in hand, firing salutes from guns of the old muzzle-loader pattern. The Inspector asked himself whether it was being part of the royal party or the way the guns were loaded that always made him feel nervous.

Behind the Artillery was an even longer line of Guardsmen presenting arms, a line of flags and then the walls, battlements and turrets of the Tower. On the greens, the hill, in windows and even on housetops, as far as the eye could see, were masses of people cheering. Sailing ships, freight ships and row boats, joined the chorus to such an extent that the great guns were almost drowned out. The Queen had remained at Windsor and Hunt wished to goodness that he was in his own mother's garden there.

Stan and Arthur heard the din while they went into the station. As they had boarded the train to take them across the river on the south bank round to Waterloo they had a ring side seat as they crossed the Thames.

The Princess Alice moved slowly off at a quarter past one after the Persian March had been played. A twenty-one gun salute was fired and the Cupid slipped into her wake.

Ted Phillips looked up at the warehouses where people were crammed in every available space.

———

323

'River's too full,' said Morris. 'There's only just room for them to pass along the lines. Every spare space is teeming with people. They're in the rigging as well, look. We'll have no chance if anything happens.'

'Let's hope it doesn't,' said Ted looking up at the cranes and the landing stages which were also covered with sight-seers.

The royal party were past Ted and Morris and approaching West India Dock. That had been Ted and Morris's destination but they would never make it now as it was impossible to get through the crowd. He spared a thought for Rose and their mother, now back from Brighton at the West India Dock cottages, as the hotel accommodation had been cancelled when the Shah did not go to Brighton. He had yet to see them but wondered what sort of a time they would be having today.

Hunt heard the crash against the side of the royal boats and instinctively threw himself and the next person down. It was the river fire-engines lashed together discharging jets of water in straight lines from five boats. Great cheers went up, including from the royal party and Hunt was left to apologise profusely to the Prince's guest and help the man up.

The Princess Alice and the Cupid stopped for several minutes as a tremendous volume of water went high into the air. Captain Shaw of the river fire brigade gave the command for the men to put full pressure on.

*

Rose, heartsick at Harry's disappearance, not having any news from him, or about him, had packed and left with her mother on Tuesday morning to return to London.

Mrs Phillips had gone to the Ship Hotel before they left, to find Sam and Mrs Curzon in case Sam could tell her anything about Harry. Like Rose and her mother Sam was none the wiser. They had assumed he must have returned to Shadwell on special duties direct from Portsmouth.

Mrs Phillips had enquired about Jack but Sam had not heard from him. All he knew from Burgess was that Jack had set off on Monday morning for Lewes. Burgess explained to Mrs Phillips that Jack had gone to old friends in Sussex and was unsure when he would be back. His room was reserved for him, Burgess had said, for a full three weeks from the sixteenth of June and some of his belongings were still in it. Mrs Phillips had thanked him and returned to Rose. Together they had travelled back to London.

Rose waited that morning for the sound of Harry's whistle bouncing off the warehouse walls on his usual walk from Poplar station. But there was nothing of him and the Dock was consumed by the arrival of the 26th Middlesex, lining up on either side of the Millwall Gates. They drilled, presented arms and a whole host of people began to arrive to take their places on platforms, drawbridges and the decks of huge ships. Rose walked to Poplar Savings Bank on the High Street to enquire if they knew what the event was. They were closing at midday they said, as the Shah and the Royals were coming to the Dock.

'Well, Mother,' said Rose as she came back into the cottage. 'The man we went all the way to Brighton to see and help protect is practically going to be at our front door. Perhaps Harry will be with him.'

But as the Princess Alice turned her head into the Millwall gates of the dock and made a circuit of it there was no sign of Harry. The whole of the basin was crammed with shipping except for a channel in the centre. The Princess Alice and her entourage went through and left by the Blackwall Gates into the Thames and then made their way to the Greenwich Hospital.

By five o'clock, Inspector Tom Hunt was on board the Cupid again, sailing back to London.

The Shah would return to Buckingham Palace after a rapid sail to Westminster Bridge followed by a carriage ride to the Palace.

Oblivious to the crowds that still lined the river, Tom Hunt found a quiet corner on deck and slumped down with the need for sleep overwhelming him. If he was lucky, he thought, he might actually get home tonight and sleep in his own bed.

*

Nineteen

Another journey was being undertaken on Wednesday. Ann Black settled into her first class seat which George had insisted on buying for her. She had given in as, otherwise, he would have come with her to Hastings at the risk of losing his position. She glanced through the window at the hills which had come into view after the dense neighbourhoods of Horseleydown and Bermondsey.

Ann's train was now beyond Peckham and she was a woman travelling alone. She had seen the expression on the two men's faces as they paused briefly at her compartment door before they moved on to the next. So be it, thought Ann, I'll have the compartment to myself.

'Situational Forensics. I have no experience of it,' Ann said aloud.

The last time she had helped Jack to understand the causes of death was in a mortuary when Ted Phillips posed as a doctor and she as his nurse. Ann had been the specialist slipping in behind Ted but pretence was essential unless she accepted arrest and he and Jack dismissal. They had got away with it and had bluffed their way out of the building. Yes, she had enjoyed that frisson of excitement, adrenalin rushing with the risk of discovery. While she valued the young Jack's opinion of herself as fully qualified the masquerade could carry consequences for them both. This time, she gathered, she would not see a corpse but Jack wanted her to look at the environment in which the body had been found. Ann was unsure of what use she could be away from a mortuary slab.

'But I can apply scientific method,' she said aloud, to her reflection in the window.

George had been against the whole idea of her disappearing down to Sussex when Jack's telegram had arrived. That morning over breakfast he had suggested he accompany her to Hastings. Ann had looked at her husband, shocked.

'No, George, there's no point in us both taking the risk of losing our positions. At least you can deny all knowledge of what I do in Hastings. If I'm discovered as something other than a scientific Doctor then I will try and cling to being Doctor Brown's assistant. That is, after all, the role he accepts for me and would endorse that I assist the police in his stead when away. But I'm sure it will be fine.'

'Well, don't take unnecessary risks. Jack is a little inclined to be over-keen to promote you as a Doctor. One word out of turn from him and you could find yourself on the wrong side of the law.' George leant across the table. 'Look why not let me come with you? It's more respectable a married couple travelling and staying together instead of you moving around with an all-male team.'

'We talked about this, George. I shall be fine. Jack fully respects me as an older, married woman, with a professional set of skills. He has a blind spot about whether a woman or a man can carry out a profession. There's never been any question of anything untoward from him, you know that.'

'You're not that much older than him. I don't know how I feel about you cavorting around with a young constable,' said George, moodily.

'I'm working professionally, not cavorting, thank-you. You're being silly. Come if you want to. How will you get off work?' asked Ann.

'I can't really,' said George.

'Exactly, so what's the point of suggesting it?' said Ann. 'Come down on Friday evening then if I'm still there. I don't know where I'm staying yet but I can make sure I meet you at Hastings. I'll get word to you where I'll be and then you can let me know the train's time of arrival.'

Her train was coming into Tunbridge and there would be a wait for the Tunbridge Wells and Hastings train. Ann had been told there was a refreshment room she could wait in. She had a medical bag with her and a carpet bag in the rack above her head. There was a half-an-hour wait before her train would leave and take the branch line to Hastings. Just time for a cup of tea and a read before she would board the next train.

The last thing she wanted was to raise Jack's expectations of what she could understand at a crime scene. Of course she would never testify. England lagged behind, as far as Ann was concerned, in recognising the importance of the medical witness in court. Italy, France and Germany were vastly ahead. She knew from her studies in Paris that the difference in the legal process meant that the decision in a French court was made by a judge instead of the English way of using a jury. This had encouraged forensic medicine to develop faster in France. English courts had long used experts but were unwilling to include a testimony which could not be understood by lay people on the jury.

The train slowed as they came into Tunbridge and Ann stood to pull her luggage from the rack. The whole area was new to her and the reading she had intended to do on the journey had been forgotten. She must catch up with it somehow. But the area was new and she may never come this way again. She wanted to savour the new area. Jack had also worked near Battle and they would pass through the station before Hastings. Ann was interested that she would shortly be able to see the views of the area from the train window, aware as she was that it was the spot where the Norman conquest had been established.

*

Jack was on the platform early after leaving Shaw to meet Field and Burgess from the Brighton direction. Emma had driven them in the Tip Cart to the Railway Station and once they were out of it had flicked the reins and sped off at a fast trot.

Train doors swung open and passengers started to descend. Steam cleared from the engine and porters attended to passenger's luggage.

Jack strained his eyes to look up the platform and spotted the woman on her own with a porter walking slightly ahead of her carrying a carpet bag and Jack enthusiastically waved a greeting. Ann quickly drew level with him and gave the porter some coins as he passed the bag to Jack's outstretched hand.

'Careful, my microscope is in it,' said Ann.

'Wonderful, all the science, eh? We can go straight to the farm where you'll be staying. It's near the place where the young woman's body was found. When you've settled in and unpacked I can show you the area,' Jack explained starting to walk. Ann fell in beside him.

'Are you staying at the farm, Jack?' asked Ann, deciding Jack looked drawn.

'I'll be down the road at friends. Constable Shaw Hockham from the Brighton police will be at the farm, and his Sergeant, who arrives shortly from Brighton, Sergeant Field. Mr Burgess is the other man coming in from Brighton today and he runs the Ship Hotel in Brighton. He'll go straight back to Brighton tonight. He was Metropolitan Police and was well known at one time for his cases. Mrs Crowhurst is the landlady at the farm and she has a daughter called Emma. So it's all respectable,' said Jack.

'Is there a Mr Crowhurst?' asked Ann.

'Not that I've seen,' Jack answered.

'I think George may come on Friday after he finishes work, but we'll move into the town for the two nights he's here,' said Ann.

'It will be good to see him again. It's been a long time,' Jack frowned at the memory of when he had last seen George. It had been at tea before Christmas, with George toasting bread over the fire in the house in Arbour Square.

Ann gave Jack an assessing once over and decided he looked as if he had lost weight across the shoulders and back.

'How are you sleeping?' she asked as she handed her ticket to a collector.

'Pretty well except for last night,' answered Jack.

'And the cough?' asked Ann.

330

'It starts when I get tired, or stressed. It's quite bad at the end of the day.'

'And are you resting each afternoon?' Ann asked, suspecting the answer.

'The last two days have been a bit difficult to do that. I didn't sleep too well last night after some news. Personal news. I feel like I could just lay down now and fall asleep where I am,' said Jack.

'Then you should take the opportunity when we get back to the farm. Use the bedroom you've given to me.'

'I don't think there'll be time, Ann,' said Jack.

'It's a priority at some point this afternoon. And the dreams?' asked Ann.

'It varies,' said Jack.

'You may get over-tired if you don't stick to Doctor Brown's advice. Rest each afternoon after lunch, or before dinner if you can't beforehand, no matter what's happening,' said Ann.

'That's proving to be easier said than done,' said Jack.

Ann mulled over how to respond. Then she thought that she had made the point and should try a different tack. 'You could start doing some Swedish "light gymnastic" exercises as well to build up again. I've got some diagrams you can have. They're done by an Institute in Sweden and are becoming popular here and in America. You can do them inside or outside. Try them once a day and then build up to twice a day. I think once you get into them you'll enjoy them and it will keep your muscle strength.'

'Sounds interesting, thank-you. I'm not sure about resting though as we're to go across to Pett Level with the Coastguard this afternoon. I'm afraid we have two murders, well three possibly,' Jack said.

'Three? Where are you finding all this Jack? Has there been an arrest?' asked Ann.

'There has for the murder of one of the crimes. The young woman but it's the wrong man. The site we'll see later at Pett Level had an older woman stabbed. The body was found later yesterday afternoon,' Jack explained.

'Do you know the area?' asked Ann.

———

331

'No, but we'll go with the coastguard who does. Our story is that we're Archaeologists or Naturalists checking the area hasn't been too disturbed,' said Jack.

Ann laughed. 'And about both those areas of enquiry do you know anything at all?'

'Well, I can recognise a flower and a fossil,' said Jack, grinning. It was good to have Ann working with him again.

Ann saw there were three men waiting at the exit of the station, watching them. The smaller one nodded in response to her gaze and she concluded these must be the two Brighton policemen and the hotelier, Jack had mentioned. The older, heavily built man, touched his hat.

'I think your friends are waiting for us,' said Ann. Jack raised a hand in greeting and he and Ann had joined the three men within a few minutes and the introductions were made. Shaw led them out of the station towards an omnibus.

'So, Jack what's our story?' asked Sergeant Field, as they walked.

'I don't think we'll need one at Lovers Seat. The place is deserted so we're unlikely to be disturbed. Ann is the one with the scientific knowledge in case we're questioned. I'm not sure how to do this if we are.'

'Mrs Black, Jack has spoken very highly of you. We're in your hands if things get technical,' said Shaw.

'Any help I can give I will but if you gentlemen are presenting as scientists then you need to have an institution behind you, or it won't be credible,' said Ann.

'I think we're in your hands, Mrs Black, where do you suggest? 'asked Burgess.

'Pick one which is unlikely to be challenged. Say it with confidence and it will be accepted. Oxford, Cambridge, that sort of place. Field survey I would suggest if you're asked, but you don't have your equipment as you're on holiday,'' suggested Ann. There was general amusement amongst the men at presenting themselves in this way.

'Is there any way we can take photographs of the crime scene at Lovers Seat and Pett Level?' asked Ann.

'I can telegraph the station at Brighton for the camera to be brought up to Lovers Seat tomorrow. Pett Level will already have undergone change with the tide which means we're already too late. Have you some experience of photography at the crime scene, Mrs Black?' asked Shaw.

'Only in France, as a medical student when assisting the police,' explained Ann. 'I was very much in the background, observing my Professor. Tomorrow it will have to be then. If we go to both sights today I can do a presumptive test to take samples if that is still possible and check if there are traces of blood at the scenes.'

'What does that test mean, Ann? asked Jack.

'It's a quick test at the site, say for haemoglobin being present. It's not one hundred per cent accurate and we'd need to follow it up afterwards. It's a test that's been around since 1863. It's the result of work by using Hydrogen Peroxide, as it reacts with haemoglobin, so we can claim blood is present,' said Ann.

'Well, it sounds like you know what you're doing. However we're unlikely to know if it's from the dead woman, Grace, are we, dear lady?' asked Sergeant Field.

Ann controlled her face at the phrase, "dear lady." She knew the Sergeant had meant it kindly.

Field nodded and excused himself and turned into the Telegraph office at the station. Burgess drew Jack on one side.

'I had some visitors late last night. Some friends of yours,' said Burgess.

Jack hesitated.

Burgess continued: 'Stan and Arthur from London and another friend whose accommodation hadn't really suited him in the last few days, Harry Franks. I hope you don't mind but they'll occupy your room for a few days until Harry can travel.'

Jack looked at Burgess curiously.

'What's wrong with Harry?'

Burgess dropped his voice further.

'He got in the way of some shot in Portsmouth in the naval review. His right arm's damaged and none too good for a stay in Portsmouth Prison. He was charged.'

Field was walking back to them and Shaw and Anne climbed up onto the omnibus and went onto the top level. Jack hung back with Burgess, letting Field on before them. They followed him on, but remained standing downstairs to continue the conversation.

'So he was one of the ones arrested. Poor Harry, how is he?' asked Jack.

'A little better this morning for a good bed and Alice's cooking. He and his friends have to disappear for a while until the paperwork disappears, so he'll use your room until you return if you don't mind. We don't want it coming out and I gather he gave a false name so in a few days the authorities will be the none the wiser,' explained Burgess.

'Good grief,' Jack exclaimed. 'Who's arranging all this to be done?'

'I wouldn't know but it has to be someone at Government level doesn't it? Harry was rather feverish when he arrived, but that was under control by this morning and I'm hopeful he'll be up and about in a few days. I saw the one called Stan before I left this morning. Interesting character but doesn't say much. He'd heard of me so I'm assuming he and Arthur are Met men. Hunt didn't say who was coming but given the closeness of the relationship with Harry I imagine they're part of a team. Stan was off to do some fishing and he and Arthur were to take it in turns to look after Harry. I've left Alice in charge anyway and she's more than a match for a bad patient.' Burgess smiled at the thought.

'Hunt must have organised this,' said Jack.

'Hunt sent Stan and Arthur. He let me know as he always does and the bill gets paid from somewhere. I don't ask too many questions, frankly Jack. As I said all I knew were two men known to Harry were coming. Tom got word to me to expect three guests. You're alright with them using your room as you're not there?' asked Burgess.

Jack nodded and swallowed. Of course Hunt would know. Burgess was right. Whoever Hunt was linked to must be very high up, he thought.

'I wondered about Rose, his fiancé, won't she be looking after Harry?' asked Jack.

'I gather she and her mother left after the Shah didn't come to Brighton. No accommodation necessary anymore, you see. They won't know what's happened and have gone back to London. Harry thinks you're with friends near Lewes by the way and will come back to Brighton at the end of the week. I haven't dissuaded him,' said Burgess.

'What about Sam and Mrs Curzon?' asked Jack.

'Sam's still with us and taking a house up at the back of St Peter's church. His mother's returned to Windsor to arrange the move from there with the other children.' Burgess explained.

'This is our stop,' Jack said, moving towards the platform at the back of the omnibus. Shaw was coming down the spiral staircase with Field and Ann.

At the farm Mrs Crowhurst had laid out a simple lunch on the kitchen table of fresh bread, a cheese and a ham from the farm and rugged wild strawberries. She and Emma were nowhere to be seen but Jack's room had been prepared for Ann while he had been out. A vase of flowers had been placed on the window ledge. Ann looked around at her room for the next few days and was pleased with the cleanliness. She opened her carpet bag and took out a smaller handbag. Inside it were the small sample bottles and phials of chemicals ready for use. Ann pushed her medical bag containing her microscope under the bed and left her carpet bag visible on the floor next to the window as it now only had her clothes in it. Satisfied that things looked normal she joined the men below.

Jack had found some muslin in a kitchen drawer and was busy cutting cheese and ham into chunks and wrapping them with the bread. Shaw had remained outside for some air and he stood looking into the distance towards the trees.

'I'm ready if you want to go now,' said Ann, picking up a strawberry. Jack looked at the small handbag that she was carrying as he had expected something which looked more medical. She smiled at him.

'I have what I need in here. No point in drawing unnecessary attention to us. It would be good if we're supposed to be checking the impact on the area of the murder and the police presence yesterday to have a notebook and pencil.'

Jack patted his chest pocket. 'In here,' he said. 'I'm never without it.'

'It's rare I'm without mine, as well,' said Field, also patting a pocket.

The light was at its best as the five of them walked towards the cliff edge and Lovers Seat. Ann peered over the edge and pointed to a mud slip below and areas where sections of the cliff had broken away at some point.

'This lovely spot won't last I fear as it's a sandstone crag. Look over there, where the dense woodland is. There's a landslip that occurred some time ago. This is so close to the edge of the cliff I'm not sure how stable it all is,' she said.

'It's certainly had some boots across it yesterday. The local constabulary were all over it,' said Shaw. Burgess chuckled, imagining what it had been like.

'Perhaps if we just stand still and look around for a while,' suggested Ann. 'The less we disturb the area the better. Thank goodness it's a bright day.'

Jack cast an eye around the group, none of whom were strangers to death in their work. Burgess had been out of it for some time but Jack suspected that this was not the first case since his retirement in which he had assisted Sergeant Field. Ann, in some ways he thought, had the hardest role of them all. Trying to prevent death and beat it must have made staring it in the face even more distressing. Field was a seasoned player and Shaw a bloodhound. Jack realised that he knew absolutely nothing about the two Brighton police officers. He had taken them on the recommendation of Burgess because Tom Hunt rated that ex-Metropolitan Police man turned hotelier.

And himself?

Looking at the romantic setting as a place of death made his chest tight. He pictured the description Edward had given him, seeing Nathan cradling Grace, half out of his mind with grief and talking to her as if she had fallen asleep. He saw himself on the seat holding Harriet and his breathing became audible. Perhaps it was the after effects of the smoke inhalation that made the coughing start. He felt a hand on his arm and Ann was at his side.

'Come and sit for a while and try and eat something,'

'I couldn't at the moment. I'd rather do something. I was wondering if the rubble over there is worth sorting through?' asked Jack.

'Good idea. You go, Jack and try and approach it from the side not across the centre area,' said Ann.

'We're happy to be directed by you, ma'am,' said Burgess.

Jack had started to remove rocks and Shaw joined him as he started to lift a boulder.

'Take it easy, my friend, no point in wearing yourself out early. Let me do the shifting of the heavy stuff,' said Shaw.

'You go first, then,' suggested Jack. Standing back he was grateful for Shaw's help. He glanced around at the footprints in the mud which had dried since yesterday. 'What do say, Shaw? Those footprints look like police boots.'

'Could well be.' Shaw looked at the area.

'Can someone sketch it as it is now and then we can compare that with any photographs tomorrow?' asked Ann.

'Good idea,' said Field, taking out his own notebook and making a start.

'It's a shame we lost Nathan Long to incarceration, as it would have been helpful to know exactly where the body was,' said Burgess.

'Edward Croft will know. The coastguard that came with Nathan. I should have thought of that and arranged for him to meet us here,' said Jack, kicking himself for not having thought of it last night. 'He'll be at the farm by two o'clock, perhaps he can show us then if we can come back.'

Ann moved forward to an area next to the pile of rubble Jack and Shaw were moving.

'It's a good job it's been dry for the last twenty-four hours,' she said, staring at the foliage at the side of the pile of footprints. One by one the men followed her direction of gaze. Ann opened her bag, bent down, and got to work.

'Is it blood?' asked Jack.

'It might be. The grass is discoloured. We'll know soon enough. Take it slowly with that pile of rubble, gentlemen, our weapon may be amongst it,' said Ann.

*

Jack and Shaw had placed three rocks on one side because parts were discoloured and one of them in particular had substances stuck to it. Field had sketched the area to the best of his ability and was roughly measuring the foot prints, most of which he was convinced were from the Hasting's force. Burgess had gone towards the Coastguard Station to see if he could collect Edward Croft early.

Ann had finished with the samples of grass and came over to where the two men continued to sort the pile of rubble. She turned the three rocks over and placed each carefully onto a piece of cloth while she examined the surfaces and then scraped areas of each into different phials. Methodically, she labelled each one and popped them into her bag. Each of the rocks would have caused damage to the head, from any angle.

'Do we know anything about Grace's injury?' asked Ann.

'I think the coastguard does as he came with the sailor after the body was found. He was a bit upset about it last night and didn't say much,' said Shaw.

'Of course, she might have fallen on them. Tripped and hit her head. Or someone hit her. It's interesting there's three rocks with the same substance on them. I think it is likely to be the same matter but we'll know later once I've got it under a microscope.' Ann paused to examine the type of cliff they were near.

'Without getting to the body we don't know if there's any way of matching up the shape of the rocks with a wound. I don't know, either where the wound is. We'll never know if its Grace's blood, of course. Sergeant Field was right when he said that. Interesting situation up here,' said Ann.

'Why?' asked Jack.

'It's romantic. Death in a romantic place is like a poem. It's a stupid place to kill someone because it *is* a romantic place. The chances of catching her alone and having the time to kill her here before someone else turns up with romantic intentions is very unlikely,' Anne said.

Jack looked at Ann. 'So it sounds unlikely that she was killed here, doesn't it? She was killed somewhere else and then the body was dumped here. Perhaps to coincide with a visit from Nathan. Are those rocks the same as the others here? Don't they look different to you?'

'I don't know, are you any good on geology? We can compare them but I wouldn't be sure. Again we can do tests but not here, it will take too long and we might invite interest,' said Ann.

'What would be the point of moving the body here?' asked Shaw.

'To frame someone that the killer knew was likely to show up here. Someone like our sailor?' suggested Field.

'Exactly. Grace must have told the killer she was meeting Nathan here, and that he was back. Perhaps the poor girl was excited and just couldn't keep it to herself. Maybe it meant a wedding and getting her baby back, assuming there was one. Shame the local force marched all over the place,' said Jack.

'Yes, we haven't got a hope of doing any meaningful check on those boot prints. Did Grace have small feet? If she did walk here we would need something clear like that to establish some of these are her shoe prints,' said Ann.

'No, Ann,' said Jack, staring at her. 'There won't be any shoe prints for Grace because she didn't walk here. She was carried here.'

'Right,' said Ann.

'Let's have a look at those rocks,' said Field.

———

'Don't we know anyone who is friendly on the Hasting's force to get at some details?' asked Jack, looking at the two men from Brighton.

'No,' said Field.

Shaw shook his head. 'Don't ask,' he said. 'They have a history of inefficient Chief Officers and the current one, Glenister, only took the appointment last year. He's an ex-inspector of the Great Western Railway.'

'What?' exclaimed Jack incredulously.

'Mind you, Shaw, he does seem to be pulling them together now. Hastings has a funny history, Jack, as a police force. The initial training was very quick, you see, back in 1836, and Sergeant Sellwood, who came down to do it from the Metropolitan Police, didn't stay long. There were only three Sergeants and nine Constables and one Inspector originally. Almost immediately that he's gone a PC was dismissed for drunkenness and sleeping on his beat. There's been a history of drunkenness in those early years and they got themselves an unfortunate reputation. By the time the railway was being built the town suffered from drunken Navvies on pay day and there were still only nine Constables so Specials were drafted in. They've twenty-nine Constables now and a new station in Bourne Street. With more time their new Chief Officer will pull them together,' Field explained. 'Now let's think about those rocks that you've taken the samples from and see if they're the same as the others here.'

Burgess and Edward Croft were approaching.

Jack made brief introductions for Edward's sake and Field and Ann shook hands with him. Edward called Jack to one side and held out a telegram to him. It was from the Coastguard Station about the yacht and the arrests. It confirmed injuries and arrests but not names.

Jack read it quickly and nodded at Edward.

'Funnily enough Burgess has just explained who the team member was. It's being sorted, that's all I dare say.'

'That's good. So, to today. What have you found?' asked Edward.

Ann explained their thoughts to Burgess and the coastguard.

'We think it's unlikely Grace was killed here. Mr Croft, you saw the body which we can't get at. Where was Nathan and Grace when you arrived here? Is there anything you can tell us about it that would help us understand?' asked Ann.

Nicely done, thought Jack. Her soft tone and gentle manner had led Edward to open up.

'She was in the rubble at the back of the seat area, Nathan had said. When I got here he was sitting on the seat holding her, rocking her. The back of the head was caved in. There was blood matted in the hair and on the clothes. I thought she'd been dead some time as rigor mortis had worn off. It didn't occur to me though that she'd not been killed here. Why did you think that?' Edward stopped.

'Because it's too popular a place. Also your point about the rigor mortis. Someone who's planned a murder wouldn't take the risk of courting couples turning up. They wanted her to be found by Nathan, I think,' said Jack.

Ann was asking Edward a question. 'The blood was matted in the hair? Then you're correct that she'd been dead some time. And you're sure there was no rigor mortis?'

'No, that was the other thing,' Edward confirmed.

'I would say you're right,' said Ann

'About two days you said last night?' asked Jack making sure he had understood.

'Yes,' said Edward, almost breathlessly.

'Excuse me asking in front of a lady, but her clothing was all right was it?' asked Field.

'Yes, nothing like that.' Edward turned away and stared out at the sea.

'What was she wearing?' asked Jack.

Edward looked at him, shocked. 'What?' asked Edward. A few seconds went by and then realization was on his face.

'It was a best dress I would say, like she was going to a party. Like she was expecting to meet her young man.' Edward smiled at Jack and looked at him proudly. 'You're good at this, aren't you?'

Jack acknowledged the compliment realising that Edward was catching up across the years.

'We'll see if we catch someone first,' said Jack, his face suddenly dour. 'We don't know but perhaps someone had sent her a message a couple of days before to expact Nathan at a particular place. She went and was attacked from behind and then stored somewhere until they could be sure Nathan would come here. Rigor mortis wears off and she's placed shortly before he arrives. The killer might even have watched him find her, and then Nathan looks around, maybe calls out, remembers there's a Coastguard Station and runs for help. I suspect he knew she was dead but there's always the hope. There's always that hope that you're in time.'

'What about Nathan's counsel? Do we know who's representing him? If we could talk to Nathan's counsel we might be able to find out details like where the wound is on the head or neck, the post mortem results, when they think she was killed, if they've made enquiries about Nathan's whereabouts at the suspected time of death,' suggested Ann.

'He may not have a counsel,' said Jack.

'Surely he has on a charge of murder? Wouldn't the Navy help him with someone?' asked Ann, incredulous at the idea of going into a murder trial without counsel.

'I don't know about the Navy, but it's still quite common for people accused of murder not to have counsel assigned to them if the judge thinks it's a straightforward case. If Nathan hasn't asked for someone to be assigned to him he'll go undefended,' explained Field.

'This is ridiculous. Can't one of you turn up pretending to be his counsel and get the facts?' said Ann.

'Well, I'm known and Shaw and Jack won't do,' said Field.

'Why not? Jack's not known is he around here?' said Ann.

'It's not that. They both sound wrong. They wouldn't be believable. The only one of us with the right sort of accent is you, Mrs Black. And there's an obvious problem with you trying to do it, if you don't mind me pointing out that women aren't appearing for the defence yet, or the prosecution either,' explained Field.

Edward Croft looked from one to the other. He was surprised that they were prepared to masquerade.

'George,' said Jack, looking at Ann. 'George could do it because he sounds right. He also stands properly with that confidence men get when they know the ropes. They'd believe he was counsel.'

'No, no, no, no, he'd never get involved and agree to lie his way into a police station. Look if Nathan hasn't got a counsel we should get him one. We only want the information the prosecution has and then we can unwind their case. How much do these people cost?' asked Ann, looking from one to the other of the three representatives of the police in front of her.

'I don't know, it's always privileged information,' said Field.

'How ridiculous,' said Ann. 'Do they want business or not?'

'I wonder if Sam could pull it off?' said Jack, staring at Ann.

'Sam's not well, Jack and if it's about accent and mannerisms how is he any different to you?' asked Ann.

'No, Ann, he's alright. He's managing with his health. And he's worked as a clerk in the City. He can imitate a toff. I've seen him do it last Christmas when we went out up the West End. Not just the accent but the way he behaved, everything. And he's got a decent suit Hunt sent to him. Burgess, what do you think?' Jack turned to the hotelier.

'I can get him across to Hastings tomorrow. I could be his clerk,' said Burgess, chuckling. 'We'd be gambling on no one checking if counsel has been appointed, and that Nathan Long will go along with the pretence. It blows our cover with him as he didn't know the police connection.'

'I don't think that matters now,' said Jack. 'And anyway neither of you have a police connection. So we're clear. It's about a man's life and finding the real murderer. Nathan will realise you're trying to be helpful. The other thing that occurs to me is about bringing forward my visit to see the old Parson at Simpson again. I'm due to go next Tuesday and he was going to make enquiries for me concerning Grace. I could risk going across tomorrow in case he's got the information we might need.'

'Is that Reverend Peter Fisher?' asked Edward.

'Yes,' said Jack, with a smile.

'We're not losing anything with you going early,' said Shaw.

'Are we done here, do you think? I've a rare appetite building for that cheese and ham,' said Jack.

'Come on back to the cottage and have some refreshment. We are due to get across to Pett Level shortly but it will be more restful for all of you to eat away from here. Jack, you're a smuggler!' exclaimed Edward. All eyes were on him. 'Of the two sides you could have come down on this afternoon I thought at first it was going to be a coastguard. But no, you've definitely got the ability to bend the law.' Edward looked round the group. 'All of you have. Jack's father and I used to lay bets as to which one he'd turn out to be in the games we used to play with him. Jack, your father's won! You're definitely a smuggler,' Edward laughed.

*

Twenty

Jack knew it was because of the effects of the fire that he still felt exhausted but he was becoming sick of the lack of strength. He had felt the adrenalin rush produced by impending action to help Nathan. Now the effect of that excitement had left him he felt drained. He ate his portion of the lunch, encouraged by Ann quietly to do so. She equally prompted him to go and rest, which he reluctantly agreed to out of respect for her profession.

'Use the room at the front, Jack,' Edward said. 'Lucy's got it ready for you for tonight.' While the others sat outside Edwards's cottage Jack made his way up the stairs.

Edward advised rubber boots explaining that it tended to be slippery at low tide around the rock pools down at Pett Level. Therefore they spent the time that Jack rested sorting through a variety available and kitted Ann out with double layers of fisherman's oiled socks to make her feet fit the smallest pair of boots. Edward apologised to her for not having anything better, aware that this woman was an educated lady. Ann thanked him for his concern and insisted what he had would be fine. Once they had acquired a pair of boots each, they sat outside and hungrily ate the supply of cheese, ham and bread which they had brought with them from the farm.

Ann gave Jack fifteen minutes from the time she had no longer heard any movements through the open bedroom window.

'Edward, I think we should wake Jack now. That sleep should be all he'll need to cope this afternoon,' said Ann. Edward went through the kitchen to call upstairs and a bleary eyed Jack appeared minutes later peering out of the bedroom window.

'Good, you've slept,' said Ann.

'That will refresh you,' added Burgess.

Jack appeared moments later and sat with the team. Edward passed him a pair of Wellington boots and socks and he started to undo his shoes.

'I thought I'd need hours,' said Jack.

'No, not now, just regular rest and fresh air. You're well on the way to recovery, Jack.' Ann said, trying some encouragement. She watched Jack's smile light up his face.

'If we're to beat the tide and see the area where the body near the rock pool was found yesterday we should go,' said Edward.

They walked in two's because the way was narrow, along the old Saxon Way towards Cliff End, with Edward leading. They passed through the village of Pett and Edward stopped to have a few words with an elderly lady sat at her front door, then they came to Pett Level, south of the village.

'It was marshland at one time and stretched along the coast towards Rye,' explained Edward. He pointed and the others followed the direction he indicated. 'The sunken forest is visible now as it's low tide.'

'Why did the sea level rise? Do you know?' asked Burgess.

'Not really sure,' said Edward. 'They say it was thousands of years ago. It wasn't the last time either that the water level changed. There was a sea port a few miles away, to do with Winchelsea, or so I've heard. It was swallowed up by the sea in 1287. Even up to the time of Queen Elizabeth there was a general influx of the water. I could show you the ruin of the Castle of Ounber, built by Henry VIII. The coast changing is still happening. Careful of slipping now as we go down towards the low flat rocks. That's where the rock pools are and the spot where Mabel Walters was found yesterday.'

'How far would we walk along the coast before we came on signs of dwellings?' asked Shaw.

'You'd reach Rye Harbour to the east. You can walk tight towards the cliffs and around to Fairlight Cove but the tide can come in and force you against the cliffs, even cutting you off. That's why I didn't choose to come that way.' Edward said, as he stopped and shaded his eyes. 'I see our friend, the historian, is down there.' He nodded towards a man on the beach. Bent double the historian moved the pebbles with both hands, stopping to make a record in a notebook with a pencil.

'Is it the man who reported the woman's body yesterday?' asked Jack.

'Yes, it is,' said Edward.

'Funny, most people would have been put off coming back so quickly,' said Jack.

'He and I have found others, washed up by the tide,' said Edward.

'Get your stories straight, as we should have a chat with this man,' said Field.

'Come on Jack,' said Ann, walking to the front of the group. Jack seized the opportunity and followed her. He took advantage of Ann's silence as they walked towards the man.

'Afternoon,' called Jack, using his wide smile. 'I understand from the coastguard, you're the man we should speak to locally about the history of the area.'

The man straightened up, initially surprised that there was other humanity on the beach. Seeing the friendly expressions of interest he touched his battered hat to Ann.

'Archaeology, Victoria and Albert Museum,' called over Jack, extending his hand. Ann glanced at him quickly, hoping there was such a department, and then smiled at the man in response to his courtesy.

'Doctor Ann George, Science, Paris,' Ann said, and Jack again smiled at the change of name but also this time because he rarely heard her present herself as a Doctor of Science. It was the truth.

'Delighted. Brian Gale, Geological Society. I had no idea our little beach was attracting such attention.' He shook hands with Jack and again touched his hat to Ann.

'Mr Croft thinks you're an historian,' said Ann, in a confidential manner.

'Well I suppose it's all linked in local eyes.' He looked across to where the others were standing and called over. 'And these gentlemen?'

'Field survey, Oxford,' called Shaw. His Sergeant cleared his throat. Edward decided to hang back and looked away to hide his expression.

To prevent the man from asking any further questions Ann said, 'I understand we're looking at finds over five thousand years old?'

'Yes, yes, yes, we believe so, although it is an estimate you understand. There have been artefacts found buried at the same depth and that is why we think the forest is thousands of years old. What are your areas of interest?'

'Decay, mainly and how to prevent it,' said Ann.

'Fossils,' Jack said.

'We have a wreck which might interest you. The coastguard has probably already mentioned it. The "Anne" funnily enough, given your own name Doctor George, a casualty of the battle of Beachy Head fighting the French in 1690. Parts of the wreck are exposed occasionally. How its survived, given the storms, might be of interest. And for your area, sir, the beach at Cliff End is full of dinosaur finds and fossils. Every time there's a storm there's some fresh treasure.'

'Thank-you I'll have a look. I understand from the coastguard there was something else rather more distressing found yesterday?' asked Jack.

'Oh my goodness, yes. I'm still recovering from the shock. A woman, a local, I'm afraid I found her. I'm here every day late June to early August and I've not see anything like it before. She was face down in the water and the tide had been in. The police surgeon when he came thought she probably drowned. Dreadful, quite dreadful.'

'How distressing for you,' said Jack, concerned as the man's hands had started to tremble. 'And yet you're back here today?'

'Of course, the work has to go on and one does find the odd body washed up on a beach in my profession, from wrecks and so on. It's always the children that are the worst I feel. The babies in particular.'

'Gracious,' said Ann, starting to fan herself with her hand and breath rapidly. Jack caught her arm as she started to sway. It was unlike her, he thought.

'Perhaps, gentlemen,' panted Ann. 'I could ask for an arm from you both to get to those rocks over there and sit for a while. Such a distressing subject.'

'Of course, my apologies, I forgot the delicacy…. Let me help you, sir,' Gale offered Ann an arm, which she took, leaning heavily on it while Jack gripped her elbow. Together Gale and Jack led her away towards an outcrop of rock across the shingle where she would be able to sit and recover.

'Nicely done,' said Burgess, and Field chuckled.

'What do you mean?' asked Edward.

'I've seen that routine pulled so many times in court for the sake of distracting the jury. She's getting him away so we can examine the area. He wasn't shifting until Domesday,' said Field.

'I wouldn't have guessed,' said Edward. 'Come on, let me show you the exact position where the woman was found yesterday, while he's occupied.'

Edward led the way across the rock pools to an area closer to the shore. The tide had brought in more sediment and the area was heavily covered by it.

'This is what happens. The storms uncover the sunken forest and change the shape of the beach but much of the time it gets covered by rubbish and sand. I'd be surprised if we find anything helpful. The police were here for hours yesterday, and I would think they've picked up anything relevant,' explained Edward.

Burgess pulled out a gardening trowel and crouched down.

'Still worth clearing what's come in on the tide and seeing what we can find. If you could screen me from view?' he asked Field and Shaw.

'Will do,' said Field. He and Shaw crouched in front of Burgess so that it would look like the three men were examining the surface level. Edward turned and looked towards the area where Ann was still attended by the two men. Burgess dug the top level and had started to uncover a darker substance under the sand. Shaw took over the scraping and Burgess stood up and stretched.

'You're getting down towards the forest. Underneath the sediment and sand there's peat,' said Edward.

'There's peat under here, is there? I'm finding spongy substances. Look if I poke my finger in it breaks.' Shaw pulled a piece away.

'That will be the sunken forest. One way you know if you've hit old sea defences, or the sunken forest, is if its spongy. Mr Gale would be creating if he could see what you're doing,' said Edward.

'Where's he from?' asked Field.

'No idea. He's been coming some years. Sometimes there's a group of them. He writes occasionally in the Hastings papers when he's found something of historical interest in the area. Sometimes he'll put on a talk in the church hall in Pett. I've seen him most days in the good weather when I've come across here,' said Edward.

'What do you know about him?' asked Field.

'He rents rooms in one of the houses in Pett. I think he's a teacher somewhere the rest of the year,' Edward explained.

'And no-one's taken him in for questioning after yesterday? Interesting. What did he say about other bodies?' asked Field.

'He mentioned finding bodies in his line of work, must mean at the coast. People drown and wash up. There's also other situations we come across. I don't like to say it really,' said Edward.

'Go on. Say it. Not much is going to upset us given what we deal with,' said Field.

'Occasionally we find a baby on the beach. Usually in a bag. Fairly young. The tide probably washes them in, chucked off a cliff somewhere up the coast,' explained Edward.

'Is this common? Why would they wash up here?' asked Burgess.

'Tidal drift, I should think,' said Edward.

'That woman found here yesterday, we were told had been stabbed,' said Shaw. 'Yet the emphasis is on her drowning. Mrs Croft said she was known as a baby farmer in the area. Not likely she was disposing of the children here is it? I mean instead of getting them adopted was she killing them and burying them?' Shaw had stopped pulling the spongy substance away. He was staring down at the area he had been clearing.

'I really don't know. Dear God, I hope not,' said Edward, staring first at Shaw and then following the direction of his gaze.

Shaw sat back on his haunches. He looked down into the expanded hole he had cleared. He sucked in the air audibly in one long breath and breathed out slowly. He put the trowel down on one side and pushed himself up. Standing away from the rock he met Burgess's eyes.

'Maybe someone found out what she was doing. Perhaps followed her and decided to finish her off in the same place as she'd been burying the babies.'

Burgess, reading the signs from the expression on the policeman's face, knelt down and with his gloved hand started to gently brush some of the peaty substances off the mounds Shaw had uncovered. But it was Shaw who spoke.

'There's several bags down here Sarg. Under where it seems to go to soil. If you pull it away where the darker substance starts and meets the sunken forest I think there's three mounds covered in some sort of cloth. Perhaps better get Doctor Ann from Paris over 'ere. And maybe think about whether we should be charging Mr Gale.'

*

Shaw stood away as if he was dazed, while Field and Burgess carried on clearing the remains of the sediment, widening the area they had started to uncover. There was darker matter which might have been peat for all they knew. It had mixed with the remains of the forest.

Edward walked towards where Ann had sat. He cupped his hands to his mouth to stop the wind from snatching his words. She stopped fanning herself and made a rapid recovery.

'Doctor George, perhaps best come and have a look at something,' called Edward. Ann, with Jack in tow, walked briskly to catch up with the coastguard. Jack looked back at Gale and registered that the man looked surprised. Could it be genuine?

Burgess had moved enough of the matter away to release one of the bags with whatever it contained in place so that he would not damage the contents further, by which time Jack was back with Ann at the rock pool. Gale had overcome his surprise at the speed Ann had moved off and was following them.

'Cut him off,' said Field and Edward moved towards Gale and turned him back.

Burgess lifted the parcel with some care and laid it onto the rock away from the pool. Two more eventually followed after he repeated the process. His face was a study of care.

'Gently does it,' called Ann, reaching into the bag she had brought with her.

'Jack, give Edward a hand to just make sure our friend doesn't come over or leave,' said Field.

Jack turned round, indicating to Edward that he would come over. Together they talked Gale out of going any closer after the shock of his find yesterday. Field, Burgess and Shaw stood waiting as Ann knelt down on the wet beach, her back to them with no thought for her dress, and blocked their view.

Gale sat down on a boulder. 'What is it?' he asked.

'Human remains, we think,' said Edward, gently.

'Again? At the same place? Oh goodness,' Gale's hands shook more visibly and Jack sat down next to him, placing a steadying hand on his arm.

'Awful shock,' said Jack.

'It's a shock again. I can't understand it, it's such a peaceful place for something so tragic to happen here. I've come to love the area you see,' said Gale.

'I'll take you back towards the cliff, no need for you to see this, really,' said Edward, giving him a hand up and leading Gale away. He complied completely with Edward and Jack watched them until the two men were across the beach in case Edward needed help with Gale. Once Jack saw them leave the beach he walked back to his other colleagues.

'Are we charging him, Sarg?' asked Shaw coming back to the team. He wiped the remaining traces of vomit away with his handkerchief.

'I don't think so,' said Field. 'Only because I think it's down to the coastguard to get the local force in now. These deaths here must be something to do with the body found yesterday. It's too much of a coincidence that the dead woman was here given her profession.'

'Like a sacrifice isn't it?' said Jack. 'Her life taken for those she'd murdered who were unprotected.'

Field looked up at him and was shocked by the hatred he saw. What was going on in that mind to react so? Almost like it was personal.

'Our objective is to get the right person responsible for Grace's death and to see Nathan released. That woman and these little children are another issue locally. If we go ahead with Shaw's suggestion we blow our cover. Mr Gale's not running and looks pretty ill to me. That coastguard is no stranger to men trying to escape and I think he'll shout pretty loud if the man tries to make a run for it. Maybe you'd be better getting the man home, Jack.'

'How do you know it's another issue?' Jack asked with some difficulty.

Field straightened up and massaged his hip, regretting the position he had adopted when he bent down.

'I'm not going down that route. We're involved because of finding the missing Brighton woman. You've kindly leant us help. The man, Gale, looks pretty rough. On the other hand we don't really want him giving information about the team of Archaeologists he met this morning to the local force do we? I suggest you get him home. How are we doing Mrs Black?' said Field, reverting to Ann's real name.

Ann sat back on her haunches and then pushed herself up. Her face was serious but controlled as she answered.

'There is rope around the necks of all three bodies. Infants, between three and six months I would say. Not possible to tell how long they've been here as it may be that the elements from the peat have permeated up and had a preserving effect. The clinging soil is likely to be post-peat organic sediments, and it's now rich and silty clay. I think if you got down another couple of feet we might hit peat properly. Given the time its assumed that the forest has been here it's likely that there's contact between post peat organics and the overlying sediment. I say this as it may have a preserving effect. And it occurs to me, Sergeant Field, I'm sorry to say, that there may be more bodies down there. I can quickly take samples if you want me to but I'm loth to disturb what I hope will be a later, thorough, examination in a post mortem. Strangling as cause of death I would say.'

'No-one to fight for them,' said Shaw.

'Exactly,' Jack agreed, 'very hit and miss existence isn't it for a child.'

Field looked at Burgess who gave a brief nod.

'The coastguard is waving,' said Burgess. 'Go over Jack, will you as you know him better and give him a hand?'

Jack looked at Burgess and frowned. Burgess had eyes full of sympathy. Jack nodded and he walked towards Edward.

'Shaw, take it easy. He's not got as much experience as you and I to handle this sort of thing. I agree by the way given the location of that woman's death, what was her name?' asked Field.

'Mabel Walters according to what Mrs Croft said last night. Might be an idea to have a chat with her by the way. She does some sort of good works with a group locally with young women who find themselves in the family way and I reckon there are suspicions about the destinations of their children.' said Shaw.

354

'Given the location of Mabel Walter's death, either through stabbing or drowning, my money's on her having been followed and caught in the act of burying the most recent body. She must have been watched, got involved in the digging and then was covering the area up when her killer struck,' mused Field.

'Jack could be right, of course, about the murder of Grace and Mabel Walters not being separate issues,' said Shaw.

'Yes, and there's three corpses as far as we know, uncovered here,' Field said. 'That means there may be other people who topped Mabel Walters.' Field shaded his eyes and stared up the beach.

'That coastguard is moving, Shaw. I think it's time for you and I to make ourselves scarce before our cousins from the Hastings force arrive,' said Field. He turned back to Burgess, and Ann: 'Mrs Black, Burgess, are you both alright to remain here and speak to the police?'

'Of course,' said Burgess. Ann met Field's eyes but gave a brief nod.

'Can I suggest you get your stories straight of why you're here,' said Field. Ann raised her eyebrows and sighed with the amount of subterfuge.

'Feeling inventive?' she asked Burgess.

'Always,' said Burgess as he smiled at her. Despite the finds she relaxed a little.

Jack had reached Edward.

'Jack, I need to get the Hasting's police over,' called Edward once Jack was in earshot. 'Mr Gale is offering to stay in his accommodation, and I've told him that he should. If you could get over to Bridge Lodge on the Pett Road and stay with him I'll get across to the first cottage at the farm to send one of the Hurst lads to the local police station. I'll be back as quickly as I can.'

'Right,' Jack said starting to move towards the track that would take him to the road.

'Alright?' asked Edward quietly, looking at the loss of colour in Jack's face. 'If you needed to rest Jack, no-one will think the less of you.'

Jack shook his head, almost irritably:

'No Edward, you don't know me, I'm not the same person as that young child you played with. There's enough hurt and death in this job to make me want to see something this tragic through. I'll see you later at the cottage.'

Bridge Lodge was on the corner of Pett Road, slightly at an angle from the church of St Mary and St Peter. Almost by the time he had reached the first dwelling in the village it was apparent that word had spread. Small communities, thought Jack. Someone may have overheard Edward sending a lad for the police. The boy had probably told his mates as he ran, such would be the reputation the boy would gain for being trusted by the coastguard.

Jack walked quite slowly into the garden of the double fronted house where Gale was staying and followed a path round the back of the property in to the kitchen. He knocked on the back door and lifted the latch to go in in case there would be any doubt. Gale had stayed in the kitchen after Edward Croft left and he now rose from his seat at the kitchen table. Jack smiled as he entered and pulled out a chair to sit down. He could see Gale's hands were still showing a tremor.

'Perhaps water?' Jack asked. There was the barest of nods from Gale and Jack pumped water into a pitcher he found on the draining board. He looked along a rack of dishes drying over the stone sink and pulled down a cup, pouring water into it for the man and filling one for himself. He sat down opposite him, pushing the cup towards him.

'The coastguard is just going for the police,' said Jack.

'Thank goodness I wasn't alone again. If I'd come across this on my own after yesterday's body I think I would have passed out. How did they find the bodies?' asked Mr Gale.

'Just digging around for artefacts,' said Jack. 'One of them saw something and went deeper.'

Gale's expression was completely confused. 'Why there?'

Jack smiled. 'As good a place as any. You know I was thinking, not much point you staying here on your own.'

'The owner's away for the summer. Just the cook's here and a woman who comes in every day,' said Gale.

'It's a peaceful spot,' said Jack. He waited until Gale had taken some sips of water and continued with a question of how Gale came to be there.

' A number of us came down some years ago in answer to an advertisement' said Gale.

'From the Geological Society in London?' asked Jack.

Gale nodded. 'I loved the quiet, so I carried on coming each summer.'

'You must have an understanding employer,' Jack said.

'I teach at Tonbridge School. The summer holidays are devoted to research,' explained Gale.

'I see, so in the term you're at the school? I would go back there, Mr Gale.'

'Why? Do you think I'm in danger? How can that be? They've arrested the murderer.' Gale's hands had started to shake again. Jack hated doing this to the man but the last thing the team wanted was Gale telling the local police there were five people on the beach that afternoon. Shaw and Field would presumably disappear shortly.

'You might be. They arrested the man suspected of killing a young woman at Lovers Seat. He's not been arrested for the death of the woman on the beach. That killer is still at large. Might have been watching us all this afternoon, ready to strike. It's upsetting but what my colleagues have uncovered look as though they may be children. Perhaps the woman you found at the rockpool was killed by someone related to one of the children? Maybe she killed the children? As you're on the beach so often, have found corpses yourself on your own admission, the police might conclude you're involved. I'd get out if I was you. I can pass on where you can be found to the coastguard if the police need to talk to you.'

'Go today? Yes, I see your point. I could get an evening train back. Yes, I will, I'll pack now. Are you sure you don't mind passing on the address?' asked Gale. The man was clearly nervous.

'Not at all,' said Jack standing to leave. 'Tonbridge School is easy enough to find if the police need to. Nice to have met you but I'm sorry it's been under such difficult circumstances. Perhaps we'll meet in London?' Jack held out his hand. Gale hesitated.

'Victoria and Albert?' Gale asked as if he was logging it away in his memory.

'That's right,' said Jack. Gale shook hands with Jack and showed him out.

Jack clicked the gate to and glanced up at the windows on the first floor. Gale was already moving back and forth across a room and Jack caught a glimpse of the man standing sideways on, concentrating on removing items from open drawers. He would be gone within the hour, Jack thought.

Jack turned into the lane and walked back through the village. Locals were out and there was a hushed silence as he passed. Strangers in their village after murder would be remembered, he thought. He did not speak and looked straight ahead, making for the path to Cliff End and from there on to Fairlight.

He felt a craving for the extensive coast line as if it could console him. But there was nothing romantic now about the scenery after the tragic picture in his mind from the rock pools. It blended with his worst nightmares of the face in the water. He could have been on any street in London dealing with the worst expression of human behaviour instead of gazing out to sea.

Jack's spirit, affected as well by what he had heard from Edward last night, would normally have lifted by the sight of the sprawling cliffs. Instead he felt all his hopes and aspirations had been buried in the sludge and residue of a dead, sunken forest and the beauty no longer touched him. The coast was deeply blood-soaked because of the vulnerability of those small beings they had found earlier and their fate had mixed with his own realisation of abandonment.

He knew the trauma of finding death as they had would have isolated each one of the team on the beach. Normally he would have worked at keeping everyone together but something had changed him last night as he had listened to the shock of the Crofts at finding he had grown up in an orphanage. The others must look to themselves today because he could not even help himself.

Jack reached Cliff End and stood on the top, under an immense blue sky, watching the uncovering of tragedy still going on. Edward had returned with two constables from the Hastings force.

Shaw must have been right as the policemen were digging. Police uniforms mingled with the figures that were Burgess, Ann and Edward. Jack knew he would never clear the view from his memory.

*

Once back at the farm Jack had given a brief explanation to Mrs Crowhurst and Emma of the afternoon's dramatic turn. He collected his bag and explained that the others would be along shortly but were helping the police at Pett Level.

'Eerie sort of place, I always thought,' said Mrs Crowhurst. 'Too deserted to let Emma go to when she was younger. Well we'll keep our eyes open and let the Coastguard know if we see anything strange. Enjoy your time with him and Mrs Croft, said Mrs Crowhurst.'

'Mrs George will be visiting an old friend of mine with me over towards Lewes tomorrow. I wonder if we might ask to be taken to the Railway Station in the morning about nine o'clock?' asked Jack.

Mrs Crowhurst agreed and he took his leave of them.

Burgess had made his own arrangements to get back for the train connection for Brighton. He and Ann arrived at the farm by six o'clock that evening exhausted for many reasons. Ann shook hands with Mrs Crowhurst and Emma and then excused herself and said she wanted to lay down for a while and make some notes about the day.

Shaw and Field materialised at the farm door having been in a position above the beach to keep an eye on progress. Field was introduced to Mrs Crowhurst and she registered that Shaw had lost his cheerfulness. Conversation turned to dinner.

'I've some Grey Gurnard tonight, a local fish, served with just butter. I hope that will suit you all?' said Mrs Crowhurst.

*

It was quite late when Burgess arrived back at the Ship Hotel. He had called in at the hotel by Hastings station and ordered himself a brandy, choosing to sit in the lounge rather than wait in the station café. It was after eight o'clock when he walked into the entrance of his hotel and Alice steered him to their private quarters.

'It's a long time since I've seen you look this grey,' said Alice. 'Get yourself to a warm bath and change, dinner's been kept for you. No work for you tonight, my dear,'

Burgess sat in his hip bath and contemplated the week it had been. Somewhere in a room on his ground floor there was a fugitive from justice.

Stan and Arthur had brought Harry Franks to the Ship Hotel from Portsmouth after dark the previous night. Burgess had been ready and Sam Curzon had received a telegram from Inspector Hunt, so he too was ready to lend assistance as the injured Detective Sergeant was brought in. Sam had wondered just how the release had been arranged but Stan had not been forthcoming.

They had indulged in a prison break, arranged by some unknown hand in government. It had gone smoothly, they were at the Ship and that was all Stan wanted to know. Hearing the clang of prison doors behind them as they half carried, half dragged Harry to a coach had terrified the hardened, rational, Police Sergeant. Arthur had gone along with it all because Stan was alright with it.

'Sam,' Stan had said with a nod, as he and Arthur had laid Harry on a bed in the room Burgess had prepared.

'This seems a bit absurd,' Sam had said.

'All I'm interested in is that it has worked. Is the doctor here?' asked Stan.

'He's on his way,' replied Burgess and then added, ' As a favour to me.'

'Slip his boots off Arthur, and cover him up. He's starting to shake,' Stan looked down at his own hand and slipped it into his pocket. No one else had seen.

'Bit of a lark, this,' said Arthur, grinning. It was the wrong response for Stan. He paced around the bedroom, taking short breaths. Arthur saw the warning signs of his Sergeant on the edge of a rage.

'Any chance we could leave Sergeant Franks to you gentlemen?' Arthur asked. 'We could do with letting off some steam and getting some air.'

'Curse it, it's a drink I want, not sea-air,' Stan said.

'On the side there,' said Burgess. 'Brandy. You get off both of you and get some rest. Food will be brought shortly to the room.'

Stan squatted on the arm of a chair and swallowed a glass of brandy. Arthur took a mouthful and grimaced.

'Swallow it,' ordered Stan. Arthur did and coughed much of it up.

'Like working with children,' Stan said to Burgess, who smiled back at him. 'Room number?'

'Sam will take you. It's Jack's room while he's staying away with friends.'

'I'll just take this with me,' said Stan, picking up the bottle.

'We'll dine out on this one, Sarg,' said Arthur.

'I will shoot you if you ever tell anyone what we have done tonight. Come on, you stink of prison. Fresh clothes and food, and then we both get a telegram to our wives about being on special duties for a few days.' Stan looked at Harry, unconscious and sweating and shaking with fever from a badly tended wound. He thought of the meeting he had witnessed through a window at the Treasury while he stood in an alley.

'I wish you hadn't told me,' he said to the unconscious Harry Franks.

*

Burgess had vanished the next morning and Sam did not see Harry until the evening. Now he heard the knock on his bedroom door quite late. He had eaten with Harry Franks alone; his mother having returned to Windsor to make preparations on packing up the home. Harry was still in pain and having difficulty in moving his fingers on the right hand. The doctor had visited, cleaned and tended the wound and fresh bandages had been applied. That morning the doctor had come back but no one except Stan, Arthur and the doctor went in or out of Harry's room. The most Sam was told was that he was making progress.

By evening Harry had sat in an armchair, after remaining in bed for much of the day. He had not spoken much, taking the broth that Alice had made from a spoon as she fed him.

Sam had just left Harry at nine o'clock, after dinner in the room, just as Stan and Arthur returned from their walk. It was good news that Harry would not undergo amputation.

Harry had said one word as Sam had started to leave: 'Rose.'

'Back at West India Dock, she and Mrs Philips,' Sam had explained.

Harry closed his eyes.

Hunt's orders were for the three men to stay put and he would liaise through Sam. Not Stan, but he, Sam and he still felt a thrill at the role he was playing. Hunt had sent through details of the diamond robbery from the Shah's belongings as well. With it was an artist's impression of a blonde man as the perpetrator of the theft, believed now to be a foreigner, possibly Dutch or Danish. Sam still waited for the information from Scotland Yard to arrive but his expectation was it would be about the same man. Hunt had sent a note for Sam to show the sketch to Jack. Sam had registered this would have to wait as he had little idea of when Jack would return. Hunt wanted to know if Jack could provide a positive match with the thief he had seen at West India Dock and the Alexandra Palace.

No word had yet been sent to Rose as to Harry's whereabouts. Sam was thinking of what they should do when there was a knock at his bedroom door

It was Burgess, looking a little grey about the gills. Sam invited him in.

Burgess unfolded the drama of Nathan's arrest and the suspicion centring around the victims found on the beach. Then he asked Sam to perform the act of being Nathan's Counsel.

Sam wanted to think it through and had gone out onto the promenade. It was dusk and not the time to advise a person to swim. The birdsong from the rooftops he had heard as he stepped out of the Ship Hotel were now drowned out by the incoming tide as it broke onto the shore. Sam walked onto the beach and turned towards the pier.

Burgess had told him there was quite a drag off shore and to be careful if he swam. The tide was in and he looked around. Always conscious of his body Sam was more so after his illness. He had never had the confidence in his strength that Jack had. He had spent too long pouring over ledgers, his only exercise having been helping his father occasionally as a Waterman.

363

He walked to the chain pier and with the shelter of the structure started to pull off his tie and shoes, followed by the rest of his clothes until he was down to his underwear. He dropped his clothes onto the shingle away from the probing tide and steadied himself on the shifting pebbles. He bore the pain on his feet until he was into the cold water.

Sam laughed.

It was more from the exhilaration that he had reached a point in his own recovery that he could swim again. Being alive and working, being wanted for his abilities, made him want to shout. Despite the knock of losing his father he knew they were, as a family, going to be alright. Shaking off the numbness in his feet he staggered up the sharp incline of the shore back to the dry pebbles. The cold water clung to him like the poison had back in January.

He quickly donned his clothes over the wet underwear and walked up the beach back to the hotel. Standing, dripping, he watched the sun sink behind the buildings further up the promenade. Once the sun had disappeared completely he turned into the hotel and went to his room to shed his wet clothes.

Thoughts of tomorrow and the charade Burgess wanted him to play troubled him. What the consequences were he could barely fathom if he and Burgess were caught. However if Nathan was innocent and Sam had not helped him the sailor's blood would be on his hands. He decided that he would play the Counsel with Burgess as his Clerk if it saved an innocent man's life. But how to present himself?

In his imagination he selected a character of young Mr Adams from his office days in the City. Sam had lightened the long working hours for himself and his fellow clerks by reducing them to hysterics as he had aped the younger partner. Sam took himself to a shaving mirror and adopted the cock-eyed smile and raised eyebrow that the man had sported. Yes, there he was in the mirror. The future hope of the Board of Directors. Adams had all the arrogance of breeding and education and the character stared back at Sam.

It was still Sam there too, the hair loss and gaunt features helped age him a little, helping to produce the future hope of the Board of Directors. Sam's characterisation conveyed the image of a man who spent long hours poring over cases. He had the mannerisms to a tee. Yes, they would lie their way in.

'We are to convince the Duty Sergeant that you've been appointed by the Judge as Counsel to Nathan. Once we've done that we want access to the police case,' Burgess had explained earlier.

Sam went to find Burgess who was in his office at the back of the reception. Sam cracked the door ajar, first knocking.

'We'll both be hanged as liars, then. I will imagine the character is convincing an investor on the worthiness of a particular stock. It may go up, it may go down, but imagine the return if the price increases.'

'And when we're done, I would advise you to follow Mrs Curzon back to Windsor until the beginning of July. Get away from this coast for the next week, just in case,' said Burgess.

'Can't be done,' Sam replied. 'My orders from Inspector Hunt are to stay with Harry. I can keep my head down around the hotel, walk at night, that sort of thing.'

Was it a trivial thing to lie? He asked himself why doing so now gave him a sense of disquiet. Such an activity for Sam he would have called "going under cover," when he had been a Metropolitan Policeman. He had longed to then, but it had been Jack that had been selected. Sam glanced at his own reflection. And why not Jack? Quite right too, he told himself. After all Sam had been the one who had had the eye for detail, and was of more use with the analysis of evidence and records. Jack, poor Jack now thought Sam, had the physical strength and was quick to act. Sam sincerely hoped that it all would return for his friend.

So why would his conscience prick? The Methodist upbringing had done too good a job on him, he told himself. He knew it was because the charade would be carried out without the direct line of authority.

Things had not turned out the way Sam had hoped in his career. Whatever was to happen in the future with this new role Hunt had given him, Sam was grateful for the opportunity. He left Burgess and once in his bedroom lay on his bed. Thanks to the physical tonic of the cold water and the swim Sam soon fell asleep.

The following morning Sam and Burgess left shortly after half-past six. Harry and his crew were still asleep and it was only the few hotel guests, up and about preparing for an early morning walk, that they met as they left. Burgess had spoken to the general staff preparing for the day as they had walked through the hotel and kissed his wife as he left reception.

He and Sam paused on the front steps to look at the day as it began.

'Lovely morning, we've got the first rays of sunshine,' said Sam as he and Burgess started their walk to the station.

'I doubt it will last. Those clouds on the horizon are lined up like an offensive about to break. I think you'll find Hastings interesting. You know the old police station used to be in the Town Hall?' said Burgess.

'I imagine the Mayor wasn't too keen on that,' Sam chuckled.

'There was also a watch house and it may have been the same one as was used before 1835. I've heard that there were four cells in there next to the gaol.' said Burgess.

They arrived in Hastings to witness a mix of bustle and calm. Burgess knew his way and led Sam through the back streets of the town, past areas that the visitors would not seek out. The cry of the gulls announced the catch arriving with the fishing fleet and above the town the ruins of the castle dominated the view.

Pausing at the door of the police station to let two constables pass Sam and Burgess briefly glanced at each other. The adrenalin was starting to pump.

'Ready?' asked Burgess.

Sam took a barely perceptible breath, nodded and they went in.

The charade began.

'Adams of Braithwaite, Houghton and Adams, Counsel to Nathan Long. This is my Clerk, Thompson.'

The Duty Sergeant took a long look at the arrogant young man with the bored expression before him. Quite well dressed, plummy accent, probably a London firm, the Sergeant thought. He gave the man standing deferentially to one side behind the Counsel a brief once over. Typical of the occupation of Clerk, he thought, overweight and a bit scruffy.

'Adams did you say?' The Duty Sergeant opened a ledger of instructions with that day's date at the top. He ran a stubby finger down the page looking for the information. It eluded him.

'We're not expecting Counsel for the prisoner. Who instructed you?'

'The Court, of course. Come man, I haven't all day. I have another five of these to do over in Brighton before I'm finished, and it will be four o'clock before I'm on a train back to London. I know you've all escaped this Shah visit down here but I'll be in the Prince of Wales party this evening and there will be a devil to play if I'm late as a result of this force's inefficiency.' Sam half turned toward Burgess and clicked his fingers several times. Burgess doubled in obeisance and dived into a well-worn satchel. He pulled out a sheaf of papers, rolled and tied with a red ribbon. Sam sniffed and started to drum his fingers on the desk. The Duty Sergeant looked down at the pale hand which had not done any manual work.

'Well, I suppose it's alright. It's just we weren't told. Come through,' said the Duty Sergeant and he admitted them into the inner sanctum of Hastings Police Station. He opened a door to a room in which a couple of constables were making tea.

'Take the Counsel and his Clerk down to the prisoner, Long. Stay outside the door and give them thirty minutes with him. Then escort them up. Excuse me Mr Adams, I'll get back to the duty desk.'

'Of course, of course. What charge have you made?' asked Sam.

'Murder and resisting arrest. He didn't come quietly. You'll see bruises, I tell you that now and that he's had the Surgeon to him. No confession, keeps alleging he's innocent of "her blood," that's what he keeps saying,' explained the Duty Sergeant.

'Evidence?' demanded Sam.

'He was there. He claims he found her as they'd arranged to meet by letter. Clear he bashed her head in and then ran for the coastguard who brought us in.'

Burgess coughed and Sam inclined his ear.

'Excuse me Sergeant,' said Burgess. 'Our physician checked the area and found three rocks blood soaked. They were not of the area implying that the body was brought there with them after the death. Also we have a sworn statement from the coastguard that the rigor mortis had worn off so death had occurred about forty-eight hours before.'

'Excellent Thompson. Clear you have the wrong man, eh Sergeant?' Sam snorted, 'Ha.'

'Well that's for the court to decide,' said the Sergeant.

'Exactly so, and it will! In the meantime there's a vicious murderer on the loose in Hastings, preying on innocent young women. What was the name of the local paper that contacted us, Thompson? Lead on Constable, take me down to my client.'

The constable unlocked the door to the cell and called into Nathan Long, 'Your Counsel's 'ere.'

They heard Nathan respond. 'Counsel? I don't have any Counsel. Is the man from the Navy?'

Sam and Burgess remained on either side of the door, side on. As the constable stepped away they both slipped into the cell keeping their faces obscured. Sam had his head turned towards the constable and he leant into the corridor, asking in his plummy voice for some privacy and for the constable to step a little further away from the cell.

The door clanged shut, the key turned and Nathan took in the hotelier, and the helpful little man called Sam that he had met in the Ship in Brighton. Sam smiled and held up a finger to his lips, waiting for the constable to put some distance between himself and the cell.

'Hello Nathan, let's see what we can do to get you out of here,' said Burgess softly.

*

Twenty-one

Sam moved quickly forward and extended his hand, taking in Nathan's physical state first. He'd put up a fight, the Duty Sergeant had said. Sam wondered how many constables were bearing the marks of that fight from the seasoned sailor.

'Have you been mistreated?' he asked.

Nathan smirked. 'I put up some resistance when they arrested me. They came off worse than me. How did you know I was here? As good as it is to see friends why are you both here? Are you a lawyer?'

'At times I could be,' Sam said. 'Have you seen the Police Surgeon?'

Nathan shook his head.

Burgess interrupted. 'We'll make sure you do before we leave. We're here because we're helping a friend in the Brighton Police, a Sergeant Field, investigating the disappearance of a number of women. Grace was one of them. We think we have evidence that can prove that you did not kill Grace.'

'Thank God,' said Nathan.

'We need to get hold of the police case against you and from what they've told us it's flawed. We can get that to the Court now and you must demand that you are represented, that the case is not straight forward,' said Sam.

'What does it matter? She's still dead.' Nathan's expression was terrible. Burgess moved forward and gripped Nathan's forearm.

'But you didn't kill her, did you?' Burgess asked the question firmly.

Nathan ran his hands through his hair and said, 'No, but it doesn't change the fact that she's dead. I've killed many people. The odds of me surviving the next skirmish must be running out by now. What are you trying to save me for? Another ship? Another war? The likelihood is I'll die anyway given where we sail next. Without Grace I won't dodge the next bullet or knife anyway so why bother fighting this.'

'Because you didn't kill her did you?' asked Sam.

'No, I've already said I didn't. Of course I didn't kill her. I've killed for Queen and Country but there's no pride in it any longer. I've killed men with families and they may have starved for all I know as a result of my action. I've killed. But not Grace. I'd not even seen Grace since I returned. There was a letter left in a makeshift post box in the cliff that we set up near Lovers Seat. It said I had a son, called Jonathan and that he already bore my name. But that there had been difficulties for her and she'd had to leave him with a woman called Mabel Walters in Hastings and there were now problems getting him back. After I came to your hotel last Monday I came over here and assumed she was in Hastings to be close to the child. I couldn't find her and I still don't know where Grace was living. We had a pact that we'd meet on set days of the year at the Lovers Seat if I came back. She'd been faithful to that, believing I'd put things right if I did return. And this time I was there but it was too late. She'd had it hard. She should never have been put through such a life. It's as much my fault for not marrying her before I left her to go back to sea. We should never have respected her father's wishes and waited. I could have set her up in Portsmouth in a lodging, with money, and she'd have wanted for nothing. I can't believe her parent's harshness and that she'd had to put the child to be nursed with a local woman to keep him alive.' His voice broke and he was silent for a while until he regained his control. Sam waited. Burgess pulled out a wrapped parcel from the satchel. He silently undid it and held it out to Nathan. There was a pie and bread. Nathan shook his head.

'Best to eat it now as they'll take it from you when we go,' said Burgess, kindly.

Precious minutes were spent as Nathan dutifully ate the food. Burgess uncorked the small bottle he had also brought and this too was consumed.

The food had started to work and Nathan resumed his story:

'Grace had paid Mabel Walters to keep the baby safe, just until she was on her feet and could look after him again, or until I returned. Whichever was the sooner. She'd got work, she said in her letter, then had gone back to get him and found that the woman had arranged an adoption, and the child had gone. Can you imagine how desperate she must have felt? Grace had never agreed to that and was after her to get the child back. I got a church last Sunday in Portsmouth, to start calling the bans and was going to surprise her that we would be married in three weeks.'

'Have you still got the letter?' asked Burgess.

'It was with everything else that the police took when I was arrested and charged,' said Nathan.

'I've met the coastguard who you brought to Lovers Seat after you found Grace. He was called to a body at Pett Level shortly afterwards. Walter's is dead, seemingly attacked from behind and left to drown, same day as Grace was found,' explained Burgess. He paused, undecided as to whether to tell Nathan about their other finds.

'Good grief,' said Nathan, sitting down. 'Found that day? What are the chances of that?'

'Yes, by a geologist on the beach. Otherwise Walters may have been washed out to sea on the tide. Whoever killed her must have known what she was doing with the children, possibly a relative.' Burgess made a decision. 'I'm afraid we found evidence of small children buried at the same spot.' Burgess stopped as Nathan buried his head in his hands and sobbed.

Sam knelt down on the cell floor and put a hand on the man's shoulder, pulling out a very clean handkerchief which he pushed into one of Nathan's hands. Burgess and he waited until the sobbing grew less.

'Is there any way to know if any of those children might be Grace's and mine?' Nathan asked.

'Not that I know of. But we have a scientist friend who might know a way,' said Burgess.

'So,' said Sam, 'The job of the police is to catch the right person. Not just clear up their charge sheet. If the real murderer is out there they have to be stopped. You need Counsel to defend you and then you carry on with your life,' said Sam.

Nathan shook his head. 'Why?'

'Because you still have life. Believe me, I know. I won't bore you with details but I do know,' said Sam, standing up. 'First thing though is to save your neck. Who's your commanding officer in the Navy?' asked Sam.

'I don't want them involved,' Nathan retorted.

'Rubbish, man,' snapped Burgess. 'They can help you. Your record alone would impress a jury.'

'Look Nathan I'm not interested in how many people you've killed or whether it was right for the English Navy to order you to do so. That's not what we're here for. Those questions will probably be asked by someone in the future.' Sam leant against the cell wall and noticing the state of it thought better of it. 'Now we'll get the details that the Duty Sergeant has given us back to Sergeant Field in Brighton, and to your commanding officers, and ask for help in your defence. We'll make sure you have a real Counsel in Court. Come on, tell us who your Commanding Officer is in the Navy?'

'If I agree to have a defence will you leave that alone? They have no influence here on shore,' said Nathan.

There was a banging on the cell door, and then it was pulled back. 'Time's up, gentlemen,' said the constable.

'Time to leave,' said Burgess, under his breath.

Nathan gripped his arm.

'They've a letter of mine, sent by Grace. I picked it up at our letter box. Can you get it?' he asked.

'I can get a copy done,' said Burgess into Nathan's ear. As the door opened he adopted the sycophantic manner of the Clerk to the Counsel.

Sam turned to the constable, becoming once more the arrogant, bored young man from the City.

'I want to see the Duty Sergeant before we leave to make a complaint on the treatment of my client. He must have the Police Surgeon today. I also want the name of the Counsel for the Prosecution. My client is now agreeing to have defence and will make a formal request through me. Lead on.'

*

Jack had been locked in a mood the previous evening after arriving at the Crofts and the evening meal placed before him was destined to proceed in quietness. But his glum expression had to be delayed for another time. Edward had started to carve meat produced for their dinner in honour of Jack coming back into their lives. Jack nodded his appreciation of the delicious aroma of lamb and being mindful of its costs nodded his appreciation to Lucy. As he came to the table Edward noted the light had come back into Jack's eyes just briefly.

Lucy went to collect the children from the front of the cottage and came through the back door with two young people holding her hands, partly hiding in their mother's skirts. The children had been briefed that there was a new "Uncle Jack," to meet.

The shy little boy who stood by his mother weighed up the visitor while his sister adopted the manner of proprietorship and clambered up on Jack's knee. Her cheek was pressed against his as small children will do when they know they are safe and loved and wish to share the benefits. Her wide-mouthed smile drew out Jack's in response. Then, and only then, did her brother come forward to show their new friend his wooden cart and horse. Martha and Andrew Croft had spun their magic and Jack's dark humour was banished. Later, after all had eaten their fill and the children were settled for the night, Jack beat Edward at cards and glanced up at Lucy with his spontaneous smile.

Much to his surprise Jack slept well and managed to produce an appetite for breakfast. He left at nine o'clock and walked across to the farm to join Ann Black for their journey to see Reverend Fisher. Emma drove them in the farm cart and they chatted about George's career expectations, careful not to wander onto the subjects within her earshot that were really exercising them both.

By the time their train towards Lewes had reached Pevensey the carriage had emptied and Ann voiced her concerns about Mabel Walters's death.

'Jack I've been waiting to tell you about a chance remark about the cause of death. One of the Hastings constables said Walters had bled into her clothing. He'd heard the pathologist had found a strange shaped wound in the back, so they were assuming the killer was a woman using a knitting needle: "One of the broken hearted mothers of those children," he said to me, "Not a man's weapon," he said. None of it made sense to them.'

'Won't take much for them to conclude that, but it clearly wasn't Grace as we know she'd been dead for two days at least. Is there any way of knowing who the babies belonged to? Scientifically I mean? Blaming a mother is nice and neat, no need to keep on looking and they'll close the case,' said Jack, cynically.

'Not at the moment, not that I know of anyway,' said Ann. She looked out at the rich pastures of the Pevensey level and thought for a few moments.

'It's a shame I can't get at the body. What was it that was said about the possibility of Mabel Walters dying of a stab wound or drowning?' asked Ann.

'She was found face down in the rock pool. It didn't need to be deep if she was unconscious. But if she'd been stabbed wouldn't she bleed to death, Ann?' asked Jack.

'Not necessarily. If she was taken by surprise, shocked, she may not even know it had happened. Whatever went on might have numbed her. She could have fallen forward and then been held down in the water. It depends on how quickly everything happened as well. If enough time goes by she would be aware of something substantial happening after a stabbing. But there may not have been much time.'

Jack nodded, taking it in. Ann continued.

'When Doctor Brown and I see someone that's been injured we always examine them from head to toe because some people just are not aware of what the injury is. We might miss an injury that will kill them. Whatever was used to stab Mabel Walters might have been used to stun her for long enough to drown her,' explained Ann.

'I've been thinking about the doctor who issued the death certificates for Mabel Walter's charges as well. He's supposed to have fallen on one of his own knives. That was the verdict. The knife wound killed him from what we heard,' said Jack.

'Well, if it had struck a main blood vessel he would have bled freely. I presume it was at the front of the body? I'd have question such as how did he fall? Did it enter a lung, for example? Either of those situations would mean he would have been in danger of dying at the scene where it happened. Do we know any details?' asked Ann.

'No nothing. That death again has been dealt with very neatly. No police enquiry after the Coroner's verdict. Accidental death. Given his role with Mabel Walters it does make me wonder. It was the first death Field mentioned and therefore may be unrelated to the baby farmer's. But it might be related. Here's the halt at Simpson now. We've a short walk to the cottage.' Jack stood and held out a hand to help Ann up.

'I can stand up on my own, Jack,' she said.

'Yes, of course you can,' he said, chastened.

'You wouldn't hold your hand out to help Ted Phillips, would you?'

'No,' said Jack, backing off.

The morning light reflected off the upper windows of the cottage as Jack and Ann walked up the lane from the railway halt. It was lined on either side by tall hedges just coming into their fullness. In another month it would need scything, Jack thought. Apart from the labourers in the field all was quiet. Ann smiled.

'What is it?' Jack asked.

'I do wonder sometimes why you've exchanged this for London,' said Ann.

'For the same reason you battle on to become a doctor. There's no future for me here as a labourer. We either stay still or we move onwards and wait for the outcome,' said Jack.

'Yes, but to leave all this, Jack? Look at those wide vistas towards the hills,' Ann breathed in the scent carried from the south.

Jack stood with his back towards the South Downs. 'Ann, you will never understand what it feels like to be at the bottom of the pile.'

'Oh, I think I do,' Ann said.

'I'm sorry, that was thoughtless of me,' said Jack.

'No matter. You and I have the same drivers you know. The reasons are different. I'm not at the bottom of the same pile as you but sometimes the effect is the same, Jack. Sometimes, both you and I are completely invisible,' said Ann.

Jack's attention was drawn to the Parson's cottage.

'The place looks closed up. I hope he's there and I've not wasted our time.'

'Someone's in the garden, a woman,' said Ann.

Jack saw the mop cap popping above the hedge as the Parson's housekeeper, Mrs Simcock, moved about the garden. He looked at the sun's position.

'Vegetables for lunch I think. That's Mrs Simcock who looks after the cottage and cooks for the Parson. The fact she's there means we can at least wait for him if he's out.' Jack pushed open the gate and called to Mrs Simcock, who was now at the far end of the garden amongst the peas.

'Marning Mrs Simcock, is the Parson at home?' called Jack.

Mrs Simcock straightened up and wiped her hands on the cloth she had draped over a bucket.

'Why sir, I'd no idea you were coming today. No sir,' she called back. 'Parson's back for luncheon about one o'clock but he went out visiting early this morning. Will you and the lady like to wait for him?'

'Thank-you we will. This lady is Mrs Ann Black, she works with the police and so is a friend and colleague of mine,'

'How do you do, ma'am,' said Mrs Simcock.

'Nice to meet you, Mrs Simcock.' Ann replied.

Mrs Simcock arranged two chairs by an old garden table for Ann and Jack and brought them tea. Jack left Ann reading a small book she had produced from her bag and joined Mrs Simcock in the vegetable garden as she continued harvesting broad beans and pulling the first carrots of the year. He cut the small crisp lettuce and picked the young peas, many of which he proceeded to pod and eat as he had done every summer from being a child.

It was nearly one o'clock before the Reverend Peter Fisher returned. The Parson paused at his gate to take in the view of the well-dressed young woman sipping tea and reading. Such elegance in his garden, he thought.

Ann looked up as she heard the latch of the gate and the dog collar the elderly man wore announced he was the clergyman Jack had brought her to meet. The Parson raised his hat to her with a little smile.

'Oh, er, Jack is here with your housekeeper,' said Ann, standing and part turning towards where Mrs Simcock and Jack were still toiling. 'I'm Anne Black. I, er, I work with Jack on occasions and assist the Police Surgeon.'

'Ah, so he's brought his lady doctor to meet me. How do you do.' Again Peter Fisher touched his hat and took the chair next to Ann. 'I may have misunderstood but I thought it was Tuesday that he was due.'

Ann sat again and said, 'Yes you're right on that but a rather urgent need has arisen on the case to do with the missing Brighton woman. That's why we've come. What a delightful spot this is.'

'Yes, I like it. You'll stay for luncheon? If Jack has left any peas for us, that is. I haven't seen him for years until this week you know. One is inclined to still see the child from eleven years ago. How do you think he is?' The blue eyes that read the soul turned to her own. Ann met them and smiled.

'Recovering. His mood is better this morning. We need to build his strength now. That sort of activity he's doing in the fresh air is exactly ideal. Ah look, they're coming over. I'm afraid we had a disturbing day yesterday and it's taken its toll emotionally.'

The Parson nodded, looking across at Jack.

'Marning Parson, it being lunchtime we've accepted an invitation from Mrs Simcock. You've got a yaffle over there you know,' called Jack.

The Parson turned to Ann to explain. 'His father used to do this with me, break into Sussex dialect because he knew I had an interest in the subject. A yaffle, Jack? Remind me what that is will you?'

'A green Woodpecker, its eating the ants,' said Jack, with a grin.

'I've never seen one,' said Ann.

'Down here,' said Jack beckoning and Ann excused herself and walked over to where the grass was full of flowers.

'Follow me in when you're ready,' the Parson called to them.

*

They had almost finished luncheon when the Parson asked Mrs Simcock to bring him the papers from his bureau. Watching him Jack had concluded that long life must be something to do with not giving up despite the body evidently starting to have its limitations.

'This tract that you asked me to look at by Wilhelm Marr. I've written what I think I can for you. Let me just say this without spoiling our luncheon. This is the sixth re-print of this work which says something about its growing popularity in Germany.' The Parson paused long enough to realise that they were still awaiting pudding.

'Mrs Simcock,' he called. 'We'll have our pudding now.'

'Right, sir,' came the reply from the kitchen.

'I suspect it's being seen as scientific, which I don't think it is,' the Parson continued, jabbing the papers with a finger. 'That's part of the reason for its popularity though. Personally I think it's drivel.' He dropped the papers in the centre of the table.

'Pass my scribblings on to your Inspector by all means,' continued the Parson. His face was grim. 'I think you're right to look at it as potentially being a cause behind the targeting of the orphanage. I don't want to go into it over the table, as it's unpleasant. There are, what I believe to be, false assumptions in it. Marr's basing his thoughts on an eighteenth century analysis of language, German of course, and he's arriving at an incorrect conclusion about different racial groups. If we're not careful it will produce a new vocabulary which is not only wrong but dangerous and venomous. I've done some research on him and the writer is a disappointed man both in his career and, I gather, his marriage. He's targeting the Jews. I hope it doesn't develop but I fear people are looking for scapegoats. Take my scribblings with my blessing and may it be useful in your work.'

'Thank-you Parson. That's good enough for me. If I come across anyone with this in London I'll pull them in,' said Jack.

'Well Jack, you are hitting the whole debate around free speech now. This sort of thing does need exposing for what it is and challenging at the right levels. I've passed the issues raised in this tract on to a friend of mine at Oxford, assuming you wouldn't mind.'

'Of course not. I'm grateful for anything you can do. Is your friend in a position to do anything?' asked Jack.

'Academically, he has the position to challenge it.'

The Parson accepted the berries from Mrs Simcock, drizzled with a home-made syrup, while he looked over his spoon at Jack. Scooping up the fruit, he asked while he chewed:

'So, your friend the Shah never arrived in Brighton?'

'No, a complete waste of time for everyone there,' said Jack.

'Well, all the members of Parliament and the Councils will soon have to go back to work. They've been kept in such a succession of parties and fêtes that they've had no inclination for knuckling down. Will you be called back now Jack?' asked the Parson.

'No, not yet. My orders were to stay and recuperate for three weeks, Parson, I've another ten days of so before I go back to London,' said Jack.

'Excellent time for another two visits then. You're coming on Tuesday aren't you? I ask because I've arranged for someone to be here for you to meet and I think you'll enjoy that visit,' said the Parson.

'I'm coming, especially if Mrs Simcock puts on another meal like this,' said Jack smiling at the lady. She did a little bob and collected the china cups and saucers from the dresser.

'Jack has to be signed off by Dr Brown, before he returns to work,' said Ann to the Parson.

'Or you,' Jack retorted.

'Only if his travels delay him longer, Jack,' Ann smiled at his ready enthusiasm to be treated by her.

'You were going to give me those exercises,' said Jack.

'Yes, I have them but was going to talk to you on our way back,' replied Ann.

'What exercises are these?' asked the Parson.

'They're Swedish exercises designed to build him back up again,' said Ann.

'Let's have a look and go out on the lawn and see if I can do them too. I'd noticed you hadn't coughed today, Jack. Good sign?' the Parson looked at Ann, who nodded.

'He'll need to be careful in the winter, though,' said Ann.

'Before we try them can I broach the subject of whether you've had the time to find anything out about Grace?' asked Jack. 'I know I've come back early but I thought I'd just ask.'

'Of course. You want it now? Alright, just a minute. I'll bring my findings out into the garden if you'd like to both go out and sit. Mrs Simcock is setting up a pot of tea out there.' Peter Fisher went towards his bureau.

'I'll get those exercises for you, 'said Ann, taking the opportunity to leave the table while the Parson was out of the room. 'They're in my bag.' She was back quickly and gave Jack the diagrams of Swedish exercises.

'I'll try them later. He's right, the Parson I mean, that I haven't coughed today,' said Jack.

'Yes he is. Perhaps have a rest here before we leave?' suggested Ann.

'If the Parson doesn't mind. I'll ask him,' said Jack.

'You could put your head back in the folding chair in the garden. It's a lovely afternoon to sit and sleep out there,' said Ann.

'I will if it won't seem rude,' said Jack.

'Unlikely to Jack, given you're with a man who knew you as a small child and I'm medically trained and used to the human body's need to rest.' Ann stood and pushed her chair closer into the table and together she and Jack walked out to the garden.

'Well, Pastor, what have you got for us,' asked Jack, as Peter Fisher joined them again. He handed a letter to Jack.

'I was sent this by return of post from a lady I know who is on the board of the Brighton Society. They basically do the poor relief in Brighton. She had passed it to them to check the writer out before they granted the application for help. See the signature?'

Jack looked at the bottom of the single page. He could make out the name Grace but could not decipher the surname. He read the sorry story, and then handed it to Ann.

"My lady, (the letter began)
My betrothed has not returned from naval service and I cannot obtain help from my family, who do not want to know me. I can barely bring myself to write to you and explain why I need help but must do so for the sake of my poor child."

'Oh dear,' said Ann, and she sighed before she continued reading.

"My lady, I have placed my child to be nursed, having paid all I had. I am not asking charity but the initial rent of a small shop in order to establish myself in business and support my child and myself. I truly believe I can make it successful and would repay the rental borrowed over time.

Should my betrothed return then I believe we will marry, such was his promise as an honourable man, and as he is a Petty Officer I believe him. There is a date soon when, if he is back, I will find a letter from him in Hastings. I would be able to repay more quickly once he returns.

I remain your servant,

Grace .... (and then the surname was illegible)."

'Poor woman. I didn't know he was a Petty Officer. Did Grace get the money?' asked Jack.

'Yes, a week ago. She apparently rented a small shop in Richmond Street quite near the Brighton Pavilion. It never opened,' explained the Pastor.

'So she was there while we were looking for her, right under our noses. And Nathan Long if he'd just stayed in Brighton and not gone off to Hastings. But Grace mentions a place where he would leave a letter for her. That must be the reason he was due to go to Hastings? You know I keep thinking that we could have prevented Grace's death if we'd not been so consumed with the Shah of flippin' Persia,' said Jack.

'You can't help that now,' said Ann. 'It was the reason you were sent here by Inspector Hunt, if we're being honest, regardless of the pressure from Doctor Brown to get you to the sea. This letter gives us a time frame Jack when she must have gone missing,' said Ann.

'After she'd got the money and rented the shop. What would a young mother do? She'd have gone to get the child wouldn't she?' mused Jack.

'And found she's too late and the child's gone,' Ann continued piecing the story together.

'Dead or adopted? Mabel Walters will have told her the child's been adopted and gone abroad. I wonder if the child was dead? Grace pushes for information and wants Mabel to get the child back.' Jack looked at Ann, who nodded.

'She undoubtedly became difficult and wouldn't leave it. I wonder if Grace told her about Nathan coming back and that he would not be pleased to find his child gone. Grace would be full of hope that everything would work out. She must have been frantic with despair at the thought of her child having been given to others. She was coming up to a date when, if Nathan is back, he'll go to the pre-arranged place. It must have been Lovers Seat,' said Ann.

'You can tell from the letter that Grace still believes that it's going to work. She's excited and maybe she told Mabel Walters that the child's father is due back. Perhaps Mabel Walters mocked her, made her angry.'

'No, Jack. The timing of Grace's death is too early for her to have killed the baby farmer,' said Ann.

'Right. Grace would still hope they'll marry and so the child has to come back so they can be a family,' said Jack.

'Dear Lord, are you telling me that the child has been killed?' the Parson asked incredulously.

'We don't know, Parson. We think that it's likely. We found corpses of young children, babies mainly, buried at Pett Level yesterday. Likely that Grace's child was amongst them. At the exact spot where the woman Mabel Walters had been murdered two days ago.'

'And Grace?' asked the Parson.

'Found dead at Lovers Seat, on the same day,' said Ann, quietly. 'Dead at least two days and brought there, she died somewhere else we think.'

'How did she die?' asked the Parson, 'not …..?'

'No, not by her own hand. She'd been murdered with a violent blow to the back of the head but several days before she was found at Lovers Seat. We think she was placed there to incriminate Nathan Long, her Petty Officer' said Ann.

'She may have told her murderer about the meeting to come with Nathan at the famous romantic spot,' said Jack. 'Mabel Walters may not have actually physically killed Grace but may have been behind the death. Nathan, of course, kept his appointment and found Grace. When the police came they arrested him and he was charged with her murder.'

Jack watched the old Parson wipe his eyes and found it difficult himself not to well up.

'Too late, too late.' Peter Fisher fumbled amongst the papers on his lap and pulled out a single sheet which he passed to Jack.

'Here is also copy of a Christening certificate for a baby called Jonathan, given the surname Long. Mother named on it is obvious. His father's surname's is there Jack, after the name Jonathon.'

'She anticipated the marriage to come. Never lost hope until it was snatched from her. She was so near. Those that abandoned her killed her,' said Jack, bitterly.

'Mabel Walters may have engineered her death but the odds were against her surviving. Crimes against the innocent,' said the Parson. His breathing was audible as he stared at Jack, and said, 'You have to catch whoever killed her, Jack, or your uniform is worth nothing. Do you recall your oath?'

Jack was shocked by the look on the Parson's face. Hatred he thought. Was it a loathing of injustice?

'Of course.' Jack said, feeling the old man's hand clasp his, he looked at Ann out of concern for the shock to the Parson.

'Tell me,' said the Parson.

'I do solemnly and sincerely declare and affirm that I will well and truly serve our Sovereign Lady the Queen in the office of constable, without fear or affection, malice or ill will: and that I will to the best of my power cause the peace to be kept and preserved and prevent all offences against the persons and properties of her Majesties subjects....'

385

'I think we need some hot sweet tea,' Ann interrupted, not liking the look of the elderly Vicar. 'Maybe brandy if you have it? Is Mrs Simcock still here?' Ann started to get up and made her way towards the kitchen, resolved to make the tea herself if the housekeeper had left.

'It's good you came back early,' said the Parson, gripping Jack's hand. Jack placed his other hand on top of the Parson's. 'I can make enquiries around the parishes for you, try and find out if anyone saw Grace between the date on the letter and when she was killed. How long did you say she had been dead before she was found?' asked the Parson.

'Two days, maybe more because the rigor mortis had worn off. So that puts death around Sunday,' said Jack.

'Tuesday last she obtains the rented shop. And it never opened.' The Parson sucked his teeth. 'That gives me my time frame. Six days. Ah, tea! But no brandy?'

'It's in the tea. Administered by Mrs Simcock,' said Ann, setting down the tray. 'And shortbread.'

'Brandy in the tea. *Sacrilege,*' pronounced the Parson.

'Just looking after you, probably,' said Ann. 'I let her put a teaspoon in, that's all.' She glanced at Jack to see how he was doing after the emotion that had been expressed. Still no cough, she thought, but it was unlikely he would sleep well now after all this.

'Medical people!' said the Parson to Jack. 'A teaspoon of brandy, I ask you. What good will that small amount do?'

'More than you think,' said Ann, passing him a bone china cup and saucer. The Parson looked at her, his eyes a watery blue.

'I wanted to tell you something, Ann, before you go. About a woman I knew as a young curate, an unusual woman in a man's world. As you've probably guessed I'm quite old. I tell you this story to encourage you, by the way, not just because I'm rambling. Phoebe Hessel is the woman,' said the Parson, but Ann laid her hand on his. He looked at her quickly.

'After you've got some of that tea inside you,' said Ann, gently.

'Ah, looking rough. Jack, one thing you'll learn with the medical profession is when you look rough. Alright Ann, I'll be good.'

Once Ann saw that one shortbread and half of the tea was consumed by the Parson, she smiled and asked:

'Why did you want to tell me about the woman, Phoebe Hessel?'

'Because she was unusual, or perhaps she wasn't. Perhaps it's just that we got to know about her. Maybe there were many other women who did the same sort of thing. Anyway I want to tell you to encourage you to keep on fighting to become a doctor. May I, now?' asked the Parson.

'Yes, I'd like to hear the story,' said Ann.

'Well, you'll find Phoebe Hessel's grave in Brighton, in St. Nicholas's churchyard. Look for it sometime will you and don't let her be forgotten. She lived to an amazing age of one hundred and eight. I met her in 1812 just as she was coming up to her hundredth birthday. She died in 1821.'

'I will go and see it. Take a sip of tea,' urged Ann.

Peter Fisher did so. As he set his cup down he explained:

'Phoebe served as a soldier initially disguising herself as a man in order to be with her soldier lover,' he said. 'Think about it, in those days, what she must have experienced, and the length of time she got away with it.' He reached for a second shortbread and Ann smiled.

'Do you mind if I dunk it?' asked the Parson.

'Good idea,' said Jack, taking a biscuit. 'I'll do the same.'

The Parson picked up his story.

'Phoebe Hessel was wounded at the Battle of Fontenoy in 1745, in the War of the Austrian Succession.' Glancing at Jack he asked: 'How's your history, Jack?'

'Local's alright but it won't be up to your standard if you're about to ask me to tell you about the Battle of Fontenoy,' said Jack, grinning.

'No? Well there were the usual allies of the Dutch, British and Hanoverian against the French. Our Phoebe was wounded, as I said. As it happens with dire consequences, because it meant she had to be examined by the surgeon so she had to reveal her sex. '

'What did they do?' asked Ann.

'The outcome was that the story came out and she and her lover were discharged from the army and they married. Her husband died by 1769 and she moved to Brighton and married a fisherman. She and her second husband were together until 1792 when he died. After that she made a living for herself hawking wares around the villages.'

'An amazing life,' said Ann. Confident of the old Vicar's recovery as his colour returned she poured herself a cup of tea.

'Wasn't it? Not the end yet. She ended up being given a pension by the Prince Regent of half a guinea a week. Half a guinea! Do you know what the annual income of a lady was in those years? Well, she lived not too badly, I can say. She survived for another thirteen years.' Peter Fisher held his shortbread over his cup as he bit into it. The crumbly nature of the biscuit meant tiny bits floated on the surface of his tea. He fixed Ann with an astute stare.

'Ann, when you face opposition, remember Phoebe and qualify as a doctor as soon as you can. Qualify! Promise?'

Ann laughed and then bent and kissed the Parson on the cheek.

'I promise. But you need to drink the rest of that cup of tea and finish the excellent piece of shortbread. Doctor's orders!' Ann said, with a smile.

*

Sam and Burgess walked quickly away from the Duty Sergeant's desk taking with them a copy of the letter Grace had sent to Nathan. The police had found it on arrest in an inner pocket when they had pinioned Nathan to the ground.

Burgess had copied the letter out while he stood at the Duty Sergeant's desk. It was dated Tuesday, seventeenth of June. Sam had distracted the Duty Sergeant by letting rip about the condition Nathan was in. It was the worst behaviour the Duty Sergeant remembered from a member of the Bar.

'Make a note of it,' Sam had barked.

'It isn't in your position to….'

'All you have to do is make a note of the request for a defence in the ledger without having an argument with me. Got it?' Sam imagined the constable behind him fighting a grin at his tone to the Duty Sergeant.

It worked. The Duty Sergeant picked up a pen and started to write in the ledger on the desk.

'Thank-you,' Sam snapped. 'Thompson, have you made a copy of the letter from the deceased to the accused?'

'Just finishing it, sir,' Burgess almost went into obeisance.

'Well get on it with it, man. Sergeant, I want you to compare the copy to the original and then sign the copy as identical content. Date it as well.' Sam snapped his fingers at Burgess who finished transcribing and pushed the copy in front of the Duty Sergeant. He scanned the original and the copy Burgess had made and signed and dated it at the bottom.

'Right, Thompson,' said Sam, tapping he desk twice. 'Our work here is done for the day. You will be hearing from us, Sergeant.'

'Bus to the Railway Station?' asked Burgess out of the side of his mouth as he and Sam walked down the steps from the Police Station.

'No, a cab,' said Sam. 'Just in case they're watching.'

*

389

Twenty-two

A light wind shared the evening with Jack and the Croft family as they took a turn across the cliff before dinner. It was far from warm though for the time of year and each one was more wrapped up against the chill than they would have imagined possible in June. The three adults were lost in reflection. Jack watched the children as they ran around their parents, seeming to have a sixth sense to remain more than three feet away from the cliff edge.

Edward broke their silence:

'It's years since we've had so much tragedy in such a short space of time.'

'Tragedy is right,' said Jack. He looked at Lucy as she played tag with Martha. The little girl ran to chase her brother as Lucy walked back to re-join Jack and Edward.

Jack decided to broach the subject of Grace.

'I saw the Christening certificate today of Grace's child. She'd named him Jonathan and given him the father's name of Long. Did you ever see the child, Lucy?'

Lucy turned and stared at Jack but she did not answer. It was a gaze of pure innocence. He half-smiled at her but her scrutiny of him held a lifetime of thought. She did not answer, choosing instead to call across to the children: 'I think we should go in now children and eat.'

Martha and Andrew changed direction and sped towards the cottage, still continuing their game of tag. Andrew overtook his younger sister and reached the kitchen door first, which made her cross.

'Do you have it with you?' Lucy asked as the children disappeared inside.

'No, I left it with the Parson,' said Jack.

'Good she did that,' Lucy said, shielding her eyes against the evening light.

They walked across the rough ground towards the coastguard station following the children back home.

'Why won't you tell me of your involvement with Grace?' Jack asked Lucy.

'Because it is a confidence. And now she is dead, and probably the baby as well, it feels like a sacrilege to have been involved in the beginning of life and to speak of it without her permission.' They had reached the cottage themselves and Lucy paused, her hand on the latch of the kitchen door. Her phrase "the beginning of life," told Jack all he needed to know. But Lucy had not finished.

'And what is the point of telling you? You cannot change anything now,' said Lucy.

'I can try and catch her murderer, and, if the baby is dead, whoever killed the baby,' Jack said, frowning at the horizon.

'It's a strange experience speaking to you now as a grown man. And a policeman. You see everything in such black and white terms. There is no law to stop the Mabel Walters of this world from disposing of children by adoption. You will never prove in a court of law that she either killed Grace, the baby, or was behind her death.'

'No, Lucy, that's not right. There are laws about harm and murder and they are very clear,' said Jack.

'Even so, you can't identify those poor little mites found yesterday on the beach, unless their mothers' are coming forward. The whole thing makes me sick at heart,' said Lucy.

They stood watching a predatory seagull on the wall in front of the coastguard station.

Jack glanced at Lucy. 'Did you help deliver the baby?' he asked.

The eyes said yes. Edward took his wife's hand.

'She was gone with him quickly though,' said Lucy, after some minutes of thought. 'We thought she may have gone back to Brighton but we weren't sure. I wondered if she had gone to take the child to her parents, hoping for a softening of their position. I don't know. I can surmise what happened but within days she was back in this area. All because her sailor would meet her at Lovers Seat when he came back. We gave her some help and the next thing I knew was the baby was with Mabel Walters and Grace had gone back to Brighton to try and make a living.'

'Would you recognise the baby?' asked Jack.

Edward came between him and Lucy. 'No, Jack, I don't want her to have to do that. It's more than you should ask.'

'I might,' said Lucy, ignoring Edward's plea. 'It's months since I saw him though. What's the point?' Lucy looked at Jack with a dead expression.

'There might be a point for the father. He can see the child identified and properly buried with Grace. It might help him,' said Jack.

Edward reached for Lucy's hand. 'You don't have to do this,' he said.

Lucy looked at her husband and squeezed his hand. 'I'll think on it, Jack,' she said.

They stood in silence, held in a mood outside the cottage. Jack broke their reflection.

'It's true there isn't a law yet about baby farming but there will be. Cases like this will change things. It will, Lucy. Maybe not quickly but it highlights the need to protect the vulnerable. Maybe people like you will change things, Lucy. Maybe I will. And maybe one day science will be able to tie back who a child's parent is. Ann says there's medical advances every week. But I can't let a murderer go free, and that's why I ask you questions.' Jack said.

'Oh, Jack, don't you see, a murderer hasn't gone free. Mabel Walters was executed by someone who found out what she was doing. I have no doubt that she killed those children. She probably was involved in getting Grace killed, even if she didn't carry out the act herself. Will you hunt the person down who killed Mabel Walters as well?' Lucy asked, defensively.

'Lucy, it's the law,' said Edward, reaching for her hand. Her eyes flashed at him and she stiffened.

'Yes,' said Jack. 'For it was not for them to do.'

'Winds getting up,' said Edward, looking at the sea. 'We should go in. Martha and Andrew will have found the pie by now and probably be half way through devouring it.' He looked from one to the other.

Jack stopped walking and coughed. He met Edward's concerned look and shrugged. 'Just the end of the day probably,' he said.

Lucy turned and looked sideways at Jack. 'I wished Mabel dead many times Jack. Where does that put me? What would the old Parson say about that?' She hesitated and controlled her own irritation. 'Come on, let's get you all fed. It's a strange thing but there's some comfort in the fact that you take the view you do.'

'Well, we'll see what's to be done tomorrow. I go over to the farm in the morning and will travel back to Brighton with Field and Shaw. Burgess has some news of Nathan by the sound of it,' explained Jack.

'And Ann?' asked Edward.

'Ann wants to try and see the pathologist who carried out the post mortem on Mabel Walters. One of the constables made a chance remark about a wound and Ann hopes to persuade the Doctor to let her see the body. Her husband, George, arrives in Hastings tomorrow night and they'll stay in the town before going back home on Sunday,' said Jack.

Edward pushed open the back door and true to form, two small children were sat at the table with a cold piece each of their mother's meat pie in front of them. The gravy oozed out of the pie and was all around their mouths.

Jack laughed and immediately went and joined them.

'Have you left some for me?' he asked.

'A bit,' said Andrew, pointing at the huge pie that was left.

'You need some vegetables with that,' said Edward.

'No, just pie,' said Martha.

'What time are you off tomorrow Jack?' asked Lucy as she removed her shawl and started to pump water.

'Before nine o'clock.' Jack said.

'Will you come back?' asked Martha, her eyes like huge saucers as she stared up at him.

'Yes, I would like to very much,' said Jack.

'There. You're locked into a promise to the children if there was any doubt that you're wanted here,' said Edward. 'Come before the summer ends and we'll take the boat out and do some fishing together. You've leave to take, I imagine?'

Jack laughed. He had not taken any leave as such except for half days with Harriet. Since the New Year 1873 Jack had worked most of his leave days. It was something Sergeant Morris was always on at him to change. Now he had a reason to do so.

'I have and I'd like to see the Parson at the same time. There's also a friend already in Brighton and an old colleague moving there with his family.'

'Well, getting out of London from time to time will do you good and you've enough reasons by the sound of it to come back apart from us. Pass your plate,' said Edward, holding out his hand ready to dish up.

'You were wrong all those years ago about Jack, Edward. You won the bet, not his father. He isn't a smuggler, he's a coastguard,' said Lucy, with a small smile.

Jack grinned and Edward slapped him on the shoulder. The children joined in and Andrew copied his father. Jack patted the two children on the shoulder as well, thankful for them.

For the dinner the three adults and two young children were at the kitchen table and it was the type of occasion that Jack sensed would come again and again for him from now on. He wondered when he would get to the point that he would feel it was a normal part of his life and to be taken for granted. That would come he was sure. At least he hoped it would. But for now it was a pleasure he savoured, as he did the meal before him.

*

During the last few days Ann had thought more and more of the possibility of she and George moving out of the city into fresher air. They needed an honest discussion about the idea and she would broach it with him tomorrow. Her few things packed and her microscope safely in its bag after being well-used she glanced for the final time under the bed, before she left the room, then in each drawer, to ensure nothing had slipped past her.

Now it was time to leave the farm and Ann carried her two bags down stairs hoping that George would remember to bring with him the extra piece of luggage she had packed for herself. It was a fancy she had to go sea swimming.

Field and Shaw had gone into Hastings the previous evening and had made their return by midnight. Their objective had really been to have a look at the new Police Station in Bourne Street to the east of the pier. Ann had asked them to take in the Albion Hotel as well, and had explained that she had written to the manager to make a booking for Friday and Saturday nights.

'Good morning, gentlemen,' said Ann as she came into the farm's kitchen. 'How was your evening?'

'A fine morning it is too, Mrs Black. It was an interesting evening. I think you'll be quite pleased with the Albion Hotel tonight,' said Shaw.

Ann smiled. 'That's good, thank-you.'

'Mrs Crowhurst has had to go to the bottom field and sent her apologies not to personally wish you a safe journey and a continuing good few days. We're to settle our accounts with Emma and then as soon as Jack arrives we will be off into Hastings. How are you feeling about today?' asked Field.

'I do feel nervous, but I'm quite resolved. The nerves are in case there's the usual battleground due to my sex. I warn you, gentlemen, I may not get anywhere with pathology,' said Ann.

'I wondered about that. Would it be helpful if I remained with you?' suggested Field.

'You're due back at the station by four o'clock though, Sarg, and we've to fit in the meeting with Burgess,' prompted Shaw.

'I know. But we need to bring this case to a conclusion,' said Field.

'Exactly,' said Ann. 'I shall be fine. I just have to prepare my mind. The worst that can happen is that I'm snubbed. Frankly, as frustrating as that would be, it's not as if I haven't experienced such treatment before. I'll do my best and if the pathologist is forward thinking I'll get the evidence we need.'

The sound of rolling wheels across the cobbles announced the arrival of their transport. Emma pulled up outside in the Tip Cart, clambered down and came into the kitchen.

'Morning Sirs, Ma'am,' she said, in her sweet way.

'Emma, we're to settle our accounts with you, I believe,' said Ann.

'Yes, Ma'am, thank-you Ma'am.' Emma picked up an account book on the dresser, turning it round for them to see.

'There's a few extra's to agree. Five shillings for yourself, Ma'am. Seven shillings and sixpence for Mr Shaw for the extra night, dinner and breakfast, laundry, and five shillings for Mr Field. I'm to write you out receipts with payment, Mother said.'

'Thank-you Emma,' said Ann, taking out her money and placing it on the book. Field and Shaw did the same.

'Extras?' enquired Field giving Shaw an inquisitive look.

Shaw flipped his bag open and revealed a small ham, several cheeses, and an item wrapped in brown paper. 'For the wife,' he said. 'Thought she'd like the items straight from the farm.'

Ann watched Emma write out the receipts. The young woman had a good hand, Ann thought. She wondered what her life would be like in years to come. She was dressed respectably and unpretentiously, ready to drive the guests into Hastings. The girl could read and write well. Would the farm come to her? Ann wondered. If she was looking to marry she would be a cut above the local labourer.

'Was there anything outstanding for Jack?' asked Ann. 'I'll settle it if there is and I can get the money back from him later.'

'Thank-you, Ma'am, but no,' said Emma.

'Talk of the very man,' exclaimed Shaw, nodding towards the open door. 'Listen, he's singing.'

'And there's the cough,' said Ann, monitoring the way it sounded.

'Marning,' said Jack, with a smile as he entered. He put his bag down and looked at each one.

'We heard you coming,' said Shaw. 'All the crows were scared off by that row you were making.'

'Ha!' said Jack. 'I need to settle my bill I think.'

'It was paid on your arrival Mr Jack,' said Emma turning to face Jack.

Ah, thought Ann, seeing the flash in Emma's eyes. Ex-farm labourer turned policeman would do you nicely, would he? But not on his part, my dear.

'I'll ride up top with Emma if you don't mind gentlemen. It's a little easier to get on the front in a dress,' said Ann. Had she imagined it? Was there a flicker of disappointment in Emma's eyes? Just for a second and then it had gone as if Ann had imagined it.

'Right, I'll bring your luggage out,' said Jack.

'Would you like me to take you to the hotel first, Ma'am?' asked Emma.

'Thank-you, that would be helpful. I can at least leave my luggage and then walk without being encumbered. I need to find the Mortuary this morning.' They clambered up and Emma looked at Ann with surprise.

'Is it dead bodies, you're wanting, Ma'am?' Emma asked, with surprise.

Ann laughed, 'Yes, that's exactly what I want today. Do you know where the Mortuary is?'

'I'll take you to what we have. No need for you to walk. But there's no plan at present for a proper Mortuary. It's to be in Queen's Road eventually. We have something that does at present. The town's grown you see. But it's not what you'll be used to Ma'am, in London.'

It seemed that they had reached the outskirts of Hastings quickly. Emma had driven the Tip Cart at a good trot and turned into the town in what seemed to be record time. She turned the rig towards the sea front for the Albion Hotel.

Because it was still early in the morning the visitors were not yet out of their hotels and Emma was able to stop a short distance from the hotel while Ann went inside to make arrangements for her luggage. It was a modest place but it would do, Ann thought.

Field insisted on carrying her luggage inside and he accompanied her to the desk. Her luggage safely in the hands of the manager, they were back clambering up into their seats in the Tip Cart. Emma turned the Tip Cart into the town and stopped outside an ordinary looking building fronting as Hasting's Mortuary.

'Thank-you Emma,' said Ann as she climbed down. 'Here's my card if ever you and your mother are in London.'

'Why, thank-you Ma'am,' the girl said, genuinely pleased. Ann paused, struck again at the lack of opportunity the girl would have.

'If you ever want to come to London on your own, I will gladly help you, if I can,' said Ann.

Emma smiled, and said, 'That's very kind, Ma'am, but there's not much time to be away from the farm.'

'Quite so. But sometimes things change,' said Ann.

'I'll keep your card, Ma'am,' said Emma.

Ann walked round to the back of the cart, and the three men clambered out to say goodbye.

'You'll telegram us later?' asked Jack.

'Yes, I'll send it to the Ship hotel for Mr Burgess. Pray for findings today and that I actually get past the reception,' said Ann.

'I will. I'll walk up with you to the door,' said Jack.

'Ann, I wanted to thank-you for everything that you've done in the last few days. I also wanted to ask your advice about what I should do as regards Harriet.'

'Your young lady?' asked Ann, raising an eyebrow.

'Yes. Would you mind?'

'No, although I doubt I can give you any advice that you haven't already worked through,' said Ann.

'Oh, I'm sure you can. From a lady's point of view should I write to Harriet and let her know where I am now? The business with the Shah is over in these parts and I can't see why I shouldn't tell her where I'm staying,' Jack asked.

'I can't see why it would matter now. She must be wondering about you. Why not? What possible harm can it do now? You could always explain that you were under orders not to let her know. But take care of yourself, rest as I've advised you, and do those exercises. I'll see you in just over a week back at Leman Street.' Ann turned to the two men waiting by the Tip Cart.

'Sergeant Field, Constable Shaw, here's to you bringing things to a conclusion. I've enjoyed working with you, said Ann.

'And you, dear lady,' said the Sergeant. 'Here's to the next time.'

'I can't imagine there will be a next time,' said Ann, smiling at the compliment.

'Well, that's for the fates to decide. As a colleague, I hope that at some point in the future we can bring your immeasurable skills to bear on other issues,' said Field.

'Take care today,' said Shaw, meaningfully.

'I will. A safe journey to you all,' Ann called as she turned into the building.

'Lovely woman,' said Field, as he clambered back into the Tip Cart.

Jack grinned at him. 'She'd rather you said she's a clever woman.'

'And so she is. But she's lovely in nature and commitment as well. That's what I meant.'

'I'll not argue with you on that,' said Jack. Climbing up next to Emma who had waited for them patiently, he had the effect of lighting up her day.

'Emma, railway next stop, please,' said Jack.

*

Inside the Mortuary reception Ann asked for the Pathologist, still maintaining her cover by giving her name as Dr George from the Sorbonne. All of it at least was true, with the exception of the surname. Whoever the Pathologist they were about to produce for her was he would expect Dr George to fit into an appropriate pigeon-hole.

She knew that she did not.

Ann sat and after some minutes took in the décor. The walls of the waiting area were decorated with the fashionable green wallpaper. Ann shuddered at the memory of historical arsenic poisoning cases she had known, the chemical absorbed innocently into the systems of unsuspecting victims as arsenic was still used for the colour green. Victims were usually small children or old people. One never knew who was susceptible, that was the problem. Again, she wondered how long manufacturers would be allowed to continue in the face of undeniable scientific evidence. Unable to stop herself, she got up from her chair and propped the door open.

'My apologies, a little air. I'm inclined to panic,' said Ann. Well partly true, but only about your wallpaper, she thought.

Fifteen minutes had gone by before the door from the corridor opened and a lively looking man with a clear eye stood looking straight at Ann. He had come through the door wiping his hands on a towel. Ann put him in his early forties.

'Doctor George?' said the man. 'I've just been reading your name in the police report funnily enough. They made a big thing about you as you're a woman scientist. It is "Dr George from Paris" said this, "Dr George from Paris," said that.' He laughed. 'I take it you're not French, but studied there?' he added.

'That's right, I did. What a coincidence that you're looking at the report,' said Ann, quite taken aback.

'Sorry, please don't think I'm rude. Doctor George, those poor men aren't used to clever women, and so everything one has said about the bodies on the beach has been recorded exactly. So in awe of you they were. I've just finished the post-mortem of the babies, you see.'

'Oh,' said Ann, frowning with the thought. 'Perhaps you'd prefer some time to reflect. I can come back .....'

'Not at all. Meeting you will be the tonic after what the Police wrote about you.'

'Well that's a new experience,' said Ann, smiling. 'But I have to confess that my name is not Doctor George. I just gave the police that name on the beach. It's my husband's name, George, and it was the first one that came into my head. I am actually a Doctor of Science from Paris but it's not recognised here. My name is actually Ann Black.'

'I see. What was the reason for the subterfuge? asked the doctor.

'I'm sorry I don't know your name,' said Ann, before she replied.

'Doctor Woodward. My apologies, I was excited to meet Doctor George! Hands are covered in alcohol so I won't offer to shake yours,' he said, holding them up to her.

'Well, Dr Woodward, I was working with some colleagues from the Metropolitan Police and the Brighton force. We were trespassing for good reason on Hastings's patch. I wondered if I could take five minutes of your time. I recalled something one of the constables said during the time on the beach. It might be of use.'

'I see. Of course, come through. My office is just down the hall. Are you still based in Paris?' Woodward asked.

'No, I work now in London. I, er, assist at times a Dr Brown who is a Police Surgeon with the Metropolitan Police.' Ann paused wondering if she should be honest with him. He seemed open. 'I also work with Elizabeth Garrett Anderson.'

They had come to a small office, just large enough to hold a desk and two chairs. The door was open and Woodward extended an arm for Ann to go in.

'Do you, I met her once. Stupid vote of the Medical Council. Just delaying things. It all has to change at some point. Very frustrating for you though. I take it then that your science degree from the Sorbonne is actually a medical degree?' Woodward asked.

'Yes,' Ann answered.

'She's not the first you know.'

'I'm sorry?' Ann said.

'Garrett Anderson. She's not the first. James Miranda Steuart Barry, she was the first. That we know of anyway. Have you come across her?' asked Woodward.

'No, I can honestly say I haven't.'

'Yes, she was definitely a female in her youth. She only died about seven or eight years ago. Did the first successful Caesarean section, out in Africa. Lived as a man both publicly and privately by all accounts. I daresay it had to be in order to be accepted at that time to study as a university student, but one simply doesn't know. Everyone only knew after her death. Took her uncle's name. I've got the article here somewhere.' Woodward pulled out a drawer and moved his fingers across the tops of neatly labelled files.

'Here we are. 1865.' He scanned an article,

'It all came out when the charwoman laid her body out after death. The family was in on it and the deception got her into medical school. Went to Edinburgh, as did I. Barry qualified in 1812 and passed the Royal College of Surgeons exam in 1813.'

He ran his eyes down the article and read it as a quote:

'By 1815 Barry was Assistant Surgeon to the Forces, which was like being a lieutenant. And then went on and worked in many parts of the British Empire.' He laid the sheet down.

'Bit of a scandal with an involvement with a high ranking male official in Africa. I think it blew over. Look, you take the article, and have a look at the rest when you leave. Interesting isn't it? Barry did a lot of good. Now that apart, tell me what the constable that you spoke to, said.' Woodward clasped his hands together and leant forward on his desk.

Ann had a great desire to laugh with relief at being so accepted, but restrained herself and smiled broadly.

'Thank-you,' she said nodding at the article. 'This is the second woman in two days that my attention has been drawn to. Now, about the constable. He referred to the only wound being a small hole in the back, as if it had been made with a knitting needle. They were assuming it was therefore a woman who was the killer. I wondered if there was any way I could see the body of Mabel Walters.' Ann held her breath.

'It's not pretty, but yes of course. We'd better get you rigged up though in different clothes. If you don't mind borrowing an apron and gloves from my nurse we can wheel Mabel out and have a look.' Woodward stood and ushered Ann out.

*

Burgess met the group in the reception of the Ship Hotel and came forward, full of bonhomie, rubbing his hands together.

'Come in, Come in. Have you eaten? No? I anticipated that would be the answer. Come through to my office and Alice has sandwiches and warmed pork pies for you all. Will you take a drop of something?'

'Thank-you kindly but no. We're both going on duty,' said Field.

'Well, another time. Strong tea is the order of the day then. Jack, how are you?' Burgess finally drew breath.

'Much better, how's Harry?' asked Jack, forgetting Field and Shaw did not know anything of the mysterious guest and his carers occupying Jack's room.

Burgess glanced at them in case they displayed interest. There was no indication of any curiosity about Jack's question.

'That guest is improving. How nice of you to have remembered him and to ask.' He led the group along the corridor and opened the door to his office. A table was laid for five and Burgess pressed a bell for luncheon to be brought in.

'Come in now. I have some good news. But first get some food into you and then there will be time enough for an update. Do you mind Sam Curzon joining us as he's been involved with our little masquerade at the police station?'

'Not at all,' said Field.

'Good. I'll send a maid to get him.' Burgess disappeared into reception to speak to a member of staff and was back within minutes.

'You'll have to let me know from where you get these pork pies with the Stilton in the top,' said Shaw, sinking his teeth into the pie as Burgess closed the office door behind him.

'It's a farm over towards Lincolnshire,' said Burgess.

It had become a party atmosphere, buoyed up by Burgess's enthusiasm. With the promise of good news the men tucked in. Sam arrived and Burgess made the introductions. Sam nodded at each in turn until it came to Jack. He enthusiastically took Jack's hand in both of his and pumped it up and down.

'You do look better, Jack,' Sam said.

'Do I? Must be Dr. Ann's care. How are things going with the move?' asked Jack, offering Sam a glass of beer.

Burgess played mine host with the tureen of lamb cutlets. Taking a leaf from Shaw's book Sam took one of the pies and chewing, nodded to Jack.

'Good,' Sam eventually said with his mouth full.

'You didn't get arrested then for impersonating Counsel?' Jack laughed.

Sam raised his eyes to the heavens and shook his head, 'No, and we managed to get a defence raised for Nathan,' he said.

'I was going to tell them that in a minute,' said Burgess, laughing. 'You're stealing my thunder.'

'Sorry, Thompson,' and Sam adopted the pose and accent of the arrogant young Partner from the City, speaking to his Clerk.

'Very good,' said Jack. 'I would never know you.'

'Come on Burgess, as good as your hospitality always is, put us out of our suspense,' said Field.

'Alright. Please help yourselves to potatoes and spring greens. ' Burgess passed an expansive hand across the table.

'As Sam correctly said we made a formal application for Nathan Long to have a Defence Counsel appointed. We also got to see Nathan. Sam here did a great performance as the arrogant young lawyer, I would say, and I think I equipped myself quite well as the fawning Clerk. But there's been more developments as the prosecution case does not hold up.'

'That's good news but in what way?' asked Field.

'It's the time of death and the delay in the body being found,' said Burgess. 'It's obvious Grace was killed up to two days before she was found and that the murder wasn't at the Lovers Seat. If Ann could get at Grace's body she has a theory that she may find fragments of the same type of rocks in the wound on the head. But there's also the point that it's such a popular place for the scene of a crime that her body would have been found almost immediately.'

'As a result, Nathan has been released into the custody of his Commanding Officer and he's back in Portsmouth aboard the lead ship of the Corvettes,' said Sam.

'Well done,' said Field, slapping Burgess on the back. Shaw raised his tea-cup to Sam, and there was a splutter of laughter from the group which generally grew as the news sank in.

'See, I told you, you should be on the stage,' Jack said to Sam, before turning to Field. 'That's what we all said, wasn't it? That the murder of Grace could not have been done at Lovers Seat because it was just too popular. The body had to be taken there at the point the murderer knew Nathan was to go and meet Grace. Plus the blood stained rocks didn't come from there and Ann more or less proved that with her tests at the farm.'

'What did she do?' asked Sam.

'No idea,' said Jack. And Burgess laughed.

'We're not putting you up as a defence witness, young Jack.'

'So, we could suggest that Grace became a nuisance in order to get the baby back and Mabel Walters was behind her death, to silence her,' said Shaw. He picked up another pork pie.

*

Ann stood back from her examination of the back of the corpse. Mabel Walters had not been a small woman and the folds of fat did not make things easy.

'Here, for the kidneys,' she said, looking up at Woodward. He bent over the body.

'Yes I see what the constable meant. That's not a knife cut.'

'It's been a sharp end though,' said Ann.

'And widened as it's gone in. I can see why the police dismissed it as a type of knitting needle. Let's see if we can take some of the skin from the area in case any substance can be traced. It might assist in finding the weapon.'

'There's a bruise on the left shoulder,' said Ann.

'Funny shape, four marks,' said Woodward.

'And a fifth under the shoulder blade.' Ann put her four fingers just above the bruises, then changed hands so that it would seem a left hand could have gripped the shoulder with another bruise under the shoulder blade. Ann's hand was too small.

'Are you right handed?' asked Woodward.

'Yes,' said Ann.

'Me too. I think the spread is too big for a woman's hand. Let me.' Woodward put the four fingers of his left hand just above the bruise marks at the shoulder of the corpse. His thumb hovered over the fifth below the shoulder blade.

'It's a man's hand,' Ann exclaimed. 'The size has to be a man's hand. It's not Grace. It's not a woman. A man has gripped Mabel Walters by the left shoulder while pushing in his weapon into the kidney area.' Ann acted the scene out. She straightened up and turned to Doctor Woodward, 'Wouldn't kill her quickly like making for the heart, but it would get her attention.'

'Create a lot of shock initially. Cause of death I would say was more likely to be drowning. This attack would disable her though. Alright. Alright. Well done Doctor Black,' Woodward slapped Ann on the back as he would have done to a male colleague. She was winded and he apologised profusely.

'I'm so sorry, I forgot myself and that you were a woman.'

'That's such a compliment,' Ann said. They both laughed.

———

'The Doctor who died on his own knife isn't here is he?' Ann asked.

'No, he was buried last week, somewhere around Lewes I think the paper said.'

'Can we dig him up?' asked Ann.

'Why?' laughed Woodward. 'It was the Coroner's decision that it was accidental death. The man fell on his own scalpel,' explained Woodward.

'I bet if we looked, working on his association with Mabel Walters, we might find the same thing as here. Small pointed weapon pushed into the back, driving him forward into his own scalpel. He probably issued death certificates for all those babies she buried. Maybe he had second thoughts, possibly blackmail? Perhaps the killer is a grieving father taking revenge. Maybe Mabel had Doctor Elm polished off for refusing to issue death certificates?'

Woodward smiled at Ann's language and enthusiasm.

'Well, I've never had to dig anyone up. Unfortunately I think we have to get permission.'

'Who gives us that?' asked Ann.

'Not sure, probably the Coroner. Maybe the Home Office. I should imagine his wife might have something to say about it too. No doubt the Church of England will have a stake in the process. There's got to be a legal process or corpses would be being dug up at the drop of a hat if there was any doubt. I've never had to ask. Perhaps we should start with the police? There's probably a vicar or two that will need to get involved.'

'We should do this, Doctor Woodward. It might be the same person you see. You said Doctor Elm was buried in Lewes? I know a Parson near there. I could send a telegram to two people. Where's the local telegraph office?'

'At the Railway Station. I'll have to inform the Inspector of our findings and suspicions,' Woodward said.

407

'Can you give me an hour before you do. I've got a Police Sergeant in Brighton and a Metropolitan Policeman waiting to hear. They may take the initiative. And my husband's due in an hour so I could kill two birds with one stone, so to speak by sending the telegrams when I meet George.' Anne was already untying her apron and walking backwards towards the doors.

'Doctor George, I mean Mrs Black, where shall I wait for you. Here?' asked Woodward.

'I shall have George with me. I don't think he'll take too kindly to starting his holiday at the local Mortuary. Would it be possible for you to come to the Albion hotel and I'll fill George in when he arrives?' Ann waited. She tapped her foot with the urgent need to get those telegrams off.

'Albion Hotel it is,' said Woodward, with a little bow of his head.

*

Burgess was at reception when Ann's first telegram arrived to tell him of the findings at the Mortuary. He excused himself from the American guest, leaving Alice to deal with her, and moved swiftly to find Field and Shaw who had just left. The sight of the portly Burgess running along the sea front caused several onlookers great amusement. He found the two Brighton men just passing the Chain Pier, Sam and Jack with them.

'It's from Doctor Ann, *success*,' Burgess panted, waving the telegram at them. 'They've found the entry wound.'

Field took charge and Shaw waited while he read the message. Jack and Sam had been on their way to the fish market to try and find Jack's fisherman with a view to taking a trip. They stood by waiting for instructions. Field handed the telegram to Shaw.

'We've an hour before the pathologist will inform Hastings Police. Ann's asking for an exhumation of Doctor Elm's body buried somewhere in the Lewes area in case the same method was used in his death. Says she's sent a message to Jack's Parson?' Field looked at Jack.

'Reverend Peter Fisher over at Simpson. He'll know what to do with that,' said Jack.

Shaw read the telegram:

'Small wound in Walters's back. Pointed tool with wide taper. Effect to stun and damage kidneys. Time provided for drowning. Five bruises on left shoulder. Man's hand.' Field looked at the others.

Then, as if choreographed, he and Jack saw the action as if it was before them. The both acted the attack out. The group disintegrated into laughter as a result, partly from relief at the findings. Field and Jack slapped each other on the back.

'It's not a knife then? What do you want to do, Sarg?' asked Shaw.

'Let's get to the station and make the request for an exhumation of Doctor Elm's body based on this evidence provided by one of our team. We think the deaths are linked. Ann says Doctor Woodward will meet her later. I'll get a response off to her to the Albion.'

'Any idea what had done it?' asked Shaw.

' It could be some sort of a workman's tool? What do you think?' asked Burgess.

'No idea at the moment. Can we do anything?' asked Jack.

'Not sure at this point, but be certain I'll ask if we need it. We'd better get going. We have little enough time before Woodward will inform Hastings. Burgess, I'll keep you informed,' said Field and he and Shaw walked away at quite a pace.

'Frustrating not to be in at the kill,' said Sam.

Jack shook his head and looked at him. 'Not this time Sam, we've done what we hoped to do. At least Nathan won't hang for a murder he didn't commit.'

'Sam's right though,' said Burgess with a sigh. 'I think I've pulled more muscles than I knew I had. I'll see you gentlemen later. What are your plans?'

'A spot of fishing if I can find a particular fisherman to take us out,' said Jack.

'Well if you catch anything good bring it back with you and I'll get it prepared for your dinner. I'd better get back. Hopefully we'll hear some news later,' Burgess started to walk back towards his hotel.

Jack and Sam stayed by the front, looking over toward the fish market for Jack's fisherman.

'There's the boat,' said Jack pointing to a particular Lugger. He and Sam approached the fisherman who agreed to take them if they would go immediately because of the tide.

'Fish are coming in to feed,' he said as a way of explanation.

'We're ready,' said Jack, proffering money.

'What's sort of fish are out there?' asked Sam clambering in and taking up position by the stern.

'Most everything,' said the fisherman. 'Certainly Mackerel and Flounder, Plaice, Sole, Garfish and more.'

'Sam Curzon,' said Sam, thinking an introduction was needed, recognising a fellow "waterman" of sorts.

The fisherman looked surprised at the introduction, but nodded and shook hands. 'Ned Pell,' he said. 'You used to the sea?'

'Not yet,' said Sam. 'I grew up on the Thames.'

'That's not a place I know. This will be different to river life. There's undertow and sea currents. If you go in, you may get caught out. Tie the line around your waists, gents,' He looked at Jack. 'Today is a bit rougher than the other day you were with me.'

'Yes I can see it is,' said Jack, steadying himself.

Ned Pell secured the end of the line which secured Jack and Sam to a rope by threading it through the middle of a strand to stop it unwinding. What most interested Jack was the preparation the fisherman went through to thread the line through what looked like a spike.

'Where did you learn to do that so fast?' asked Jack.

'I've always done it as far back as I can remember. You've just got to be careful not to blunt or bend the point.'

'Would every fisherman know how to do that?' asked Jack.

'Depends on the training,' explained Ned Pell. 'Different knots for different needs and the tools to do the work. I've a good knife, a fid and a marlin spike. But then I was in the navy at one time and was learned in handling knots and splices. A good knot must hold fast without slipping and you must be able to untie it quickly.'

'These other fishermen on-shore, would they know the same as you?' asked Jack, standing up and starting to untie the line around his waist.

'Some might, depending on what they've done in their time at sea. If we're going it should be now,' said Ned Pell.

'Interesting tool, isn't it Sam, see how it thickens as you move away from the point. Sharp point too. Bet that could go into your foot if you dropped it pointed down,' Jack asked.

'If there was some height behind it,' said Ned Pell.

'I think we need to get off. I'm sorry, I know we've delayed you and I don't want the money back but we can't go fishing. I've learnt enough and I've work to do. Come on Sam we need to go.' Jack jumped down into the water.

'You're very safe, I know these waters well,' called Ned Pell.

'It's not that. I have to do something quickly,' said Jack.

Sam had stood as Jack disappeared over the side into knee deep water. He called quizzically:

'You may have learnt enough but I would like to know what the hell's going on. I'm very sorry, Ned, he's not been well. Keep the money, his money, for your trouble.' Sam followed Jack, jumping down into the water, muttering about the effect on his boots of so much sea-water.

Jack waded up the beach partly obscured by the craft moored there and waited for Sam to join him.

Finally struggling up the beach Sam reached Jack and stood waiting for an explanation, his arms akimbo, frowning at his friend.

'We need to go to the coastguard station over there,' said Jack.

Sam stared at Jack, unable to work out what was going on. 'Coastguard station? This is ridiculous. Just stop at once and explain what is going on!'

'There's not enough time to explain, just come with me to the coastguard and you'll hear what's going on when I explain it to him.' Jack started to walk away.

'Jack! Jack!' There was no response and Jack kept walking. 'Just explain!' shouted Sam.

Jack had already walked past the fish market and had reached Brighton's Coastguard Station. Sam bit at his nails and tersely exclaimed, 'Oh, ….. very well then.' Frowning he followed Jack.

*

Jack had gone towards the Coastguard station before he had worked out what he was going to say. The realisation of the murder weapon potentially being a marlin spike had seemed fantastic. Until Ned Pell had mentioned the Navy. He leant against the counter and waited. He was about to accuse a man of a murder, possibly two if the same wound was on Doctor Elm's body and he knew instinctively that Nathan had executed the two people for their destruction of life. How ironic, thought Jack, to throw yourself in the way of harm at a point when you believed you had paradise within your grasp. It must have been seeing Mable Walters at Pett Level. But why the doctor? Nathan must have believed that the police would never act.

'Excuse me!' Jack called, and he heard a movement from a room at the back of the counter.

Sam came in looking as if he needed resuscitating.

'Are you mad?' he said, breathless and indignant. 'Would you have the courtesy to explain to me what is going on.'

Jack did not answer. He looked around to check if there was a telegraph facility. 'Good,' he said as he saw it. 'We can get a message to Edward at Fairlight.'

'Will you tell me why we need the coastguard? Did the fisherman do something wrong?' asked Sam.

'In a minute, my friend,' Jack said to Sam. 'The coastguard's coming.' Jack smiled at the Brighton coastguard, now standing in front of him.

412

'Good afternoon, I and my colleague here work for the Metropolitan Police. I am Constable Jack Sargent, Second Class, Reserve.'

'Yes?' asked the Coastguard, looking Sam and Jack over. 'What can we help you with?'

'We've reason to believe that the lead Corvette of the fleet at Portsmouth that will be bound for the South American end of the Atlantic, should be boarded to arrest a sailor called Nathan Long for a murder at Pett Level this week. We know his rank as Petty Officer. I have no identification with me, neither does my colleague here, but you can verify who I am if you will telegraph Edward Croft at Fairlight.'

'Mr Croft knows you?' asked the coastguard.

'Yes, he does. I was staying with him and his wife until this morning.'

'And you're saying there's a Royal Navy sailor on board the lead Corvette of the fleet who you want to arrest for murder?'

'That's right, on the fleet bound for South America,' said Jack. 'In your telegram would you ask Mr Croft to instruct Spithead Coastguard?'

'I can tell him that's what *you're* asking. Whether that's what he'll do is up to him.'

Sam finally understood what had clicked in Jack's mind. He turned and gaped at Jack. Although he did not perform the manner and the accent, Jack saw Sam's alter ego of the young partner of the City Firm was coming to the fore as he faced the coastguard.

'We have reason to believe it's the murder committed at Pett Level of Mabel Walters. The weapon used was a marlin spike. I'm sure we don't have to emphasise to you that a Royal Navy sailor would have the expertise to use one as a weapon? That's right, isn't it Jack?' Sam asked.

'Yes, and it's the murder of a civilian.' Jack said.

The coastguard nodded and took in the way Jack and Sam were dressed. 'What happened to your boots?' he asked.

'We were on board a fishing boat. We had to jump into the water to come here,' Sam explained.

413

'Anyone speak for you here in Brighton?' asked the coastguard.

'Sergeant Field and Constable Shaw Hockham, Brighton Police,' said Jack.

'Also the hotel manager Mr Burgess at the Ship Hotel,' added Sam.

'And you have evidence of this murder? If we're to board a Naval vessel we have to be sure what we're doing,' said the coastguard.

'The pathologist in Hastings has the evidence,' said Jack.

The coastguard thought about what they were saying and came down on the side of contacting Edward Croft.

'Alright, take a seat. I know both those policemen and Mr Burgess. I'll see if I can get an answer from Mr Croft.'

Fifteen minutes turned to twenty and then the twenty-five minute mark was passed. Twice the telegraph sprang into action but the coastguard wore an impenetrable expression. Jack and Sam sat on the wooden bench in the front office and waited.

'You'd think it would be quicker, given it's just up the coast. They've laid submarine telegraph lines to India and Australia now,' said Sam, completely dejected.

Jack nodded. 'I know. There's activity going on though Sam. The answer will come,' he said.

'Of course I realised that's why Nathan was shocked that the body had been found,' Sam said.

Jack started. 'When was this?' he asked.

'In Hastings. When Burgess and I went to see him. We were only focusing on Grace's death. I should have noticed at the time. When I said that they'd found the body of the Baby Farmer on the same day as Grace was found he went shaky and commented on the fact that the body had been found. He mentioned the tide. Of course he was probably banking on the tide carrying the body out to sea. Do you think he knew the woman had killed Grace?'

'No. I think he saw the dead children she was burying. Maybe because Grace couldn't find out where their baby had gone he assumed one of those children was their baby. He may have lost his senses. He wouldn't have known Grace was dead at that point,' said Jack. He thought about the scene on the beach that day, Ann bent over the tiny mounds they had uncovered.

'Why would he have killed the doctor?' asked Sam.

'We don't know that he did yet,' said Jack. 'Maybe something had happened with Grace.'

'Ann must suspect that the pathologist will find the same type of mark and wound on the body. She wouldn't be so intent on exhumation of the body otherwise,' said Sam.

'But until it's done we can't assume it was murder or that Nathan is guilty of that death,' said Jack.

The coastguard came back into the front office.

'Mr Croft has responded. He's described you,' said the Coastguard. 'And given your full name. Can you tell me what it is, please?'

'John William Sargent,' said Jack.

'Right, that's fine. Mr Croft has said to let you know he's telegraphed to Spithead. They'll get onto it now. He's also contacting Brighton Police Station and sending a message to Sergeant Field. He said to tell you he's on his way to Portsmouth with a full crew. He'll be in touch with the Ship Hotel as soon as he knows what's happening. Thank-you very much. Good afternoon.'

'Is that it?' said Sam.

'Yes,' replied the coastguard, surprised. 'Nothing else to be done from here. It's just a matter of time.'

'Right, thank-you.' said Jack.

Outside both men sniffed the wind.

'How far is it to Portsmouth?' asked Sam.

Jack motioned irascibly. 'Too far Sam. With a fair wind Edward will make it faster and I'm not sure what we could do even if we went. Better to wait to hear from Edward or Field.'

'And you're happy with that, are you?' asked Sam.

Jack knew what Sam was saying and looked at his friend.

'Honestly? No, but I've done that journey to Portsmouth and the train stops everywhere possible. If we were sure that the fleet for the South Atlantic was to stay indefinitely I'd be glad to go. As it stands we could be too late.' Jack gave Sam a sideways look. 'You were encouraging me to rest last Sunday.'

'I know. I just find the fact that we can't take action deeply frustrating,' said Sam.

'Here's something you should do. It's probably time we came clean with Inspector Hunt about this case. You're his man here. Why don't you work on a suitably worded briefing for him?'

'Are you sure? You said he specifically told you not to contact the Brighton Police or get involved in local matters,' said Sam.

'Well I didn't.' Jack grinned. 'They contacted me. Anyway my link is via Burgess on this but I think Tom Hunt wouldn't expect me to ignore a multiple murder. Apart from that Burgess reminded me Tom Hunt is his friend. You know better than I do what the Inspector's movements are. Have you heard what the Shah is doing now?'

'Last contact I had with him was on the twenty-fourth. There was a stink about police being withdrawn from ordinary duties at Kensington Gardens due to the large crowds in Hyde Park. They were all waiting to witness the return of the Shah from the Windsor Review. Even questions in the House of Commons about the gates at Kensington Palace closing forty minutes later than usual as a result. Apparently Inspector Hunt has been commended for the fact that there were no incidents from Westminster to Staines throughout the last week,' said Sam.

'No-one deserves it better than him. Part of me wishes I could have seen it and the other part is glad to be have been out of it,' said Jack.

'One thing you do need to know. Hunt has asked why Ann Black has been down here. I've replied that I haven't see her, which is true.'

'Well Ann reports to Dr Brown so I think I shall be silent on that. I wonder how Ann is getting on? She must have met up with George by now,' said Jack.

*

Twenty-three

'Ann, for heaven's sake, we were supposed to be having a holiday together, not becoming immersed in one of your police cases,' exclaimed George Black.

Ann had been stopped at reception as she and George arrived and handed a telegram. She waited until they were in their room, which was pleasant enough with a view of the sea, the unread message burning a hole in her pocket. With one eye on the time she had even waited for George to unpack the few things he had brought, had let him hang her fresh outfit in the wardrobe for her and listened to his humorous account of the exchange with a client. Then, and only then, did she turn her attention to the telegram from Sergeant Field. The application for the exhumation was underway, and there was progress on the type of weapon used to make the mark on Mabel Walters's body through a discovery Jack had made. Sergeant Field believed an arrest was imminent.

Ann glanced at the clock in the room. She had ten minutes before Doctor Woodward arrived.

George, for his part, had enjoyed the journey and the clear views cross the countryside with high blue skies, in comparison to the heavy, smog-laden skies in London. It was a charming afternoon, although not as warm as he had hoped. He momentarily had thought of hiring transport, arranging a hamper and going to the South Downs for the afternoon.

Ann looked lovely as always as George had caught sight of her waiting for him at the exit to the platform, although he sensed that her excitement was not just because he had come. He had half-expected that she would be full of news about the previous few days but Ann said little, letting George tell her about the end of his week. He had heartily looked forward to a restful weekend with fresh air and good food. When she received the telegram in the hotel he felt himself tense but Ann had put it straight into her pocket and George had relaxed into the time they would have together.

When Ann gave him the news of her morning's activities and the fact that she was about to have a meeting with the Hastings pathologist he started to dread the weekend ahead. With incredulity he listened to her account about the baby deaths, two murders unsolved and Jack's relationship with Coastguard Edward Croft and officers from the Brighton Police. In triumph she passed him the telegram to read.

George held the telegram and stared at Ann.

'Aren't you going to read it?' Ann asked, the excitement in her eyes. He knew his face had set. Trying to mask the disappointment he opened the telegram out and slowly read it, nodding as he did so.

'Of course, this is so clever,' said George. 'Well done, as always. Well done. But why?' he asked simply, as if in pain.

'I'm not sure I understand your question,' Ann said, concerned at the way he looked.

'Why am I here?' George asked.

'George what a funny thing to say. We're going to have time here together. I thought it would be good for us to be out of the city in clean air, some exercise and rest. The last time we were away was at Christmas after all,' said Ann.

'Ah, rest. Yes, rest and exercise. Except you're not resting are you Ann? And it sounds as if I will be doing all those activities alone.'

'George! It's one more meeting and that is my part done. The exhumation will be nothing to do with me,' Ann said, earnestly trying to reassure him.

'Why do I not believe that? As soon as you get anywhere near Jack Sargent all thought of yourself and remaining safe goes by the board. It's as if your compass shifts. He consistently puts you in danger of arrest by your masquerading as a doctor. He encourages you to break the law Ann, which is *ironic*, given he's a policeman. He plays to your weakness, that mis-placed sense of inferiority, by flattering you professionally.' George walked to the bedroom window and stared out at the sea, which was busy with the fishing fleet.

'George, this is ridiculous,' said Ann, an edge creeping into her voice.

'Is it? Is it, Ann? Well, I must be ridiculous then,' George said. There was silence between them for several minutes. Ann stared at her husband's back working through how quickly the afternoon had been spoilt.

'I'm at a loss to know what to do or say in case I make this worse,' she began. 'Because I asked him to come here instead of seeing him at the mortuary I think I should go down and see Doctor Woodward. In my way I was actually trying not to exclude you. Would you care to join us? This will be all that I will do. It will be rude if I don't go and see him. Then, I promise, that there will be nothing else for two days.' Ann turned the bedroom door knob and partially opened the door when George said:

'Yes, yes, of course you must. No I don't think I'll join you. I think I'll go for a walk to the pier and probably go up to the Castle. You've no doubt seen them. I don't want to bore you if you have. I'll see you back here for dinner.' He turned to pick up a silver topped mahogany walking stick he had brought with him.

Ann stopped in the doorway.

'George, I haven't been to the pier or the castle. I would love to see them with you and, by the way, you never bore me. I don't think I shall be long with Doctor Woodward. Then I'll come and find you.'

'I'll wait at the pier, then,' George said, flatly avoiding her eyes.

'That will be lovely,' said Ann, giving him a concerned smile.

George looked away as he could not bear what he had just done but he was angry. Inexplicably angry at the younger man who managed to place his wife into the professional position that she always longed for while he, George, had trapped her in a domestic role. He knew he was being ridiculous but it was too late. He heard the door click to as Ann left the room.

420

Woodward was waiting in the small lounge at the front of the building. He stood as Ann entered, his face alive with the news he had to share. Ann forced a smile and they shook hands, Woodward a little too vigorously.

'Doctor George, I think that is what I will have to call you, regardless of the fact it's an alias. Great news! The process has begun and Brighton Police have made a formal application in the last few hours to get Doctor Elm's body exhumed. You must come down and assist when we have a date.'

'Ah, I don't think that can happen,' said Ann, imagining George's reaction.

'But it has to. Without your expertise it wouldn't be happening at all,' exclaimed Woodward.

'That's very kind but I don't see how I can possibly be involved any further. Doctor Brown would have to give his permission and we are so busy. I think my part in this case is done. Would you think me rude if I hurry away? My husband has only just arrived and it's the end of a very busy week for him. I really wish you well in the investigation,' said Ann.

Woodward paused, slightly taken aback at the change.

'Well, that won't be the end of our association,' he said. 'I shall contact Doctor Brown and issue an invitation and I assure you I will ask for you to come back and assist.'

Ann shook her head and looked away. Woodward thought for a moment and saw a solution.

'I'll issue the invitation to Doctor Brown, and we'll make a party of it. My wife's always saying she never meets my colleagues so now she can. He can bring Mrs Brown and you bring your George. Yes, that's what we'll do. Look, I'll let you go and I'll be in touch,' Woodward grasped Ann's hand between both his own. Beaming, he pumped her hand up and down again. Ann was unsure if she should laugh or cry.

*

Jack, Sam and Burgess, were like dogs chasing their own tails until dinner. Suddenly, every activity seemed an irrelevancy while they tried to occupy themselves.

Burgess appeared at reception to check if there was news from Field every ten minutes. Aware he was harrying the staff, Alice intervened and suggested that he chat to the guests who were enjoying the view of the evening sky from the hotel lounge.

By six o'clock Jack and Sam moved into the lounge themselves. Jack found a novel in the bookcase and proceeded to read the same paragraph over and over again before he abandoned the book onto the sofa.

Sam sat in the window seat and checked over his mother's figures for the cost of curtain materials, arriving at a different total each time. Abandoning the fifth attempt at concentration he folded up the list and replaced it in his inside pocket.

'Have you any idea how long it would take to sail from Fairlight to Portsmouth?' Sam said to Jack. Glad of a reason to move Jack joined his friend in the window.

'Absolutely no idea,' said Jack.

'Fancy eating?' asked Sam.

'Not yet,' Jack answered. 'Let's give it until seven.'

'We could walk up the pier,' suggested Sam.

'We could. I think I should go and see Harry instead. Which reminds me where are Stan and Arthur?' asked Jack.

'Walking every day, or fishing off the pier. They vanish shortly after breakfast each morning. Arthur says it the only way Stan exorcises his devils is to keep active. I gather Stan needs to walk miles to keep him equitable. Getting out onto the hills does mean they stay out of the crowds and no one asks any questions,' explained Sam.

'I can imagine Stan's seen a thing or two after all these years,' said Jack. 'Have you been in to see Harry today?' asked Jack.

'Yes, first thing,' answered Sam. 'I helped when the doctor called this morning. Burgess hasn't let anyone into the room from the staff. He and Alice clean it and change the bed between them. Stan collects Harry's breakfast and Arthur's been helping Harry with his personal care before they go out.

'Do you know if Rose knows where Harry is, Sam?' asked Jack.

'No she doesn't,' said Sam. 'Just the few of us and Hunt. But let's go and pay a visit as I'm sure Harry will be glad to see you back here.'

Jack thought Harry looked grey as he saw him dozing in the chair by the window. There were dark hollows in his cheeks and his usual good complexion was lost in pain. The window was wide open and Harry's head was against one of the large wings of the armchair as he dozed. The rug, which had been place lightly over his knees by Alice as the wind had brought the change in the tide, was half on the floor and half draped over one of his legs. Jack picked up the rug and covered Harry's legs.

'I'll go and get his dinner tray,' whispered Sam. Jack nodded and quietly sat on the end of the bed opposite the drawn looking man as Sam left the room. Jack looked around at the side of his old bedroom occupied by Stan and Arthur. Two temporary camp beds had been put up for them and the few belongings they had managed to bring with them were around each bed in serried ranks.

The door opened and Stan filled the space, initially doing a double take on seeing Jack as if he was out of place. Arthur followed his Sergeant in and exclaimed a little too loudly.

'Why Jack! When did you get back?'

Harry's eyes opened and he brought Jack into focus.

'You're back, lad,' he said.

Jack smiled, 'Yes,' he said. 'Earlier this afternoon.'

'Feeling better?' asked Harry.

'Much better, thank-you. The cough still comes when I get tired, but I can recognise that now. But what of yourself, Harry? Burgess tells me strange things have happened to you since Sunday.'

Harry grimaced and shook his head. 'The worst thing is that I have to endure Stan's snoring. And Rose not being here to calm the savage breast. Everything else will mend with time.'

'Time is what he has to have as well, young Jack, so no stories of yours. He's a sharp temper at the moment,' Stan explained and Jack knew from his expression that Burgess had explained everything to Stan.

'How quickly can you return to London, Harry?' asked Jack.

'You see, I told you he'd want his room back,' Harry managed a wan smile. 'Hopefully by the end of next week. We'll have a better feel for time when the doctor removes the bandages on Monday. However it will be another week before I can go to my home and also see Rose. She mustn't guess. While the Shah is still in England we have the perfect excuse for my absence. I could do with dinner. Arthur, could you see Burgess for it?' said Harry.

'Sam's gone to the kitchen to collect a tray for you. We'll not tire you by staying, but I wanted to see you for myself.' said Jack, standing.

'How was your few days away?' Harry persisted.

'Very fruitful,' said Jack, glancing at Stan's frown. 'I found my "family." People who knew me as a child and were close to my parents. There's an old Parson at Simpson who I'll go back and stay with on Tuesday for a night. And also my father's great friend, who is at Fairlight outside Hastings. He has a young family now and they seem to want me to visit again. I stayed with them this week and plan to go again later in the summer.'

'Those are good developments for your life. It shows in your face, Jack. You've had rest too. Don't take health for granted,' said Harry.

'I've had good advice,' said Jack, thinking of Ann Black. 'I've started some Swedish exercises to start building up again.'

'Where did you come across those?' asked Arthur.

'Oh, from a doctor I spoke to in the week,' said Jack. Stan cleared his throat which Jack knew was an indication that he'd said enough. 'I can show you after dinner if you're interested.'

Arthur nodded.

The door opened and Sam appeared with a tray on which were covered dishes, a small glass of fortified wine and a carafe of water. Arthur moved across to where a camping table leant against the wall. He set it up at Harry's side.

'Well, well Harry, you're looking braver every minute. Dinner also looks good. What say you Jack if we go and eat now and we can catch up with Stan and Arthur later?' suggested Sam.

Harry smiled. 'One thing before you go. Jack. I had a premonition before the 'accident' that I would have been safer had you been there. I'm sorry I took you off the team. I thought it was for your good. In fact it proved to be a mistake for me I suspect. I wanted you to know that.'

'Don't worry about that now, Harry. You were right to do it for my recovery. I've had a very fruitful week personally. If I'd stayed here those opportunities I now have would have been lost. The benefit of hindsight, as they say,' said Jack.

Harry winced at some pain in his arm, and Jack thought it was time they left.

'Come on Sam, I could eat a horse. Rest well and we'll see you tomorrow, Harry,' said Jack.

*

Burgess joined Sam and Jack for dinner, occasionally moving across to other tables of guests to chat or chivvy his staff. By eight o'clock there was still no word from Field or Edward Croft.

Sam suggested a game of draughts and the three men moved into the lounge. Burgess set up the board and Jack excused himself, sitting slightly apart, saying he had to write two letters.

When he had done Jack sat with both sealed before him, each addressed to a different woman. Sam, never one for games that did not involve money, was distracted by a clatter of carts outside and lost to Burgess. He glanced across, saw the names on the envelopes and looked quizzically at Jack, trying to imagine the contents.

425

Jack had written to Harriet and explained that his duties and convalescence were largely over but that if she could visit Brighton within the next week they could spend a long-awaited day together. He had added that on his part it was very much long awaited. That was all he said, enough he hoped, but without putting Harriet under pressure.

The second letter was to Mary and was much lighter in tone. Largely because there was no personal commitment on Jack's part except friendship for Mary. It suggested they meet towards the end of next week for a walk before he returned to London. This he intended to hand deliver personally to the Royal, with a large tip to ensure that she received it. He decided he would set himself the walk to fill the time.

'Jack?' asked Sam. 'Letters to two ladies?'

'One is to a friend, the other to the woman I will marry. What's wrong?' asked Jack.

'I wondered which way round it is, or whether it's like shifting sand?' asked Sam.

Jack gave his friend a knowing look and stood to go. 'There's nothing spoiling if I walk over now to the Royal, is there? I feel the need to do something rather than sitting and waiting.'

'Of course, it's a good idea. I can get that other one sent off for you if you leave it with me. London is it?' asked Burgess.

'Thank-you,' said Jack, handing over his letter to Harriet.

'I too am corresponding with a lady,' said Sam with a comical look on his face. 'Although she actually wrote to Mother. It's a family Mother met on a train on one of her outings with you. She must have told them where she was staying and the lady mentions the house we are to take. We're invited to tea. Here, have a look at the name.' Sam pulled the letter from his pocket and pushed it across the table to Jack.

Jack picked up the two sheets of clear script and turned them over to find the signature of the music teacher, Eleanor Davies.

'Oh that's good she's honoured her promise. You must go, you'll like her,' said Jack, handing the letter back to Sam.

'I have your permission then, to get to know the lady?' asked Sam cryptically.

'It's nothing to do with me Sam,' said Jack, frowning.

———

426

'No? Although on page two she mentions that she hopes my Mother's son with the fair hair now feels better. Are you about to add a third lady to your circle?' Sam winked at Burgess.

'It was a misunderstanding,' said Jack. 'Mrs Curzon had mentioned her sons, and Miss Davies jumped to a conclusion. You should answer that and accept. Nice for your mother to get to know them and I think you'll like Eleanor Davies, and she will like you. Tell her in the letter I'm not part of the family. I'd better get off up to the Royal, Sam, and I expact I'll be about half an hour.' Jack pocketed the letter to Mary and left the lounge.

*

Glancing at the change in the sky Jack wondered how Edward's sail to Portsmouth had gone. And Field and Shaw? Where were they now? Perhaps they had already started back, Nathan with them, in custody. What would be the next step?

Jack turned onto the beach having decided to prolong his walk after delivering his letter and call in at the Coastguard station. At the Royal he had given the letter to a young boy in the hotel's uniform. Jack tipped him well and the boy had winked, jumping to all the wrong conclusions. Jack hoped the good tip would buy his silence for Mary's sake. The Coastguard station was locked and deserted, their boat gone. Answering a call, he thought. Hours had gone by since the telegrams had been sent. It seemed one of the longest evenings of his life.

Although it was approaching ten o'clock there was still a great movement of people promenading and locals working. Sightseers and residents busied themselves with the social requirement of being seen as the evening grew cooler. The fishermen were still on shore making final preparations to put out at dawn on the tide.

How much of this case had been chance? he asked himself as he took in the view. Was it arrogant of him to think he had the right answer about the marlin spike? If he was wrong was an innocent man under arrest again tonight?

427

And why had he decided to pursue Nathan Long as Mabel Walters's killer? After all they had decided to only focus on finding Grace's murderer. He had set in train a manhunt that afternoon. Was it fair and justified?

Jack bought cockles from a man near the Flagstaff by the West Pier and sat on a low wall to eat them. Realising he was near Regency Square and Westfield Gardens he decided at the last minute to have a walk around them before starting back to the Ship Hotel. He had seen them from a distance from the fishing boat that day with Mrs Curzon when he had reviewed the security and had wanted to walk the area at some point. With only just over a week left of his time in Brighton now was as good a time as any. He would settle better to sleep, he thought, with fresh air and more of a good walk.

The fairness and justifications of pursuing the case did not matter if they were on the right track. In a way it dawned on Jack why it mattered to pursue Nathan despite relating to the man and having empathy for his love of Grace. Jack could almost put himself in Nathan's shoes with the desire to protect. But there was more than protection in these deaths. Information must have been given about Grace and the baby and Jack believed that Nathan had initiated executions. Mabel Walters had been stabbed from behind. Even if the cause of death was drowning, whoever had stabbed her had facilitated the death and walked away.

His mind turned to the death of Doctor Elm. If Ann's instinct was right and they managed to get the body exhumed there just might be the same type of stab wound in the back. Cause of death was falling forward on a knife in that case. Jack had heard it called a scalpel. Had that been engineered? If all the facts fitted and it was the same type of rear attack as that of Mabel Walters, the same type of wound, with the person walking away, Jack knew why he was pursuing the case. It was a most cynical, calculated couple of attacks leading to deaths which could have been stopped. The perpetrator had taken the law into his own hands.

Both Walters and Elm could have been charged instead of the killer pursuing self-perceived justice without any legal authority to do so. The killer had taken vengeance and wreaked punishment. And it was not his place to do so. That was why catching the killer mattered to Jack.

How much of his thought processes were as a result of the last nine to ten months Jack was not sure. He suspected that there were values that he had brought with him, quite rational, coherent, although unsophisticated, but ways of settling differences with reference to a higher authority.

*

It was close to eleven o'clock when Jack returned to the Ship Hotel. Sam and Burgess had stayed in the lounge. Alice had taken over the supervision of the staff and the front door was to be locked at eleven. Sam had had no inclination to go out and had continued with half his mind on the accounts for the move of his family to Brighton and half on the outcome of the expedition underway to Portsmouth. He and Burgess had talked a little of general things in the lounge, too aware of being overheard. The room had steadily emptied after ten o'clock and Sam finally broached the subject on both men's minds.

'Odd there's no word,' said Sam.

'Yes. I suspect that does not bode well,' said Burgess.

The lounge door opened and Jack came in.

'Anything?' Jack asked, as he joined the two men in the lounge.

'No. We were just saying it seems odd,' said Burgess.

'Let's give it until midnight,' suggested Sam. 'I doubt Field and Shaw would disturb us after that.'

'I went by the Coastguard station but it was shut up and the boat had gone. I wondered if Edward had called it over to Portsmouth,' mused Jack.

'Of course something may have happened, and they may have been delayed,' said Burgess.

'It seems only a little blowy down at the water. Would Portsmouth be that different?' asked Jack.

'On shore it can be a little more gusty than Brighton. But if they've gone out windspeed can triple,' said Burgess.

Alice came in with a plate of sandwiches for the three men. She put her hand on Burgess's shoulder and looked at each of them.

'I wasn't sure if you were going to make a night of it,' said Alice. 'I thought the young men would need something if they were to stay awake,' she said.

'Not just the young men,' said Burgess with a mock expression of offense.

Jack took a sandwich and tucked in, relishing the butter and the ham, but Sam declined.

'I think I will go to bed,' said Sam, standing up. 'You may be right about a delay. Shall we meet at seven for breakfast, in case anything has happened?'

'If I could hasten things I would,' said Burgess. 'The problem is we have no idea where our friends are at this moment.'

'Well, whatever the outcome it may take the night to emerge,' said Jack. 'I'll follow you shortly Sam. Thank-you Alice for the sandwich.'

'He always did this,' said Alice, nodding at her husband. 'When he was still in the police. He'd wait up until news of the arrest came in. I always made him sandwiches.' Alice smiled at her husband and he patted her hand.

Jack and Burgess decided to sit a while longer and doze in a chair, with the remains of the sandwiches on the table in front of them. As the clock in reception struck the half hour Jack excused himself and left Burgess to his vigil. The corridors were deserted as Jack made his way to his new room, this time, on the first floor and at the rear of the building. There was some noise in the street but he trusted that it would not keep him awake.

*

430

At seven o'clock the following morning the sounds of the tradesmen delivering to the rear entrance woke Jack, with the realisation that he had overslept if he was to breakfast with Sam. Even with all their noise the tradesmen were still quieter than in London.

Other tables were surprisingly full as Jack entered the breakfast room. Departing guests clearly had an early start to their homeward journey on Saturday morning. Jack joined Sam who had almost finished. Within minutes tea was brought for Jack and a bowl of hot, milky, porridge.

'The Kippers are good,' suggested Sam.

'Kippers it is,' said Jack to the waitress.

Sam pulled a telegram from his pocket and pushed it across the table to Jack.

'The message came by telegram from Edward Croft at Spithead at six o'clock this morning. Here, have a look.'

It read:

"Fleet sailed. Reached them outside English waters. Outside range of coastal weapons. Refusal to surrender Petty Officer Long. Will answer on return. Turning for home."

Jack read it and looked at Sam. 'Has Burgess seen it?' he asked.

'No, he waited up until two in the morning and Alice hadn't the heart to wake him,' explained Sam. 'What does, "Will answer on return" mean?'

'Perhaps Edward has more to explain. I suppose he will have sailed for Fairlight this morning. We can probably expect a visit from Field and Shaw at some point.' Jack looked through the window at the day.

'Well that's it then. The case dies. How very frustrating,' said Sam.

The second message was a carbon copy of the first. However this came in human form as, by eight o'clock, Sergeant Field arrived in the reception with eyes that testified to a sleepless night. He had a copy of the same telegram from Edward. Alice directed him to the breakfast room and he joined Jack and Sam who were still at their table.

'We've received a copy as well. Has anything else happened?' asked Jack.

'Nothing. Shaw and I left Portsmouth just before midnight, explained Field. 'We snoozed a lot. I was wishing for a sleeping car like the one introduced by the North British Railway this year. We got in about three o'clock this morning and I've had about four hours sleep. Shaw has a rest day today and I've ordered him to keep it.'

'Here's Burgess, now,' said Sam, nodding towards the door. Field held out the telegram for Burgess to read. The hotelier took it as he pulled out a chair. Slowly, his eyes scanning Edward Croft's message, he lowered his ample body onto the cushioned seat.

'Well there's no point in any of us losing sleep over this one now is there?' said Burgess. Jack heard the disappointment, however. 'After all we were trying to find Grace initially and that is what we did. Everything else was extra. You've a town to police and I've a hotel to run. Life carries on,' said Burgess to Field. He turned and looked at Jack. 'I learnt that the hard way.

'None of us have had much sleep,' said Sam factually after looking into Field's blood shot eyes.

'No,' said Field.

Burgess indicated to a staff member to serve Field quickly.

'Talk us through what happened after you left Brighton?' asked Jack.

Field waited as tea was poured for him. He spooned sugar into the hot liquid and scalded his mouth before he began his account.

'We left here by train. We had no idea that Nathan's Corvette had already set sail. I gather Edward Croft sailed to see if he could intercept before they left coastal waters. He'd a chance you see if they hadn't. But it was too late and although he went alongside there was no reason why the Captain had to give Nathan up. His response was that the man would return after his tour of duty and answer any charges at that point. As far as the Captain was concerned he was innocent until proven guilty and was needed on duty.'

'When do they come back?' asked Jack.

'Could be two years,' said Field. 'We waited for Edward's boat to return to the Spithead Coastguard's station and then we went for the last train. Edward tied up until this morning and they were to leave on the tide. There's a letter that was passed to Edward from the Corvette. I don't know who it's for though, as it's addressed to Adams of Braithwaite, Houghton and Adams, Counsel, and Thompson, his Clerk.'

Sam paused. He stared at Burgess.

Slowly, Sam held out his hand for the letter, aware all eyes were on him. Field gave it to him and Sam fingered it. He put it down on the table and ran his finger along the names.

'That's you and I,' Sam said to Burgess. 'Somehow I don't want to read this.' He looked up at Jack.

'Are you going to open it Sam?' asked Jack.

'No,' said Sam. 'Not here. Nathan has written to the two men who got him released. His Counsel and the Counsel's Clerk.'

'But he knew that you weren't those things,' said Field.

'Yes, he knew our names. But he's not written to Sam Curzon or Mr Burgess, he's written to his Counsel.' Sam frowned as Field held his hand out for the letter.

'I think,' said Sam, pocketing the letter. 'I think that Burgess and I need to read this first. Not in the presence of policemen, and then we'll know what to do. Excuse me, won't you.' Sam stood and withdrew.

Jack stared after him, aware his mouth had fallen open. Burgess pushed back his chair and followed Sam without a word.

'Apart from arresting them I can't think what to do,' said Field.

*

Twenty-four

Burgess followed Sam through reception and motioned to Alice to have tea brought into their private courtyard garden. He caught up with Sam and steered him down the corridor to a door. As they went through it Sam saw a wrought iron table and chairs in the centre of a walled garden. He dropped the unopened letter onto the table and stared at it.

'It's not for you and I to take this on, son,' said Burgess.

'It would seem a breach of trust to have opened it with Jack and Field, somehow.' Sam almost whispered his reply.

Tea arrived and Burgess indicated to the maid to place the tray on a side table. He did not want to run the risk of a cup being knocked over the letter.

Both men had now sat but in their minds they were lost in the cell with a young sailor. There they sat, two ex-policemen. Burgess, who had been laughed out of the police force for his obsession about a case and his ensuing depression, and Sam, whose life had almost been lost. It was to these two men Nathan Long had chosen to write.

Burgess poured tea but Sam shook his head. Eventually, the letter was released from its prison.

He read:

'I have written to you both as the two men who tried to help me find my Grace, and who acted as my Counsel earlier this week. Thanks to you I was released back to the Navy, with all charges for Grace's murder dropped, and by the time that you read this I will have left these shores, perhaps forever.

Providence will decide if I live or die as I again may go into battle. Indeed it is more than likely I will do and I have little care for my life without Grace. I ask you to read this letter with that in mind.'

'I think I will have some tea after all,' said Sam, laying the letter down. He got up to pour himself a cup of tea.

'Good,' said Burgess. 'How about a biscuit?'

'Perhaps later,' said Sam. 'Would you mind continuing reading it?'

Burgess picked up the letter and heard Nathan's voice begin:

'By now, no doubt, there will be some clever mind that will have turned towards the death of Mable Walters.'

'Here we go,' said Burgess. Sam moved behind Burgess and started to read over his shoulder:

'You told me that Walter's body was discovered at Pett Level, on the same day that Grace's was found. This did come as quite a shock as I had assumed that the baby farmer, as she was called locally, would either recover sufficiently to get off the beach or she would succumb to the wound to be washed out on the tide. There was a chance of either. But I run ahead of myself and there is another situation I must first explain.

In the post box that Grace and I had made at Lovers Seat I found her letter written ready for the first earliest date I could return. She had no doubt checked as we had arranged, to see if it had been collected each month, but had not added any other until hers had been picked up and a response left for her by myself. I took her letter away to read and held it close.

Shortly before I met you in Brighton I had left a letter for her explaining that I had indeed returned and was still of the same mind to wed. I explained that I had understood the reason her parents had not supported her and was anxious for her well-being and that of the child I suspected she had borne in my absence. I said I would meet her as soon as she could come. I arranged for the Bans of marriage to be read at Portsmouth. I left a guinea for her, being all the coin I had on that day, and assured her that she would be well supported from then on. I suggested a day we meet. It was the very day that I found her dead. I know, therefore that someone else either read that letter, or Grace had confided in them.'

'How dreadful,' said Sam. Burgess nodded but did not speak. He did not want to break the spell that Nathan's letter wove. It continued:

'She found my letter as she left another, telling me of my son Jonathan and her attempts to survive. How that broke my heart! That dear, sweet, girl left abandoned by the people closest to her.

She also explained that the woman, Mable Walters, who had the care of the child while Grace made a living, had told her the baby had been adopted by people overseas. Grace had not been able to support the child further, or pay any more to Mable Walters and so the woman had accepted an offer of a fee from an English couple working overseas who did not have any children. This was the baby farmer's story and Grace had resolved to get our son back before she met me.

Grace was, she said, hopeful as Mable had suggested she meet her to take the child. I did not know where that meeting place was to be or I would have gone there. This, I suspect, was the day when Grace met her death.

Her letter explained that she had asked for help from the doctor who had treated her shortly after the birth and was beside herself with excitement that the three of us would be reunited as a family and that we would wed. She told me that this Doctor Elm had challenged Mable Walters about the children for whom she was arranging adoptions.

Once I knew his name I decided to go and see him myself.

I must say, at this point, that I still did not know where Grace was living. Indeed I never discovered this. When I came to the Hotel it was a genuine search for her. I never, to this day found out her address.

I met Doctor Elm and he acknowledged treating Grace after the birth, but not being at the delivery. Grace, he told me, had been helped by some kind women from a charity and they had been at the birth and given her the after-care.'

436

Sam paused and exhaled. He said, 'That's Lucy Croft and the charity she helps with. Jack told me she had known Grace and the child.'

Burgess nodded but still did not speak. They went back to Nathan's letter:

'I visited the Doctor and frankly, found him callous. I told him I knew of the adoption and asked his help and was shocked by the response. He actually laughed. He called us fools for believing the woman was having the children adopted. He said that the death rate of the children was too high. Even though they were neglected, it was still too high and he had started to question Mable Walters himself. He had signed cause of death certificates in the past but was now refusing to certify any more deaths. He seemed only concerned with his professional reputation as each certified death was published in the local paper. Without his help he feared that she was taking matters more into her own hands, claiming the children were being adopted.'

'I think it's time we got Jack and Field in here. I could also do with a walk before we read anymore. How about you?' asked Burgess.

'Yes, I agree,' said Sam. 'I'm going to get Jack and Field. This is a police matter now, don't you think?'

Burgess agreed. 'I do. Then we can finish it and we'll know what to do.'

Burgess walked as far as the Chain Pier. He watched the visitors enjoying the water lapping at the shore and sucked in the clean, fresh, air. Setting his face against the memories of the past he turned back towards his hotel. He hung his hat on a peg outside his office and walked out into the courtyard garden much treasured by Alice. Every plant had been carefully chosen by her.

Field and Jack were already there and they had caught up with the letter so far. Burgess sat opposite Jack at the tiny garden table and remembered being the same age. Jack, with his career ahead of him, young and keen, but his health already carried a question mark for the future. Burgess's reflection was interrupted by Sergeant Field, his face indicating a bad smell.

'You know when I was a child I never read a whole story. I always skipped to the end. What do you think, shall we read the last page?'

'How can we?' asked Sam. 'Surely we need to understand the mind of the man?'

Jack screwed up his face as he looked round at Sam. 'Last page, Sam, and then more tea if you don't mind.'

Field placed the letter back in the centre of the table and the four men gathered round.

'Well that isn't helpful,' said Jack, reading the last page. 'It's an addition to the letter about a bequest of money for a grave for Grace and if necessary, all those children buried at Pett Level, if they can't be identified. It's witnessed and dated, look. Nathan says he's notified his bank in Portsmouth to make funds available. He wants the children buried on the beach to be with a mother and not alone,..... *damn it.*' Jack had started to fill up. Sam heard the voice break as Jack covered his eyes with a hand. Sam put a hand on his shoulder.

Field turned the letter over so a blank page faced the sky. Burgess poured tea for them.

'If anyone prefers not to continue I'll read it myself. I'll not think the less of anyone,' said Field.

'No, let's see it through,' said Jack, his blue eyes turned more brilliant by the water in them. He stared at the Police Sergeant, wondering if he too would get to a point in his career when he would be able to hide the effects of a case.

'Alright, there's nothing for it but to read the lot,' said Field. With resignation he pulled up a chair and looked at each of the other men.

'One thing I must say,' declared Field. 'Whatever reasons the writer of this letter has for what he has done it's a question of what he has done. We need to cut through the accompanying story of why and look at the actions and if he meant to do whatever the letter will tell us he's done. Alright?'

They all nodded and Field picked up the letter and started to read it aloud:

'I questioned the doctor about how many death certificates he had signed. He said as recently as a week ago there had been three. Before that another three....'

Jack tapped the table with his finger and said, 'Perhaps that's the six we found.'

'But why get death certificates for them if she's burying them on the beach? No, I'm afraid there were more than six,' said Burgess.

Sam looked at them and held a finger to his lips trying not to break the mood painted by the narrative. They went back to the letter:

'I gave him my name and asked if Jonathan was amongst them? He said that he had not signed any cause of death for a child called Jonathan Long. Then he added that he was certain that meant nothing and he suspected more had been disposed of. He said unpleasant things about the young women who were the mothers, stating it was a fate worse than death to have left a child in Mable Walter's care. I stared him down at that point and became resolved.

I told you in the police cell that I have killed a great many people. You reminded me that I did so in the name of my country as service, and you were right. But Grace was my country, as was my child, vulnerable to be defended and I had failed them both thus far. But regardless of the reasons I can give you I know a death is still a death.

———

My will at that time was paramount. No matter what the doctor's education and position I challenged him that because of it he should have had the best interests of his charges in mind. I had no knife or gun, but my tools were with me as they always were. He turned his back on me and had picked up something from his case. I could not see it. I drove one of my tools into his back, to wound not to kill and left him. I thought, as a doctor, he would have something to deal with that caused him physical pain. I read later that his death involved falling on his own knife and I concluded that it must have been a surgeon's knife that he took from his bag.'

Burgess sneezed, which broke the mood. Field took the opportunity to get up and move his chair into the sun.

'Chilly,' he said.

'Can't you feel the pain he's in?' exclaimed Sam.

Jack nodded. 'Yes, but it's still being done consciously isn't it. He means harm and we know from his own admission that he's used a "tool," he had, which is likely to be the marlin spike as we thought. What his action and mindset is called is up to the lawyers. He's not defending himself either, Sam. It's building, isn't it, to be uncontrollable anger, perhaps fed by his experiences in the Navy. Its calmly explained though and I don't think he's out of control.'

'Let's go on, shall we?' suggested Burgess, turning the page for Field.

Field read aloud, his tone flat:

'I spent the rest of the time up to when I found Grace at Lovers Seat tracking Mable Walters as she moved around the area. I became convinced that the doctor was right. I saw no visiting couples seeking to adopt in a week. At the end of that time I decided to confront her about Jonathan.

I went to the house early morning to be told by a girl giving some care to the infants there that Mable Walters had just left and had deliveries to make of three children for adoption. Part of me hoped that Jonathan was therefore alive and that I might persuade the woman to part with him to me if I paid her.

I had followed this woman for seven days and knew her movements. She was a heavy woman, cumbersome and so was not moving quickly. If she had three children with her, it was unlikely they would be silent and that she would need transport.

I stopped at the local carrier and he said Mable Walters had indeed taken a cart towards Rye. He confirmed that she had three children with her as they were squawking. I paid for the hire of a horse and rode out of Hastings on the only way she could have gone in a cart. I reached Winchelsea but there was no sign of her so I doubled back but on a lower road.

I followed the track along the Military Canal and asked the bargees if they had seen her. None had. I rode across country becoming more and more concerned for those children in her charge, imagining one of them was my son. I will never know if he was there. I was beside myself by the time I turned for the village of Pett.

A woman at her door told me that she'd seen a burly woman in a cart go past on the way to Pett Level. My worst fears for those children were fulfilled for when I arrived at the beach there was a huddled figure by the rock pools and there were no children visible.

Killing in the service of the Queen has become the way to save my own life, or that of my companions at arms. There is horror to it, but also the exhilaration of survival. I was not the one under threat that day. I believe I was already too late to save the children but a madness had seized me.

I approached Mable Walters from behind, knowing she had finished hiding her charges. She didn't even know I was there as I drove the marlin spike into her back.

She made a terrible noise almost an utterance and then collapsed onto the area she had been covering. If my son was there I had at least taken vengeance for that innocent life.

I wanted to punish, to avenge and I wanted her to suffer. But more than that I felt pleasure at first at what I had done. No other child would die at this woman's hand. I sat on the beach next to her while she begged for help, wounded. I told her the sea would help her soon as I realised the tide was coming in. I could have helped her but I had gone mad. As the sea rushed in across Pett Level I walked around and around the rock pools, laughing. I can still hear the things I shouted. After a while the sea was at ankle depth and with no thought for Mabel Walters lying face down in the sea water I walked back to my horse and rode towards Hastings.

The horror of what I had done slowly came over me as I rode and I turned back. Regardless of these actions I have done, I believe, my training started to bring me back to reason and as a Petty Officer in the Queen's Navy, that some sense started to whisper into my mind.

Yes, I am battle damaged. I admit that. But I was now guilty of wanting to murder and having carried the act out. By the time I got back I was too late and the sea had rolled in and her body was covered. She would have drowned or bled to death and I hoped, beyond hope, that the tide would move her body further down the coast, and with it cleanse my guilt. From there I rode to Fairlight to another utter tragedy.

So, you see, Sam, my Counsel, the shock I experienced in the cell that day when you told me that Mable Walters was found at Pett Level. As you know it was on the same day I discovered my Grace at Lovers Seat.

As to my love, I cannot write it. I was too late and my sentence is one for life. No one loved me as Grace had. She gave me everything and I gave her nothing. I cannot begin to think what the child she had born had gone through. That is why I say to you that I commit my life to the will of Providence now and if I live I will face the penalty on my return, whatever it may be. I rather think though that as I go into the way of harm again that the whole issue of my guilt will be taken care of in some fighting action or other. I do not expect to return.

Thank-you my friends for exonerating me from Grace's murder. Wherever I die I will not carry the stain of Grace's death on my head.

I remain, Petty Officer Nathan Long.'

The additional final page they had already looked at.

Field put the letter on one side. Burgess offered to keep it in the safe if the men wanted time to think.

'I think we should respond,' said Jack.

'In what way?' asked Sam.

'That we have all read his letter. And that we'll be waiting if he does return,' said Jack.

'What does that mean?' asked Sam.

'What it sounds like. The two policemen present here will be waiting for him,' said Jack, looking at Field.

Field nodded. He picked up the final page and looked over the details again.

'I think we should make this letter available for Edward Croft to read. Spithead Coastguard will be the first to know when the Corvette returns. As to the bequest, I can safely say that he's given some thought to it. Who is going to carry it out though?' asked Field.

'Let me speak to the Parson when I see him on Tuesday. I suspect he will help. Nathan's requests about the children will be honoured that way if they can't be identified, or a parent doesn't come forward,' said Jack. 'The children must be at the Mortuary. If you're going to let Edward Croft see the letter we could ask Lucy Croft if she would be prepared to identify any of the children. I know she helped deliver Jonathan as she told me the other night.' Jack paused to think.

'It's possible that the charity she works for may have others who would be prepared to try and identify the six children,' Jack continued. 'And they may have contact details for the mothers. I suspect Edward will not be happy at her being asked but I think we should try.

'As regards burying them with Grace, that could be more difficult,' said Jack. 'If no-one identifies them or comes forward that's the only way I can see we can make it happen. But Grace's parent's probably have first call on her burial don't they?'

'I would imagine so,' said Burgess. 'They may not be interested however, having made their decision. You see your Parson and I'll get across to Fairlight and have a word with Edward and Lucy Croft.'

'Meanwhile, I and a few colleagues will make a call on the property being used as the baby farm,' said Field, looking at his pocket watch.

*

Sitting in the lounge on the Monday morning of his last week in Brighton Jack picked up a copy of the Times. Nathan Long and his corvette, he thought, were already far away.

Jack glanced out through the rain on the windows towards a grey skyline which melted seamlessly into a grey sea. Neither Field nor Shaw had been in touch since the morning of Nathan's letter and Jack had to content himself that he had no further role to play in the case. He was passing time, waiting for the post to be sorted by rooms, and for Sam to return with the keys to the new house he had taken. Jack would then go with him to open it up. Mrs Curzon was on her way from Windsor with the younger boys and her mother, and today would be the last luncheon he would share with Sam for some time.

June 30th it was, and Jack could not believe so much had happened since his arrival in Brighton. Sam had intimated that Inspector Hunt had taken a special commission for Harry and Jack, which would involve him coordinating, but that was all he knew. Hunt would brief Jack and Harry on their first morning back in London.

Jack knew he was much better and only coughed uncontrollably when he was really tired. The dreams were still a problem and had taken their natural development with the investigation into Grace's murder.

He read the first column in the paper and noted that today was the last public appearance for the Shah in London. The weather was unpromising if it was anything like the day they were having in Brighton. Extensive preparations had been made, according to the Times, for the visit of the Imperial visitor to Crystal Palace.

London in the rain, thought Jack. Rivulets of muddy water flowing down the streets and smoke clogging the damp air. He could picture the depressed faces trying to get on omnibuses rattling along with signs of: "Full inside."

Perhaps Ann had a point. How could he turn his back on Sussex? Still, he had made his choice and chosen London and a career.

Jack scanned the columns in the paper. Sir Samuel Baker, the Governor General of the Nile Basin had not after all been assassinated. He was in Khartoum in good health and reported that the slave trade had been put down.

It just shows, thought Jack, one can never really trust the news. It was just like all those reports he had read a couple of years ago about Doctor Livingstone who was supposed to have been murdered again and again. Then suddenly he was reported to be alive and well. He continued scanning: Sir Samuel Baker was apparently a member of the National Geographical Society. His thoughts went to the historian at Pett Level and Jack wondered how Gale was sleeping.

He forced himself to concentrate. Another column stated on good authority (without citing from whom) that the Shah of Persia had enjoyed his visit to Manchester and had offered a number of the skilled workers the opportunity of trips to Persia to teach the workmen there.

On he read finding the account that the naval review at Spithead had been the most enjoyable of all the sights witnessed by the Shah. But not by Harry, thought Jack, and as he looked up over the top of the paper he saw Harry's sidekick, Stan, walking towards him.

'How's our patient doing this morning?' asked Jack.

'Steadily improving. We'll try him outside tomorrow. You around?'

'Not tomorrow, I'm off to stay with an old friend,' said Jack. 'I was just reading that the Spithead naval review was the Shah's favourite event, although how the reporter knows that is a mystery. I doubt our patient would agree.'

'Dreadful place. I'll never show my face there again,' said Stan.

'Spithead?' Jack asked, surprised.

'Portsmouth. We came very close Jack to ending up inside. It was touch and go getting out of there, I can tell you. I'll never forget the sound of those gates clanging behind us,' Stan had dropped his voice.

'Really? I heard Hunt was looking for volunteers to escort the Shah there for his departure shortly to France. I wondered if you'd like your name being put forward?'

Stan blinked rapidly which was never a good sign. Jack regretted his attempt at humour.

'If we weren't in a public place you would not be breathing,' said Stan.

Jack grinned as the response was always over the top from this man. He passed Stan the paper.

'I should think Hunt's exhausted, trailing around after a bunch of royals on this caper,' said Stan.

'Hunt is?' asked Jack.

'Didn't you know?' Stan looked round but the nearest people to them were leaving the lounge.

'Queen's request,' Stan said, dropping his voice to a whisper. 'And that's not all he's up to I can tell you. Does the area, Whitehall, mean anything to you?'

'I know where it is,' said Jack, equally quietly.

'Yes, well. Going into that with you is probably a step too far. Hunt's had special duties to protect the Prince of Wales in the last few weeks. He grew up on the Windsor Estate which is the biggest hint I can give you why he's been selected. His mother still lives there and he visits regularly. His work in the last few weeks has been by royal request. He used to recite to the Prince Consort and her Majesty when he was growing up on the Windsor estate. Can you imagine the work on Hunt's desk piling up while he treks around after that royal pleasure seeker, the Prince of Wales? To say nothing about the bastard at the top we're after being left alone for the last few weeks.' Stan picked a piece of bacon out of his teeth and examined it.

'I didn't know any of that,' Jack exclaimed.

'And you still don't. Anyway,' Stan continued. 'Soon be over and the Shah will be gone. You should have seen the crowds in London, Jack. Unbelievable that nothing nasty started. We'd never have protected the Royals properly, you know. The Queen had the right idea keeping out of it all. London season is almost over and they'll all leave for their estates in the country. Have you had the post yet?'

'No, that's what I was waiting for,' said Jack, looking sideways at Stan. He dropped his voice. 'Am I supposed to know that about Hunt?'

'No, so keep it under your hat. I'm telling you for a reason. I decided it was important you knew who Hunt mixes with. Affects some of the things we get asked to do. Like me and Arthur round Spithead, and our poor patient. Can you shoot, by the way?' asked Stan.

'No,' said Jack, surprised. 'Why are you asking?'

'Well, our patient's quite attached to you. Might need to be with you under some circumstances soon. Problem is his right hand is unlikely to return to full function from what the doc here says. 'Course, his own doctor might disagree. Shooting might be a problem, I'll go and check at reception if the post has come.' Stan got up and took the Times with him.

Jack watched him go, his mind moving to Sam's explanation that Hunt had a special commission for Harry and Jack. His thoughts were interrupted as he heard jangling from the corridor and Sam appeared behind a huge grin and a large ring of keys.

'Got them,' said Sam, shaking the keys again.

'Wonderful,' replied Jack. 'Do you want to go now, or after luncheon?'

'Luncheon feels like waiting for next week, too long. Let's go now. Mother and the boys will be here about five o'clock,' said Sam.

'That's fine with me. We can keep our eyes open for supplies on the way. I'll just check if there's a letter in the post for me and I'll be with you,' said Jack.

Alice saw him coming and held up a letter for Jack. She raised her eyebrows and closed her eyes as she smelt the perfume from the envelope. Jack laughed as he took it from her, knowing the handwriting was Harriet's. He put it in his pocket deciding he would not hold Sam up by stopping to read the letter now. It was enough at the moment that Harriet had written. Alice gave him a knowing look from the expression on his face and Jack turned back to collect Sam.

They left in the direction of St. Peter's church as the house was over in that part of Brighton. It was as Sam had originally described it and Jack thought it a fine church, now made the Parish Church of Brighton that very year.

'We'll make it our church now,' Sam said.

Jack was taken aback by the house, which had five storeys. Sam unlocked the kitchen door and they went in.

'Sam, it's huge,' said Jack. 'Now I understand how you can get all those people in and do paying guests. Can you afford it, really?'

Sam looked at Jack and pushed his glasses to the back of his nose.

'Yes, for we have our lodger. I hadn't said anything but Mrs Phillips is to come. I don't think Rose knows yet and Harry certainly won't mind his mother-in-law not living with them. It's just that she and Mother get on so well and Mrs Phillips has fallen in love with Brighton. So she will join us in two weeks. That's how we can afford it. As long as I have work, and we have a paying guest too, we can make ends meet. But in August we will take our first holiday makers and, look Jack, I have here the first bookings.' Sam pulled out of his wallet two letters requesting different weeks in August. Jack took them, nodded and smiled, as he handed them back.

Sam led him through room after room uncovering the furniture that the Landlord had provided.

Jack said: 'I'm away tomorrow but I can help you today. You've whitewash ready I see. The kitchen could do with it. I can get that done before your mother arrives. At least it will give it a fresh look.'

'There's a fair bit to do. It's good of you but I don't want you to exhaust yourself and start the cough off again. If you get something done in the kitchen I can start upstairs to arrange the rooms so that there's bedrooms ready for the boys tonight. Would you light the range although it's June?' asked Sam.

'Yes, I would get it going,' replied Jack. It will give the place chance to warm through. It's a shame it's a wet day as we could have had the windows open. It feels like it's been empty some time. If I get it going you can boil water for tea and for cooking as well.' Jack looked at the range which was freshly blackened. He opened it and pulled out a kettle and a large pan.

'Are you sure you're alright to do this?' asked Sam.

'Yes I think so. If I start coughing I'll just stop for a while,' said Jack. He thought for a few moments and then continued, 'I'd like to do this for you all. That business with Nathan Long has left some sadness, Sam. Physical work sometimes acts as a soothing balm. My father always said that more problems were solved in his head when he dug over ground and planted new seedlings than any other way.'

Sam took a deep breath. 'He was right. I'll get started upstairs.'

*

Towards the end of the morning Sam went out and introduced himself in the local shops. He bought cheese, bread, milk and tea and placed orders to be delivered later. It gave him great pleasure to place money on the counter and to set up an account to be settled each month.

The kitchen had a pump with a supply of fresh water so once the range was lit the kettle was put to good use. Sam produced two tin mugs bought from a Ship's Chandler near the sea front earlier that morning. He and Jack sat on the front wall like two children and munched the bread and cheese.

By five o'clock the entire belongings of the Curzon family arrived in front of the house along with loud banging on the front door. Sam's young brothers who were the eldest of the four, Dan and Tom, had discovered the back gate and flew into the kitchen, stopping briefly as they encountered Jack clearing away the last evidence of whitewash. Sam appeared and made the introductions and Jack found himself roped into a promise to take them all fishing on Saturday. A grateful Mrs Curzon took possession of the kitchen and the two younger boys carried in a dining chair each. Jack thought how they all looked like future clerks.

The older Mrs Curzon who quickly was introduced as Grandma proved as good a labourer as any and her first task was to get the pie into the range to re-heat, and the potatoes, which had part boiled that morning, were simmering away before Jack knew it.

'You'll eat with us?' asked Grandma. He was already in her good books for getting the range going.

'If you've enough, I would be happy to,' said Jack.

Cake was produced to celebrate and lasted very little time between the eight of them. Mrs Curzon knew just where she had packed the cups, and the kettle went into production again.

Rain had stopped earlier in the afternoon and by seven o'clock the Curzon family and Jack were seated on up-turned boxes in the garden eating hot meat pie and potatoes.

'I could turn that piece of ground over for you later in the week,' said Jack. 'Get some planting done. Now's the time for it if you're to have any vegetables this year.'

'A whitewashed kitchen and an offer of a vegetable garden in one afternoon! Can you live with us?' asked Grandma.

Jack laughed, but Sam answered quickly.

'He will stay, hopefully, many times, Gran,' said Sam.

'Can I dig it with you?' asked the youngest brother, whose name had escaped Jack. He had been trying to remember the names and thought this might be Peter. Mr and Mrs Curzon had given their children Bible names so it was just a matter of working through the well-known ones before Jack got it right.

'Of course you can, Peter,' said Jack.

'I'm Luke,' said the boy.

'Luke. I'll get it right next time I come. I must away now. I've a letter to read,' said Jack.

'From Harriet?' asked Sam.

Jack put down his cup and stood to go. 'Yes, I hope it's her Sunday off this week and she might come down.'

'If its Sunday you must bring her to tea. I mean it Jack. It's time I met the future Mrs Sargent,' said Sam.

'And your plans tomorrow?' asked Mrs Curzon.

'Yes, what time are you off to Lewes?' asked Sam, starting to stand.

'I'm on the nine o'clock train. I'll wave as I ride by,' said Jack.

'No you won't, you'll come to breakfast if you're passing the house,' said Grandma. 'What takes you to Lewes?'

'I get the train to a village just after Lewes to see an old family friend. I could catch it from the terminus. The Lewes Road Station near here won't open until September first but I could call in here first.' Jack explained.

'Are we to have a station near here?' asked Grandma.

'Yes. Takes you round to Eastbourne and Hastings. Nice day out if you fancy it. Are you sure it's no trouble to call in?' asked Jack.

'You've seen the way these boys eat. What is one more. And we've always kept open house in Windsor haven't we Sam,' said Mrs Curzon. 'It will make the house seem like home if you come, Jack.'

'Alright, I will. Many thanks, and see you in the morning.'

Sam walked with Jack as far as St. Peter's and they parted with a handshake.

*

Jack checked the clock and decided he would see if a visit to Harry was acceptable after he had read Harriet's letter. The paper smelt of rose as always and he closed his eyes and could imagine her in the very presence of the scent. Once in his room he spent time unsticking the envelope so that the whole piece was undamaged.

There was noise in the street and he shut the window to allow him to give his full attention to Harriet's letter. A knock at the door announced Burgess with news of dinner. Jack excused himself explaining that he's eaten with Sam and the family.

'How has their move gone?' asked Burgess.

'Well. I'm sure they'd love it if you and Alice called. Helps it feel like home,' said Jack.

'Remind me where they are?'

'Brunswick Place, near St Peter's Church,' said Jack.

'I know it. I'll leave you to your letter, Jack. Let me know if there's anything else you fancy later. After that business of Nathan's letter I may need a nightcap,' said Burgess.

'Yes, I may join you with one,' replied Jack.

'I shall miss Sam and his cheeriness,' said Burgess and he left the room, pulling the door to as he went.

Jack took the notepaper out of the envelope and read:

Jack,

I think it extraordinary that you have written now after so long. So much has happened and I hardly expected to hear from you.

I am dismissed, Jack. Your letter came to me by hand from the Grove, which was kind of them. But they will not welcome letters sent for me again.

I am at Georgina's until next week when we leave for Honiton for her wedding to Arscott. Then I will stay with Mother for the rest of the summer until I can find other employment. I have one kind reference from the Grove but not from the Housekeeper. Georgina has been making enquiries for me.

I do not want to go into details as it was all my fault. I should never have behaved as I did in trying to see Sergeant Phillips to make contact with you. I am so mazed with myself. To tell you the truth about my dismissal I lied and said I was ill and could not work one day. One of the other maids, Clara, covered up for me and she was dismissed as well.

As to you and I. I hardly know how to begin.

I understand that you have a new friend, called Mary, and have been walking out with her in Brighton. I hear she is very lovely and Georgina thought her elegant and kind to you and could tell she was in love with you. I am glad of that. You know I liked you but I do not know if it was love.

Arscott had mentioned to Georgina that he had met you with a friend. Georgina, of course had to see, and in some ways I wish she had not as I have found it hard to know the tenderness with which you and Mary spoke to each other. She carried a rose apparently and it has tormented me that it was probably from you. Perhaps I loved you after all?

I have decided that we cannot go on and that I must concentrate on getting work if I am to achieve my ambitions. I know you wanted to marry me and that I held you off. It all seemed too soon to me. I should have been more honest with you and refused you earlier. But Jack I thought I loved you. I suppose it is inevitable that another will cross your path. I am glad for you and hope that she is more ready to wed than I.

———

453

As to my need for work I should not have forgotten myself and acted dishonestly. I have been very upset about everything that has happened with the Grove. Georgina is very encouraging but says that I may need to start again as a Scullery Maid and work up.

You will not be surprised then that I will obviously not be coming to Brighton. I could not afford the train fare now anyway.

I wish you well. I am sorry Jack.

I cannot think how to sign this letter except to say it is from:

Harriet.

*

Twenty-five

As he neared Lewes Jack felt he had to part from all the acrimony and heart-breaking anguish that had drowned him through the night. The relationship with Harriet had begun so well last year but one letter had separated them. He had been deceiving himself for some months he realised. She would never have married him. Her words that she had, "thought that she loved him," mingled with Ted's voice in Jack's head, "She's very young, Jack."

Whatever the future held for him it would be worlds apart from Harriet unless he could talk her round. That fact last night had left him with an ache which had made him howl like a wounded animal and he had sobbed noisily, as a thwarted child would, wishing that his life had ended in the Alexandra Palace fire. What was the point of it all? The struggle, the fight, if he was to be perpetually alone? Then the uncontrollable coughing had begun and he had retched.

Burgess had been called after a complaint from a guest at the noise from room ten. When he entered Jack's room Burgess found him sitting on the floor, doubled up trying to get his breath. Burgess opened the window, poured water and knelt down beside him, putting an arm around his shoulders to straighten him up. He got Jack to take sips of water slowly, encouraging him to breath steadily. Gradually the cough subsided and Jack's breathing settled to a more normal pattern.

Seeing the letter, then discarded on the floor, Burgess had picked it up and handed it to Jack, catching sight of the signature. Jack let it fall on the bed.

So that was it, Burgess thought, girl trouble. He opened the door and peered up the corridor. There was a maid at the far end who was about to go into another room to turn down the coverlet, and light the lamps.

'Get my wife quickly, will you, a guest is unwell,' he called.

Alice came with brandy and a teaspoon and made Jack take it like dosing with medicine. Jack gave her a vacant look, eyes still liquid, but a small smile of thanks eventually came.

'You're always so kind,' Jack said.

'And why shouldn't we be?' said Alice, firmly.

Burgess started to clear up the mess.

'Now you get your shoes on and come to our sitting room,' Alice said.

And there Jack had remained for the night. Burgess and he had talked into the early hours, and Jack grew more verbose as the level of brandy at his side diminished. By one o'clock, exhausted and slightly drunk, Jack had fallen into a restless sleep.

Burgess sat for an hour opposite Jack to ensure he was not likely to wake. He raked the fire so that the grey ash fell through the grate into the tray beneath and put more coal on to keep it in until the fresh one was laid, covered Jack's knees with a lamb's wool rug and settled down himself to get what little sleep was left to him.

Jack woke at seven to the sounds of plates being put onto a side table next to him and the smell of breakfast pervading the sitting room.

'If that's for me I really can't eat anything,' he said to Alice.

'Nonsense, you have to keep your strength up. Come on, you're no good to anyone if you let this situation finish you. Burgess says he thinks it's a young lady. Well, at your age and with your looks and prospects, there'll be plenty more. Now take some tea, and try this toast.'

At first Jack shook his head but Alice would not take no for an answer. She sat next to him and coaxed him sip by sip, mouthful after mouthful.

'She doesn't want me,' said Jack.

'Well, more fool her,' said Alice. 'Believe me, at my age, I know a good bet when I see one.'

Jack managed a slight smile.

It was half past seven when Burgess came in. Jack thought he looked tired and felt that he should apologise.

'I've caused you a bad night,' he said.

'Think nothing of it. You're over the worst this morning. The sun is shining and we should get you out shortly and on your way to your Parson,' said Burgess.

'I should go and try and see her,' said Jack, his hands shaking. 'I should go to London and speak to Arscott and find out where Harriet is.'

Burgess saw the hands, as did Alice. She moved forward and took both of Jack's in her own hands and held them tightly.

'Grip my hands,' she said to Jack.

Jack did until his knuckles turned white. Realising he may be hurting Alice he loosened his hold. The shaking of his hands had stopped although Alice's hands were red with the pressure.

'Come on, lad, time to get cleaned up. You've a train to make haven't you?' asked Burgess.

Jack stared at him, wondering what to do. Burgess held out a hand to pull him up and Jack stared at it as the door opened and Stan came in.

'Well, Jack. How are you?' asked Stan.

'What – do you know?' Jack ran his tongue over his lips.

'I thought it wise to let Stan know that you'd had bad news. He's the only superior officer of sound body and mind available,' said Burgess.

'Sound body I would agree with you. There are times when I do wonder about my mind,' said Stan, putting a hand under Jack's elbow. 'Come on, lad. I'm going to travel with you this morning and when you leave the train at Selmeston I'll do some walking. I've a fancy to see Firle and Glynde for the next two days. Arthur's enough to help Harry now so they won't miss me here. If we're to make the train you need to get ready and pack an overnight bag.'

'Stan, Harriet won't marry me,' Jack said as Stan hauled him up onto his feet. There was the name. Alice and Burgess gave each other a knowing look.

'I know, lad. Well that's the way sometimes, said Stan. 'We have to take today minute by minute and not think too much. Now is the time to get yourself cleaned up and dressed. When you've done that we'll talk about what we do next. Don't try and think too far ahead is my advice. Minute by minute.'

———

457

From the Ship Hotel Jack and Stan walked up to Sam's in Brunswick Place. Jack had insisted that he must let the Curzon's know he was not coming for breakfast. Stan had been all for sending a note but Jack would not have it.

'Sam's been through a worse time than anything I'm going through. His family have been kind to me,' said Jack.

Stan took it as a good sign that Jack could compare his grief about Harriet with another's difficulties and so they stood on Sam's new doorstep and explained Jack was not too well after some personal news.

Jack interrupted. 'Stan's being polite. The truth is that Harriet has been told a story about me walking out with Mary. She's lost her position as well and it all sounds very mixed up. Her sister was there at the Brighton exhibition, Sam and although it was meant as friendship on my part it's all been misunderstood.'

Sam was warm in his response. 'I'm truly very sorry,' he said, gripping Jack's forearm. 'I know we bantered the other day about ladies but that was all it was. I knew you were true to Miss Harriet. And she must know that at the back of her mind. Perhaps with time she'll realise that this tale she's heard is a load of nonsense. I don't doubt the feeling on Mary's side, Jack. I could see it that day. But from you I know there's nothing other than your warm friendship for her. Look Jack, there's no need for you to be on your own when you come back tomorrow. If you don't mind the madcap household we have you are welcome to stay.'

Jack felt himself well-up and half turned away. He nodded his thanks.

Stan shook hands with Sam and wished the family well. 'We should get going,' he said. 'We've a journey to do and I've Firle Beacon to see.'

'Have a safe journey. I noted from the paper this morning that there have been so many rail accidents this year,' said Sam. 'Hold on, I'll give you a key as I've a spare.'

Sam disappeared into the hall and returned with a large wooden pot, painted yellow with a carved key on the top. He removed the lid and dug his fingers into a pile of keys, eventually pulling out the one he was searching for.

He reached forward for Jack's hand and pressed a front door key into it. Jack nodded his thanks, overwhelmed at the kindness and the three men parted.

Selmeston emerged as the sun burnt off the cloud from the hills. Jack and Stan walked from the halt rather than ride with the cart that had waited for the train. It was earlier than he had arranged with Reverend Peter Fisher and they were killing time. Stan's advice had been to get on this morning so that there was less time to sit around and reflect. Jack could not remember another time when Stan had been so conversational. At first he had responded with nods or shakes of the head but as the journey proceeded Jack had started to engage.

'You should give some thought about your career long-term,' said Stan.

'I have a little. It seems early days to be planning though. Surely I just need to get more experience.' Jack shifted his bag to the other hand.

'Nothing wrong with having a plan. Few more years and you should be trying for Sergeant. You want to make Inspector after that,' said Stan.

'Sounds a bit ambitious. I had thought about getting to Sergeant but Inspector feels a long way off, if ever I even consider it. Look we're here. I hope the Parson won't mind me being so early. You'll come in and meet him?'

'I would like to, and then I'll get off and leave you to your day.' Stan slipped his bag off his shoulder and stood slightly to one side as Jack knocked on the door.

Mrs Simcock opened the door and exclaimed:

'Oh sir, you're early! Reverend Fisher is still out on his rounds. And you've brought another friend. He'll like that. Do come in and I'll get you some tea.'

'I hadn't thought to stay,' said Stan. 'I'm just travelling this way to do some walking. Will the Reverend be long?'

'He should be back shortly. He goes with the milk round each morning. It's his way. I'll bring your tea.'

'Funny thing to do,' said Jack.

'I suspect he's looking after his beat,' said Stan. 'Seeing who's around, and those who are up and about have the chance to have a friendly word instead of facing the day of troubles alone. Not much different to us you know.'

'Higher authority you could argue, though,' said Jack.

Stan nodded, noting the sense of humour was returning.

Mrs Simcock brought the tea and they settled into well-used armchairs.

'The Reverend wouldn't have a local map would he?' asked Stan.

'Yes sir, there are his own he has drawn over many years. They're up on the shelf above the desk.' Mrs Simcock pulled a thick file down for Stan. 'Were you interested in any area in particular?'

Stan noted there was no sign of any dust.

'Firle Beacon and Glynde,' said Stan.

' A new one came from Ordnance Survey yesterday but I won't give you that one as Reverend Fisher hasn't studied the changes yet. He shouldn't be long now. I'll be doing him breakfast when he comes. Can I make it for you gentlemen as well?' Mrs Simcock asked.

Jack paused, aware unusually that he had no appetite.

Stan cut in before Jack could refuse: 'If it's no trouble that would be very welcome.'

'You'll tell the Reverend won't you, Jack?' said Stan, as he looked down the garden towards the hedge separating it from the lane. An elderly man, nearing eighty Stan thought, told the horse to whoa. He was wearing a dog collar, so Stan did not win any prizes in his assessment. The clergyman climbed down from the seat next to the milkman and his boy. The rest of his clothes were more akin to a farm labourer.

Jack rose from his chair as the kitchen door opened.

'Marning Parson,' Jack said. 'I'm sorry I'm so much earlier than we arranged.'

'No worries on that score,' said Peter Fisher. 'Good to see you anytime. I'll be in as soon as I've got my boots off.'

The Parson came through from the kitchen eyeing Stan with a completely expressionless face which it had taken years to master. There was a hint of a smile as Peter Fisher walked towards him to shake his hand.

'No matter, Jack, about being early. You've brought a new friend for me to meet, so you are forgiven. How do you do, sir, you're another policeman, I take it?'

'I am Reverend. Sergeant Stan Green from Shadwell. Jack and I work together from time to time. I travelled with Jack this morning and will go walking to Firle Beacon. Your housekeeper kindly let me look at your maps.'

'Oh you must have the new one from Ordnance Survey then. Just a minute let me get it for you.' Peter Fisher removed a crisp envelope from a drawer and handed it to Stan.

'That's quite a walk for you. Will you go back tonight? I take it you've been part of the group at Brighton?'

'I've been in at the end of things,' said Stan.

The Parson noted the deliberately vague answer.

'Will you return tonight?' Peter Fisher repeated the question, adding, 'Or are you in need of accommodation?'

'Jack mentioned an inn in Lewes. I'd like to see Glynde tomorrow and had thought to enquire at the inn later,' said Stan.

'No need if you can cope with a camp bed and my small study. You're welcome to join us this evening. We have something to celebrate today but I won't give the game away and spoil that yet,' explained Peter Fisher.

'Have you had some good news, Parson?' asked Jack.

'Yes, and I will share it at eleven which is the appointed hour for another guest to arrive.' The Parson studied Jack's face and registered he was not looking well.

'How is your health progressing Jack?' he asked.

'It's been improving. I had a bad night, that's all,' said Jack.

'I had a telegram from Doctor Ann,' said the Parson. 'I've made enquiries and her assumptions about Grace were right. She did look for help in various parishes and I've a list of dates and locations for you. That should help pin it down, I think, and ensure Nathan does not take the blame for her death,' said Peter Fisher.

Jack glanced at Stan.

Stan remained quiet and looked at the ordnance survey map but the reference to "Doctor Ann" and a person not being blamed for a death, was sufficient for him to understand that Jack had not been simply staying away with friends. He said nothing and traced the contours on the map with a finger. The smell of bacon had slowly invaded the parlour. Now Mrs Simcock appeared from the kitchen and announced breakfast was ready if the gentlemen would like to come to the small table in the garden. The tea pot and crockery was already laid for three.

'Help yourself, gentlemen,' said Peter Fisher, taking the covers off the two dishes full of bacon and egg. Jack poured himself tea and added sugar. Stan made up a plate of bacon and eggs and offered it to Jack. Their eyes met and Jack shook his head. Stan started to tuck into it. Peter Fisher noted it all and drew his own conclusion about the poor appetite.

'So are you going to tell me why you had a bad night and why you arrived so early?' asked the Parson. 'As delighted and interested as I am to meet Sergeant Green I sense from the look of you that there is a reason why he is with you.'

Jack looked at Stan and then back across at Peter Fisher. The old clergyman stirred his tea and waited. Jack looked for some minutes at the movement of the trees as the wind got up along the valley. Why did he always think of the tide changing when he saw trees move like that?

'I had some bad news yesterday. From my young lady. Harriet, that I told you about. There's been a misunderstanding and she wrote to say that she doesn't want ….' Jack gripped the teaspoon until it was entirely obscured by his hand. His knuckles turned white.

Peter Fisher looked at Stan who wrinkled his nose up and shook his head. Jack reached into an inside pocket and passed Harriet's letter to the clergyman.

Minutes went by as Peter Fisher read Harriet's letter. He went through it once, looking at Jack as he came to the part about Mary, and then started to read it through again, momentarily pausing two or three times. Not once did his expression change.

Feelings of frustration at himself for not taking any action to get to Harriet had started to build in Jack before he and Stan had left Brighton. It reached its peak like a hiatus hernia at that breakfast table. He stood and walked away staring at the hills beyond from the edge of the garden. He should not have come but should have caught the London train. He could trace Georgina and see Harriet, sort the mess out. The agitation he felt started to bring on the cough.

Peter Fisher got up and followed Jack down the path. He held out the letter without a word and Jack put it back in the inner pocket of his jacket.

'What do you want to do?' asked Peter Fisher.

'Go to London,' said Jack, stifling his cough. 'Talk to her.'

'Go?' said the Parson, surprised. 'What, go to London now? To Harriet?'

'I should talk to her, explain it's not true. None of its true.'

'You didn't walk with a young lady in Brighton, give her a rose? Laugh? Be comfortable together? It's all a figment of her sister's imagination?' Peter Fisher paused. He had started to half turn back towards the breakfast table. Stan was stirring his tea, not looking at Jack.

'Not like you make it sound. Not like Harriet's been told,' said Jack, sourly.

'No?' Ah, I see. Tell me how it was while we eat breakfast. Come back and have something. Important to keep up your strength,' suggested Peter Fisher. Jack followed him to the table.

'What can I give you Jack?' asked Stan offering a plate again.

'I'll just have some toast,' Jack said.

Peter Fisher looked at Jack. 'Well, someone has orchestrated a story after seeing you with the "lovely" young woman in Brighton. I believe you by the way. I think you'd be straight with a young woman.' The clergyman glanced at the untouched toast on Jack's plate. Stan helped himself to another egg.

'Of course there's more than the grief about your supposed infidelity in that letter,' said Peter Fisher. 'Forgive me, Jack if I eat, won't you? I was up at five.'

'Of course, you must,' said Jack.

Peter Fisher helped himself to the cooked food. He ate and made quick work of his breakfast. Placing his knife and fork perfectly centre he said: 'And perhaps one day when Harriet has got over the other two griefs she's experiencing she will work all this out for herself. But there's more going on for that young lady than just you. She's lost a great deal and, reading between the lines, I don't think she's very well at the moment. Her relationship with you is just part of the London she's been experiencing and, I don't mean this to cause you offence, it's not the main part yet. Now she's lost her dream. And I don't think you were it, by the way. The way the letter's written tells me that. It's all over the place.' Peter Fisher reached across to a plate covered in slices of fried bacon and removed two pieces from it onto a separate plate. He proceeded to butter slices of thick, farmhouse bread and put the bacon between them to make a sandwich.

'Last time I made you a bacon sandwich was when you were nine. Do you remember?' asked Peter Fisher, pushing the plate across to Jack.

Jack looked at him in surprise and shook his head.

'You told me then it was your favourite way of eating it. Is that still true?'

Jack looked at the plate and then back into the clear gaze. He picked up one of the halves and bit into it. His stomach reacted with the expectation of food long needed. He nodded.

'What is needed with this young lady,' said the Parson, 'is kindness, rather than you arriving to scale the castle wall and set fair maiden free. A gentle letter leaving things open, if that's how you feel, is what I would advise. And time.'

'It feels so weak. Surely if I loved her I would go?' said Jack.

'Surely if you loved her you would wait?' said the old vicar, firmly. 'Unless you are more interested in your own well-being than hers? In your intense loneliness is the idea of letting someone else be for a while, so unbearable?'

Jack pushed himself back on the chair until the back legs only were on the ground. His wounds this time were emotional and he was unsure how to cope with them.

Stan remained silent, slowly and carefully helping himself to food to ensure he did not break the spell.

'There is another issue of course. Is the sister older?' asked Peter Fisher.

'Some years, yes. Why?' asked Jack.

'Perhaps years bring an understanding of people. Perhaps then she saw something in the other woman's gaze when she looked at you which you do not see. The letter says she is lovely and it was clear she was in love with you. Sometimes it takes a woman to see these things. You aren't looking for it that's quite clear,' said the Parson.

'It's rubbish. Mary is a nice girl, just lonely. Yes she's lovely if you like her type. She could have any man. She works hard and doesn't have any life outside the hotel where she works. It was the Exhibition in Brighton and the place was full of people. The whole town was there. I hadn't gone alone with her. We were part of a group and there were two other ladies present. She's no young man to give her a rose and I felt she should have one. There were flower stalls and many young ladies carried roses. You'll remember her, Stan. You remember Mary from the Mason's Arms on the Commercial Road?' Jack looked at Stan.

Stan sat back and put his knife and fork down. 'That Mary?' he said. He looked at Peter Fisher, who registered the implications.

Jack swallowed a cough and could not speak for a short while, as he struggled with the attempt to control it. The natural break in the conversation put a distance into his decision making about leaving for London and Jack felt defeated by his own body more than the arguments put to him.

'Later, if you feel like it, I can help in the tone of a letter if you feel you are ready to write one. It won't matter if you want to leave it for a few days, but I do think it will have to be written,' said Peter Fisher.

'I should be going,' said Stan, standing up. Jack was in good hands and he knew he could go now. 'If your housekeeper can give me something to wrap this sandwich in I'll take it with me and enjoy it at the Beacon.'

'Yes, please do,' said the Parson. 'The paths at the lower levels can be muddy after the rain we've had. The gamekeeper's cottage for Firle Place is up there and you can certainly get fresh water from them, if not hot tea, if you mention you're a friend of mine.'

'Thank-you. I'd like to take you up on your offer of staying overnight if that's still open, Reverend,' said Stan.

'Of course, delighted. You'll find the climb up to the Beacon tiring so we'll wait supper for you. If I may I'll walk up the lane with you to the point where you go across the field,' said Peter Fisher.

'Great shame this business with the young lady,' said Stan, as he and the Reverend walked.

'It is, it is indeed. Ann Black had obviously done a great deal with Jack regarding his health last week, but this business has knocked him back. We will do what we can and I have a visitor relating to affairs of Jack's parents coming today, which will be good news for him. But I must not tell you before he's heard himself.'

'It's a good day for something encouraging. You met Ann Black?' asked Stan.

'Yes, remarkable woman. Jack brought her to meet me last week. Made a great difference to the findings about that poor woman Grace and the baby farming. I hope my small part helped. At least we can say with some certainty that Grace's movements indicate Mabel Walters had had her killed, or committed the act herself. It exonerates her fiancé from blame at least. Three murders though, terrible. To say nothing of all the poor children. I've got the diocese onto the exhumation of the doctor's body.' Peter Fisher stared into the distance.

Stan stood and sniffed the wind which carried the smell of baking. The Parson obviously thought he knew what had been going on. He wondered if the wind carried information about his evening meal to come. If he stood a little longer he wondered what else the Reverend would disclose. Honest people always did. So, Jack, thought Stan, while we all thought you were off visiting friends and relatives you've been tracking down multiple killers. And getting Ann Black down for her forensic skills to boot. Stan turned to the Reverend and extended his hand.

'Thank you for your hospitality, I'll look forward to this evening. Remind me before I go was it Mabel Walters who was to be exhumed?' Stan laughed and shrugged. 'I'm a little hazy on who's who.'

'No, no, the doctor. Doctor Elm,' said Peter Fisher, shaking Stan's hand. 'Sadly died on his own scalpel but it's possible that he was stabbed with a marlin spike before he fell on it. Its whether or not there's bruising anywhere on the back or shoulder to indicate a man gripped him before he drove the marlin spike into the back.' Peter Fisher acted out the forceful push into the back. He said: 'If there is its cause of death apparently then. Similar you see to the way Mabel Walters was killed. Doesn't look good for Nathan. Well I must let you go.'

'They did well, Ann and Jack,' Stan called as he started to turn.

'All of them, Burgess had a good instinct to keep on with it. And those two policemen from Brighton, Field and Shaw, I think were their names. I hope my little part helped.'

'Undoubtedly. It's always the civilians that make the difference,' said Stan. 'Just one question.'

'Yes, of course,' Peter Fisher waited.

'You mentioned children?'

'That's right. Didn't he tell you? Probably six, maybe more, disposed of by the baby farmer, Walters. Grace's child undoubtedly. That must have been what drove Nathan to kill her. Very sad,' said Peter Fisher.

'And the significance of the marlin spike?' asked Stan.

'Grace's young man, Nathan, is in the Royal Navy,' explained Peter Fisher.

'Ah, I see. He finished off the baby farmer, as you call her, and possibly the doctor. Do you know what's happened to him?' asked Stan.

'Not yet, I was hoping Jack had news this morning.'

'Save it for tonight, eh? I'd like to hear the outcome from Jack too,' said Stan.

Peter Fisher nodded and waved as he walked away.

As he started the climb Stan went over the numbers in his mind. Jack had been busy. Eight murders dealt with in one week, with the possibility of Doctor Elm as well once the exhumation was completed. And Harry thought young Jack had been resting when he took him off the team. Instead he and Ann Black, who had surprisingly taken a holiday at the same time as Doctor Brown, had been working on an investigation. Stan thought he would like a chat with Burgess. Knee deep in bodies they'd been. Stan logged the names of Field and Shaw from Brighton away. He decided he would like to meet them before he went back to London.

*

Out of respect for the visitor due at eleven o'clock the Reverend changed into his clerical "uniform" as Jack called it. Jack had slept for more than an hour after Stan had left, his brow at times contorted into a deep frown, murmuring occasionally. Mrs Simcock did what she could to keep the room quiet for him, draping a light blanket over his legs.

He had slept deeply and was withdrawn when he woke. Peter Fisher thought that he still looked ill and decided not to explain the purpose of their visitor due to arrive in ten minutes time. Mrs Simcock brought tea and the warm Queen Drop biscuits that had taken just ten minutes to cook.

'I can go out and give you some privacy while your visitor is here,' Jack offered.

'No, no, you must be here. You have a role to play this morning in this visit,' the old vicar said. 'I'll call you in when it's time.'

At ten minutes to eleven a horse and rider came up the lane and stopped by the gate to the cottage. Jack could see the rider had a good cut to his clothes and carried a messenger bag slung across his body. He dismounted and went round to the front door. Something official, thought Jack as that was not the action of a friend.

Fifteen minutes followed and Jack waited. Conscious that he had little patience with his thoughts he decided to occupy himself with pulling the weeds in the border. His cough still lurked despite the sleep. Jack decided to seek refuge in activity. He had cleared part of a border when Mrs Simcock came into the garden to collect him.

'The Reverend asks would you care to join him and Mr Layton in the study now, sir,' she said.

Jack stood and wiped his hands on his handkerchief, following her towards the kitchen. As he slipped off his boots at the step Jack could hear the two men discussing the state of business in Lewes. Jack went through to the study and waited by the open door until Peter Fisher saw him and called him in.

'The boundaries will need enlarging with all that implies politically,' Langton was in the process of saying.

'Well it's inevitable the town will grow. Now, Jack, *come in.* Do you remember Mr Langton at all?'

'I'm sorry, sir, but I don't,' said Jack, shaking hands with Langton, who studied the young man before him.

'No, of course you won't. It was my partner who dealt with your father. I remember you as a small boy though. You're like your father was at your age.'

'Did Father supply your business?' asked Jack.

'In a manner of speaking.' Langton smiled. 'We are Solicitors, Commissioners of oath etc. There were a few pieces of business we performed for your parents, for your mother, unusually then, was a partner in the business, you know.'

'I didn't know that, but it makes sense. She was the one with the business head.'

'Also the one who put in the capital, as financially your mother was well set up,' said Langton. 'When they married she brought four thousand pounds with her. She was older than your father by a good fifteen years and had the care of her father's books for his business. Thoughts of marriage were long gone in her mind and she had focussed on being a woman of means. Her father, your grandfather as he would have been had he lived, had discouraged many a man. Selfishly, I think with the benefit of hindsight, as she had a good business head, your mother. I understand the money had to be invested in property according to his will after he died and that is why there was the house with the ten acres that your mother and father turned into a market garden business at Bexhill.'

'I didn't know any of that,' said Jack.

'No reason why you should have done, you were a small child. She was a woman who knew her own mind and she took a fancy to your father. It wasn't easy for her. There were objections in those days. They formed a partnership and fell in love. Had she lived your mother would have explained it to you eventually. It was always her intention to train you to manage what they had.'

Jack sat at the table as Langton held out a chair for him. He looked at Peter Fisher, whose eyes were twinkling.

470

'I must not get distracted. Shall we begin?' Langton suggested with a look at the clock. 'I must be away by one o'clock, I'm afraid, which means an early luncheon.'

'No matter. I'll let Mrs Simcock know,' said Peter Fisher, rising from his chair.

'Reverend Fisher contacted me when you wrote to him that you were coming. He said in his letter that at last John William Sargent was found! The reason for our meeting concerns a will.' Langton smiled at Jack.

Jack nodded, 'Am I here to witness it?' he asked.

'Goodness me, no. It's your father's will. In fact it's a will trust your father made. It was your mother who would have had care of it but as she died within a day after him you became the beneficiary,' said Langton.

'So there was a will,' said Jack.

'Oh yes, of course. Your mother was no fool and as the law passed her property and money to her husband in those days it would be under the care of trustees had she lived. It's been kept in the safe in the office for the last eleven years. In September you will be twenty-one and we will read it then. I have it here to show you it exists.' Langton opened the leather messenger bag and took out a brown envelope which he placed between Jack and himself.

'Am I only to look at it now?' asked Jack.

Langton smiled and pulled it from its bound envelope. The document remained folded except for the first paragraph which plainly contained his father's name, his mother and names of trustees.

'Of course, we don't usually do this before the date but given the, er, circumstances which Reverend Fisher explained to me since that day your aunt came to the office with you, we are making an exception,' said Langton, he kept a hand on the document.

Jack looked at him in a lifeless quietness. Peter Fisher came back into the room and placed his hand on Jack's shoulder.

'Well Jack, it will all come right now. Mr Langton's explained what this is presumably?' said the old vicar.

'It's the will trust my parents left,'said Jack, glancing up at Peter Fisher.

'You're the sole beneficiary.' Peter Fisher was interrupted by a cough from Langton. 'Come, come man, what does it matter now. In a few months you'll read out all your complicated language on chattels and so on.'

'It's "need to know only" at the moment Reverend,' said Langton, exasperated.

'Exactly. He needs to know,' said Peter Fisher. 'He should have known years ago instead of ….. well, anyway, he needs to know something.' He patted Jack's hand.

Langton sighed. 'Let me explain it then. That way we won't breach anything.' The solicitor looked at Peter Fisher. He began to unfold the story:

'Your Aunt was to have the care of you while you were under age and submit accounts to the trustees. Unfortunately we lost contact with her after the meeting on the day of your parent's funeral. We assumed, wrongly, that she had you with her. We could not have known that she had abandoned you. We tried to locate her as the years went by but all leads led to dead ends. We began to assume that she may have married and emigrated. Had we known …. But there's no point in dwelling on the past,' said Langton.

'No indeed, if I'd known you were going to get sloppy I could have carried on and explained it myself. Get on with it, man and cut your long-winded way,' Peter Fisher cut in.

'No need, no need,' said Langton firmly, giving the vicar a look. He started to explain again:

'Because of the investment boom in the 1860's your trust did rather well. No need to go into details but the partners did work for you. Of course the fees had to be paid out of the proceeds and we were to take that every year but it was a small management fee and has not affected the growth of the capital accumulating for you.'

'Say it as he'll understand it, man,' shouted the Parson.

Langton gave the vicar a look.

'In addition as there were no demands on the capital for your support we decided to wait until the year you came of age. This year in fact. As I said, after our initial meeting with her we never heard from your aunt again,' Langton paused, and took a sip of the elderflower cordial that had been placed at his elbow by Mrs Simcock.

He continued:

'We wrote to your aunt at the only address we had, of course, as she was told that your father's expectation of her was that she would care for you, submit bills as regards schooling and clothing and we would pay the supplier direct. One of the trustees, you will see here,' said Langton, pointing at the first page, 'is Reverend Fisher, a second is my partner, and Edward Croft was to be the third.'

Jack smiled. 'I'm glad I know them again before I've heard this. It feels right. All the time I thought I was alone people were trying their hardest for me.'

'Exactly,' said Peter Fisher. 'It was always your parent's intention that we would oversee your education, take you out for tea for iced buns and that sort of thing that small boys always want.'

Langton looked at the clock on the mantlepiece and frowned. 'If I may? There was no need for your aunt to be out of pocket provided everything was bona fide. She was to marry she told us and we suspect now that the gentleman would not include a child in the arrangement. Perhaps he would have felt differently if she'd free access to the money. That is the only reason we can think of for her to be so angry at the meeting with my partner. It was unforgiveable that you were placed in an orphanage. Had the wretched woman told us that she couldn't care for you and marry at the same time we could have made alternative arrangements. We knew nothing and we deeply regret what happened.'

'I didn't remember her as an aunt. I remembered the woman telling me I was to go to an orphanage and there was no one left to care for me. It must have been your offices that we visited, after the funeral,' said Jack.

'Yes. She may, of course, be anywhere now. She may be dead. She no doubt married and it may be possible to look for a change of name. I daresay we can have her traced through an agent if you want to know her?' suggested the lawyer.

Jack ignored Langton's last question. The complication of an unreliable relative was the last thing he wanted.

'What I don't understand is if the trust falls due when I'm twenty-one what would you have done with it if you couldn't have found me?' asked Jack.

'Oh we're used to that sort of thing. I mentioned using a tracing agent just. We'd have found you alright. We'd have advertised in the London Gazette, contacted the police, that sort of thing. As it happens we'd have picked you up easily as you were in the papers, you know, ' said Langton. He smiled and turned to the back page of the trust. There, in a separate pile of papers was tucked the newspaper article from the Coroner's hearing after the Alexandra Palace Fire. The artist's impression was a good likeness.

'My partner saw the commendation from the Coroner of your actions in the Alexandra Palace Fire. It's an excellent artist's impression, of course. Here it is: Constable John William Sargent, Second Class Reserve, Metropolitan Police. My partner read it out. Said at the time it had to be our John William. Time will tell, I said. Time will tell. And of course it has.'

'The great thing to me isn't the little bit of money but the fact that they tried. My parents really tried to set up everything. They couldn't have known it would turn out badly,' said Jack.

'No, that's right,' said Peter Fisher. 'But in my experience, and probably as you are finding in your work now, the great unknown is always human behaviour. Experience and old age has taught me there is no limit to the diabolical way a human being can be. However I am still surprised at times at the depth of the horror inflicted on another by one of our kind.'

'We should probably talk about the case later then,' said Jack.

'We have the rest of the day,' said Peter Fisher, 'Stan was quite interested. I thought we could chat when he's back later.'

Jack froze and then found the fact that his Parson had shared information with Stan intensely funny. It was the opposite side of the coin. He could equally have sobbed. Instead he laughed almost hysterically until the coughing took over. Langton's face made him worse for a while, as Jack could see the solicitor was doubting his sanity. It was difficult to calculate the emotions Jack was experiencing. There had been too much in the last twenty-four hours to deal with. Peter Fisher poured him brandy but Jack waved it away. He had consumed enough recently and wanted no more.

He frowned as he stared at the legal document on the table between him and Langton. It was not the paper that brought the frown. How to deal with Harry and Hunt once they knew, as they surely would after Stan had briefed them was a conundrum.

Seeing all the conflicting emotions on Jack's face the lawyer said, 'It's all been rather a shock I suspect. Think on things and if there's something you want to ask in the next few weeks or months here's my card. We're effectively working for the beneficiary. That's you, and we've had years of having it easy on this case. We will give you whatever help you want.'

'It's not this situation that I was thinking about. I have something to deal with at work that I hadn't expected. But, frankly, after losing Harriet and then finding that there's a will rather makes me feel what will happen next. Perhaps, if anything, can you just give me some feel for what's in the papers?' suggested Jack.

'Yes, I can speak in general terms at this point. The exact details must wait until your twenty-first birthday on September seventh,' explained Langton.

'Would I be able to buy somewhere to live? It matters, you see, to have my own home,' said Jack.

'Then I'll tell you now that financially, you are better off than you thought yourself to be. It should ease your burden about your future considerably,' said Langton.

'But could I buy a home?' asked Jack.

'As to buying a property I would say it will depend on what and where.' Langton weighed up how much he should say. 'However I assure you that you would be able to afford a modest property by putting some of the capital into bricks and mortar. It remains within the trust of course, but you would have the benefit for your lifetime. We should make a will for you as soon as your birthday is here. I suggest that we meet on your birthday and we can present the final investment outcome at that date for you. There has been some diversification in order to help the capital to grow. Your father's business was sold, you see, and the property. That was his wish thinking that if he died first the capital, which had been your mother's, would return to her to live on. I shouldn't say more now. We can meet on the morning of September seventh with all the trustees in place and the will trust can be read for you at that point.'

'It's a good feeling,' said Jack. 'The first today.'

Peter Fisher asked: 'Can you tell him at least what the capital was?'

'There is little point as eleven years has lapsed. It bears no resemblance to the picture now. No, I don't think it wise, Reverend,' said Langton.

'It's alright, Parson,' said Jack. 'I know what I wished to know. I see Mr Langton can't say anymore. It's enough for me at this time to know my parents made some provision. Ironic isn't it on a day I thought I had lost everything. Even my health takes its time to recover. The other problem you've given me good counsel on and I'll be grateful for your help with a letter later. I'm not saying I accept what's happened with Harriet as it seems like weakness to accept it but the word you said, "kindness," rings in my ears. I will be kind and I will hope.'

'That's the way, Jack. Now we must do the luncheon some justice to satisfy Mrs Simcock as Mr Langton must go soon. I had thought to open a good bottle of wine but the news in the last two days has been mixed for you. With your permission I still can.'

476

'Forgive me but I'd like to wait 'til September seventh,' said Jack.

'Quite right,' said Peter Fisher. 'Once the full details are yours we can celebrate properly.'

*

Stan sat down amongst the scrub, having found a clear view. He ate the sandwich he had made at the Reverend's cottage and drank the water the gamekeeper from Firle Place had given him. As soon as he started to think about what he and his men had been involved in he knew it was time to be walking again. A good walking pace was the solution, he knew, to the nightmares of the last few weeks and the rescue he and Arthur had brought off from Portsmouth. He hoped he would never see the last warder again. Stan had a feeling he had been the sort not to forget a face.

Stan had been going for hours and could see the sun had moved west. It was time to get off the Downs and turn back for Selmeston and what Stan was sure would be a good dinner. How to play the work Jack had been doing bothered him. Stan strode out to shorten the time and thought of the two colleagues who had been damaged physically in the last few weeks. Harry Franks, whose hand the doctor seemed to think would not recover properly and the young, enthusiastic, constable Stan had met last December, now broken hearted at the loss of his love and still suffering from the effects of the smoke inhalation. Well, time may heal both, he thought. Harry would see Doctor Brown when he was back in London and Jack? Yes, perhaps Jack would find solace in the arms of the lovely Mary. Who knew on that score? Stan, who had long realised that his wife and children were what kept him sane, hoped Jack would not spend his life alone with just a career.

The sun had gone behind the beacon as he reached the lower levels. From the chimney of the small cottage near the church in Selmeston came a spiral of smoke. Even in June the cottage walls would keep out the day's warmth. Stan turned into the garden and saw a figure bending over a garden fork turning the soil.

'You getting some rest, aren't you Jack?' Stan called.

'This isn't hard, Stan,' Jack replied. 'I'm better working than just sitting. Reverend Fisher's inside if you want to go in. I'll be about a quarter of the hour and then I'm done with this bed. I thought I'd do it for him as the Parson can't bend too well these days. He's suggested fishing tomorrow.'

Stan nodded and unlatched the kitchen door. He nodded to Mrs Simcock and slipped his feet out of his muddy boots at the step. She smiled, recognising the training of a wife present in his behaviour not to dirty the kitchen floor.

'Kettle's hot if you'd like a tea making?' she asked.

'I can do it as you're busy,' said Stan, picking up the kettle and pouring scalding water into the tea pot to warm it. 'Can I pour one for you?' he asked.

'Thank-you sir, but I won't. I'll be going home shortly as soon as the pie has baked. The Reverend will serve up dinner for you all. I've my young'uns to see to.'

'Have you many?' asked Stan.

'Four at school now and still at home. Two working in Eastbourne. Lucky though as they're apprenticed and not on the land. Farming's been hard for the last year or so.' Mrs Simcock folded up her apron and used it to protect her hands as she opened the range door.

'There that will keep hot now for when you want to eat it,' she said. 'Potatoes in the dish and the gravy is in a jug on the griddle. Cheese is in the pantry with a nice cheese from the Weald. I'll just go through and say good evening to the Reverend and leave you gentlemen to yourselves. Your bed is made up, sir, in the study. I hope it fits you as it looks a little small against your height.'

'I'll be fine, thank-you. It will be the lap of luxury in comparison to some of the places I have laid my head in the last few weeks,' said Stan.

Mrs Simcock nodded her head. The Reverend had mentioned these men had been involved in a special police team. She did not claim to understand it but she appreciated they may have been in danger.

'Well, sir, dinner with the Reverend will be a blessing and I hope the food is too. I'll just go through, and I will be here early in the morning.'

'A good evening to you and your family,' said Stan.

The kitchen door opened and Jack moved quietly in. Stan thought how much better he looked in comparison to that morning.

Jack threw water over his hands and forearms, leaning over the sink. He damped down a cloth on the draining board and wiped over his face and neck and then sank into a chair.

'Did you make it to Firle Beacon?' Jack asked.

'Yes – about ten miles in total I reckon I've done today. It's grand country but it's a steep climb and seen some rain by the state of the tracks.'

'You've done a lot of walking Stan, since you've been here,' said Jack.

'It's how I manage my mind,' said Stan. 'You look better than you did earlier as well.'

'Do I? Good. I've had some encouraging news about the future although I don't yet know the full extent of it. The Parson had knowledge of a will left by my parents. I've seen a solicitor who drafted it for Father this afternoon and when I turn twenty-one in a few months the full picture will become clear.'

'News like that changes things for you, Jack, despite the sadness you had last night. I'm glad for you. Things might come right with Harriet at some point. But if they don't there's others that might suit you better.'

'I've written to her with the Parson's help. Now I must leave it for a while. Perhaps I'll hear. I hope I do. But don't think I would marry unless it was her,' said Jack.

'I've never believed in the idea of there being only one person for each of us. I think that's something manufactured by the writers of novels. Give it time, lad and focus on your career. You're only just starting and you've had quite a time of it in the last month.'

'Would you say that of your own wife?' asked Jack.

'There's more to it than romantic love, Jack. There's the children and the home we've built. We work together to keep it going. Yes, if I never heard her voice again I'd find it impossible. But it has to become more than a burning passion when a woman walks into the room. She's now as much part of me as I am of her. The air I breath would not be the same unless she was there and that's hard to explain. She and the children are the reason why I walk the dark moods off that the job has produced over the years.'

Jack nodded. 'Parson said he'd mentioned the case about Grace and the babies,' said Jack.

Stan nodded. 'Sounds like there's to be another commendation for you if I was Hunt. Fill me in, won't you?'

'Ah, there you both are,' called the Parson, from the doorway. 'Putting the world to rights?'

'I could say, I hope so,' said Jack.

*

Acknowledgements

Chapter One

Stanford's library map of London and its Suburbs 1872.

British-history.ac.uk: some liberty has been taken with the timing of the development of the West India Dock Offices and the location of customs. The Dock cottages were never as homely as are implied with Mrs Phillips.

Glove manufacturers in Millau, France during the nineteenth century.

A Dictionary of the Sussex Dialect and Collection of Provincialisms in Use in the County of Sussex, Reverend William Douglas Parish.

Chapter Two

The Jewish Orphan Asylum:
www.childrenshomes.org.uk

Wilhelm Marr 1873.

American depression 1873-1896.

Chapter Three

The Telegraph, June 10 1873.

The Eastbourne Chronicle, Saturday June 14 1873

The 19th century Herne Hill Society. Retrieved 3/5/2012 by Wikipedia.

Bradshaw's Descriptive Railway Handbook 1863.

The Alphabetical Railway Guide, W. Tweedie, 1870 p 55.

"The Amazons Within, Women in the BMA 100 years ago."
Tara Lamont, BMJ.com 19-26 December 1992.

Herne Hill Society 2003, p.10.

"The London, Chatham and Dover Railway". The Building
News, 10.27.9 Jan 1863.

A Devon Dialect taken from "The County of Devon" by G.A.
Cooke (written about 1816-1820.)

Chapter Five

'Disused stations,' source Nick Catford. Disused-stations.org

Htpps://www.biography.com/people/louis-pasteur-
94334402

Victoria and Albert Museum 'Health and Medicine in the 19th
century.

Bradshaw's Descriptive Railway Hand-book of Great Britain
and Ireland 1863.

bbc.co.uk 24/9/14 Devon: My Home Town, article by Ian
McNab

Chapter Six

Fairbrass is mentioned in "The Great British Bobby, A history
of British Policing from the 18th century to the present." Clive
Emsley, paperback 2010.

Chapter Seven

History of Victorian seaside fashion: fashion-era.com

Map LXVI Sussex surveyed 1873-75, published 1880.

Chapter Nine

"Brighton and Hove, Historic Character Assessment Report," March 2007. R.B. Harris. Westsussex.gov.uk

Hazlitt, mentioned in Bradshaw's Handbook 1863.

Chapter Ten

The Royal Archives: Queen Victoria's Diamond Jubilee Scrap Book 1897.

Historic medals: Timothy Millett Ltd.

Royalcollection.org.uk: Illustrated London News 28/6/1873.

The Theatre Royal, Brighton, published July 1st 1866, from the ERA.

Hansard 1803-2005 – 1870s – 1873. 9 June 1873 vol 216 cc638-712 Commons Sitting – visit of the Shah of Persia.

Hansard 1803-2005 – 1873. 19 June 1873 vol 216 cc1150-1– Lords sitting – visit of the Shah of Persia – The Naval Review at Spithead.

Chapter Eleven

The Eastbourne Chronicle 28 June 1873.

The Cambrian, Swansea, 20 June , 1873.

The New York Times, 19 June, 1873

Stanford's Map of London and its suburbs 1872. Historic-UK.com

Duncan Gardham (12 June 2008) "David Davies Victorian Inspiration," The Daily Telegraph.

Sanchez Manning "Britain's Colonial Shame: Slave-owners given huge pay-outs after abolition" Independent on Sunday, 24/2/13.

Chapter Twelve

Summer Exhibition Royal Pavilion 19th June 1873.

Labour and the London Poor, 1861, Chapters 1-7; H. Mayhew. Penguin.

Plain Cookery Recipes. Nelson: London, UK: 1875.

NCBI.NLM.NIH.GOV: How the mid-Victorians Worked, Ate and Died. Paul Clayton and Judith Rowbotham.

The Met Office historic UK climate records archives.

Hansard: June 19 1873 vol 216 cc1151-6 Visit of the Shah of Persia.

Hansard HC debate 19 June 1873 vol 216 cc1174. Shah of Persia's visit to the City.

Chapter Thirteen

TheRoyalSchool.org.uk: founded in 1846 by Queen Victoria and Prince Albert for the permanent education of the children of the families in royal service within the Great Park.

Newspapers.library.wales. The Cambrian, Swansea June 20 1873.

The Cardiff Times, Saturday June 21 1873.

Illustrated London News, volume LXII, June 28 1873.

Edward VII: The last Victorian King. By Christopher Hibbert

The Letters of Queen Victoria, by Queen Victoria. A Biographical Companion.

Chapter Fourteen

1850-1899: Historical weather events: 1872-1879. Metoffice.org.uk

The London Gazette March 1873

The County Ground, Eaton Road, Hove, was the home to the Sussex county club from 1872 after the lease ran out on their former ground. West Sussex.gov.uk

Persia and the Victorians, by Marziah Gali.

Chapter Fifteen

Rev. Peter Fisher is a fictional character.
The Rev. W.D. Parish, Vicar of Selmeston, Sussex, was the author of 'A Dictionary of the Sussex Dialect and Country Provincialisms in use in the County of Sussex,' published by Farncombe and Co in Lewes in 1875.

Selmeston.info: The Parish Church.

Hansard 25 July 1873 House of Lords debate, vol 217 cc964-6

Collections.rmg.co.uk HM Turret Ship "the Devastation"

Portsmouthdockyard.org.uk

The Cambrian, Swansea, June 27th 1873:
Newspapers.library.wales

Chapter Sixteen

Hastingschronicle.net Hastings Coastguards and Smugglers Chronicle.

The High Weald Coast from Hastings to Pett. Classic landforms of the Weald. Landform guide number 4 pp 39-43. D.A. Robinson and R.B.G. Williams, University of Sussex. Sussex.ac.uk

Chapter Seventeen

Hastings Coastguards and Smugglers Chronicle. Hastingschronicle.net 1850-1899.

Hastings Chronicle April 30 1862.

Discovering Fossils: discoveringfossils.co.uk
The geology at Fairlight.

Shorehambysea.com

"Little known about ancient Pett Level sunken forest" 14/8/13 BBC News, by Tanya Gupta.

Exploreforensics.co.uk: the four manners of death by Jack Claridge, 6/1/17.

Webarchive.nationalarchives Pett Level (SSSI)

Chapter Eighteen

Persia and the Victorians by Marzieh Gail, volume 6, 1951.

The Argus, (Melbourne, Vic: 1848-1957 Monday 8 September 1873 page 6;
Monday 22 September 1873 page 4.

The Persian March: Johann Strauss II.

The Cambrian, Swansea, June 27 1873

Chapter Nineteen

The Lancet.com Peter Vanezis "Forensic Medicine Past, Present and Future. 2004.

Pehr Henrik Ling 1776-1839 pioneered the teaching of physical education in Sweden.

A History of Archaeology in Great Britain, Springer.com

David Rowland, History of Hastings Police 1836-1967.

English Criminal Justice in the nineteenth century, David Bentley.

Toff: it was a mid-eighteenth century word for a rich or upper-class person. It was perhaps an alteration of "tuft," used to describe a golden tassel worn on the cap by titled undergraduates at Oxford and Cambridge.

Chapter Twenty

Sunken Forest is Revealed, The Rye and Battle Observer, 15/1/2014.

Content.historicengland.org

Chapter Twenty-One

Writersforensicsblog D.P.Lyle.MD.

Jewishvirtuallibrary.org Wilhelm Marr 1819-1904.

Folding chairs were popular in the American Civil War with officers who could fold and carry them.

Mendicity Society Brighton: The Letter in the Attic Project. Mybrightonandhove.org.uk

The oath is derived from the oath Metropolitan Police Officers were asked to swear before God from 1829 onwards.

Phoebe Hessel's Grave, St Nicholas's church, Simon Carey, Geography Britain and Ireland

Chapter Twenty-Two

James Miranda Steuart Barry, du Preez and Dronfield 2016.

Marlinspike Seamanship, found on globalsecurity.org.

Hansard.parliament.uk June 30, 1873. Vol 216.

Dictionary of Sussex words and phrases and Devon words: as they appear in the book.

Dupping: walking quickly

Lear: thin.

Pemsey: Pevensey.

Mesh: Marsh.

Maize: stupid. (D) maized as a bezom.

Mock-Beggar Hall – a farm near Rye, Sussex, had this name in the nineteenth century.

Nunty: in east Sussex it was used to describe a shabby state of dress.

Old-Father; the person who gives away the bride at her wedding. It was not usually the father of the bride. In mid Sussex among labourers in the nineteenth century it would often be the sweetheart of the bridesmaid.

Sen: since.

Abouten: on the point of doing something.

Coolthe: coolness.

Abusefully: abusive.

Afeared: afraid

A sky as black as a hat: is a thundery sky. (D)

Dutch cousins: great friends.

Wide-of: out of the direct road but not far off.

Gaffer: grandfather or master.

Adle-headed: stupid

Avised: aware of, or to know for a fact.

Neglact: neglect; before ct, e became pronounced as a.

Effact: effect, see the note after Neglact.

Ache: tired

Leave off the Sherry: Jack may have said adone.

Expact: expect.

Printed in Poland
by Amazon Fulfillment
Poland Sp. z o.o., Wrocław

55011437R00275